Wish You Were Here

BY JODI PICOULT

Wish You Were Here
The Book of Two Ways
A Spark of Light
Small Great Things
Leaving Time
The Storyteller
Lone Wolf
Sing You Home
House Rules
Handle with Care
Change of Heart
Nineteen Minutes
The Tenth Circle
Vanishing Acts
My Sister's Keeper
Second Glance
Perfect Match
Salem Falls
Plain Truth
Keeping Faith
The Pact
Mercy
Picture Perfect
Harvesting the Heart
Songs of the Humpback Whale

FOR YOUNG ADULTS

Off the Page
Between the Lines

AND FOR THE STAGE

Over the Moon: An Original Musical for Teens
Breathe: A New Musical

JODI PICOULT

Wish You Were Here

ALLEN&UNWIN
SYDNEY • MELBOURNE • AUCKLAND • LONDON

First published in Australia and New Zealand in 2021 by Allen & Unwin
First published in the United States in 2021 by Ballantine Books, an imprint of Random House, a division of Penguin Random House LLC, New York

Allen & Unwin
83 Alexander Street
Crows Nest NSW 2065
Australia
Phone: (61 2) 8425 0100
Email: info@allenandunwin.com
Web: www.allenandunwin.com

 A catalogue record for this book is available from the National Library of Australia

ISBN 978 1 76052 878 2

Internal design by Caroline Cunningham
Title page and part opener ornament: iStock/mysondanube
Printed and bound in Australia by Griffin Press, part of Ovato

10 9 8 7 6 5 4 3 2 1

The paper in this book is FSC® certified. FSC® promotes environmentally responsible, socially beneficial and economically viable management of the world's forests.

For Melanie Borinstein, soon to be the newest member of our family.

There's no one else I'd rather run a quarantine salon with.

According to Darwin's *Origin of Species*, it is not the most intellectual of the species that survives; it is not the strongest that survives; but the species that survives is the one that is able best to adapt and adjust to the changing environment in which it finds itself.

—LEON C. MEGGINSON

ONE

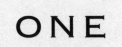

ONE

ONE

March 13, 2020

When I was six years old, I painted a corner of the sky. My father was working as a conservator, one of a handful restoring the zodiac ceiling on the main hall of Grand Central Terminal—an aqua sky strung with shimmering constellations. It was late, way past my bedtime, but my father took me to work because my mother—as usual—was not home.

He helped me carefully climb the scaffolding, where I watched him working on a cleaned patch of the turquoise paint. I looked at the stars representing the smear of the Milky Way, the golden wings of Pegasus, Orion's raised club, the twisted fish of Pisces. The original mural had been painted in 1913, my father told me. Roof leaks damaged the plaster, and in 1944, it had been replicated on panels that were attached to the arched ceiling. The original plan had been to remove the boards for restoration, but they contained asbestos, and so the conservators left them in place, and went to work with cotton swabs and cleaning solution, erasing decades of pollutants.

They uncovered history. Signatures and inside jokes and notes left behind by the original artists were revealed, tucked in among the constellations. There were dates commemorating weddings, and the end of World War II. There were names of soldiers. The birth of twins was recorded near Gemini.

An error had been made by the original artists, so that the painted zodiac was reversed from the way it would appear in the night sky. Instead of correcting it, though, my father was diligently reinforcing the error. That night, he was working on a small square of space, gilding stars. He had already painted over the tiny yellow dots with adhesive. He covered these with a piece of gold leaf, light as breath. Then he turned to me. "Diana," he said, holding out his hand, and I climbed up in front of him, caged by the safety of his body. He handed me a brush to sweep over the foil, fixing it in place. He showed me how to gently rub at it with my thumb, so that the galaxy he'd created was all that remained.

When all the work was finished, the conservators kept a small dark spot in the northwest corner of Grand Central Terminal, where the pale blue ceiling meets the marble wall. This nine-by-five-inch section was left that way intentionally. My father told me that conservators do that, in case historians need to study the original composition. The only way you can tell how far you've come is to know where you started.

Every time I'm in Grand Central Terminal, I think about my father. Of how we left that night, hand in hand, our palms glittering like we had stolen the stars.

It is Friday the thirteenth, so I should know better. Getting from Sotheby's, on the Upper East Side, to the Ansonia, on the Upper West Side, means taking the Q train to Times Square and then the 1 uptown, so I have to travel in the wrong direction before I start going in the right one.

I *hate* going backward.

Normally I would walk across Central Park, but I am wearing a new pair of shoes that are rubbing a blister on my heel, shoes I never would have worn if I'd known that I was going to be summoned by Kitomi Ito. So instead, I find myself on public transit. But something's off, and it takes me a moment to figure out what.

It's quiet. Usually, I have to fight my way through tourists who are listening to someone singing for coins, or a violin quartet. Today, though, the platform is empty.

Last night Broadway theaters had shut down performances for a month, after an usher tested positive for Covid, out of an abundance of caution. That's what Finn said, anyway—New York–Presbyterian, where he is a resident, has not seen the influx of coronavirus cases that are appearing in Washington State and Italy and France. There were only nineteen cases in the city, Finn told me last night as we watched the news, when I wondered out loud if we should start panicking yet. "Wash your hands and don't touch your face," he told me. "It's going to be fine."

The uptown subway is nearly empty, too. I get off at Seventy-second and emerge aboveground, blinking like a mole, walking at a brisk New Yorker clip. The Ansonia, in all its glory, rises up like an angry djinn, defiantly jutting its Beaux Arts chin at the sky. For a moment, I just stand on the sidewalk, looking up at its mansard roof and its lazy sprawl from Seventy-third to Seventy-fourth Street. There's a North Face and an American Apparel at ground level, but it wasn't always this bougie. Kitomi told me that when she and Sam Pride moved in in the seventies, the building was overrun with psychics and mediums, and housed a swingers' club with an orgy room and an open bar and buffet. *Sam and I*, she said, *would stop in at least once a week.*

I was not alive when Sam's band, the Nightjars, was formed by Sam and his co-songwriter, William Punt, with two school chums from Slough, England. Nor was I when their first album spent thirty weeks on the *Billboard* charts, or when their little British quartet went on *The Ed Sullivan Show* and ignited a stampede of screaming American girls. Not when Sam married Kitomi Ito ten years later or when the band broke up, months after their final album was released featuring cover art of Kitomi and Sam naked, mirroring the figures in a painting that hung behind their bed. And I wasn't alive when Sam was murdered three years later, on the steps of this very building, stabbed in the throat by a mentally ill man who recognized him from that iconic album cover.

But like everyone else on the planet, I know the whole story.

The doorman at the Ansonia smiles politely at me; the concierge looks up as I approach. "I'm here to see Kitomi Ito," I say coolly, pushing my license across the desk to her.

"She's expecting you," the concierge answers. "Floor—"

"Eighteen. I know."

Lots of celebrities have lived at the Ansonia—from Babe Ruth to Theodore Dreiser to Toscanini to Natalie Portman—but arguably, Kitomi and Sam Pride are the most famous. If my husband had been murdered on the front steps of my apartment building, I might not have stayed for another thirty years, but that's just me. And anyway, Kitomi is finally moving now, which is why the world's most infamous rock widow has my number in her cellphone.

What is my life, I think, as I lean against the back wall of the elevator.

When I was young, and people asked what I wanted to do when I grew up, I had a whole plan. I wanted to be securely on a path to my career, to get married by thirty, to finish having kids by thirty-five. I wanted to speak fluent French and have traveled cross-country on Route 66. My father had laughed at my checklist. *You,* he told me, *are definitely your mother's daughter.*

I did not take that as a compliment.

Also, for the record, I'm perfectly on track. I am an associate specialist at Sotheby's—*Sotheby's!*—and Eva, my boss, has hinted in all ways possible that after the auction of Kitomi's painting I will likely be promoted. I am not engaged, but when I ran out of clean socks last weekend and went to scrounge for a pair of Finn's, I found a ring hidden in the back of his underwear drawer. We leave tomorrow on vacation and Finn's going to pop the question there. I'm so sure of it that I got a manicure today instead of eating lunch.

And I'm twenty-nine.

The door to the elevator opens directly into Kitomi's foyer, all black and white marble squares like a giant chessboard. She comes into the entryway, dressed in jeans and combat boots and a pink silk bathrobe, with a thatch of white hair and the purple heart-shaped spectacles for which she is known. She has always reminded me of a wren, light and hollow-boned. I think of how Kitomi's black hair went white overnight with grief after Sam was murdered. I think of the photographs of her on the sidewalk, gasping for air.

"Diana!" she says, as if we are old friends.

There is a brief awkwardness as I instinctively put my hand out to take hers and then remember that is not a thing we are doing anymore and instead just give a weird little wave. "Hi, Kitomi," I say.

"I'm so glad you could come today."

"It's not a problem. There are a lot of sellers who want to make sure the paperwork is handed over personally."

Over her shoulder, at the end of a long hallway, I can see it—the Toulouse-Lautrec painting that is the entire reason I know Kitomi Ito. She sees my eyes dart toward it and her mouth tugs into a smile.

"I can't help it," I say. "I never get tired of seeing it."

A strange flicker crosses Kitomi's face. "Then let's get you a better view," she replies, and she leads me deeper into her home.

From 1892 to 1895, Henri de Toulouse-Lautrec scandalized the impressionist art world by moving into a brothel and painting prostitutes together in bed. *Le Lit,* one of the most famous in that series, is at the Musée d'Orsay. Others have been sold to private collections for ten million and twelve million dollars. The painting in Kitomi's house is clearly part of the series and yet patently set apart from the others.

There are not two women in this one, but a woman and a man. The woman sits propped up naked against the headboard, the sheet fallen to her waist. Behind the headboard is a mirror, and in it you can see the reflection of the second figure in the painting—Toulouse-Lautrec himself, seated naked at the foot of the bed with sheets pooled in his lap, his back to the viewer as he stares as intently at the woman as she is staring at him. It's intimate and voyeuristic, simultaneously private and public.

When the Nightjars released their final album, *Twelfth of Never,* the cover art had Kitomi bare-breasted against their headboard, gazing at Sam, whose broad back forms the lower third of the visual field. Behind their bed hangs the painting they're emulating, in the position the mirror holds in the actual art.

Everyone knows that album cover. Everyone knows that Sam bought this painting for Kitomi from a private collection, as a wedding gift.

But only a handful of people know that she is now selling it, at a unique Sotheby's auction, and that I'm the one who closed that deal.

"Are you still going on vacation?" Kitomi asks, disrupting my reverie.

Did I tell her about our trip? Maybe. But I cannot think of any logical reason she would care.

Clearing my throat (I don't get paid to moon over art, I get paid to transact it), I paste a smile on my face. "Only for two weeks, and then the minute I get back, it's full steam ahead for your auction." My job is a strange one—I have to convince clients to give their beloved art up for adoption, which is a careful dance between rhapsodizing over the piece and encouraging them that they are doing the right thing by selling it. "If you're having any anxiety about the transfer of the painting to our offices, don't," I tell her. "I promise that I will personally be here overseeing the crating, and I'll be there on the other end, too." I glance back at the canvas. "We're going to find this the perfect home," I vow. "So. The paperwork?"

Kitomi glances out the window before turning back to me. "About that," she says.

"What do you mean, she doesn't want to sell?" Eva says, looking at me over the rims of her famous horn-rimmed glasses. Eva St. Clerck is my boss, my mentor, and a legend. As the head of sale for the Imp Mod auction—the giant sale of impressionist and modern art—she is who I'd like to be by the time I'm forty, and until this moment, I had firmly enjoyed being teacher's pet, tucked under the wing of her expertise.

Eva narrows her eyes. "I knew it. Someone from Christie's got to her."

In the past, Kitomi has sold other pieces of art with Christie's, the main competitor of Sotheby's. To be fair, everyone assumed that was how she'd sell the Toulouse-Lautrec, too . . . until I did something I never should have done as an associate specialist, and convinced her otherwise.

"It's not Christie's—"

"Phillips?" Eva asks, her eyebrows arching.

"No. None of them. She just wants to take a pause," I clarify. "She's concerned about the virus."

"Why?" Eva asks, dumbfounded. "It's not like a painting can catch it."

"No, but buyers can at an auction."

"Well, I can talk her down from that ledge," Eva says. "We've got firm interest from the Clooneys and Beyoncé and Jay-Z, for God's sake."

"Kitomi's also nervous because the stock market's tanking. She thinks things are going to get worse, fast. And she wants to wait it out a bit . . . be safe not sorry."

Eva rubs her temples. "You do realize we've already leaked this sale," she says. "*The New Yorker* literally did a feature on it."

"She just needs a little more time," I say.

Eva glances away, already dismissing me in her mind. "You can go," she orders.

I step out of her office and into the maze of hallways, lined with the books that I've used to research art. I've been at Sotheby's for six and a half years—seven if you count the internship I did when I was still at Williams College. I went straight from undergrad into their master's program in art business. I started out as a graduate trainee, then became a junior cataloger in the Impressionist Department, doing initial research for incoming paintings. I would study what else the artist was working on around the same time and how much similar works sold for, sometimes writing up the first draft of the catalog blurb. Though the rest of the world is digital these days, the art world still produces physical catalogs that are beautiful and glossy and nuanced and very, very important. Now, as an associate specialist,

I perform other tasks for Eva: visiting the artwork in situ and noting any imperfections, the same way you look over a rental car for dings before you sign the contract; physically accompanying the painting as it is packed up and moved from a home to our office; and occasionally joining my boss for meetings with potential clients.

A hand snakes out of a doorway I am passing and grabs my shoulder, pulling me into a little side room. "Jesus," I say, nearly falling into Rodney—my best friend here at Sotheby's. Like me, he started as a college intern. Unlike me, he did not wind up going into the business side of the auction house. Instead, he designs and helps create the spaces where the art is showcased for auction.

"Is it true?" Rodney asks. "Did you lose the Nightjars' painting?"

"First, it's not the Nightjars' painting. It's Kitomi Ito's. Second, how the *hell* did you find out so fast?"

"Honey, rumor is the lifeblood of this entire industry," Rodney says. "And it spreads through these halls faster than the flu." He hesitates. "Or coronavirus, as it may be."

"Well, I didn't *lose* the Toulouse-Lautrec. Kitomi just wants things to settle down first."

Rodney folds his arms. "You think that's happening anytime soon? The mayor declared a state of emergency yesterday."

"Finn said there are only nineteen cases in the city," I tell him.

Rodney looks at me like I've just said I still believe in Santa, with a mixture of disbelief and pity. "You can have one of my rolls of toilet paper," he says.

For the first time, I look behind him. There are six different shades of gold paint rolled onto the walls. "Which do you like?" he asks.

I point to one stripe in the middle. "Really?" he says, squinting.

"What's it for?"

"A display of medieval manuscripts. Private sale."

"Then that one," I say, nodding at the stripe beside it. Which looks exactly the same. "Come up to Sant Ambroeus with me," I beg. It's the café at the top of Sotheby's, and there is a prosciutto and mozzarella sandwich there that might erase the look on Eva's face from my mind.

"Can't. It's popcorn for me today."

The break room has free microwave popcorn, and on busy days, that's lunch. "Rodney," I hear myself say, "I'm screwed."

He settles his hands on my shoulders, spinning me and walking me toward the opposite wall, where a mirrored panel is left over from the previous installation. "What do you see?"

I look at my hair, which has always been too red for my taste, and my eyes, steel blue. My lipstick has worn off. My skin is a ghostly winter white. And there's a weird stain on the collar of my blouse. "I see someone who can kiss her promotion goodbye."

"Funny," Rodney says, "because I see someone who is going on vacation tomorrow and who should have zero fucks left to give about Kitomi Ito or Eva St. Clerck or Sotheby's. Think about tropical drinks and paradise and playing doctor with your boyfriend—"

"Real doctors don't do that—"

"—and snorkeling with Gila monsters—"

"Marine iguanas."

"Whatever." Rodney squeezes me from behind, meeting my gaze in the mirror. "Diana, by the time you get back here in two weeks, everyone will have moved on to another scandal." He smirks at me. "Now go buy some SPF 50 and get out of here."

I laugh as Rodney picks up a paint roller and smoothly covers all the gold stripes with the one I picked. Once, he told me that an auction house wall can have a foot of paint on it, because they are repainted constantly.

As I close the door behind me, I wonder what color this room first was, and if anyone here even remembers.

To get to Hastings-on-Hudson, a commuter town north of the city, you can take Metro-North from Grand Central. So for the second time today, I head to Midtown.

This time, though, I visit the main concourse of the building and position myself directly underneath the piece of sky I painted with my father, letting my gaze run over the backward zodiac and the ckles of stars that blush across the arch of the ceiling. Craning my neck back, I stare until I'm dizzy, until I can almost hear my father's voice again.

It's been four years since he died, and the only way I can garner the courage to visit my mother is to come here first, as if his memory gives me protective immunity.

I am not entirely sure why I'm going to see her. It's not like she asked for me. And it's not like this is part of any routine. I haven't been to visit in three months, actually.

Maybe *that's* why I'm going.

The Greens is an assisted living facility walkable from the train station in Hastings-on-Hudson—which is one of the reasons I picked it, when my mother reappeared out of the blue after years of radio silence. And, naturally, she didn't show up oozing maternal warmth. She was a problem that needed to be solved.

The building is made out of brick and fits into a community that looks like it was cut and pasted from New England. Trees line the street, and there's a library next door. Cobblestones arch in a widening circle from the front door. It isn't until you are buzzed in through the locked door and see the color-coded hallways and the photographs on the residents' apartment doors that you realize it's a memory care facility.

I sign in and walk past a woman shuffling into the bright art room, filled with all sorts of paints and clay and crafts. As far as I know, my mother has never participated.

They do all kinds of things here to make it easier for the occupants. Doorways meant to be entered by the residents have bright yellow frames they cannot miss; rooms for staff or storage blend into the walls, painted over with murals of bookshelves or greenery. Since all the apartment doors look similar, there's a large photo on each one that has meaning to the person who lives there: a family member, a special location, a beloved pet. In my mother's case, it's one of her own most famous photographs—a refugee who's come by raft from Cuba, carrying the limp body of his dehydrated son in his arms. It's grotesque and grim and the pain radiates from the image. In other words, exactly the kind of photo for which Hannah O'Toole was known.

There is a punch code that opens the secure unit on both sides of the door. (The keypad on the inside is always surrounded by a small zombie clot of residents trying to peer over your shoulder to see the numbers and presumably the path to freedom.) The individual rooms aren't locked. When I let myself into my mother's room, the space is neat and uncluttered. The television is on—the television is *always* on—tuned to a game show. My mother sits on the couch with her hands in her lap, like she's at a cotillion waiting to be asked to dance.

She is younger than most of the residents here. There's one skunk streak of white in her black hair, but it's been there since I was little. She doesn't really look much different from the way she did when I was a girl, except for her stillness. My mother was always in motion—talking animatedly with her hands, turning at the next question, adjusting the lens of a camera, hieing away from us to some corner of the globe to capture a revolution or a natural disaster.

Beyond her is the screened porch, the reason that I picked The Greens. I thought that someone who'd spent so much of her life outdoors would hate the confinement of a memory care facility. The screened porch was safe, because there was no egress from it, but it allowed a view. Granted, it was only a strip of lawn and beyond that a parking lot, but it was something.

It costs a shitload of money to keep my mother here. When she showed up on my doorstep, in the company of two police officers who found her wandering around Central Park in a bathrobe, I hadn't even known she was back in the city. They found my address in her wallet, torn from the corner of an old Christmas card envelope. *Ma'am,* one of the officers had asked me, *do you know this woman?*

I recognized her, of course. But I didn't *know* her at all.

When it became clear that my mother had dementia, Finn asked me what I was going to do. *Nothing,* I told him. She had barely been involved in taking care of me when I was young; why was I obligated to take care of her now? I remember seeing the look on his face when

…e realized that for me, maybe, love was a quid pro quo. I didn't want to ever see that expression again on Finn, but I also knew my limitations, and I didn't have the resources to become the caretaker for someone with early-onset Alzheimer's. So I did my due diligence, talking to her neurologist and getting pamphlets from different facilities. The Greens was the best of the lot, but it was expensive. In the end, I packed up my mother's apartment, Sotheby's auctioned off the photographs from her walls, and the result was an annuity that could pay for her new residence.

I did not miss the irony of the fact that the parent I missed desperately was the one who was no longer in the world, while the parent I could take or leave was inextricably tied to me for the long haul.

Now, I paste a smile on my face and sit down next to my mother on the couch. I can count on two hands the number of times I've come to visit since installing her here, but I very clearly remember the directions of the staff: act like she knows you, and even if she doesn't remember, she will likely follow the social cues and treat you like a friend. The first time I'd come, when she asked who I was and I said *Your daughter,* she had become so agitated that she'd bolted away, fallen over a chair, and cut her forehead.

"Who's winning *Wheel of Fortune*?" I ask, settling in as if I'm a regular visitor.

Her eyes dart toward me. There's a flicker of confusion, like a sputtering pilot light, before she smooths it away. "The lady in the pink shirt," my mother says. Her brows draw together, as she tries to place me. "Are you—"

"The last time I was here, it was warm outside," I interrupt, offering the clue that this isn't the first time I've visited. "It's pretty warm out today. Should we open the slider?"

She nods, and I walk toward the entrance to the screened porch. The latch that locks it from the inside is open. "You're supposed to keep this fastened," I remind her. I don't have to worry about her wandering off—but it still makes me nervous to have the sliding door unlocked.

"Are we going somewhere?" she asks, when a gust of fresh air blows into the living room.

"Not today," I tell her. "But I'm taking a trip tomorrow. To the Galápagos."

"I've been there," my mother says, lighting up as a thread of memory catches. "There's a tortoise. Lonesome George. He's the last of his whole species. Imagine being the last of anything in the whole world."

For some reason, my throat thickens with tears. "He died," I say.

My mother tilts her head. "Who?"

"Lonesome George."

"Who's George?" she asks, and she narrows her eyes. "Who are *you?*"

That sentence, it wounds me.

I don't know why it hurts so much when my mother forgets me these days, though, when she never actually knew me at all.

When Finn comes home from the hospital, I am in bed under the covers wearing my favorite flannel shirt and sweatpants, with my laptop balanced on my legs. Today has just *flattened* me. Finn sits down beside me, leaning against the headboard. His golden hair is wet, which means he's showered before coming home from New York–Presbyterian, where he is a resident in the surgery department, but he's wearing scrubs that show off the curves of his biceps and the constellation of freckles on his arms. He glances at the screen, and then at the empty pint of ice cream nestled beside me. "Wow," he says. "*Out of Africa . . . and* butter pecan? That's, like, the big guns."

I lean my head on his shoulder. "I had the shittiest day."

"No, I did," Finn replies.

"I lost a painting," I tell him.

"I lost a patient."

I groan. "You win. You always win. No one ever dies of an art emergency."

"No, I mean I *lost* a patient. Elderly woman with LBD wandered off before I could get her in for gallbladder surgery."

"Little black dress?"

A smile tugs at Finn's mouth. "Lewy body dementia."

This makes me think, naturally, of my mother.

"Did you find her?"

"Security did," Finn says. "She was on the labor and delivery floor."

I wonder what it was that made her go *there*—some internal GPS error, or the kite tail of a memory so far in the clouds you can barely see it.

"Then I *do* win," I say, and I give him an abbreviated version of my meeting with Kitomi Ito.

"Okay," Finn says, "in the grand scheme of things, this isn't a disaster. You can still get promoted to specialist, when she eventually decides to sell."

What I love most about Finn (well, all right, *one* of the things I love most about Finn) is that he understands that I have a detailed design for my future. He does, too, for his own. Most important, mine and his overlap: successful careers, then two kids, then a restored farmhouse upstate. An Audi TT. A purebred English springer spaniel, but also a rescued mutt. A period where we live abroad for six months. A bank account with enough padding that we don't have to worry if we need to get snow tires or pay for a new roof. A position on a board at a homeless shelter or a hospital or cancer charity, that in some way makes the world a better place. An accomplishment that makes someone remember my name.

(I had thought that Kitomi Ito's auction might do that.)

If marriage is a yoke meant to keep two people moving in tandem, then my parents were oxen who each pulled in a different direction, and I was caught squarely in the middle. I never understood how you could march down an aisle with someone and not realize that you want totally different futures. My father dreamed of a family; to him art was a means of providing for me. My mother dreamed of art; to her a family was a distraction. I am all for love. But there is no passion so consuming that it can bridge a gap like that.

Life happens when you least expect it, but that doesn't mean you can't have a blueprint in your back pocket. To that end, while a good number of our friends are still racking up expensive degrees or swiping left or figuring out what sparks joy, Finn and I have *plans*. But we don't only have the same general timeline for our lives, we also have the same dreams, as if we're dipping into the same bucket list: Run a marathon. Know how to tell a good cabernet from a bad one. Watch every film in the IMDb top 250. Volunteer at the Iditarod. Hike part of the Appalachian Trail. See tulip fields in the Netherlands. Learn how to surf. See the northern lights. Retire by age fifty. Visit every UNESCO World Heritage Site.

We're starting with the Galápagos. It's a hellishly expensive trip for two millennials in New York; the cost of the flights alone is exorbitant. But we've been saving up for four years, and thanks to a deal I found online, we managed to fit a trip into our budget—one that has us based on a single island, rather than the more expensive island-hopping cruises.

And somewhere on a lava-sand beach, Finn will drop to one knee and I will fall into the ocean of his eyes and say *yes, let's start the rest of our lives*.

Although I have a schedule for my life that I have not deviated from, I'm treading water, waiting for the next milestone. I have a job, but not a promotion. I have a boyfriend, but not a family. It's like when Finn is playing one of his videogames and he can't quite level up. I've visualized, I've manifested, I've tried to speak it into the universe. Finn is right. I will not let a little hiccup like Kitomi's uncertainty derail me.

Derail *us*.

Finn kisses the top of my head. "I'm sorry you lost your painting."

"I'm sorry you lost your patient."

He has been idly tangling his fingers with mine. "She was coughing," he murmurs.

"I thought she was there for her gallbladder."

"She was. But she was coughing. Everyone could hear it. And I . . ." He looks up at me, ashamed. "I was scared."

squeeze Finn's hand. "You thought she had Covid?"

"Yeah." He shakes his head. "So instead of going into her room, I checked on two other patients first. And I guess she got sick of waiting . . . and walked off." He grimaces. "She has a *smoker's cough,* and a gallbladder that needs to be removed, and instead of thinking of her health I was thinking of mine."

"You can't blame yourself for that."

"Can't I? I took an oath. It's like being a fireman and saying it's too hot to go into a burning building."

"I thought there were only nineteen cases in the city."

"Today," Finn stresses. "But my attending put the fear of God into us, saying that the emergency department will be swamped by Monday. I spent an hour memorizing how to put on PPE properly."

"Thank God we're going on vacation," I say. "I feel like we both need the break."

Finn doesn't answer.

"I can't wait till we're on a beach and everything feels a million miles away."

Silence.

"Finn," I say.

He pulls away so that he can look me in the eye. "Diana," he says, "you should still go."

That night, after Finn has fallen into a restless sleep, I wake up with a headache. After I find some aspirin, I slip into the living room and open my laptop. Finn's attending at the hospital made it clear, in no uncertain terms, that taking time off at this moment would be *greatly discouraged.* That they were going to need all hands on deck, immediately.

It's not that I don't believe him, but I think of the deserted train station, and it doesn't make sense. If anything, the city looks empty— not full of sick people.

My eyes jump from headline to headline: State of emergency declared by de Blasio.

The mayor expects a thousand cases in New York City by next week.

The NBA and NHL have canceled their seasons.

The Met has closed to all in-person visits.

Outside, the horizon is starting to blush. I can hear the rumble of a car. It feels like an ordinary Saturday in the city. Except, apparently, we are standing in the eye of the storm.

Once when I was small my father and I went with my mother to shoot pictures of the drought in the Midwest, and we got caught in a tornado. The sky had gone yellow, like an old bruise, and we took refuge in the basement of the B&B, pressed up against boxes marked as Christmas decorations and table linens. My mother had stayed on ground level with her camera. When the wind stopped shrieking and she stepped outside, I followed. She didn't seem surprised to see me there.

There was no sound—no humans, no cars, and oddly, not a single bird or insect. It was like we stood beneath a bell jar.

Is it over? I asked.

Yes, she said. *And no.*

Now, I don't realize Finn is standing behind me until I feel his hands on my shoulders. "It's better this way," he says.

"To go on vacation by myself?"

"For you to be in a place where I won't worry about you," Finn says. "I don't know what I might wind up bringing home from the hospital. I don't even know if I'll be *coming* home from the hospital."

"They keep saying it'll be over in two weeks." *They,* I think. The news anchors, who are parroting the press secretary, who is parroting the president.

"Yeah, I know. But that's not what my attending's saying."

I think about the subway station today. About Times Square, devoid of tourists. I'm not supposed to hoard Lysol or buy N95 masks. I've seen the numbers in France, in Italy, but those casualties were the elderly. I'm all for taking precautions, but I also know I am young and healthy. It is hard to know what to believe. *Whom* to believe.

If the pandemic still feels distant from Manhattan, it will probably

n nonexistent on an archipelago in the middle of the Pacific
ean.

"What if you run out of toilet paper?" I say.

I can hear the smile in his voice. "*That's* what you're worried about?"
He squeezes my shoulders. "I promise I will steal rolls from the hospital if fights start breaking out in the bodegas."

It feels wrong, so wrong, to go without Finn; it feels even more
wrong to think about bringing a friend along as a substitute—not
that I know anyone who could leave for two weeks with zero advance
notice anyway. But there is also a practicality to his suggestion that
sinks its claws into me. I already have the vacation time blocked off.
I know we can get a credit on Finn's airfare, but the fine print on our
amazing travel deal was no refunds, period. I tell myself that it would
be stupid to lose that much money, especially when the thought of
showing up for work on Monday makes my head throb harder. I
think of Rodney telling me to snorkel with the iguanas.

"I'll send pictures," I vow. "So many you'll have to get a better data
plan."

Finn bends down until I can feel his lips in the curve of my neck.
"Have enough fun for both of us," he says.

Suddenly I am gripped by a fear so strong that it propels me out
of my chair and into Finn's arms. "You'll be here, when I get back," I
state, because I cannot bear the thought of that sentence being a
question.

"Diana," he says, smiling. "You couldn't get rid of me if you tried."

I honestly do not remember getting to the Galápagos.

I have the Ambien to blame for that, I suppose. I took it as soon
as I got on the flight. I remember packing, and how at the last minute I took my guidebooks out of my carry-on and put them in my
luggage. I remember checking three times that I had my passport. I
remember Finn getting paged back to the hospital, and how he
kissed me goodbye and said, "Victoria Falls."

"You've already forgotten my name," I joked.

"No, that's the next UNESCO site we visit. Except, for that one, go to Zimbabwe and you stay here. Fair's fair."

"Deal," I promised, because I knew he wouldn't leave me behind.

After that it is all bits and pieces: the crazy bustle of the airport, as if it is holiday season and not a random weekend in March; the bottle of water I buy and finish on the flight and the *People* magazine I never crack open; the jolt of the wheels that whips me out of a dream state full of facts I'd read about my destination. Still logy, I stumble through the unfamiliar airport in Guayaquil, where I will stay one night on mainland Ecuador before my connecting flight to the Galápagos.

I remember only two things about landing: that the airline has lost my luggage, and that someone checks my temperature before letting me into Ecuador.

I don't have enough Spanish or bandwidth to explain that my flight for the islands leaves early tomorrow, but surely this has happened before. I fill out a report at baggage claim, but based on the number of people who are doing the same thing, I don't have high hopes for being reunited with my bag in time. Wistfully I think of the guidebooks I packed in there. Well, that's all right. I'll be discovering places firsthand; I don't need to read about them anymore. I have the essentials in my tote—toothpaste and toothbrush, phone charger, a bathing suit I packed in case *this very thing* happened. I'll come back to the airport in the morning and fly to Baltra on Santa Cruz Island in the Galápagos, then take a bus to the ferry to Isabela Island, where I'll stay for two weeks. Hopefully my bag will catch up with me at some point.

After I shower, I braid my hair, connect to the shitty hotel Wi-Fi, and try to FaceTime Finn. He doesn't answer, and then a few minutes later, my phone starts to ring. When his face swims onto the screen, it is hidden behind a face shield, and he's wearing a surgical mask. "You made it," he says.

"I did," I tell him. "My suitcase, though, wasn't as lucky."

"Wow. You mean, not only did I give up a vacation in paradise . . . I also gave up a vacation where you'll be walking around naked?"

smile. "I'm hoping it doesn't come to that." Suddenly I feel very
red, and very isolated. "I miss you," I say.

The sound of an ambulance siren swells through the speaker.
Finn's eyes cut to the left. "I have to go."

"Are you seeing it yet?" I ask. "The virus?"

His eyes meet mine, and behind the Plexiglas shield I notice the
faint circles underneath them. It's ten P.M. While I've been asleep on
a plane, I realize, Finn has not left the hospital for twelve hours. "It's
all I'm seeing," he says, and then the line goes dead.

The next morning, my flight to Santa Cruz goes off without a hitch.
But there is a sea lion between me and the ferry to my final destination.

It sprawls across the dock in the sunshine, a slug of muscle, whiskers twitching. I edge closer toward it with my camera, thinking I
can send a picture to Finn, but the minute I'm within striking distance its head and shoulders swoop upward and its eyes fix on me.

I run, leaping over its tail as it lets out a yawp and a roar, and I
nearly drop my phone.

My heart's still pounding when I reach the boat. I glance over my
shoulder, certain that the beast is right on my heels, but the sea lion
is immobile again, splayed on the bleached boardwalk like a lazy dog.

There are only two ferries a day to Isabela Island, but the afternoon trip isn't as crowded as I expect it to be. In fact, there's only me
and two other passengers. In broken Spanish, I ask the man who
helps me board if I am on the right boat, and get a sharp nod. I take
a seat outside. And then, suddenly, we're afloat and Santa Cruz Island starts to get smaller and smaller.

The Galápagos are a collection of islands flung into the ocean like
a handful of gems on velvet. They look, I imagine, the way the world
did when it was newly born—mountains too fresh to gentle into
slopes, mist spitting in valleys, volcanoes unraveling the seam of the
sky. Some are still spiky with lava. Some are surrounded by water
that's a dozy turquoise, some by a dramatic froth of waves. Some, like

Isabela, are inhabited. Others are accessible solely by boat, and home only to the bizarre collection of creatures that have evolved there.

For two hours on the ferry I am sprayed, jerked, and yanked through choppy waters. One of the passengers, who looks to be a college kid backpacking around, is an unsettling shade of green. The other is a girl with the smooth brown skin of a local. She seems young—maybe twelve or thirteen?—and she is wearing a school uniform: a knit polo shirt with a school crest embroidered over the heart and a pair of black pants. In spite of the heat, she is also sporting a long-sleeved sweatshirt. Her shoulders are hunched, arms clutching a duffel; her eyes are red. Everything about her says: *Leave me alone.*

I keep my eyes on the horizon of the water and try not to throw up. I mentally compose a text to Finn: *Remember the time we took the ferry from Bar Harbor to Nova Scotia for your roommate's wedding and everyone on board got sick?*

The ferry does not, as it turns out, go all the way to Isabela. It stops at a mooring, and then the backpacker, the girl, and I share a water taxi the final leg of the journey—a short distance to Puerto Villamil. I am squinting at the sugar-sand beach and palm trees when the backpacker beside me laughs with delight. "Dude!" he says. He grabs my sleeve and points. Swimming beside the boat is a tiny penguin.

As we get closer, the mass of land differentiates into individual sensations: hot gusts of wind and hooting pelicans; a man climbing a coconut tree and tossing the nuts down to a boy; a marine iguana, blinking its yellow dinosaur eye. Sidling up to the dock, I think that this could not be any more different from New York City. It feels tropical and timeless, lazy, remote. It feels like a place where no one has ever heard of a pandemic.

But then I realize that there is a horde of people waiting to secure the services of the water taxi. They have the sunburned look of tourists who are already refitting themselves into the mindset of home, shoving and yelling over each other. One man holds out a fistful of cash, waving it at our driver, who looks overwhelmed. "What's going on?" I ask.

"*La isla está cerrando,*" he says.

Cerrando, I think, rummaging through my limited Spanish vocabulary.

"I don't understand," I say.

The young girl is silent, staring at the dock ahead. The backpacker looks at me, and then at the crowd. He speaks in Spanish to our taxi driver, who responds in a stream of words I don't know.

"The island's closing," he says.

How does an island *close?*

"They're locking down for two weeks," the boy continues. "Because of the virus." He nods at all the people waiting on the dock. "They're all trying to get back to Santa Cruz."

The girl shuts her eyes, as if she doesn't want to see any of them.

I can't imagine how all these people are going to fit on the small ferry. The taxi driver asks a question in Spanish.

"He wants to know if we want to go back," the boy says, glancing in the direction of the ferry, still moored a distance away. "That's the last boat off-island."

I do not like it when plans change.

I think of Finn, telling me to leave New York City. I think of the paid-in-full room waiting for me within walking distance of these docks. If the island is locking down for two weeks, then they must be assuming that's how long it will take for the virus to be controlled. I could spend those two weeks fighting with this angry mob to get a seat on a flight back to New York, and hole up in our apartment while Finn works.

The boy tells the driver something in Spanish, then turns to me. "I told him you'll probably want to go back."

"Why?"

He shrugs. "Because you look like someone who plays it safe."

Something about that smarts. Just because there's a small glitch doesn't mean I can't adapt. "Well, actually, you're wrong. I'm staying."

The backpacker's brows rise. "For real? Shit," he says, with grudging admiration.

"Well, what are you going to do?" I ask the kid.

"Go back," he says. "I've already been in the Galápagos for a week."

"I haven't," I reply, as if I need an excuse.

"Suit yourself," he says.

Two minutes later, the girl and I get off the water taxi onto Isabela Island. The knot of anxious travelers parts and flows around us like a current as they hurry to board the small boat. I smile at the girl shyly, but she doesn't respond. After a while I realize she isn't by my side anymore. I glance back and see her sitting on a wooden bench near the pier, her duffel beside her, wiping tears off her face.

Just then, the water taxi pulls away from the dock.

Suddenly it hits me: in an effort to seem more chill than I actually am, I have just stranded myself on an island.

I have never really traveled on my own. When I was little I went on location with my father when he went to restore works of art—at museums in Los Angeles, Florence, Fontainebleau. When I was in college, my roommates and I spent spring break in the Bahamas. I spent one summer with friends, working in Canada. I've flown to Los Angeles and Seattle with Eva to schmooze potential clients and evaluate pieces of art for auction. With Finn, I've driven to Acadia National Park; I've flown to Miami for a long weekend, and I was his plus-one at a wedding in Colorado. I've met women who stubbornly insist on traveling by themselves to the most remote places, as if belligerent self-sufficiency is even more Instagrammable than foreign landmarks. But that's not who I am. I like having someone share the same memories as me. I like knowing that when I turn to Finn and say, *Remember that time on Cadillac Mountain* . . . I do not even have to finish the sentence.

You are on an adventure, I remind myself.

After all, my mother used to do this effortlessly, in places that were far less civilized.

When I look back at the pier again, the girl is gone.

I slide my carry-on tote onto my shoulder and walk away from the docks. The town's small buildings are jumbled like a puzzle: brick walls with a thatched roof, a brightly painted pink stucco, a wooden

breezeway with a BAR/RESTAURANT sign above it. They are all different; the only thing they have in common is that the doors are firmly
shut.

La isla está cerrando.

Land iguanas wriggle across the sand street, the only signs of life.

I pass a *farmacia* and a store and several *hostales*. This is the only
road; it stands to figure that if I stay on it, I will find my hotel.

I keep walking until I spot the boy I saw from the boat who has
been catching the coconuts. *"Hola,"* I say, smiling. I gesture up and
down the road. "Casa del Cielo . . . ?"

There is a light thud as the man who has been in the coconut tree
drops down behind me. "Casa del Cielo," he repeats. *"El hotel no está
lejos, pero no están abiertos."*

I smile at him, all teeth. *"Gracias,"* I say, even though I have no clue
what he said. I wonder what the hell I was thinking, coming to a
country where I do not speak the language.

Oh. Right. I was thinking that I was coming with Finn, who *does*.

With a little polite wave, I continue in the direction he's pointed.
I have gone only a few hundred yards when I see a faded wooden
sign, carved with the name of the hotel.

I reach the front door just as someone is exiting. She is an old
woman, her face so creased with wrinkles that it looks like linen; her
black eyes are bright. She calls back to someone still inside the building, who answers in Spanish. She is wearing a cotton dress with the
logo of the hotel over the left breast. She smiles at me and disappears
around the side of the building.

Immediately following her comes another woman—younger, with
a rope of hair down her back. She is holding a set of keys, and starts
locking the door behind her.

Which seems really strange, for a hotel.

"Discúlpame," I say. "Is this Casa del Cielo?"

She cranes her neck, as if to look at the roof, and nods. *"Estamos
cerrados,"* she says, and she looks at me. "Closed," she adds.

I blink. Maybe this is a siesta kind of thing; maybe all businesses
on the island close at (I glance at my watch) . . . 4:30.

She gives the door a sharp tug and starts walking away. Panicked, I run after her, calling for her to wait. She turns, and I rummage in my tote until I find the printed confirmation from the hotel; proof of my two weeks, paid in advance.

She takes the piece of paper from me and scans it. When she speaks again, it is a river of Spanish, and I recognize only a single word: *coronavirus*.

"When will you be open again?" I ask.

Then she hunches her shoulders, the universal sign for *You are shit out of luck*.

She gets on a bike and pedals away, leaving me in front of a rundown hotel that has charged me in advance for a room they won't give me, in a country where I don't speak the language, on an island where I am stranded for two weeks with little more than a toothbrush.

I wander behind the hotel, which backs up to the ocean. The sky is bruised and tender. Marine iguanas scuttle out of my way as I sit down on an outcropping of lava and take out my phone to call Finn.

But there's no signal.

I bury my face in my hands.

This is not how I travel. I have hotel reservations and guidebooks and airline mileage accounts. I triple-check to make sure I have my license and passport. I organize. The thought of wandering aimlessly through a town and rolling up to a hotel and asking if there are vacancies makes me sick to my stomach.

My mother had once been in Sri Lanka photographing water buffalo on a beach when a tsunami hit. *The elephants,* she said, *ran for the hills before any of us even realized what was coming. Flamingos moved to higher ground. Dogs refused to go outside. When everything else is running in one direction,* she said, *it's usually for a reason.*

At the touch of a hand on my shoulder, I jump. The old woman who exited the hotel is now standing behind me. When she smiles, mostly toothless, her lips curl around her gums into her mouth. *"Ven conmigo,"* she says, and when I don't move, she reaches out a bony hand and pulls me to my feet.

She holds on to me as if I am a toddler, leading me further down the sandy street of Puerto Villamil. It is not wise, I know, to allow myself to be dragged somewhere by a stranger. But she hardly fits the profile of a serial killer; and I am out of options. Numbly, I follow her past the locked shops and closed restaurants and silent bars, which give way to small, neat dwellings. Some are fancier than others, hiding behind low stucco walls with gates. Others have bicycles rusting against them. Some have yards made of crushed seashells.

The woman turns toward one little house. It is square and made of concrete, painted pale yellow. It has a small porch made out of wood, and wrapped around the legs of its columns are vines thick with a riot of flowers. Instead of climbing the steps, though, she takes me around the back of the house, which slopes down toward the water. There is a courtyard with a metal café table and a rope hammock, some potted plants, and a break in the knee-high wall that leads directly onto the beach. The waves are spreading rumors down the shore.

When I turn around, the old woman has stepped through a sliding glass door and is waving me closer. I walk into a tiny apartment that looks both lived in and not. There is furniture: a worn, ugly brown plaid couch and a driftwood coffee table, scattered rag throw rugs. There is a rickety table big enough for two, with a blushing conch shell in the center holding down a stack of paper napkins. There's a refrigerator and an oven and a stove. But there are no books on the shelves, no food in the open cupboards, no art on the walls.

"You," she says, the English sharp on her tongue, "stay."

I can't help it, my eyes fill with tears. "Thank you," I say. "I can pay you. *Dolares*."

She shrugs, as if it is absolutely normal for a stranger to offer up a home for a displaced traveler, and money is beside the point. Then again, maybe on Isabela, it is. She smiles and pats her own chest. "Abuela," she says.

I smile back at her. "Diana," I reply.

The apartment is a little mystery. There is a twin mattress, and I hunt down sheets in a linen closet. Buried in the back beneath the towels are three T-shirts, soft and faded—one with a flag I do not recognize, another with a black cat, a third with the logo of a company over the breast. That same logo is on a box of oversize promotional postcards that I find in a box—easily several hundred of them. G2 TOURS, surrounded by pictures of a volcano and a tortoise and a rocky beach and a beady-eyed blue-footed booby. In a pitted armoire in the bedroom I find a pair of flip-flops that are too big for me, and a mask and snorkel. In the bathroom, there is a half-empty tube of toothpaste in a drawer and a bottle of generic ibuprofen. The refrigerator has a few random condiments—mustard, Tabasco—but nothing I can eat.

It is that which drives me out of the relative comfort and safety of the apartment. When my stomach growls so loud I can't ignore it anymore, I decide to go in search of food and a decent cellphone signal. I peel off the shirt I've been wearing for two days and change into the tee with the logo, knotting it at my waist. Then I exit the sliding glass door, and find myself standing at the edge of the world.

The ocean is flirting with the shore, rushing over it and then retreating. A movement draws my attention as a ragged outcropping of rock suddenly animates—not lava rock, as it turns out, but a tangle of marine iguanas that slide into the waves, diving down. I try to follow their trajectory but I lose sight of them when the water gets deep. I shade my eyes with my hand, and try to pick out another island on the horizon, but I can see only an indistinct blur where sea meets sky. I can totally understand how a captain might have charted that point, and believed he could sail over the edge.

I suddenly feel very, very far away from my real life.

It seems like I'm the only person on the beach, but then gradually I notice someone running far in the distance, and if I concentrate, I can hear the whoop of children playing somewhere. When I turn back to the house, upstairs, there is a silhouette of someone—Abuela, I assume—behind a pale curtain.

I could go up there, and mime hunger, and Abuela would likely sit me down and cook me a meal. But it feels rude, especially since she has already given me shelter. I also know, because I just walked through town, that all the businesses are shuttered. Maybe there's a restaurant or a market in the opposite direction? So I channel my inner Elizabeth Gilbert/Amelia Earhart/Sally Ride and strike out into the unknown.

The only road out of town winds past cacti and tangled brush and brackish water. Flamingos blush, walking on water, the cursive loops of their necks forming secret messages as they dive for shrimp. At certain points the road narrows and is edged with black stones. At others, it is littered with fallen leaves. Everything is green and red and orange; it is like stepping into a Gauguin. My phone has only one bar the entire time.

Finn will freak out if he doesn't hear from me. On some rational level he knows that there is limited Wi-Fi in the Galápagos. I literally told him on the phone, yesterday, before we were cut off. Plus, the guidebooks all mention it as a caveat and say your best bet is spotty service at your hotel . . . or suggest turning off your phone, and simply enjoying your vacation. To Finn and me, that sounded like heaven. But that was when we thought we would be *together* inside this bubble of solitude.

If it were the other way around—if *he* were the one who was stuck somewhere without cell service—I would be worried. I console myself with a pep talk: he knows I landed safely; it has been only a day; I will figure out a way to reach him tomorrow.

By the time I've walked for twenty minutes, it's nearly sunset. The jaunty arms of the cacti re-form in the low light into strangers following me; when iguanas scissor in front of me I jump. I should turn around before it's too dark for me to find my way back. I am about to resign myself to going to bed hungry when I see a little shed further up the road. I squint, but I can't quite make out the sign.

By the time I can read it, I know that it's not a restaurant or a convenience store. CENTRO DE CRIANZA DE TORTUGAS GIGANTES. There is a translation in English—GIANT TORTOISE BREEDING CENTER—and just to be extra clear, a picture of a tortoise hatching from an egg.

There is no gate, so I wander into the open-air courtyard. The main building is closed up for the night (or longer?), but a horseshoe of enclosures surrounds me. Each pen is gated by a concrete wall that is a few feet high—certainly big enough for me to lean over, but too high for the tortoises to escape.

I approach one wall and find myself face-to-face with a prehistoric-looking tortoise. Its slitted eyes stare at me as it moves closer on padded feet and stretches its neck up from the hump of its shell. I look at its flat head and dinosaur skin, the black ridges of its toes, its Voldemort nose. It opens its mouth and sticks out a spear of tongue.

Delighted, I lean down on my elbows and watch it turn away, loping across the dusty ground toward another tortoise in the distance. With lumbering underwater movements, it crawls up the shell of the second tortoise, anchoring her so they can mate. The male I've been watching curves his neck toward his partner, tendons stretching. His thick arms look like they are covered in chain mail. He grunts, the only sound he'll make in his life.

"You go, buddy," I murmur, and I turn away to give them privacy.

In the other enclosures are hundreds of tortoises of varying sizes. They look, heaped, like a collection of army helmets. Some sleep, some are surprisingly limber. Others seem world-weary, as they crawl out of a puddle electric green with algae, or maneuver stalks of food into their mouths. Even the smallest ones remind me of old men, with the wrinkled skin of their throats and bald pates.

In one of the enclosures, a few of the tortoises are chewing on apples. The apples are small and green and seem to have fallen from a tree beyond the concrete pen. I watch the reptiles use their powerful jaws to grind.

My stomach rumbles, and I glance at the tree.

I'm not the kind of person who eats berries off random trees; I'm a New Yorker, for God's sake, and most of nature looks like a hazard to me. But if the tortoises are eating these, then they have to be safe, right?

I can't quite reach the fruit. The branches that hang into the pen have already been stripped by the greedy tortoises, so I find myself climbing onto the little wall to grasp an apple.

"*Cuidado!*"

I turn, almost toppling into the tortoise pen with surprise. The dark has settled like a net, casting shadows, so I can't see who's calling to me. I hesitate, and then turn back to the apple tree.

My fingers have just brushed against the skin of the apple when I am yanked off the wall and lose my balance, then find myself sprawled on the dusty ground with a man looming over me. He is yelling in Spanish, and I cannot see his face in the dark. He leans down and grabs my wrist.

I wonder why I assumed it was safe to wander an unfamiliar island by myself.

I wonder if I escaped a pandemic at home only to get attacked here.

I start fighting. When I land a good punch in his ribs, he grunts, and holds me tighter.

"Don't hurt me," I cry out. "Please."

He twists my wrist, and for the first time I feel the burn in my fingertips where they brushed against the skin of the apple. They are blistered and red.

"Too late," he says in perfect English. "You already did that yourself."

TWO

I scramble to my feet, cradling my hand. My fingertips throb.

"They're poisonous to the touch," the man says. "The apples."

"I didn't know."

"You should have," he mutters. "There are signs everywhere."

Poison apples, like a fairy tale. Except my prince is stuck in a hospital in New York City and the evil witch is a six-foot-tall galapagueño with anger management issues. I look at the tortoises, still blissfully feasting, and he follows my gaze. "You're not a tortoise," he says, as if he knows exactly what I'm thinking.

By now my skin feels like it's on fire. "How poisonous?" I ask, starting to panic. Do I need to go to the hospital?

Is there even a hospital?

He takes my hand and peers down at my fingers. He has dark hair and darker eyes and he is wearing running shorts and a sweaty tank. "It'll go away, the burn, the blisters. Soak in cold water if you have to." Then his eyes narrow on my breasts. I yank my hand away and fold my arms over my chest. "Where did you get that?"

"Get what?"

"That shirt."

"I borrowed it," I say. "My luggage got lost."

His scowl carves deeper lines in his face. "You're on vacation," he mutters. "Of *course* you are."

He says this like it is a great personal affront to him that I, an outsider, am on Isabela. For a country whose main source of revenue is tourism, this doesn't exactly feel like a warm welcome.

"I hate to break this to you, but everything on the island is closed for two weeks, including this place."

"*You're* here," I point out.

"I live here, and I'm on my way home. Like you should be. Or haven't you heard there's a pandemic?"

At that, I bristle. "Actually, yes, I have heard. My boyfriend is on the front lines treating it."

"So you decided to bring the virus here."

As if I am Typhoid Mary. As if I am intentionally trying to hurt people, instead of attempting to stay safe.

"*Maldita turista,*" he mutters. "Who cares what happens, as long as you get your vacation."

My eyes widen. He might have kept me from eating something poisonous, but he's still a complete asshole. "As a matter of fact, I don't have Covid. But you know, just to make sure, we can socially distance right now by putting the entire island between us."

I pivot and march away from him. My blistered hand, dangling at my side, has its own heartbeat. I refuse to turn around to see if he's watching me leave, or if he's continued toward his home. I don't stop moving until I reach the entrance of the center. Just beside the sign I saw when I first arrived is another sign, this one with a picture of an apple and a red X covering it. CUIDADO! LOS MANZANILLOS SON NA-TIVOS DE LAS GALÁPAGOS. SOLAMENTE LAS TORTUGAS GIGANTES SON CAPACES DE DIGERIR ESTAS MANZANITAS VENENOSAS. And then in perfectly clear English: CAREFUL! MANCHINEEL TREES ARE NATIVE TO GALÁPAGOS. ONLY GIANT TORTOISES CAN DIGEST THESE POISON-OUS LITTLE APPLES.

I hear a muffled snort and look up to see him standing ten feet away from me, arms crossed. Then he heads off deeper into the is-land, until the dark swallows him whole.

By the time I return to the apartment, it's night. Unlike in the city, where there's always a glow from a billboard or a storefront, here the dark is comprehensive. I navigate by the moonlight, which is bouncing on the ocean like a skipping stone. When I reach the stretch of beach in front of the apartment, I take off my sneakers and wade in ankle deep, bending to hold my singed fingers in the cold surf. My stomach growls.

I retreat to the little knee wall that divides the yard from the beach and pull out my phone. It sits in my palm, bright as a star, fruitlessly searching for a signal.

I miss you, I type in a text thread to Finn, and then erase the letters one by one. Somehow, it's worse trying and failing to send a text than to never send it at all.

If Finn were here, we would have laughed the whole way back to our hotel room, bonding over poisoned apples and rude locals.

If Finn were here, he would have given me half of the KIND bar he always carries on a plane, just in case.

If Finn were here, maybe I'd be engaged, and getting ready to start the rest of the life I've planned.

But Finn isn't here.

The whole point of traveling with someone from home is to remind you where you came from, to have a reason to leave when you begin to lose yourself in the lights of Paris or the majesty of a safari and think, *What if I just stay?*

But given that I don't have a hotel room and I'm starving and I have blisters on my hand from a killer native tree, there isn't much that makes me want to remain on Isabela. Except for the fact that I literally can't leave.

I am so out of my comfort zone that all I want to do is curl up in a fetal position and cry. I slip through the sliding glass door and turn on a light. On the kitchen table, beside the conch shell, is a plate covered by a tea towel. Even from across the room, I can smell something delicious. When I pull off the towel, the table rocks unevenly.

On the plate is a quesadilla of sorts, stuffed with cheese, onions, to-matoes. I eat all six slices standing up.

I take the box of G2 Tours postcards and set them on the kitchen counter. Pulling one from the stack, I use a pen from my tote and write a message. GRACIAS, I scrawl, and sign my name, and then trudge barefoot up to the front entrance of the home. It's dark inside, so I slip the message under the front door.

It's possible that for every angry asshole on this island, there's someone like Abuela.

Back in my apartment, I write a second postcard—this one to Finn—before I pull off my clothes and slip into bed and fall asleep to the bated breath of the overhead fan.

Dear Finn,

It feels really old school to be writing a postcard, but even if this island is a technology desert, the mail is supposed to work, right? First, I should tell you that I'm fine—there's no evidence of the virus anywhere here. The ferries stopped running for two weeks, presumably to keep it that way. It's not going to be the vacation I expected—tourism (and everything else commercial) is shut down here. But I'm renting a room from a nice old lady and what's cooler than living as a local, right?! I'm just going to have to explore Isabela on my own, but that means I'll be an expert when you and I take a trip back here. ☺

It is dramatically gorgeous here—I keep thinking that a painting wouldn't do it justice, because you'd never capture the black of the rocks that glint in the sun, or the turquoise of the water. It feels kind of . . . rugged and unfinished. There are iguanas just hanging out every-where, like they own the place. I'm pretty sure there are more of them than there are human residents.

Speaking of residents—I hope you're okay. I hate not being able to hear your voice. Yes, even when you're singing off key in the shower.

Love, Diana

From preschool, at my first easel, it was clear that I had some kind of gift for art. My father was the one who worked on paintings—from ceiling frescoes to giant canvases, doing conservation—but he would have been the first to tell you that he was not a creator, but a re-creator. When I was a freshman at Williams and one of my paintings was chosen to be part of a student exhibition, my father proudly came to the opening, wearing the only suit he owned.

My mother did not attend. She was embedded in Somalia, chronicling their civil war.

My father spent twenty minutes absorbing my piece. He stared at it as though he had been told that the world was about to go black and white, and this was his last chance to see color. Several times I saw his hand twitch as he reached toward the frame, and then settle at his side again. Finally, he turned to me. *You have your mother's eye,* he said.

The next semester, instead of signing up for more art studio classes, I filled my time with art history and media and business courses. I did not want to spend my life being compared to my mother, because I was determined to be nothing like her. If that meant finding a different branch of the art world to perch on, so be it.

I wasn't surprised to be selected for a summer internship at Sotheby's when I was a rising senior, because I had structured my entire college career around being accepted to their program. On my first day, I was shuttled into a large room full of equally bright-eyed summer interns. I sat down beside a Black man who—unlike the rest of us, in our conservative blazers and tailored trousers—was wearing a purple silk shirt and a midi skirt printed with enormous roses. He caught me staring, and I jerked my head toward the front of the room, where the directors of the different departments were lining up, calling out interns' names.

"If I didn't want people looking," he whispered, "I wouldn't have worn it. McQueen."

I held out my hand. "Diana."

"Oh, honey," he said. "No. The designer of the skirt is Alexander McQueen." He reached out his own hand—beringed, with silver polish on his nails. "*I'm* Rodney." Then he cataloged me from my neat part to my sensible heels. "Middlebury?"

"Williams."

"Hmm," he replied, as if I might be wrong about my own college. "First rodeo?"

"Yeah. Yours?"

"Second," Rodney said. "I was here last summer, too. They work you like a three-legged husky at the Iditarod, but I've heard Christie's is worse." He raised a brow. "You know how this goes, right?"

I shook my head.

"It's like Harry Potter's sorting hat. They call out your name, and your department. No trades." He leaned closer. "I'm a design major at RISD and last year I got placed in *Fine Wine*. Wine. What the hell do I know about wine? And no, before you ask, you don't get to drink it."

"Impressionism," I told him. "That's what I'm hoping for."

Rodney smirked. "Then you'll probably wind up in Space Exploration."

"Musical Instruments." I grinned.

"Handbags."

He reached into a satchel and pulled out a foil-wrapped package. "Here," he said, breaking off a piece of cake. "Drown your sorrows preemptively."

"Cake makes everything better," I said, taking a healthy bite.

"So do hash brownies."

I choked, and Rodney whacked me on the back.

Diana O'Toole, I heard, and I popped up out of my chair. "Here!" I called.

Private Collections.

I looked down at Rodney, who pushed the rest of the brownie into my hand. "Could have been Rugs and Carpets," he murmured. "Chow down."

As it turned out, I did not finish the hash brownie, even as I sat at the front desk, where I had been assigned to answer phones and direct visitors to floors of a company I didn't yet know. I routed calls and read obituaries in *The New York Times*, circling in red pen the obits of rich people who might have estates to be auctioned. Then, one afternoon, a man who was nearly as wide as he was tall strode up to the desk holding a frame wrapped in linen. "I need to see Eva St. Clerck," he announced.

"I can make you an appointment," I offered.

"I don't think you understand," he said. "This is a Van Gogh."

He began to unwrap his frame, and I held my breath, anticipating the signature broken brushstrokes and thick blocks of color. Instead, I found myself staring at a watercolor.

Van Gogh did paint over a hundred watercolors. But I didn't see the explosion of color that might have confirmed the origin of the piece for me, and it wasn't signed.

Of course, it also wasn't my department—or my job—to assess it.

But what if? I thought. *What if this is my big break, and I'm the standout intern who identifies a diamond-in-the-rough Van Gogh and becomes a legend at Sotheby's?*

"Just a moment," I said.

With my hand wrapped around the receiver, I called Eva St. Clerck, who was a senior specialist in Imp Mod back then. I introduced myself and had barely begun to explain when she said, "Oh, for fuck's sake," and hung up the phone.

Two minutes later, she was striding out of the elevator bank. "Mr. Duncan," Eva said, her words frosting over. "As I told you last week and the week before that and the week before *that*, we do not believe that this is an original—"

"She said otherwise," the man said, jabbing a finger at me.

My eyes widened. "I did *not*."

"*She,*" Eva said, "is a nobody. She is not qualified to assess a ham sandwich, much less a piece of art."

I blinked. This was the woman I'd hoped to work for that summer; maybe I had dodged a bullet.

Suddenly a hand grabbed my arm. "Get up." I was so caught up in the drama unfolding before me that I hadn't even noticed my *actual* boss approaching from the other direction. Jeremiah was a senior specialist in Private Collections, and he had been tasked with finding things for me to do, like play receptionist at the front desk. "We need you now."

"But the desk—"

"I don't care." Jeremiah pulled me away, talking as he led me down a rabbit warren of hallways. "The Vanderbilts are deciding between us and Christie's to sell their estate. It's all hands on deck."

Jeremiah opened the door to a conference room. A frazzled group of estate sales specialists looked up. "That's the intern?" one of them said. I was led to a computer in the corner, and told to start entering the hundreds and hundreds of pages of notes on art and property and belongings that were part of the estate. While I typed and double-checked my work and inventoried the list, the group behind me tossed out pitches that might convince the Vanderbilts to choose Sotheby's over Christie's.

For days I organized oils by Dutch Masters and Rolls-Royces and gilded horse carriages and listened to Jeremiah and the other senior specialists dream up a breathtaking pitch for an auction. Stepping into that room was like being wrapped by electricity; it was the confirmation I needed that the buzz provided by art did not begin and end at its creation.

The Vanderbilts picked Sotheby's the day before my internship ended. There was champagne and speeches and a round of applause for me, the draft horse who had labored nights and weekends on the grunt work.

No matter what Eva St. Clerck thought of me.

I stole a bottle of Moët and drank it with Rodney in the handicapped bathroom. Over the course of the summer we'd become inseparable. He had been assigned to Islamic Art, but somehow convinced his senior specialist to let him hang out with the design team that structured the rooms and displays in which auctions took place.

We wandered through the Met and the Whitney on weekends and made it our mission to find the best avocado toast in the city. I got him drunk when his boyfriend dumped him via text; he dragged me to sample sales and Cinderella-ed me out of my chinos and into deep-discount Max Mara and Ralph Lauren. "Here's to Fine Wines," I said, lifting the bottle to my lips.

"Here's to *us:* future graduates of the Sotheby's master's class of 2013," Rodney countered. Our plan was to matriculate in the company's art business degree program together, get hired for real, and take over the art world.

Privately, I also wanted Eva St. Clerck to know who I was, and what I was capable of.

Nine years and several promotions later, Eva St. Clerck knows who I am: the protégée who secured Kitomi Ito's Toulouse-Lautrec . . . and lost it.

When I wake up the next morning, the sun is swollen in the sky and beating so hot it makes the air ache. I pull on the bathing suit I had the uncanny prescience to pack in my carry-on, grab a towel, and walk to the edge of the ocean, dancing faster when the soles of my feet start to burn. The blisters on my hand have flattened into calluses.

The difference between the broiling air and the cold waves makes me gasp, but I draw in a deep breath and run into the surf, three long strides, and then dive underneath. When I surface, my hair is slicked back from my face, and I float on my back with my eyes closed. The salt dries on my cheeks, tightening my skin.

How long could I stay like this, suspended, blind? Where would I wind up?

I let my legs sink with gravity and squint at the horizon. I wonder if that's the direction Finn's in.

It feels like massive cognitive dissonance to be in this tropical paradise and to know, half a world away, New York City is bracing for a pandemic.

When you're surrounded by desert, it's inconceivable to think there are places that flood.

I wade out of the ocean, wrap myself in the towel, and wring out my ponytail. Suddenly all the hair stands up on the back of my neck, as if I am being watched. I whirl around, but there is no one on the beach. When I turn back toward the apartment, I see a blur of movement, but it is gone before I get close enough to see.

It isn't until I'm in the shower that I realize I have no shampoo and no soap. And of course, no food, since I ate everything that Abuela left me last night. With my skin and hair still unwashed, I pull on my jeans from yesterday and a fresh T-shirt from the stash I found in the linen closet and walk back into Puerto Villamil. I'm hoping something is open now. My goal is to stock up on supplies and provisions, and to find a post office where I can get stamps and mail the postcard I wrote to Finn. If I can't get texts or emails or calls out to him, at least he will have an old-fashioned letter.

But Puerto Villamil is a ghost town. The bars and restaurants and hostels and shops are all still dark and closed. The post office has a locked metal gate pulled down over its entryway. For a heart-stopping moment I wonder if maybe I've slept through an evacuation, if the entire island is empty except for me. Then I realize that one of the businesses, while still dark inside, has someone bustling around.

I knock on the door, but the woman inside shakes her head at me. *"Por favor,"* I say.

She puts down the box she is holding and unlocks the door. *"No perteneces aquí. Hay toque de queda."*

It is, I realize, a market. There are baskets on the counter filled with fruit, and a few narrow aisles sparsely lined with shelved dry goods. I pull cash out of my pocket. "I can pay."

"Closed," she says haltingly.

"Please," I say.

Her face softens, and she holds up a hand with her fingers outstretched. Five items? Five minutes? I point to a yellow fruit in a basket at the counter. Guava, maybe. The woman picks it up. "Soap?" I say. "Sopa?"

She reaches onto a shelf and holds out a can of soup.

Well, I'll take it, but I can't shower with it. I mime scrubbing my hair, and under my arms, and she nods and adds a bar of Ivory to my pile. I say every Spanish food item in my narrow vocabulary: *agua, leche, café, huevo*. There is little that's fresh, which limits my options, and which makes me wonder how or if the people on Isabela will get shipments of perishables like milk and eggs. For every item I manage to communicate, there are two that she doesn't have; the locals must have known things were closing down and stocked up. "Pasta?" I say finally, and she finds three boxes of penne.

There are worse fates than having to eat only pasta.

"Stamps?" I ask. I hold out my postcard and point to the corner.

She shakes her head, and points across the street to the closed post office.

On the counter is a small stack of newspapers. I cannot read the Spanish headlines, but the picture makes it clear—it is a priest in a church in Italy, blessing scores of coffins filled with Covid casualties.

This is what is coming to America. This is what Finn will be dealing with.

And I am stuck here.

The shop owner holds out her hand, the universal symbol for payment. I offer a credit card and she shakes her head. I don't have any Ecuadorian money and I still haven't found an ATM. Panicked, I peel off two twenties and hand them to her before she can renege and take away my groceries. She locks the door again, and I head off with my plastic bag.

I'm halfway down the main street when I hear a ping on my phone. I pull it out of my pocket and watch a torrent of messages from Finn roll onto my screen.

I lost you.

Hello?

Tried FaceTiming but . . . ?

Bad Wi-Fi? Will try you tomorrow.

He's texted multiple times since then, and finally seemed to realize that I still didn't have cell service. The last message says that he'll send an email instead, in case I find an internet café.

I look up and down the street at the tightly closed storefronts and snort.

But apparently, I am sitting in the one hot spot of service in Puerto Villamil, because when I check my inbox, somehow there is an email that has downloaded from Finn. I sit down cross-legged and start to read, absorbing his words like they are an oasis in a desert.

To: DOToole@gmail.com
From: FColson@nyp.org

I can't believe it's only been two days. The schools are already shut down here, and bars and restaurants. We've got 923 cases in the city alone. Ten deaths. The subway is empty. It's like New York is a shell, and all the people are in hiding.

Not that I'd know, because I haven't left the hospital. They scrapped the model for surgical residents. You know how I used to bitch about being a junior resident, because I'd have to do nights and ED consults while the senior residents scrubbed in to the actual surgeries—and how you said that one day it would be my turn? Well, nope. I may be a fourth-year resident but that's gone. No one is doing surgery anymore. All elective procedures—and even emergent ones, like appys and gallbladders—have been canceled, because the surgical ICU is filled with Covid patients. Residents are expendable, I guess, so we've all been reassigned to Covid, too.

To be fair, it's the only illness we're seeing. But I was trained as a surgeon, and suddenly I'm supposed to be an internal med doc treating infectious disease, and I have no idea what I'm doing.

Neither does anyone else.

I'm on hour 34 of my 12-hour shift, because there aren't enough of us to take care of the patients. They started arriving and they haven't stopped. They all show up gasping and by the time they get here, they're already screwed. They try to suck in air, but there's nowhere for the air to go, so they wind up damaging more lung—it's this vicious cycle. Normally, we'd put patients like that on high-flow nasal cannulas, which can get them ten times as much oxygen, but they also would aerosolize the virus all over the place. So instead we use non-rebreather masks or small nasal cannulas. They don't work. Nothing in our bag of tricks does. People are crashing left and right because they aren't getting enough oxygen, and the only thing left to do is intubate. Which is the most dangerous thing of all, because we can't get a patient on a vent without literally spreading the virus all over ourselves.

So we have armor, I guess, even though there's not enough of it. Now, just to see a patient, I have to put on my hair covering, my N95 mask, then my face shield, then my paper gown over scrubs, then two pairs of gloves. We were sent videos to memorize the order, and we have spotters watching us to make sure we haven't forgotten anything before we march into battle. It feels ridiculous, that this little filter over my face is the only thing protecting me from this virus. It takes six minutes to get into PPE, but twelve minutes to get it off, because that's when you are more likely to infect yourself. It's hot and itchy and miserable and I worry what it must feel like for the patients—we are acting as if they have the plague.

Which, maybe, they do.

We try not to stay in their rooms. We don't touch them unless we have to. No one really knows how long the virus lasts on surfaces, so we assume the worst. When we come out we take off our gloves, toss them into the trash, and wash our hands. Then the cap goes into the trash, and we wash our hands. The gown is placed in a plastic bin, and we wash our hands. Then the shield comes off, and we wash our hands. Our N95 masks we have to reuse, because there aren't enough. So we take them off and stick them in little cubbies, tagged with our names, and wash our hands. In Italy, docs are wearing hazmat suits like they're entering a nuclear reactor, and I'm washing down my face mask with a fucking wipe.

My knuckles are cracked and bleeding.

I should not complain.

Today I had to do an emergency cricothyrotomy on a Covid patient. He was crashing, minutes away from going into cardiac arrest. I called RICU—the respiratory team—stat, but the guy's neck
was too thick and the anesthesiologist couldn't get a good visual
to intubate him fast enough. It was just me and the anesthesiologist and the nurse and the man gasping for air. I had to step in and
do the emergency cric to secure the airway and get him intubated
before it was too late. I was terrified, because, you know, if you do
it wrong, if you miss one detail, you might get infected. I had to
squeeze my hands together to keep them from shaking before I
made the incision. I kept telling myself to do this efficiently and
quickly and to get the fuck out of that room and sanitize myself.

When it was over the anesthesiologist and I left like we were on
fire. I pulled off all my gear in the right order and scrubbed my
hands and used Purell afterward and then I realized that the nurse
was still in that room, with all those airborne molecules of virus.
She was all of maybe 25. She was stroking the patient's arm, and I
saw her brush a tear from the man's cheek, even though he was
fast asleep. She was talking to him, even though he was sedated
and couldn't hear her.

Here I am bitching about wearing a paper space suit and making a cut, and she was providing real, true patient care.

And I thought: She's the fucking hero.

I don't know why I'm telling you this. It feels good, though, to
know you're listening.

I don't know how long I sit on the main street in Puerto Villamil
rereading Finn's email, the sun baking the back of my neck and the
crown of my head. His description of the city and the hospital feels
unreal, dystopian. How could so much change in just forty-eight
hours?

Suddenly it feels juvenile and entitled to be upset about not staying in the hotel I booked, or being hungry. There is no way in hell I'm going to complain to Finn.

It's so beautiful here, I type. *It's hard to know where to look—there's water so clear you can see fish on the bottom and crazy dramatic hunks of lava rock and iguanas crossing Main Street.*

The people are superfriendly too, I write.

I describe the sea lion on the dock in Santa Cruz and the choppy ferry ride and I completely leave out the mob of frantic tourists that met me when I reached Isabela.

The only bad thing, I add, *(aside from the lack of cell service) is that you're not with me.*

I hate that I'm here, and that you're in the thick of it. I wish I could be there for you.

I do not tell him that even if I decided to head home, there's no way for me to get there.

I hit send.

I stare at the screen, holding my breath, until the notification pops up: *No internet connection.*

In the field of auctions, video representation is nowhere near as important as the physical catalog. It's far more important to have your clients pore over the stunning photographs, read the copy about the object's provenance, to determine—from the placement in the book—how important the piece might be. After graduating from Sotheby's with a master's in art business, and training for a year, I was hired in 2014 as a junior cataloger in Imp Mod. My job was to write the words that accompanied the photos. A specialist might bring in the painting, but it was my task to bring it to life.

The library at Sotheby's isn't really a library, but rather stacks of bookshelves that line the hallways of every floor of the office. As a cataloger, I would scour the materials, trying to piece together initial research on the market value of a piece, how much money similar works had sold for, and whatever little tidbits I could add. The way to hook people on a piece of art is to find a detail that sticks in their minds—something that can personalize the work: this was painted the day before he met the mentor who would sponsor him as an artist; this was the first painting he did in oils; this image was influenced by Degas, Gauguin, Cézanne. Every snippet of copy was reviewed and edited and arranged to grab the interest of the buyer and keep him turning pages.

What this meant for me, practically, was that I rarely sat down during the day, unless it was to type a revision, and then I'd run mock-ups and edits from one specialist to another, to the marketing people, and to the art department that organized the catalog for printing. Also, we were always on a strict deadline to get the catalog off to the printer in time for the actual auction.

That was the reason I didn't take the elevator one day, three years into my tenure at Sotheby's. By then my boss—Eva St. Clerck—was the head of sale for Imp Mod. I was running something to her to meet a deadline, and with the elevator stuck on another floor, I opted for the emergency staircase instead. But I was in such a hurry, I missed a step and found myself tumbling down the stairs, breaking my fall with my left arm outstretched.

I landed in a tangle at the landing, my tights torn, my knee skinned. As I lay sprawled, I considered running back upstairs to change into the spare pair of tights I kept in my desk to prevent Eva St. Clerck from taking one look at me and raising a disappointed eyebrow. I tried to push myself upright and nearly blacked out from the wave of pain that swallowed me.

When I could breathe again, I wriggled my phone out of the pocket of my jacket and texted Rodney with a single hand. *Help.*

By the time he located me in the stairwell, I was propped against the wall with my legs splayed in front of me, cradling my left arm with my right. He hauled me up and marched me toward the closest elevator bank. "We're going to the ER," he announced, looking down at my wrist and wincing. "That is not a natural angle."

"I can't just leave. Eva—"

"Does not want to incur a lawsuit because you fell down the stairs when you were trying to appease Her Majesty." When we reached street level, Rodney bustled me through the lobby and out the front door. The emergency department of New York–Presbyterian was only a few blocks away; we heard the ambulance sirens all the time.

The waiting room was half-full: there were mothers cradling crying toddlers, an elderly man with a bad cough, a couple whispering furiously in Spanish, a man in construction gear holding a bloody towel to a gash in his thigh. The triage nurse took my information down, and forty-five minutes later, my name was called. "Do you want me to come with?" Rodney asked, and even though it was exactly what I wanted, I decided to act like a grown-up and shook my head.

"Good," he said, "because this *People* magazine from 2006 is impossible to put down."

I was brought through the double doors to a little curtained cubicle, where I sat on a gurney, trying not to jostle my arm. It felt like fire under my skin, and all of a sudden it was too much: the pain, the catalog deadline, a potentially broken bone. Tears streamed down my cheeks, my nose started running, and when I tried to reach out with my nondominant hand for a tissue beside the gurney, the box fell onto the floor, and I started to cry harder.

Which was the moment the doctor entered. He was tall and blond, with hair that kept falling in his eyes. "Ms. O'Toole? I'm Dr. Colson, and I'm a resident in . . ." he said, looking down at my chart. "I understand that you fell—" He glanced at my face, and his brows shot up. "Are you okay?"

"If I was okay," I sobbed, "I would not be in the emergency room."

"Tell me what happened," he said.

So I did, as he gently touched my elbow and wrist, moving it incrementally, stopping when I gasped in pain. His fingers were warm and sure. He asked me questions as he checked me for concussion, examined the scrape on my knee, and a bruise that was blooming on my hip. "So are you always in a hurry?" he asked.

The question surprised me out of my discomfort. "I guess?"

For the first time since he had entered the cubicle, his eyes met mine. "I suppose that's not a bad thing, if you know where you're headed," he said.

"Is that the current way of saying take two aspirin and call me in the morning?"

"No. You're not getting out of here without an X-ray." He smiled a little, the corner of his mouth quirking up on one side. "The bad news is I'd lay odds that your arm is broken. The good news is that if you can make jokes, you probably won't die on my watch."

"Great," I murmured.

"It is," he said. "I'd hate to see my Yelp rating tank." He leaned out of the cubicle and spoke with a passing nurse. "We'll get you down to radiology for imaging, and then I'll come back."

I nodded. "My friend's in the waiting room," I said. "Can someone tell him what's going on?"

He straightened. "I can get word to your boyfriend."

"He's just a co-worker," I corrected. "Rodney. He brought me here. He'll be the only one in the waiting room wearing couture."

The doctor grinned. "You gotta love a hero in Prada."

It took an hour for my X-ray to be performed and read and for Dr. Colson to come back to my cubicle. I was lying down by then, trying not to move my arm. He showed me the scans on an iPad, the clean white line of the break in my bone. "It's a simple break," he said.

"It doesn't feel simple."

"That means you don't need an ortho consult. I can put a cast on you, and you can be on your way."

He showed me how to hold up my arm, thumb out, while he gently slipped a stockinette on like an evening glove. He took a roll of cotton and wound it up and down again, mummifying my arm. The whole time, he asked me questions: How long had I been at Sotheby's? Did I study art at school? Did I prefer modern art, or impressionist art? He told me that he was a surgical resident, but that it was his first year, and he was doing a two-week rotation in the ED. He confessed that this was his first cast.

"Mine, too," I said.

The fiberglass wrap he used was already stiffening in place. For the final layer, he offered me a choice of blue, hazard orange, camouflage, hot pink.

"I get to *pick*?"

He smiled. "A perk for our first-time customers."

"Pink," I said. "Although Rodney would say that'll clash with my wardrobe."

"Choose something you won't get sick of looking at for the next six weeks," he suggested. "If you want something matchy, go with blue. It's the same color as your eyes."

As soon as he said it, he flushed and ducked his head, laser-focused on the last layer of wrap.

Finally, I was able to turn my wrist a little to look at his handiwork. "Not bad for a novice," I said. "Five stars on Yelp for sure."

He laughed. "Whew."

"So," I said, looking up at him. "That's it?"

"One more thing," he said, and he took a black marker from his white coat pocket. "Can I sign your cast?"

I nodded, smiling.

FINN, it read. And a phone number.

"In case there are complications," he said, meeting my gaze.

"I feel like that's a HIPAA violation or something," I said.

"Only if you're my patient. And lucky for me," he said, handing me my discharge papers, "you are no longer my patient."

By the time I walked into the waiting room again, we'd planned to meet for dinner the following night, and I barely noticed the throbbing in my arm. Rodney was lying on his back across four chairs. He took one look at my face, and the signature on my cast. *"Girl,"* he said.

After reading Finn's email I decide I'm going to get back to America if I have to swim. I return to the apartment to get my carry-on tote and then double back into Puerto Villamil. There are very few signs of life on Isabela, but I have the best chance of finding an exit to the mainland if I'm in town.

I have to wait only an hour on the pier before a small boat approaches, its engine chugging. There is one person in it, but I can't see him clearly from this distance. I hurry down the dock, waving, as the man hops out of the boat, turns away from me, and ties it securely on a mooring.

"Hola," I say tentatively, wondering how I am going to communicate beyond a simple greeting.

When he stands and wipes off his damp hands on his shorts, then turns around, I realize it is the man from the tortoise breeding site who tackled me yesterday. *"No es cierto,"* he mutters, closing his eyes for a second, as if he could blink me away.

Well. At least I already know he speaks English.

"Hello again," I say, smiling. "I wonder if I could rent your boat."

He shakes his head. "Sorry, it's not my boat," he says, and he shoulders past me, walking away.

"But you were just in—" I run after him, to catch up. "Look. I realize we got off on the wrong foot. But this is an emergency."

He stops, folding his arms.

"I'll pay you," I try again. "I'll pay as much as you want to get me to Santa Cruz." I don't have very much cash left, but there *have* to be ATMs there, at least.

He narrows his eyes. "What's in Santa Cruz?"

"The airport," I say. "I have to get home."

"Even if you got to Santa Cruz, there are no flights in or out."

"Please," I beg.

His face softens, or maybe it's just an illusion. "I can't take you there," he says. "We're in the middle of a strict quarantine. There are federal officials enforcing it."

By now, I'm fighting back tears. "I know you think I'm a stupid tourist," I admit. "I should have left with the last ferry. You're right. But I can't stay here for God knows how long while people I love are stuck . . ." My words evaporate; I swallow hard. "Haven't you ever made a mistake?"

He flinches as if I've hit him.

"Look, I don't much care what happens to me," he says. "But if you're arrested for traveling to Santa Cruz, that's not going to get you home, either." His eyes roam over me, from the crown of my head to my sneakers. "I hope you figure something out," he adds, and with a brief nod, he leaves me standing alone on the pier.

By the late afternoon, I am not only wondering if I can get off this island, I'm wondering if I'm the only one *on* it.

Even though I know it can't be true, it feels like I'm the last person on earth. Since being dismissed by the man from the tortoise breeding center, I have not seen a single soul. There is no movement or light in Abuela's part of the house; the beach is entirely empty. Even if there are no tourists descending on Isabela Island—even if people are being cautious because of coronavirus—it feels as if I've been dropped onto the set of a dystopian movie. A beautiful set, but a very lonely one.

I find myself walking in the same direction I went yesterday, toward the tortoise breeding center, except I get lost and wind up instead on a wooden walkway through a mangrove forest, with long-fingered tree branches bleached and twisted above me, knuckles bent. It is desolate and oddly beautiful; it's the place in the fairy tale where the witch appears. Except there is only me, and an iguana perched on the handrail of the walkway, its Godzilla hackles rising as I walk past.

When I see the sign for Concha de Perla, my memory is jogged: I had bookmarked this page in the travel guide that is still lost somewhere with my luggage, as a place for Finn and me to visit. It's known as a snorkeling haunt, arms of lava encircling a small part of the ocean to create a natural lagoon. I do not have a snorkel with me, but I am sweaty and hot, and diving into cool water becomes a mission.

I read the sign diligently, thinking of poisoned apples, but there is nothing warning me off. The walkway ends in a small, enclosed dock that looks out over the water. Two sea lions are sprawled on the boards, the wood still wet around their bodies, like a crime scene outline. They do not even twitch as I pass to lean over the railing and peer at the water: green-tinted but clear, with a family of sea turtles swimming just below me.

Well. If I'm the last person in the world, there are worse places to be.

I toe off my sneakers and peel off my socks, hiding them under the bench of the dock. It feels exhibitionistic to undress, but there's no one else here, and I have too limited a supply of clothing to get it wet. When I'm down to my athletic bra and panties, I start descending the staircase into the water. I let it lap at my shins, and then do a shallow dive into the lagoon.

The water is cool on my skin, and when I stand, I can almost brush the sandy bottom with my toes. There are mangrove trees at the edge of the pool, and through the ripple of the water are black shadows of lava. Some of them are large enough to rise from the surface, jagged as teeth. I tread water for a few moments and then start to swim in the direction of the lava outcroppings. The sun is so strong that it feels like a coronation. I lean back, floating, blinking up at the clouds that drift across the sky.

When I feel myself being poked, I startle violently, swallow water, and come up sputtering. Two penguins bob in front of me, seemingly as surprised to see me as I am to see them.

"Hey there," I whisper, grinning. They are the size of my forearm, tuxedoed formally, their pupils yellow dots. I stretch out my hand gently, inviting them to swim closer. One of the penguins dives under the water and reappears to my left.

The other one pecks me hard enough to draw blood.

"Jesus Christ!" I cry out, kicking away from the penguin, clapping a hand over my shoulder. It's barely a scrape, but it hurts.

I think of all the children's stories about penguins, which are clearly doing a disservice by making them seem friendly and cuddly. Maybe in real life they're territorial; maybe I've committed an infraction by swimming into their part of the lagoon. I distance myself from them, moving a little further out of reach of the dock toward the tangled roots of the mangroves.

I paddle around lazily, wary of penguins. I also have the sensation again that I'm being watched.

I'm wearing my underwear, which is basically equivalent to a bikini, but it's still not the way I'd like to be discovered unawares. Twice, I glance over my shoulder, but even from this distance I can see there's no one on the dock.

Splash.

The sound comes from behind me and when I whip around, the spray of water keeps me from seeing anything.

I turn away and it happens again.

But this time when I turn, I'm a foot away from the curious stare of a sea lion.

His eyes are black and soulful, his whiskers bob. Under the water his body looks like one compact, undulating muscle, the tail sweeping powerfully to keep him upright.

One flat platter of a fin breaks the water and he splashes me again.

So I splash him back.

For a moment we just stare at each other. His nose twitches. He slaps his fin on the surface again and sends a shear of water into my face.

I burst out laughing and he does a backward dive, reappearing a few feet away from me. With a grin, I fling myself backward underwater, too. When I come up, pushing the hair out of my face, the sea lion is a foot away. This time, I hold my breath and somersault underwater, opening my eyes beneath the surface to watch him do the same thing.

It's almost like we're having a conversation.

Delighted, we play together, mimicking motions. Worn out, I start swimming back to the dock. For a while, the sea lion follows me. We surface underneath the raised wooden dock, breathing hard. He smells of fish.

I slowly stretch out my hand, thinking that maybe he will let me pet him, now that we have established a friendship of sorts. But before I can reach the silk of his wet fur, a drop of blood materializes in the center of my palm.

Shocked, I pull my hand back—Did I cut it on lava? Was it the penguin?—just as a second drop splats into the water, diffusing like dye.

I glance up and realize it's coming from above the dock.

Scrambling up the slippery steps I see a girl sitting with her back to the post that forms a corner of the dock. She is young, on the cusp of being a teenager. She seems just as surprised to see me as I am to see her, and she immediately yanks down the sleeve of her sweatshirt, but not before I get a glimpse of the ladder rungs of cuts, one still bleeding.

"Are you okay?" I ask, moving toward her, but she hunches up her knees and slips her hands in the pockets of her sweatshirt.

I never self-harmed, but I remember a girl from my high school who did. Her mother was dying of ovarian cancer and once, we were both waiting for the guidance counselor on a bench outside her office. I looked over and saw the girl picking at scars on her forearm that reminded me of the height marks my father made on my bedroom doorframe every year on my birthday to chart my growth. She stopped when she saw me staring. *What?* she said.

This girl has black hair in a messy braid, and she isn't crying. In fact, she looks pissed off to have had her hiding spot trespassed upon. "What are you doing here?" she accuses.

"Swimming," I say, and my cheeks burn as I remember what I'm wearing, and what I'm not. I grab my borrowed T-shirt from where it sits, under the bench, and pull it over my head.

"It's closed," the girl says, and suddenly I realize why she looks familiar: she was the third passenger on the ferry yesterday. The one who was crying.

"Did you hurt yourself?" I ask.

She continues as if I haven't spoken at all. "The whole island is closed," she says. "Because of the virus there's a curfew after two P.M."

I look at the sun, slung low in the sky. I begin to understand why the island feels like a ghost town. "I didn't know," I say honestly. Then my brows draw together. "If there's a curfew, what are *you* doing here?"

She stands up, her hands still buried in her pockets. "I didn't care," she says, and she runs down the wooden walkway.

"Wait!" I cry, trying to follow her, but the wood burns the bare soles of my feet and, wincing, I have to stop in a puddle of shadow. By the time I limp back to the dock to put on my jeans and sneakers, the sea lion has disappeared, too.

I am halfway back home before I realize that this mystery girl spoke English.

I hear the shouting before I even reach Abuela's house. She is stand-ing on the front porch, trying to placate a man who is arguing with her. Every time she touches his arm, trying to calm him down, he releases a torrent of Spanish. *"Hey!"* I yell, jogging faster as I watch Abuela bend like a willow under his frustration. "Leave her alone!"

They both turn at the sound of my voice, surprised.

It's that same guy . . . again. "You?" I say.

"This is not your business—" he says.

"I think it is," I interrupt. "What gives you the right to scream at a woman who's—"

"My grandmother," he says.

Abuela's face creases into the soft lines of a thousand wrinkles. *"Mijo,"* she says, patting his arm. "Gabriel."

I shake my head. "I'm Diana. Your grandmother very kindly of-fered me an apartment when my hotel closed down."

"It's my apartment," he says.

Is he kicking me out? Is that why they're arguing?

"My apartment," he repeats, as if I am too slow to understand. "The one you're currently squatting in."

"I can pay you," I say, scrabbling in my jeans pocket for money. I peel off most of what's left.

Abuela sees the money in my hand and shakes her head, pushing back at my fist. Her grandson—Gabriel—turns slightly, speaking quietly to her. *"Tómalo; no sabes por cuánto tiempo serán las cosas así."*

She nods and flattens her mouth into a thin line. She takes the money from my hand, folding it and tucking it inside her dress pocket.

Abuela responds to Gabriel, her eyes flashing, and for a moment, he has the grace to look embarrassed. "My grandmother," he says, "wants me to tell you that I moved out a month ago and that she can give the space to anyone she wants." He narrows his eyes at me. "Why aren't you *in* the apartment?"

"I'm sorry," I say. "I can't quite keep up. *Do* you want me there, or *don't* you?"

"There's a curfew." His eyes narrow on my wet hair. "You're dripping. Onto *my* shirt."

My God, everything is a personal affront to this man.

Suddenly Gabriel's face changes. *"Jesucristo,"* he swears, as he rushes past me and grabs the shoulders of someone in the street. He looks like he can't decide whether to hug or throttle them.

I watch as relief wins out in him. His arms circle tightly, and on the porch, Abuela's eyes fill with tears. She crosses herself.

I don't know what Gabriel is saying, because he is speaking Spanish. But from this angle, I can see the face of the person he's embracing. It's the girl from the dock at Concha de Perla, her sweatshirt still pulled past her wrists, her eyes fixed on mine, silently begging me to keep her secret.

THREE

For the next few days, I slip into a routine. In the mornings, I go for runs. I go as far as I can along the beach; I hike past the tortoise breeding center and Concha de Perla; I take paths that lead me into the heart of Isabela and to its cliffed edges. Sometimes I see locals, who nod at me but don't speak. I am not sure if they are keeping their distance because of the virus, or because I am a foreigner. I watch fishermen leave the pier in Puerto Villamil in little *pangas*, heading out to catch food for their families.

I wake before the sun and go to sleep before eight, because I can only spend half the day outside. After the two P.M. curfew, I stay indoors, reading on my Kindle—until I run out of downloaded books. Then I creep onto the postage-stamp yard of sand that abuts the beach, swing in the hammock, and watch Sally Lightfoot crabs scuttle away from the surf.

Abuela brings me a meal sometimes, and it is a nice alternative to the pasta that is my main food group.

I do not see her grandson or the girl.

I start talking to myself, because my voice has gone rusty with disuse. Sometimes I recite poetry I memorized in high school as I walk in the thorny desert of the center of the island: *Had we but world enough, and time; this Coyness, Lady, were no crime.* Sometimes

I hum when I wring out my clothes, washed in the sink, and hang them to dry in the hot sun. Sometimes I let the ocean harmonize as I sing into its roar.

Always, I miss Finn.

I still haven't been able to talk to him, but I have written him post-cards every night. I hope to get stamps and mail them, and maybe find a cellphone store in town where they can work out a way for me to text internationally. I also need clothing, because rinsing out my limited supply every night isn't ideal. The few stores that are still open do not seem to have regular hours, and I keep timing it wrong. While trekking into town, I have seen intermittent signs of life at the pharmacy, a shawarma stand, and a church. I decide that, later today, I will try my luck again in Puerto Villamil.

Before dawn, I go for a run, until my lungs are burning. When I reach a spiky black monolith of lava, I sit down on the sand and watch the stars burn out of the sky, like sparks on a hearth. By the time I walk back home, the tide is coming in. It erases my footprints. When I look back over my shoulder, it's as if I was never there.

I take another blank postcard from the G2 Tours box and sit down on the hammock outside my apartment to finish my latest missive to Finn; then something at the edge of the water catches my eye. In the hazy blue light, rocks look like people and people look like monsters, and I find myself walking closer to get a better look. I am almost at the shoreline before I realize it's the girl from Concha de Perla, carrying a trash bag. She straightens, as if she can sense me coming up behind her. She is holding a plastic water bottle with Mandarin characters on the label. "It's not bad enough that the Chinese fishing fleets are poaching," she says in perfect English. "They have to throw their crap overboard, too."

She turns to me and jerks her chin along the rest of the beach, where other bottles have washed ashore.

She continues to pick up trash as if it's perfectly normal for her to be here at the crack of dawn, as if I haven't seen her cutting herself or being yelled at by Gabriel.

"Does your brother know you're here?" I ask.

Her wide black eyes blink. "My brother?" she says, and then she huffs a sharp laugh. "He is *not* my brother. And it doesn't really matter if he knows or not. It's an island. How far away could I even get?"

When I was in school and that girl was harming herself, I felt like our paths kept crossing. Probably they had before, too, but I hadn't been aware. One day, as we passed in the hallway, I stopped her. *You shouldn't do it,* I said. *You could really hurt yourself.*

She had laughed at me. *That's the point.*

I watch this girl pick up a few more plastic bottles and jam them into her bag. "You speak English so well."

She glances at me. "I'm aware."

"I didn't mean—" I hesitate, trying to not say something inadvertently offensive. "It's just nice to have someone to talk to." I reach down and grab a bottle, holding it out for her bag. "I'm Diana," I say.

"Beatriz."

Up close, she seems older than I first thought. Maybe fourteen or fifteen, but petite, with sharp features and bottomless eyes. She is still wearing her sweatshirt, arms pulled low beyond her wrists. There is a school crest over her heart. She seems perfectly content to ignore me, and maybe I should respect that. But I am lonely, and just days ago, I watched her self-harming. Maybe I am not the only one who needs someone to talk to.

I also know, based on our previous interactions, that she is more likely to flee than to confide in me. So I choose my words carefully, like holding out a crust of bread to a bird and wondering if it will dart away, or hop one step closer. "Do you always pick up the trash here?" I ask casually.

"Someone has to," she says.

I think about that, about all the visitors, like me, who descend on the Galápagos. Economically, I'm sure it's a boon. But maybe having all the boats and tours suspended for a few weeks isn't a bad thing. Maybe it gives nature a moment to breathe.

"So," I say, making conversation. "Is that your school?" I point to my chest, in the same spot where the logo is on her sweatshirt. "Tomás de Berlanga?"

She nods. "It's on Santa Cruz, but it shut down because of the virus."

"So that's where you live?"

She starts walking; I fall into place beside her. "During the school year I live with a family in Santa Cruz," she says quietly. "*Lived* with."

"But this is where you were born?" I guess.

Beatriz turns to me. "I do not belong here."

Neither do I, I think.

I follow her further down the beach. "So you're on vacation."

She snorts. "Yeah. Like *you're* on vacation."

Her barb hits home; as holidays go, this isn't exactly what I hoped for. "How come you go to school off-island?"

"I've been there since I was nine. It's like a magnet school. My mother enrolled me because it was the best chance of getting me out of Galápagos forever, and because it was the last thing my father wanted."

It makes me think of my own mother and father. Separate circles that didn't even overlap to form a Venn diagram where I could nestle into both their spaces.

"He's your father," I guess. "Gabriel?"

Beatriz looks at me. "Unfortunately."

I try to do the math; he seems so young to be her parent. He can't be much older than I am.

She starts walking away. "Why was he yelling at you?" I ask.

She turns. "Why are you following me?"

"I'm not . . ." Except, I realize, I am. "I'm sorry. I just . . . I haven't had a conversation with anyone in a few days. I don't speak Spanish."

"Americana," she mutters.

"I wasn't planning on coming here alone. My boyfriend had to back out at the last minute."

This, she finds intriguing; I can see it in her eyes. "He had to work," I explain. "He's a doctor."

"Why did you stay, then?" she asks. "When you found out the island was closing?"

Why *did* I? It's been only a few days, but I can barely remember. Because I thought it was the adventurous thing to do?

"If I had anywhere else to go, I would," Beatriz says.

"Why?"

She laughs, but it's bitter. "I hate Isabela. Plus, my father expects me to live in a half-finished shack on our farm."

"He's a *farmer*?" I say, my surprise slipping out.

"He used to be a tour guide, but not anymore."

Likely, I think, *because he was so unpleasant to his clientele.*

"My grandfather owned the business, but when he died, my father closed it down. He used to live in the apartment you're in, but he moved to the highlands, to a place without water or electricity or internet—"

"Internet? There's internet on this island?" I hold up the postcard I am still clutching. "I can't send email, and I haven't been able to call my boyfriend, either . . . so I was writing him. But I can't buy stamps . . . and I don't even know if there's still mail service . . ."

Beatriz holds out her hand. "Give me your phone." I hold it out, and she taps through the settings. "The hotel has Wi-Fi." She nods toward a building in the distance. "I put in their password—but it shits out more often than it works, and if they're closed, they probably turned off the modem. If you still can't connect, you could try getting a SIM card in town."

I take back my phone, and Beatriz reaches for another bottle. A rogue wave soaks her arm, and she pushes her sleeve up before she remembers the red weals left by the razor blade. Immediately, she claps her palm over them, and juts her chin up as if daring me to comment.

"Thank you," I say carefully. "For talking to me."

She shrugs.

"If you wanted to, you know, talk . . . again . . ." My eyes flicker to her arm. "Well, I'm not going anywhere in the near future."

Her face shutters. "I'm good," she says, yanking down the wet fabric. She looks at the postcard, still in my hand. "I could mail it for you."

"Really?"

She shrugs. "We have stamps. I don't know about the post office, but fishermen are allowed off-island to deliver what they catch, so maybe they're taking mail to Santa Cruz."

"That would be . . ." I smile at her. "That would be amazing."

"No big deal. Well. Gotta go check in with the warden."

When I glance up, I realize we have walked all the way to town.

"Your father?" I clarify.

"*Tanto monta, monta tanto,*" she says.

I wonder if the reason Gabriel is keeping such a tight rein on Beatriz is because he knows she's cutting. I wonder if he isn't angry, but desperate.

"Could you stay with your mom instead?" I blurt out.

Beatriz shakes her head. "She's been gone since I was ten."

Heat rushes to my face. "I'm so sorry," I murmur.

She laughs. "She's not dead. She's on a Nat Geo tour ship in Baja, fucking her boyfriend. Good riddance." Without saying another word, Beatriz slings the bag over her shoulder and walks down the middle of the main street, scattering startled iguanas in her wake.

The proprietor of Sonny's Sunnies speaks English and sells more than sunglasses and sarongs. She also sells T-shirts and neon-bright bikinis and SD cards for cameras and, yes, SIM cards for international calling—although there are none in stock at the moment. I can't believe my continued streak of bad luck. She's right there where Beatriz said I'd find her, on the main street of Puerto Villamil, just before noon. The door is wide open and Sonny is sitting behind the cash register, fanning herself with a magazine. She is round everywhere—her face, her arms, her swollen belly—and she peers at me over an embroidered mask. "*Tienes que usar una mascarilla,*" she says, and I just stare at her. The only word I understand in her sentence sounds like eye makeup, and I'm not wearing any.

"I . . . *no habla español,*" I stammer, and her eyes light up.

"Oh," she says, "you're the *turista*." She points to her face. "You need a mask."

I glance around the store. "I need more than that," I tell her, making a small pile on the counter—Galápagos tees, two pairs of shorts, a sweatshirt, a bikini, a face mask made of cloth with little chili peppers printed on it. I add a guidebook with a map of Isabela. When I show her my phone, she shows me a SIM card that will let me make local calls on a local network, which I buy even though I can't imagine who I'll be calling or texting locally. No, she tells me, she doesn't sell stamps.

Finally, I pull out a credit card. "Do you know where there's an ATM on the island?"

"Oh," she says, putting my card in one of those old machines that create a carbon copy of it. "There's no ATM."

"Not even at the bank?"

"No. And you can't use a credit card there to get cash."

I look at the minuscule amount of money I have left, after paying Abuela—thirty-three dollars. Minus ferry fare returning to Santa Cruz . . . as I do the math, my heart starts pounding. What if my cash supply doesn't last me for another week and a half?

My panic attack is interrupted by the jingle of the bell on the door. In walks another woman in a mask, carrying a toddler. He squirms in her arms, calling out to the shop owner until he is set down on the floor and races toward her, clinging to her leg like a mollusk. She swings him onto her hip.

The woman who carried in the little boy unleashes a torrent of words I cannot understand and then she seems to notice me.

She looks familiar, but I can't figure out why until she snaps toward the proprietor, and her long, black braid whips behind her. The woman from my hotel, whose name tag read Elena. Who told me they were closed.

"You are still here?" she says.

"I'm staying with . . . Abuela," I reply. That means *grandmother*, I know. I'm embarrassed to not know her real name.

"*La plena!*" Elena scoffs, throws up her hands, and slams out of the store.

"You're staying in Gabriel Fernandez's old place?" the shop owner asks, and when I nod, she laughs. "Elena's just pissed because *she* wanted to be the one sleeping in his bed."

I feel my cheeks heat. "I'm not . . . I don't . . ." I shake my head. "I have a boyfriend at home."

"Okay," she says, shrugging.

To: DOToole@gmail.com
From: FColson@nyp.org

I keep checking my phone to see if you've texted. I know it isn't your fault, but I wish I knew for sure you are okay. Plus, I need some good news.

This virus is like a storm that just won't ease up. You know on some rational level that it can't stay like this forever. Except, it does. And gets worse.

The easy-to-diagnose Covid patient has fever, chest pain, a cough, a loss of smell and a metallic taste in their mouth, hypoxia, and fear.

The ones that aren't as obvious arrive with abdominal pain and vomiting.

The ones you get Covid from have no symptoms and go to the ER because they cut their hands slicing a bagel.

My attending said we should assume everyone in the hospital has Covid.

He's pretty much right.

But weirdly, the ER isn't very busy. No one's just *walking in* any-more, they're too scared. You never know if the guy with the bro-ken leg sitting next to you in the ER is Covid-positive and asymptomatic. God forbid you cough, even if you have a common cold. You'll be looked at like you're a terrorist.

Since no one wants to risk coming to the hospital, most of the patients arrive by ambulance, coming only when they're unable to breathe.

I've been assigned to one of the Covid ICUs. It's loud AF. There are beeps and alarms that go off any time a vital sign changes. The ventilator makes a noise every time it breathes for a patient. But there are no visitors. It's weird for there to be no crying wives or family members holding a patient's hand.

Oh, and every day, treatment changes. Today we're giving hydroxychloroquine. Tomorrow: whoops, no, we're not. Today we're trying remdesivir, but antibiotics are out. One attending is pushing Lipitor, because it lowers inflammation. Another's trying Lasix, used for heart failure patients, to help remove fluid from around Covid lungs. Some docs think ibuprofen is doing more harm than good, although no one knows why, so they're giving Tylenol for fever instead. Everyone wants to know if convalescent plasma helps, but we don't have enough of it to know.

When I'm not with a patient, I'm reading studies to see what other docs are doing in other places, and what clinical trials are available. It's like we're throwing shit at a wall to see if anything sticks.

Today, I had a patient who was bleeding through her lungs. Normally, we'd give a thousand milligrams of steroids to stop the hemorrhage, but my attending was waffling, because based on previous flu studies, we're worried that steroids might make Covid worse. I kept watching him wrestle with a course of action, and all I could think was: does it matter, if she's dead either way?

But I didn't say anything. I left the room and did my rounds, listening to lungs that couldn't push air and hearts that barely were beating, checking vitals and fluid status, hoping that the patients I was checking on could ride out the virus before we run out of beds. There is a thousand-bed Navy ship being sent to NYC but it won't get here till April; and based on estimates, the hospitals in the city will max out of beds in 45 days.

It's only been a week.

I decided I'm not listening to the news anymore, because I'm basically living it.

God, I wish you were here.

In 2014, one of the plaster rosettes fell from the ceiling of the Rose Main Reading Room of the New York Public Library and shattered on the floor. When the city decided to inspect it, they also inspected the ceiling in the adjacent Blass Catalog Room. The ornate plasterwork of that ceiling was touched up and tested for weight and strength. The 1911 James Wall Finn trompe l'oeil mural of the sky on canvas, however, couldn't be restored because it was too fragile. Instead, my father spent nearly a year re-creating the image on canvas that would be set in place on the ceiling, and could be easily removed for touch-ups in the future.

When the canvases were being installed in 2016, he was there directing the operation. Because he was a perfectionist, he insisted on climbing up a ladder to illustrate how the edge of the canvas had to align, flush, with the gilded satyrs and cherubs of the carving that framed it.

That same day, I was in East Hampton, at the second home of a woman who was auctioning off a Matisse with Sotheby's. Our protocol required someone from the auction house to be present when a piece was transported, and since I had just been promoted to a junior specialist in Imp Mod, I was given the assignment. It was mindless work. I would take a company car to the site, meet the shipping company there, and before it was packed up I'd use a printed copy of the painting to mark down any scratches or peels or imperfections. I'd oversee the careful packing of the piece, watch it get loaded into a truck, and then I would get back into my company car and return to the office.

The job, however, was not going according to plan. Although our client had said her housekeeper would be expecting us, her husband was also home. He'd had no idea that his wife was selling the Matisse, and he didn't want to. He kept insisting that I show him the contract, and when I did, he told me he was going to call his lawyer, and I suggested he should maybe call his wife instead.

The whole time, my phone was buzzing in my pocket.

When I finally answered, the number was not one I recognized.

Is this Diana O'Toole?

I'm Margaret Wu, I'm a doctor at Mount Sinai . . .

I'm afraid your father's been in an accident.

I walked out of the house in the Hamptons, dazed, completely oblivious to the man still on the phone with his lawyer and the movers awaiting my approval to wrap up the painting. I got into the company car and directed the driver to take me to Mount Sinai. I called Finn, whom I'd been dating for several months, and he said he'd meet me there.

My father had fallen off a ladder and struck his head. He was hemorrhaging in his brain, and had been taken directly into surgery. I wanted to be there holding his hand; I wanted to tell him it was going to be all right. I wanted my face to be the first thing he saw in the recovery room.

The traffic on Long Island was, as usual, a disaster. As I cried in the backseat of the company car, I bargained with a higher power. *I will give You anything,* I swore, *if You get me to the hospital before my father wakes up.*

Finn stood up as soon as I walked through the sliding glass doors, and I *knew.* I could tell from the look on his face and the speed with which he wrapped his arms around me. *There was nothing you could have done,* he whispered.

That was how I learned that the world changes between heartbeats; that life is never an absolute, but always a wager.

I was allowed to see my father's body. Some kind soul had wrapped gauze around his head. He looked like he was asleep, but when I touched his hand, it was cold, like a marble bench in winter that you will not linger on, no matter how weary you might be. I thought of how his heart must have caught when he lost his footing. I wondered if the last thing he saw was his own sky.

Finn held my hand tight as I signed paperwork, blinked at questions about funeral homes, answered in a daze. Finally, a nurse gave me a plastic bag with the hospital logo on it. Inside was my father's wallet, his reading glasses, his wedding ring. Identity, insight, heart: the only things we leave behind.

In the taxi on the way home, Finn kept one arm anchored around me while I clutched the bag to my chest. I reached into my purse for my phone and scrolled to the last text my father had sent me, two days ago. *Are you busy?*

I had not answered. Because I *was* busy. Because I was going to his place for dinner that weekend. Because he often decided he wanted to chat in the middle of business hours, when I couldn't. Because there were any number of items on my to-do list that took precedence.

Because I never thought that I'd run out of time to respond. The story of our life was a run-on sentence, not a parenthetical.

Are you busy?

No, I typed in, and when I pushed send, I started sobbing.

Finn reached into his jacket, looking for a tissue, but he didn't have one. I scrabbled inside my own coat pocket and came up with the rectangular printout of the painting I had gone to pack up just that morning, a thousand years ago. I looked at the red circles and arrows meant to signify the marks and chips on the frame, the nick on the canvas, as if they meant anything.

As if we don't all have scars that can't be seen.

Dear Finn,

Well, it's still beautiful here, and I'm still the only tourist on this island. In the mornings, I go out for runs or hikes, but in the afternoon the whole place is locked down. Which feels redundant, when you're this isolated.

Sometimes I find myself eye to eye with a sea lion or sharing a bench with an iguana and I'm just blown away by the fact that I'm that close, and there's no wall or fence between us, and that I don't feel threatened. The fauna was here first, and in a way they still lord it over the humans who now share the space. I wonder what it would be like if I wasn't the only one marveling over them. I mean, the locals are all used to it. I'm a one-woman audience.

The great-granddaughter of the woman who is renting me a room speaks English. She's a teenager. Talking to her makes me feel less lonely. I hope I do the same for her.

Every now and then I get a hiccup of cell service and one of your emails arrives in my inbox. It feels like Christmas.

Are you getting any of these postcards?

Love, Diana

The next morning, when Beatriz rounds the corner with her trash bag—a one-girl recycling crew—I am sitting at the shoreline, making a drip castle.

From the corner of my eye, I see her, but I don't turn. I can feel her watching me as I scoop up a handful of wet sand, and let it sift through my fingers, creating a craggy turret.

"What are you doing?" she asks.

"What does it look like I'm doing?" I say.

"It doesn't even look like a castle," she scoffs.

I lean back. "You're right." I hold out my hand for her plastic bag. "Do you mind?"

She hands it to me. Mixed in with the same plastic water bottles from the Chinese fishing fleets are twist ties, burlap curled with seaweed, scraps of foil. There's a broken flip-flop, green plastic soda bottles, red Solo cups. There's electric-blue netting from a bag of oranges, and a tongue of rubber tire. I pull all of these out and use them to fashion flags on my castle turret, a moat, a drawbridge.

"That's trash," Beatriz says, but she sinks down cross-legged beside me.

I shrug. "One person's trash is another person's art. There's a Korean artist—Choi Jeong Hwa—who uses recycled waste for his installations. He made a massive fish puppet out of plastic bags . . . and a whole building out of discarded doors. And there's a German guy, HA Schult, who makes life-size people entirely out of garbage."

"I've never heard of either of them," Beatriz says.

I take the thong off the flip-flop and create an archway. "How about Joan Miró?" I offer. "He spent the end of his life on Mallorca, and he'd walk the beach every morning like you, but he'd turn the trash he collected into sculptures."

"How do you even *know* this?" she asks.

"It's my job," I tell her. "Art."

"You mean, like, you paint?"

"Not anymore," I admit. "I work for an auction house. I help people sell their art collections."

Her face lights up. "You're the person who says *I have one dollar, one dollar, do I hear two . . .* "

I grin; she does a credible job of imitating an auctioneer. "I'm more behind the scenes. The auctioneers are kind of the rock stars of the industry." I watch Beatriz take a handful of tiny shells and line the moat with them. "There was this one British auctioneer we all had a crush on—Niles Barclay. During auctions, I was usually assigned to be on the phone with a collector who wasn't physically present and make bids on his or her behalf. But once, I was pulled to be Niles Barclay's assistant. I had to stand on the podium with him and mark down the sales price of the item on the information sheet when the bidding closed, and hand him the next information sheet to read out loud. Once, our hands touched when I was passing him the paper." I laugh. "He said, *Thank you, Donna,* in his amazing British accent, and even though he got my name wrong I thought: *Oh my God, close enough.*"

"You said you had a boyfriend," Beatriz says.

"I did. I do," I correct. "We gave each other one free pass. Mine was Niles Barclay; his was Jessica Alba. Neither one of us has cashed in on our pass." I look at her. "How about you?"

"How about me what?"

"Do you have a boyfriend?"

She flushes and shakes her head, patting the sand. "I mailed your postcard," she tells me.

"Thanks."

"I could stop by, if you want," Beatriz says. "Like, I could come to your place every now and then and pick them up, if you're sending any more."

I look at her, wondering if this is an offer of help, or a need for it. "That would be great," I say carefully.

For a few moments, we work in companionable silence, forming crenellated walkways and buttresses and outbuildings. As Beatriz stretches, reaching into the trash bag, her sleeve inches higher. It's been a few days now since I saw her cutting herself. The thin red lines are fading, like high-water marks from a flood that's receded.

"Why do you do it?" I ask softly.

I expect her to get up and run away, again. Instead, she digs a groove into the sand with her thumb. "Because it's the kind of hurt that makes sense," she says. She angles her body away from mine and busies herself by connecting some twist ties.

"Beatriz," I say, "if you want—"

"If I were making things from trash," she interrupts, shutting down the previous line of conversation, "I'd make something useful."

I look at her. *We're not done talking about the cutting,* I say with my eyes. But I keep my voice casual. "Like what?"

"A raft," she says. She sets a leaf on the water of the moat, which keeps seeping into the sand until one of us refills it.

"Where would you sail?"

"Anywhere," she says.

"Back to school?"

She shrugs.

"Most kids would be thrilled with an unscheduled break."

"I'm not like other kids," Beatriz replies. She adds a bit of yellow plastic hair to her twist tie creation, which is a stick figure with arms and legs. "Being here . . . feels like moving backward."

I know that feeling. I hate that feeling. But then again, these are circumstances beyond normal control. "Maybe . . . try to embrace that?"

She glances at me. "How long are *you* going to stay?"

"Until I'm allowed to leave."

"Exactly," Beatriz answers.

When she says it, I realize how important it is to have an *out*. To know that this is an interlude, and that I'm going home to Finn, to my job, to that plan I set in place when I was her age. There is a profound difference between knowing your situation is temporary and not knowing what's coming next.

It's all about control, or at least the illusion of it.

The kind of pain that makes sense.

Beatriz sets her little figure atop the castle: a person in a building without doors or windows or ladders, a structure surrounded by a deep moat.

"Princess in a tower?" I guess. "Waiting to be rescued?"

She shakes her head. "Fairy tales are bullshit," Beatriz says. "She's literally made out of trash and she's stuck there alone."

With my fingernail, I carve out a back door to the castle. Then I wind some seaweed around a plastic spoon, dress it in a candy wrapper, and set my figure down beside hers—a visitor, an accomplice, a friend. I look up at Beatriz. "Not anymore," I say.

To: DOToole@gmail.com
From: FColson@nyp.org

The hardest hit are Hispanics and Blacks. They're the essential workers, the ones who are in the grocery stores and mailrooms and fuck, even cleaning the hospital rooms we're using. They take public transportation and they're exposed to the virus more frequently and there are often multiple generations living under one roof, so even if a teenage Uber Eats driver contracts Covid and doesn't show symptoms, he might be the one who kills his grandfather. But what's even worse is—we're not seeing these patients until it's too late. They don't come to the hospital, because they're afraid ICE is hanging out here, waiting to deport them, and by the time they can't breathe anymore and they call an ambulance, there's nothing we can do.

Today I watched a Hispanic lady who's part of the cleaning crew at the hospital wipe down a room. I wondered if anyone's bothered to tell her to strip in her entryway when she gets home and shower before she lets her kids hug her.

We finally got a new shipment of PPE. But it turns out that instead of N95 masks, which is what we really need, they sent gloves. Thousands and thousands of gloves. The guy who accepted the delivery is the chief of surgery and every resident I know is terrified of him because he is so intimidating, but today, I saw him break down and cry like a baby.

We have a new trick: proning. It's tummy time, for adults. Its mortality benefit has been around in studies since 2013, but it's never been used as much as it is now. We do it for hours, if the patient can take it. The way your lungs work, when you're on your belly they have more room to expand and the blood flow and airflow are equilibrated enough to hold off intubation for a while. We've learned that patients can seem to tolerate a huge decrease in air exchange so now instead of only looking at the numbers for gas exchange, we look to see which patients are worn out from breathing, and they're the ones who get intubated. That's the good thing. The bad thing is that if someone decompensates, and needs intubation after a trial of no intubation, they will certainly die, because when lungs are already damaged by quick breathing, by the time they're ventilated, it's too late. We are basically playing Russian roulette with people's lives.

One of the three patients of mine that died today was a nun. She wanted last rites and we couldn't find a priest who was willing to come into the room and administer them.

Sorry if there are typos—I keep my phone in a Ziploc bag when I'm at the hospital. I'm wiping down the bills that come in the mail. A nurse told me she washed her broccoli with soap and hot water. I can't remember the last time I ate a cooked meal.

I wish I knew for sure that this was getting through to you.

And I wish you'd answer back.

Dear Finn,

I wish I could tell you how badly I'm trying to reach you, although the fact that I can't is sort of the point. Remember how we thought it would be so romantic to be shut away from the outside world? It doesn't feel that way when I'm alone on the outside, banging to be let back in.

It makes for some pretty weird self-reflection. It's like I am in some parallel universe where I am aware of other things going on, but I can't respond or comment or even be affected by them. LOL, is the world even turning, if I'm not really a part of it?

The girl I told you about, she says that being here feels like moving backward. I know I should be grateful to be safe and healthy and in a gorgeous bucket list destination. I know this was the perfect time for this to happen, with my job in limbo and you stuck at the hospital. I also know that when you're in the thick of living your life, you don't often get to push pause and reflect on it. It's just really hard to sit in the moment, and not worry if pause is going to turn into stop.

Jesus, I am bad at having downtime. I need to find a way to keep myself occupied.

Or I need to find a plane. A plane would be good, too.

Love, Diana

After I've been on the island for a little over a week, Abuela invites me to lunch.

I have not been inside her home before now. It is bright and cozy, with a tangle of plants on the windowsills and yellow walls and a crocheted afghan on the couch. There is a ceramic cross hanging over the television set, and the entire space smells delicious. On the stove is a pan; she walks to it and moves the contents around with a spatula before lifting the utensil and pointing at the kitchen table so I will sit down.

"*Tigrillo,*" she says a moment later, when she sets a plate down in front of me. Plantains, cheese, green pepper, onions, and eggs. She motions for me to take a bite, and I do—it's delicious—and then with satisfaction, Abuela turns back to the stove and loads a second plate. I think she is going to join me, but instead she calls out, "Beatriz!"

Beatriz is here? I haven't seen her for four days, not since we built the sandcastle together.

I wonder if she ran away from her dad's farm again.

From behind a closed door on the other side of the living room comes a flurry of angry response I cannot understand. Abuela mutters something, setting the plate on the table and resting her hands on her hips in frustration.

"Let me try," I say.

I pick up the plate and walk to the door; knock. The response is another muffled stream of Spanish. "Beatriz?" I say, leaning closer. "It's Diana."

When she doesn't answer, I turn the knob. She is lying on a bed that's covered by a plain white cotton blanket. She is staring up at the ceiling fan, while tears stream from the corners of her eyes into her hair. It is almost as if she doesn't realize she is crying. Immediately I set the plate on a dresser and sit next to her. "Talk to me," I beg. "Let me help you."

She turns onto her side, presenting her back to me. "Just leave me alone," she says, crying harder.

After a moment, I stand up and close the door behind me again. Abuela looks at me, her heart in her eyes. "I think she needs help," I say softly, but Abuela just cocks her head, and my worry is lost in translation.

Suddenly the front door opens and Beatriz's father stalks in. *"Ella no puede seguir haciendo esto,"* he says. Abuela steps forward, putting a hand on his arm.

He makes a beeline for the bedroom door. Without thinking twice, I step directly in his path. "Leave her be," I say.

Gabriel startles, and I realize he has been too furious and single-minded to clock my presence. *"Porqué está ella aquí?"* he asks Abuela, and then looks at me. "What are you doing here?"

"Can we talk?" I say. "Privately?"

He stares at me. "I'm busy," he grunts, trying to dodge around me for the doorknob.

I realize I'm not going to be able to divert him, so I pitch my voice lower, assuming that Abuela cannot understand English any better than I can understand Spanish. "Do you know that your daughter cuts herself?" I murmur.

His eyes, already nearly black, manage to darken. "This is none of your business," he says.

"I just want to help. She's so . . . sad. Lost. She misses her school. Her friends. She feels like there's nothing for her here."

"*I'm* here," Gabriel says.

I don't respond, because what if that's the problem?

A muscle tics in his jaw; he is fighting for patience. "What makes you think I would listen to a *Colorada*?"

I have no idea what that is, but it can't be a compliment.

Because I was a kid once, I think. *Because I had a mother who abandoned me, too.*

Instead, I say, "I guess you're an expert on teenage girls?"

My words do exactly what my physical interception didn't: all the anger leaches from him. The light goes out of his eyes, his fists go slack at his sides. "I am an expert on nothing," he admits, and while I am still turning this confession over in my mind, he reaches past me for the doorknob.

I do not know what I expect Gabriel to do, but it's not what he actually *does:* He goes into the room and sits gingerly on the bed. He brushes Beatriz's hair back from her face until she rolls over and looks up at him with her swollen, red eyes.

I feel a shadow at my back, and Abuela walks into the bedroom. She stands behind Gabriel, her hand on his shoulder, completing the circuit of family.

I feel like I am in the middle of a play, but nobody has given me a script. Silently, I back away and slip out the front door.

Isolation, I think, is the worst thing in the world.

To: DOToole@gmail.com
From: FColson@nyp.org

Before the mayor closed all nonessential businesses in the city
today, I went to Starbucks on my way to work. I was in my scrubs,
and I was masked, of course. I don't go anywhere without a mask.
The barista was joking around. She said, *I sure hope you don't
work with Covid patients.* I told her I did. She literally fell back three
feet. Just . . . fell back. If that's how I'm being treated—and I'm not
even sick—imagine how it feels to be one of those patients, alone
in a room with nothing but stigma to keep you company. You
aren't a person anymore. You're a statistic.

The Covid ICU, which used to be the surgical ICU, is just a long
line of patients on ventilators. When you walk into the ward it's like
a sci-fi movie; like these very still bodies are just pods incubating
something terrifying. Which is kind of the truth.

We're trying to be more careful about intubating because
based on our experience, once a person's on a vent he's less likely
to get off it. By now, I could identify the lungs of a Covid patient in
my sleep (and some days, it kind of feels like that's what I'm doing).
It's this vicious cycle—if you can't breathe deeply, you breathe fast.
You can only breathe 30 times a minute for so long before you ex-
haust yourself. If you can't breathe, you can't stay conscious. If you
can't stay conscious, you can't protect your airway, so you might
aspirate. And that's how you wind up being intubated.

We give etomidate and succinylcholine before we put the
GlideScope down the throat and bag the patient, because there's
a slight delay before getting hooked up to a ventilator. Ideally, you
want to keep the patient comfortable but able to open his eyes
and follow basic commands. The problem is that Covid patients
have such low oxygen levels they are delirious—and we have to sedate them deeper in order to control their breathing and make
sure they're not fighting the ventilator. So that means doses of pro-
pofol or Precedex or midazolam, some kind of ketamine for

sedation—plus analgesics like Dilaudid or fentanyl for pain—and on top of that, if they're restless, we will paralyze them with ro-curonium or cisatracurium so they aren't trying to overbreathe the vent, and inadvertently damaging themselves. They're on a whole cocktail of drugs . . . and not a single one actually treats Covid.

Man. What I'd give to know what your day was like. What you're thinking. If you miss me as much as I miss you.

I hope you don't. I hope wherever you are right now, it's better than this.

The next morning, I open the sliding glass door for my morning run down the beach and nearly collide with Gabriel. He is carrying a big cardboard box that is overflowing with vegetables and fruits, some of which I don't even recognize. I am certain I am dreaming this, until he reaches out one hand, steadying me so we do not crash. "These are for you," he says.

I'm not sure what to say, but I take the box from him.

He runs a hand through his hair, making it stand on end. "I am *trying* to say I'm sorry."

"How's it going for you so far?"

Two bright burns of color stain his cheeks. "I should not have . . . treated you as I did yesterday."

"I only wanted to help Beatriz," I say.

"I don't know what to do for her," he says quietly. "I didn't know she was hurting herself . . . until you said so. I don't know what's worse—that she's doing it, or that I didn't even notice."

"She hides it," I tell him. "She doesn't want anyone to know."

"But . . . you do."

"I'm not a psychologist," I say. "Is there someone here she could talk to?"

He shakes his head. "On the mainland, maybe. We don't even have a hospital on island."

"Then you could talk to her."

He swallows, turning away. "What if talking about it makes her do more than just . . . cut?"

"I don't think that's how it works," I say slowly. "I knew a girl who did this, back when I was younger. I wanted to help. A school counselor told me that if I reached out to her, it wouldn't make her do it more, or do something more . . . permanent . . . but it might make her take steps to stop."

"Beatriz won't talk to me," Gabriel says. "Everything I say makes her angry."

"I don't think she's angry at you. I think she's angry at . . ." I wave my hand. "This. Circumstances."

He tilts his head. "She told me about the sandcastle. About people who make art . . . out of garbage." Gabriel clears his throat. "She hasn't given me more than two or three words at a time since she got back to the island a week ago, but last night, she wouldn't stop defending you." He catches my gaze. "I've missed hearing my daughter's voice."

As an apology goes, that one hits the target. He is staring at me fiercely, as if there is more to say, but he does not know how. I break away, glancing down at the box in my arms. "This is too much," I tell him.

"They're from my farm," he says, and then adds, with a hint of a grin, "since I couldn't get you an ATM."

That surprises a laugh out of me. "Does everyone know everyone's business here?"

"Pretty much." He shrugs. "You won't want to leave those in the heat," he says, then reaches behind me and pulls open the slider, so I can carry the box inside. I set it on the kitchen table gingerly, wondering if I should broach the topic of Beatriz again. Last night, I had thought maybe the girl was running away from her overbearing father; now I am not so sure. Either Gabriel is the world's greatest actor, or he is just as lost as his daughter is.

He looks at the box of blank postcards on the kitchen table. "What are you doing with those?"

"Basically, they're my paper supply. I've been writing to my boyfriend."

Gabriel nods. "Well. At least they're still good for something."

"Oh!" I say. "Wait." I whirl around, dart into the bedroom, and return with the neatly folded pile of very soft T-shirts I'd co-opted. "I wouldn't have borrowed them if I knew they were yours."

"They're not." He makes no move to take them from me. "Burn them, if you want." He looks at my face, then sighs. "My wife used to sleep in them. I wasn't upset because you borrowed them. It just . . . was like having a ghost walk over your grave."

He says the word *wife* like it is a blade.

Suddenly he bends down, manipulating the wobbly leg of the table. "I should have fixed this before you moved in."

"You didn't know I was moving in," I reply. "And you weren't particularly thrilled by the idea, as I recall."

"It is possible I judged—how do you say it?—the book by its jacket."

I smile faintly. "By its cover." I think about him sneering at me for being a tourist, for being an American. I start to feel indignation percolating inside me, but then I remember that every time our paths have crossed, I've made poor assumptions about him, too.

He rips off a piece of the cardboard box, folds it, and uses it to balance the table. "I'll come back this afternoon and fix it properly," he says.

"Maybe Beatriz could join you," I offer. "I mean, if she wants to."

He nods. "I will ask."

Something blossoms between us, delicate and discomfiting—a silent second start, a willingness to give the benefit of the doubt, instead of expecting the worst.

Gabriel inclines his head. "I leave you to your morning, then," he says, and he turns.

"Wait," I call out, as his hand grasps the sliding door. "If you're a tour guide, why do you hate tourists so much?"

Slowly, he turns. "I'm not a tour guide anymore," he says.

"Well, since the island is closed," I reply, "technically . . . I'm not a tourist."

He smiles, and it is transformative. It's like the first time you see a falling star. Every night after that, you find yourself searching again, and if you don't see one, you feel crestfallen. "Maybe, then, one day, I can show you my island," Gabriel offers.

I lean against the table. It is, for the first time in a week, sturdy. "I'd like that," I say.

FOUR

A lot of people would think a vacation alone with nothing to do is heaven.

I am not one of those people.

I do not go to movies by myself. If I walk in Central Park, it's usually in the company of Finn or Rodney. If I travel for work, and stay overnight at a hotel, I will always choose room service over eating alone at a restaurant.

The idea of being by yourself on a desert island has a romantic cachet to it, but the reality is less attractive. I find myself looking forward to my mornings on the beach, because Beatriz meets me there almost every day, and then follows me home to collect my daily postcard to Finn. I find reasons to hover around the front door of Abuela's place, so that we can have our odd conversation made of charades, and because it almost always ends in a dinner invitation. I engage Gabriel in discussions about when the island might reopen, when the ferry will return to take me back to the mainland.

Twice I've found enough of a cell signal to call Finn, but he hasn't answered. Once, a flood of texts and emails came through, but they were garbled, symbols and gibberish instead of sentences. When I can, I send responses back into the void. *I shouldn't have gone. I miss you. I love you.* Here, too, I might as well be shouting into a canyon, and hearing only an echo.

There are some days when I don't speak a single word out loud, and I restlessly move from the apartment to the beach or go for a run just to stop myself from having to think about Finn, about how long it's been since I heard his voice, about my job, about my future. With every passing hour, all of that feels hazier, as if the pandemic is a fog that's rolled in from nowhere and nothing looks quite the way it used to.

When I have no alternative, I sit by myself and wonder how far I've been blown off course.

> *Dear Finn,*
>
> *I've been thinking about how I left things at work. If the situation is really bad in the city, then maybe Kitomi was right to hold off on the private auction. But then again, if it's really bad there, Sotheby's is going to need that sale more than ever.*
>
> *By the time I get back, I may not even* have *a job.*
>
> *Which is . . . strange. For so long I've known what I want to do and who I want to be when I grow up—I can't imagine not being an art specialist. It's not like I've always secretly dreamed of being an astronaut and now this is my big opportunity to strike out in a new direction. I* liked *the direction I was headed.*
>
> *I will say this, though—sometimes I look at the neon-orange Sally Lightfoot crabs polka-dotting black lava, or the pattern of spots on the back of a ray underwater, and I think: art is everywhere, if you know to look for it.*
>
> *I miss you, goddammit.*
>
> *Love, Diana*

I didn't expect to like Kitomi Ito.

Like the rest of the world, I saw her as she'd been cast: the villain in the story of the Nightjars, the quiet psychologist-turned-siren who'd ensorcelled Sam Pride and led to the breakup of arguably the best band in the history of rock and roll. Whatever she'd done with her life since then—which included opening an ashram and writing three bestsellers about expanding one's consciousness—paled in comparison to how she had affected Sam Pride. There were die-hard Nightjars fans who blamed her for his murder, because she was the reason Sam relocated from the UK to New York City.

To be fair, I also didn't expect my boss to take me to Kitomi Ito's apartment when she was trying to get Kitomi to commit to an auction at Sotheby's. But Eva had been hinting for a while that since I was now an associate specialist in Imp Mod, I should be getting more responsibility. She started dragging me to meet with art collectors and their collection managers—not because she enjoyed the pleasure of my company, but to groom me for a more senior position.

I was flattered, and I was stoked. If I could be promoted to specialist—becoming an assistant vice president before I turned thirty—I would be ahead of my own ideal career schedule.

For several weeks now, Eva had been courting Kitomi as a potential client, taking her to lunch at Jean-Georges and The Modern. Given what Kitomi was floating for potential auction—a Toulouse-Lautrec original with an unparalleled history—I wondered if she ever had to make herself a meal, period. I was sure Phillips and Christie's were wining and dining her as well; it was all part of the process of building a relationship with a seller—in the hope that the first piece they consigned for sale might not be the last. It was called the long game, and everyone in the business played it.

Just the fact that Eva commanded me to tag along, however, did not mean that she had developed any sudden affection for me. She was still the same frighteningly efficient, untouchable boss that (who was I kidding) I wanted to be one day. Like Eva, I wanted to walk down the hall at Sotheby's and hear interns whisper. I wanted my name inextricably tangled with works of great art. I wanted to make the Fortune's 40 Under 40 list.

"When we get there," Eva instructed, as we sat in the back of the car that was taking us to the Ansonia, "you are effectively mute. Understand?"

"Got it."

"Not even a hello, Diana. Just nod."

"What if she—"

"She won't," Eva says.

The Ansonia settled across the entirety of a block, a grande dame at a ball surveying the frenzy she would never deign to take part in. Kitomi Ito's apartment was the penthouse, and to my surprise, when the elevator doors opened she was waiting for us herself. Eva shook her hand and smiled. "This is Diana O'Toole," she said. "She's an associate specialist on our team."

Kitomi was so much smaller than I had anticipated, just a hair above five feet tall. She wore a floor-length embroidered robe over jeans and a white T-shirt, and her purple glasses. "Nice to meet you," she said, with a slight accent, and I realized in that instant that in all the photographs and grainy video clips where I'd seen her with Sam Pride and the Nightjars, I had never actually heard her voice. She was part of a music legend, but she had no sound of her own.

I opened my mouth to say hello, and then snapped it shut and smiled.

Kitomi had a traditional Japanese tea set out in her living room— handleless cups and squat teapots wreathed with delicate painted flowers. She led us right by it, down a little hallway, to where the painting was hanging. I couldn't tear my eyes from it, and I got the same flutter in my stomach I always got when I first saw a piece of art that was legendary. The smudges of color at the edges of the frame became crisper in the middle, where the lovers were depicted. Clearest of all were their eyes, riveted on each other. Suddenly I was *there*, in the way that art can make you time-travel: I could imagine the painter, mixing his palette; could smell the attar of roses on the bedsheets; could hear the thumps of the prostitutes entertaining their clients in the rooms on either side.

Part of my job surrounding this acquisition had meant learning as much as possible about Henri de Toulouse-Lautrec and his work, so that I could assess how it fit into the impressionist canon. Over the past few weeks I'd done research at the office, at NYPL, at Columbia and NYU. Born in France to a comte and comtesse who were first cousins, Toulouse-Lautrec had a skeletal dysplasia that left him only five feet tall with an adult-size torso, child-size legs—and, allegedly, oversize genitals. His father was embarrassed by his choice to become an artist; his mother was concerned for the company he kept. He had a reputation as a ladies' man. His first liaison was with Marie Charlet, a seventeen-year-old model. Another lover, Suzanne Valadon, tried to kill herself when their relationship ended. The red-headed model Rosa la Rouge, a prostitute, was likely the one who gave him the syphilis that led to his death.

Like other artists, he was intrigued by Montmartre—the bohemian part of Paris, jammed with cabarets and prostitutes. The Moulin Rouge commissioned him to create posters and saved a seat for him always. For weeks at a time, he would move into brothels, painting the reality of the lives of sex workers—from boredom to health checks to the relationships they had that were not commercial transactions. He was much more interested in the difference between how a person acts in a certain environment and how they do when they're alone—the space between the showman and the self; the gap between the private and the professional.

His work was described as painterly, relying on long, unblended brushstrokes. His art was more a blur than a snapshot, like scanning a crowd and having your gaze snag on something—the green, looming face of a woman, the bright red tights of a dancer. He was much more interested in individuals than in their surroundings, so there was usually a certain feature that he felt was distinctive and he accentuated that, letting the rest of the field float away. His gaze was not romanticized, but practical and dispassionate.

Around 1890, he painted a series—*Le Lit*—that featured prostitutes in bed in quiet moments of intimacy. The women were pastel, because they used to powder themselves to look whiter and younger and healthy, but the surroundings were comparatively brighter, to contrast between where they were and who they were. *What you see,* Toulouse-Lautrec seemed to say, *is not what you're really getting.*

There was no question that Kitomi Ito's painting fit into this series, with one startling departure: here, Toulouse-Lautrec had painted himself into the frame.

Beside me, I heard Eva draw in her breath, and I remembered that this was the first time she'd seen the piece in person, too.

She cleared her throat, and I shook myself out of my reverie. I had work to do. It was my responsibility to assess the condition of the painting: Was the paint peeling? Was the frame sound? And the signature—did it look like his other signatures: *T-Lautrec,* the *T* and dash almost forming an *F,* the sharp acute angle of the *L,* the tiny loop of the *t* at its cross mark. While I was doing this, Eva had her own job: convincing Kitomi Ito that Sotheby's was the right auction house to sell the piece.

We knew that in the past, Kitomi had sold through Christie's. But for this painting, she had invited other auction houses to make their pitches. "It's breathtaking," Eva said, and when she did, I didn't look at the artwork but at Kitomi Ito's face. She looked like a mother who had made the decision to give a baby up for adoption, only to realize that it was harder than she thought to let him go.

"Sam used to say," she said, "that when he turned eighty, he'd never do another interview. Never sit in front of another camera. He wanted to go to Montana and raise sheep."

"Really?" Eva asked.

Kitomi shrugged. "We'll never know, I suppose."

Because thirty-five years ago, her husband had been murdered. She turned, leading us down the hallway again to the table for tea.

"Is there a particular reason you decided to sell the painting?" Eva asked.

Kitomi looked up at her. "I'm moving."

I could see Eva doing calculations. If Kitomi was going to leave New York City, there would be other things in the apartment she might want to sell.

The tea steamed in front of me. It smelled like green grass. "It's sencha," Kitomi said. "And there's Scottish shortbread, too. Sam was the one who got me addicted to *that.*"

I sat with my hands folded in my lap, listening with half an ear to

Eva's pointed questioning: *Have you had the painting appraised? Has the piece been moved? Has there been any restoration done on it? What other players do you work with in the art field—does someone manage your collection? What do you hope to achieve through auction?*

"What I want," Kitomi said, "is for this painting to close one chapter, so I can open the next one."

Her words sounded like the break of a bone, sharp and irrevocable.

Eva began to pitch the marketing campaign she and other senior associates had been fine-tuning since the first call from Kitomi. The plan was to wrap Sam Pride's name all over the auction, because value is added for a celebrity—part of the reason the Vanderbilt estate had sold as well as it did years ago was simply the name Vanderbilt in the descriptions. "At Sotheby's, we know art. So naturally, we would write up the history of the time of Toulouse-Lautrec's life and pitch it to the top five Imp Mod collectors in the world, and we would give the painting the cover of the catalog. But we also know this is special. This piece is like nothing we have ever auctioned, because it is a link between two icons of their times. It's not just Toulouse-Lautrec who should be spotlighted, but Sam Pride. At the auction, we would lean into the moment at which this painting intersected with Sam's life."

Kitomi's face was unreadable.

"Nineteen eighty-two," Eva continued, "when the album came out with this visible in the cover photo. We would also reunite the surviving Nightjars as a precursor to the auction—art begetting art."

Eva reached into a leather folio to present the formal write-up of the pitch to Kitomi: the multimillion-dollar estimate of the painting's value that would be presented to the public, what we thought the market value actually was, and the reserve—the secret amount Sotheby's would keep as the price below which we would not sell.

I rose from my seat, about to ask for a restroom when I remembered I wasn't supposed to speak. Kitomi looked up, her eyes black buttons. "It's down the hall," she said. "Left at the end."

I nodded and slipped away. But instead of going to the bathroom, I found myself standing in front of the painting.

A lot of Toulouse-Lautrec's work was about movement. His earliest art captured horses, then he focused on dancers and the circus and bicycle racing. But even later paintings felt like they were kinetic. *At the Moulin Rouge, The Dance*—one of his most famous paintings—showcases a tilted perspective on the floor to make the viewer feel off-kilter and a little drunk—while the eye is drawn to the red of the dancer's stockings and to the pink of a fine lady's dress and then to the gentleman she is watching and then to the flurry of another dancer's petticoat behind him—all these angles make you feel like you are spinning, like you are in this loud room moving about, as small details catch your eye.

Kitomi Ito's painting, on the other hand, was all about stillness.

It was the moment after intimacy, when you weren't joined to your lover anymore, but still felt him beating like blood inside you.

It was the moment where you had to remember how to breathe again.

It was the moment where nothing mattered more than the moment ago.

The model had red hair, and it was one of the only splashes of color on the background, which was tan, like cardboard. The field was white with bits of pastel in it. The woman—Rosa la Rouge—sat up half-nude. Behind her was a mirror, reflecting the direct gaze of the man who faced her from the bottom right of the painting: Lautrec himself, turned to the side, so you saw his bared shoulder and his profile, his beard and the wire edge of his glasses. The artist's shoulder—a pallid green—was the only other bleed of color in the painting. I wondered if it was meant to flag illness, like his bent legs under the covers; or jealousy over this woman who would ultimately be the end of him.

Or maybe it was a flash of the hidden heart of a man most often described as aloof.

I shook myself away from the painting and continued down the hall to the bathroom, passing an open doorway. The room was familiar to anyone who had ever seen the Nightjars' final album, with Kitomi and Sam Pride in that very bed. The only thing missing, of course, was the painting that, for the album cover, had been hung behind Kitomi.

But there were things in the room now that were not part of that photo. On one side of the bed was a nightstand with a stack of books, a glass half-full of water, a pair of purple reading glasses, some hand cream. On the other was a nightstand with only one item on it: a man's wedding ring. Neatly aligned on the floor was a battered pair of men's leather slippers.

I backed away, feeling even more voyeuristic now than I ever had seeing Kitomi half-naked on an album cover, and went to the bathroom. When I emerged, Kitomi herself was standing in front of the painting.

"His cousin was a medical student," she said. "He let Henri scrub in and do paintings of surgery." She turned, a smile in her eyes. "I've always thought of him by his first name, not Toulouse-Lautrec," she said. "He was hanging over my bed for years, after all."

I took a few steps toward her. I wondered if I should tell her that I knew all that. But Eva had warned me to stay silent.

"He was placed in a sanitorium because of alcoholism and syphilis, and to prove to doctors he was sane enough to leave, he painted images of the circus from his memory. But he still died at thirty-six." Kitomi's mouth twisted. "Some people burn too bright to last long."

Her voice was so soft I had to strain to hear it. "Auctioning it off feels like an amputation. But it doesn't seem right to have it in Montana, either."

Montana.

I thought of Kitomi saying she wanted to turn the page.

This was not, I realized, a woman who wanted a clean break, a new life. This was a woman who was so tied to her dead husband she was going to live out the dream he didn't.

I thought: *Eva is going to kill me.* But I turned and said, "I have an idea."

On the way to El Muro de las Lágrimas, or Wall of Tears, Beatriz and I detour past the remains of a mermaid. Yesterday, she stretched at the edge of the beach where the dry sand met the wet. Scales of shells mounded her tail; her hair was a tangle of seaweed. But today, our sand art has been all but swallowed by the sea.

"I bet it's totally gone by curfew," Beatriz says.

"Tibetan monks spend months making sand mandalas and then they brush them away and throw them into a river."

She turns, pained. *"Why?"*

"Because it's not permanent and that's the point."

Beatriz looks at the ruins of our sculpture. "That's the stupidest thing I've ever heard," she says, and she picks up her water bottle and starts walking. "Are you coming, or what?"

Today she is taking me to a site that is part of a former penal colony. It's a two-hour hike through parched terrain, past scrub and cacti and, yes, poison apples. Even though we have left early, the sun is strong enough to make my shirt stick to my back with sweat, and I can feel my scalp burning where my hair is parted.

Beatriz is still cagey with me, but there are moments when she lets down her guard. Once or twice I've made her laugh. It may be foolish to think that she's any less sad in my company, but at least I have eyes on her. And as far as I can tell, there aren't any fresh cuts on her arms.

"I thought art was supposed to be something you left behind so everyone would remember you," Beatriz says.

"Something doesn't have to be finished and hanging on a wall for you to remember who made it," I say. "You ever heard of Banksy? He's a British street artist and activist. One of his paintings—*Girl with Balloon*—was auctioned off by my company in 2018. Someone bought it for $1.4 million . . . and as soon as the gavel came down, the canvas started to slip out of the frame, in shreds. On Instagram, he posted *Going, going, gone,* and said he'd built a shredder into the frame intentionally, in case the work ever sold at auction."

"Were you *there?*"

"No, it happened in England."

"What a waste of money."

"Well," I say, "actually, it went up in value when it was torn into ribbons. Because the real art wasn't the painting—it was the act of destroying it."

Beatriz glances at me. "When did you know you wanted to sell art?"

"In college," I admit. "Before that I thought I'd be an actual *artist*."

"Really?"

"Yeah. My father was a conservator. He restored paintings and frescoes that needed fixing."

"Like the Banksy?"

"I guess, although that wasn't glued back together. Conservationists usually focus on really old art that's literally crumbling to pieces. He'd bring me to his sites, when I was little, and let me paint over a tiny bit that wouldn't mess anything up. I'm sure he didn't tell his bosses. The best days of my life were the ones where I got to go to work with him, and he'd ask me things as if my answers really mattered: *What do you think, Diana, should we use the violet or the indigo? Can you make out how many claws are on that hoof?*"

I feel the same black shadow that always comes on the heels of a memory of my father: the acrid smoke of unfairness, the knowledge that the parent I wish was still here is gone.

"Does he still let you do it? Paint with him?"

"He died," I say. "He's been gone about four years now."

She looks at me. "I'm sorry," she says.

"I am, too."

We walk a little further in silence. Then Beatriz says, "Why don't you paint anymore?"

"I don't have time," I reply, although that's not true.

I haven't made time, because I haven't wanted to.

I remember the exact day I put away my painting supplies, the shoebox with its arthritic tubes of acrylics and the palette with layer after layer of dried moments of inspiration, like rings on a tree. It was after the student exhibition at Williams, when my father said my painting reminded him of my mother's work. But I somehow couldn't bring myself to throw away the tools of the trade. When I moved to

New York, the shoebox came with me, still unopened. I set it on the highest shelf of my closet, behind sweatshirts from college I no longer wore but couldn't bear to donate to Goodwill, and the winter hiking boots I bought but never used, and a box of old tax records.

Beatriz is looking at me with sympathy. "Is it because you weren't good at it?" she asks. "That you stopped painting?"

I laugh. "You could argue that any time someone intentionally leaves a mark behind, it's art. Even if it's not pretty."

She tugs her sleeves down over her wrists. Even in this heat, she has chosen to hike in a sweatshirt, rather than show me the scars on her arms. "Not every time," she murmurs.

I stop walking. "Beatriz . . ."

"Sometimes I can't remember her. My mother."

"I'm sure your father could—"

"I don't *want* to remember her. But then I think . . ." Her voice trails off. "Then I think maybe I'm just easy to forget."

I reach for her arm and push her sleeve up gently. We both stare at the ladder of scars, some silver with age, and some still an angry red. "Is that why you cut?" I ask quietly.

At first I think she is going to pull away, but then she starts speaking, fast and low. "The first time I did it, I guess. And then . . . I stopped for a while. At school, it was easier to distract myself. But then, right before I came back here . . ." She shakes her head, swallows. "How come the people who don't even notice you exist are the ones you can't stop thinking about?"

"My mother was never home when I was a kid. In fact, I used to think she *looked* for reasons to travel so she could get away from me."

The words come out in a rush of air, a popped balloon of anger. I don't think I've ever said it out loud before to anyone. Not even Finn.

Beatriz stares at me as if all my features have rearranged. "Did she run off with a photographer from a Nat Geo ship?" she asks drily.

"No. She just decided that everything in the world—literally—was more important than I was. And now she has dementia and has no idea who I am."

"That . . . sucks."

I shrug. "It is what it is," I tell her. "The point is, if someone abandons you, it may be less about you and more about them."

I stop speaking as we come upon a wall that rises from the scorched earth. It's made of volcanic rock and towers over us a good sixty feet, stretching further than my eye can see. It does not, I realize, enclose anything. "The inmates built it in the forties and fifties," Beatriz says. "It wasn't for any real purpose, except to create work for punishment. Tons of prisoners died while they were building it."

"That's grim," I mutter.

There are two ways of looking at walls. Either they are built to keep people you fear *out* or they are built to keep people you love *in*.

Either way, you create a divide.

"They only got one ship full of cargo a year—the prisoners and the guards were all starving. To stay alive, they hunted down land tortoises to eat. There's rumors that the place is full of ghosts, and you can hear them crying at night," Beatriz says. "It's creepy as fuck."

I step closer, walking the length of the wall. Some of the stones are etched with symbols, letters, dates, patterns, hatch marks to count time.

If you define art as something made by the hands of men, something that makes us remember them long after they're gone, then this wall qualifies. The fact that it is unfinished or broken doesn't make it any less striking.

When my phone starts buzzing in my pocket, I jump. It has been so long. I pull it out with a cry of surprise and see Finn's name.

"Oh my God," I say. "It's you. It's really you!"

"Diana! I can't believe I got through." His voice is scratchy and pocked by static and so, so dear. Tears spring to my eyes as I struggle to hear him: "Tell me . . . and every . . . you . . . it's been."

I'm missing half of what he says, so I curl myself around the phone and experimentally move along the wall hoping for a stronger signal. "Can you hear me?" I say. "Finn?"

"Yeah, yeah," he responds, and I can hear the relief in his words. "Christ, it's good to talk to you."

"I got your emails—"

"I didn't know if they were going through—"

"The service here is terrible," I tell him. "I wrote you postcards."

"Well, nothing's been delivered yet. I can't believe there's no internet there."

"I know," I say, but that's not what I want to talk about, and I don't know how long this magical, elusive signal will last. "How are you? It sounds—"

"I don't even have words for it, Di," he says. "It's . . . endless."

"But you're safe," I state, as if there is no alternative.

"Who knows," he says. "I read Guayaquil's getting slammed. That they're stacking bodies on the streets."

At this, my stomach turns. "I haven't seen anyone sick here," I tell him. "Everyone wears masks and there's a curfew."

"I wish *I* could say that." Finn sighs. "All day long it feels like I'm sandbagging against a wave and then I walk outside and realize that it's a fucking tsunami and we don't stand a chance." His voice hitches.

I look around at the curl of clouds in the sky, the sun glittering on the ocean in the distance. A picture postcard. Just a few hundred miles away this virus is killing people so fast that they don't have room for bodies, but you would never know it from where I stand. I think of the empty shelves of the grocery mart, the people like Gabriel growing their own food in the highlands, the fishermen that have to carry the mail to the mainland, the tourism that dried up overnight. The curse of being on an island is inaccessibility, but maybe that is also its blessing.

Finn's voice wavers, cutting in and out again. "Pregnant women . . . labor alone . . . ICU, the only time family is allowed . . . gonna die in the next hour."

"You're breaking up—Finn—"

"Nothing changes and . . ."

"Finn?"

". . . all dead," he says, those words suddenly clear and crisp. "Every time I finally get to come home and you aren't there, it feels like another slap in the face. You don't know how hard it is being alone right now."

But I do. "You're the one who told me to go," I say quietly.

There is a silence. "Yeah," Finn answers. "I guess I just assumed . . . you wouldn't actually listen."

Then you shouldn't have said it, I think uncharitably, but my eyes are burning with guilt and frustration and anger. *I can't read your mind.*

Which suddenly feels like a much bigger problem, a seed of doubt that sprouts the very moment it's planted.

"Di—a?" I hear. "Are . . . still . . . ?"

Although I have not budged, I've somehow lost the connection. The line goes dead in my hand. I slip the phone into my pocket and trudge back toward the wall to find Beatriz sitting in its shadow, scraping the edge of one pointed piece of basalt against the smooth belly of another.

"Was that your boyfriend?" she asks.

"Yeah."

"Does he miss you?"

I sit down beside her. "Yes," I say. I watch her create a hashtag on a rock, and color in each alternate square like a chessboard. "What are you doing?"

She slants her gaze my way. "Art," she says.

I lean my back against the sharp stones of the wall. There are endless ways to leave your mark on the world—cutting, carving, art. Maybe all of them do require payment in the form of a piece of yourself—your flesh, your strength, your soul.

I reach for a rock. I start to carve my name into another loose stone. When I'm finished, I write BEATRIZ on another. Then I stand up and pick at some of the pebbles and sand in the surface of the wall, making space to wedge the name rocks into it. "What are *you* doing?" Beatriz asks.

I dust my hands off on my thighs. "Art," I reply.

She scrambles to her feet, following me as I step a distance away. The rocks I've carved are pale gray, completely different from the bulk of the dark wall. They are, from back here, unnoticeable. But when you walk closer, you cannot miss them. You just have to take those few steps.

The first time I saw impressionist art, I was with my father at the Brooklyn Museum. He covered my eyes with his hands and guided me up close to Monet's *Houses of Parliament. What do you see?* he asked, removing his hands when I was inches from the canvas.

I saw blobs. Pink and purple blobs and brushstrokes.

He covered my eyes again and drew me further away. *Abracadabra,* he whispered, and he let me look again.

There were buildings, and smog, and twilight. There was a city. It had been there all along, I'd just been too close to see it.

Squinting at the lighter shards in the wall that have our names on them, I think that art goes both ways. Sometimes you have to have the perspective of distance. And sometimes, you cannot tell what you're looking at until it's right under your nose.

I turn to find Beatriz with her face tipped up to the sky. Her eyes are closed, her throat stretched like a sacrifice. "This would be," she says, "a good place to die."

Dear Finn,

    By the time you get this postcard, you probably won't even remember what you said when we finally actually got to speak to each other, even if it was only for a minute.

    I never chose to go anywhere without you.

    If you didn't really want me to go to the Galápagos by myself, why did you say it?

    I can't help but wonder what else you've said that you didn't really mean.

Diana

Toulouse-Lautrec rarely painted himself, and when he did, he hid the flaws of his lower body. In *At the Moulin Rouge,* he put himself in the background next to his much taller cousin, but hid his deformed legs behind a group of people at a table. In a self-portrait, he depicted himself from the waist up. There is a famous photograph of him dressed as a little clown, as if to underscore that people who focused on his disabilities formed an inaccurate impression of him.

All of this made Kitomi Ito's painting even rarer. This was the only work of Toulouse-Lautrec's where he was literally and figuratively baring himself, as if to say that love renders you naked and vulnerable. There were other differences, too. Unlike most of his work, which had been exhibited after his death in Albi, his birthplace, at a museum funded by his mother, this one disappeared from the public eye until 1908. Until then, it had been stashed away with a friend of Toulouse-Lautrec's, an art dealer named Maurice Joyant. With the painting had come the express directive of the artist: sell this only to someone who is willing to give up everything for love.

The first owner of the painting was Coco Chanel, who received it as a gift from Boy Capel, a rich aristocrat who bought it to lure her away from her first lover, Étienne Balsan. Chanel fell madly for Capel, who financed her foray into clothing design and her boutiques in Biarritz and Deauville. Their relationship was intense and sizzling, even though Capel was never faithful to her and married an aristocrat and kept another mistress. When he died at Christmas 1919, Chanel draped her windows with black crepe and put black sheets on her bed. *I lost everything when I lost Capel,* she once said. *He left a void in me the years have not filled.*

Years later, Chanel had an affair with the Duke of Westminster, who took her aboard his yacht, the *Flying Cloud.* Long after that, the duke offered up his yacht for a friend who needed a place for a tryst—Edward VIII, briefly the king of England, who was obsessed with the American divorcée Wallis Simpson. Although they didn't wind up using that yacht, they did have an affair—one that led him to give up the throne. Months later, in 1937, Edward VIII bought the Toulouse-Lautrec painting for Wallis Simpson, negotiating with Chanel through their mutual friend the duke. Chanel wanted it out of the house, she said, because it broke her heart.

In 1956, Wallis Simpson was said to be jealous of Marilyn Monroe because Marilyn had pushed her off the front pages of the newspapers. She invited her nemesis for tea, choosing to keep her enemies close. While at Simpson's home, Monroe was left breathless by the Toulouse-Lautrec painting. In 1962, when Joe DiMaggio was trying to get Monroe to remarry him, he convinced Simpson to sell him the painting. He presented it to Marilyn three days before she died.

No one knows how Sam Pride and Joe DiMaggio crossed paths, but in 1972, Pride bought the painting from DiMaggio, and gave it to Kitomi Ito as a wedding present. It hung over their bed until he was killed, and then she moved it into the hallway of their apartment.

There is a small matte smudge on the frame of the painting, from where Kitomi Ito touches it as she passes, drawing her like a lodestone, or a statue you rub for good luck.

Provenance, in art, is a fancy word for the origins of a work. It's the paper trail, the chain of evidence, the connection between then and now. It's the unbroken link between the artist and the present art collector. The provenance of Kitomi Ito's painting is devotion so fierce, it scorches the earth with tragedy and lays waste to those who experience it. Starting, of course, with the man who'd caught syphilis from his paramour . . . but who stared at her from the corner of the painting with single-minded focus, as if to say, *For you, love, I would do it all again.*

To: DOToole@gmail.com
From: FColson@nyp.org

Six of my patients died today.

Their families were allowed to come in here and say goodbye the hour before they died—and that's an improvement over what it was last week, when they had to do it over FaceTime.

This last patient was on ECMO. Everyone's talking about vents and how we're running out of them but no one is talking about ECMO—which is when your lungs are so bad, even the vent doesn't work anymore. So you get a giant-ass cannula in your neck and one in your groin and the blood gets pumped through a machine that acts like your heart and lungs. You get a Foley catheter and a rectal tube and a nasal gastric tube for nutrition—we are literally outsourcing their bodies.

This woman was twenty years old. TWENTY. All that bullshit about how the virus is killing old people? Whoever's saying that isn't working in an ICU. Of my six patients who died, none were over 35. Two were Hispanic women in their twenties who developed Covid bowel necrosis, which required surgical resection—they made it through surgery but died from complications. One was an overweight man, 28—overweight, but not obese. One, a paramedic, bled into her lungs. One guy I thought was gonna make it, until his pupils blew out—the heparin we gave him so the ECMO could do its work without clotting gave him a brain bleed.

Why am I telling you all this? Because I need to tell *someone*. And because it's easier than what I *should* be saying.

Which is: I'm sorry for what I said to you. I know I'm the reason you're where you are now. It's just that nothing's the way it is supposed to be, goddammit.

Sometimes I sit and listen to the whir of the ECMO machine, and I think, *This person's heart is outside his body, and I understand completely.*

Because so is mine.

The night before my two-week anniversary on Isabela, Abuela throws me a goodbye dinner. Gabriel comes with Beatriz, who clings to me when I leave to go down to my apartment. I've given her my cellphone number, but also my address, to stay in touch. Gabriel walks me to my door that night. "What will you do back home?" he asks.

I shrug. "Get on with my life," I tell him. But I am not quite sure what that is anymore. I don't know if I'll have a job, and I am nervous about seeing Finn again, after our weird phone conversation.

"Well," he says, "I hope it's a good one, then. Your life."

"That's the plan," I say, and we say good night.

It does not take long for me to pack—after all, I have nearly nothing—but I clean the kitchen countertops and fold the towels I've washed and fall asleep dreaming of my reunion with Finn. Normally, I would have checked on my flight home, but without internet, I have to just hope for the best.

The next morning when I open the sliding door, my tote stuffed and settled on my shoulder for the walk into town to the ferry dock, Gabriel and Beatriz are waiting. Beatriz looks happier than I have ever seen her look. She throws her arms around me. "You have to stay," she says.

I look over her head at her father, and then hold her at arm's length. "Beatriz," I tell her, "you know I can't. But I promise to—"

"She's right," Gabriel states, and something deep in my chest vibrates like a tuning fork.

I glance at my watch. "I don't want to miss the ferry—"

"There is no ferry," Gabriel interrupts. "The island isn't opening."

"What?" I blink. "For how long?"

"I don't know," he admits. "But there aren't any flights out of Santa Cruz . . . or even Guayaquil, for that matter. The government isn't letting any incoming planes land, either."

I let my tote slip from my shoulder to my elbow. "So I can't get home," I say. The words feel like they're being torn from my throat.

"You can't get home *right now*," Gabriel corrects.

"This isn't happening," I murmur. "There has to be a way."

"Not unless you swim," Beatriz says, sunny.

"I have to get back to New York," I say. "What am I supposed to do about work? And *Finn*. Oh my God, I can't even tell him what's going on."

"Your boss can't be mad at you if there's no way for you to get back," Beatriz reasons. "And you can call your boyfriend from Abuela's landline."

Abuela has a landline? And they're just telling me *now*?

My life has been a series of telephone poles one after the other, benchmarks of progress. Without a road map of the steps that come next, I am floundering. I do not belong here, and I cannot shake the feeling that at home, the world is moving on without me. If I can't get back soon, I might never catch up.

I've been on an island for two weeks, but this is the first time I've really ever felt completely at sea.

Gabriel looks at my face, and says something to Beatriz in Spanish. She takes the tote from my arm and carries it into the apartment while he leads me upstairs to Abuela's. She is sitting on her couch watching a telenovela when we come in. Gabriel explains to her why I'm here, again in language I don't understand.

Oh, God. I'm stuck in a country where I can't even communicate.

He bustles me into the bedroom, where there is a phone on the nightstand. I stare at it. "What's the matter?"

"I don't know how to call home," I admit.

Gabriel picks up the receiver and punches a few buttons. "What's his number?"

I tell him and he hands the phone to me. Three rings. *This is Finn; you know the drill.*

When I glance up, Gabriel is shutting the door behind himself.

"Hi," I say out loud. "It's me. My flight's been canceled. Actually, every flight's been canceled. I can't get home now, and I don't know when I'll be able to. I'm sorry. I'm so fucking sorry." A sob rises like a vine through my sentences. "You were right. I shouldn't have left."

I am so mad. At Finn, for telling me to go. At myself, for not telling Finn to go fuck himself when he said it. So what if we would have forfeited money on a vacation? In the grand scheme of things, losing dollars is nothing compared to losing time.

I know I'm not thinking rationally—that Finn isn't the only one to blame. I could have told him that if things were going to be worse, I would rather have shouldered them by his side than been somewhere less risky without him. I could even have been smart enough to get right back on the ferry that was dropping me off on Isabela as soon as I learned that the island was about to close.

What I'm truly angry about is that when Finn told me to go, he meant the opposite. When I said I'd leave, I wanted to stay. And even though we'd been together for years, neither one of us read between the lines.

There's really nothing else I have to say, which surprises me, because it's been so long since we have truly talked. But Finn is drowning in reality and I'm in a holding pattern in paradise. *Be careful what you wish for,* I think. When you're stuck in heaven, it can feel like hell.

"As soon as I find out more, I'll tell you. Not that I know how," I mutter. "This whole situation is just insane. I'll keep sending post-cards. Anyway. I thought you'd want to know." I stare at the receiver for another moment and then hang it up and afterward realize I hadn't said *I love you.*

When I step into Abuela's living room, Gabriel is sitting next to her on the couch. He stands when he sees me. "All good?"

"Voicemail," I say.

"You'll stay in the apartment, obviously," he says, as if he's trying to make up for his reaction when he first found me here.

"I don't have any money—" That jogs a new worry in my mind—as sick as I am of eating pasta, I don't even have enough cash to feed myself.

"And we'll make sure you have food," Gabriel says, reading my thoughts. He bends down and kisses Abuela on the cheek. "I don't want to leave Beatriz too long."

I follow him out the front door, onto the porch. When he jogs down the steps, headed toward my apartment in the rear, I call his name. He turns, looking up at me, impatient.

"Why are you doing this?" I ask.

"Doing what?"

"Being nice to me."

He grins, a streak of lightning. "I'll try to be more of a *cabrón,*" he says, and when I blink, he translates. "Asshole."

"For real, though," I press.

Gabriel shrugs. "Before, you were a tourist," he says simply. "Now, you're one of us."

What I want to do: crawl underneath the covers of my bed, and pretend that when I wake up, I'll realize this was all just a nightmare. I will breeze down to the dock, board a ferry, and begin the first leg of my journey back to New York City.

What I do instead: accompany Gabriel and Beatriz to a swimming hole inland. Beatriz says that if I'm all by myself I will just wallow in my misery, and I cannot contradict her because it's the rationale for every outing I've dragged her on this past week—when *she* was the one who needed distraction. She is carrying a snorkel and mask looped onto her arm, and it bounces against her hip as we hike. "Where are we going?" I ask.

"We could tell you," Beatriz says, "but then we'd have to kill you."

"She's not entirely wrong," Gabriel adds. "Most of the island is closed because of the pandemic. If the park rangers find you, they'll *fine* you."

"Or take away your tour guide license," Beatriz tosses over her shoulder.

Gabriel's shoulders tense, then relax again. "Which I am not using anyway."

She turns on a heel, walking backward. "Are we or are we not going to a secret place you used to take clients?"

"We are going to a secret place I used to go to as a boy," he corrects.

We finally reach a brackish pond with water that is the color of rust and bordered by brush and thickets of fallen, twisted branches. As Isabela goes, it is far from the prettiest of landscapes. Beatriz begins to strip down to her bathing suit and long-sleeved rash guard, leaving the rest of her clothes in a pile. She fits her snorkel and mask to her face, then dives into the muddy lagoon.

"Maybe I'll just wait here," I say.

Gabriel turns in the act of pulling his shirt over his head and smiles. "Now who is judging a book by its cover?"

He kicks off his shoes and splashes into the water, and reluctantly I peel down to my bathing suit and wade in. The bottom drops away sharply, unexpectedly, and I find myself swallowed up by the water. Before I can even panic, a strong hand grabs my arm, holding me up as I sputter. "Okay?" Gabriel asks.

I nod, still choking a little. My fingers flex on his shoulder. This close, I realize that he has a freckle on his left earlobe. I look at the spikes of his eyelashes.

With a strong kick I free myself, and start swimming in the direction Beatriz went.

Gabriel overtakes me quickly; he is a stronger swimmer. He's headed straight for a wall of tangled mangrove roots, or so it seems, near which Beatriz's snorkel bobs. She lifts her face when we get closer, her eyes huge behind the plastic of the mask. The snorkel falls from her mouth as she scrambles up a makeshift ladder of roots and disappears into a fold in the brush. After a moment, her head sticks back out again. "Well?" she says. "Come on."

I try to follow, but my foot keeps slipping on the branches below the water. Gabriel's hands land square on my ass and he shoves, and I whip around fast with shock. He raises his brows, all innocence. "What?" he says. "It worked, yes?"

He's right; I have cleared the surface. I bang my knee and feel a scrape on the bare skin of my thigh but after a moment, I find myself on the other side of the mangrove thicket, staring at a twin lagoon. In this one, the water is almost magenta, and in the center a sandbar rises like an oasis. On it, a dozen flamingos stand folded like origami as they dip their heads into the pool to feed.

"*This,*" Gabriel says from behind me, "is what I wanted you to see."

"It's amazing," I say. "I've never seen water this color."

"*Artemia salina,*" Beatriz says. "It's a crustacean, a little shrimp, and it's what the flamingos eat that makes them pink. The concentration in the water makes it look so rosy. I learned that in class." At the mention of her studies, her face changes. The buoyancy of her shoulders seems to evaporate.

If I can't get off this island to go home, she also can't get off it to return to school.

She curls her fingers around the edges of her rash guard sleeves, pulling them more firmly down over her arms.

As if the mood is contagious, Gabriel's face shutters, too. "*Mijita,*" he says quietly.

Beatriz ignores him. She snaps on her snorkel, dives into the pink pool, and kicks as far away from us as she can, surfacing on the other side of the oasis.

"Don't take it personally," I say.

Gabriel sighs and rubs a hand through his wet hair. "I never know the right thing to say."

"I don't know if there's a *right thing*," I admit.

"Well, there's definitely a *wrong* thing," Gabriel replies, "and it's usually what comes out of my mouth."

"I haven't seen any new cuts," I tell him.

"I know she talks to you," he says, "and those conversations are for you to keep."

I nod, thinking of what Beatriz told me about her mother, and how that doesn't feel like a confidence I should break.

Gabriel takes a deep breath, as if he is gathering courage. "But will you tell me if she brings up suicide?"

"Oh my God, of course," I say in a rush. "But . . . I don't think that's why she cuts. I think for her . . . it's the exact opposite of being suicidal. It's to remind her that she's here."

He looks at me as if he is puzzling through my English. Then he tilts his head. "I'm glad you're staying," Gabriel says softly, "even if it is selfish of me."

I know he is speaking of whatever fragile thread I've spun between me and Beatriz, who clearly needs a confidante. But there is more to those words, a shadow crossing my senses. I feel my cheeks heating, and I quickly avert my face toward the flamingos. "What are those?" I ask, pointing to the small gray-and-white mottled birds that hop on the sand between the legs of the flamingos. "Finches?"

If Gabriel notices me trying to change the conversation with the finesse of a wrecking ball, he doesn't comment. "That's a mockingbird."

"Oh. And here I was, feeling Darwinian." I smile, trying for a joke.

Galápagos is, of course, famous for its finches—and for Charles Darwin. I'd read about him in every tour guide that was packed in my lost suitcase. In 1835, he came to the islands on the HMS *Beagle,* while just twenty-six and—surprisingly—a creationist who believed that all species were designed by God. Yet in the Galápagos, Darwin began to rethink how life had appeared here, on a spit of volcanic rocks. He'd assumed that the creatures had swum from South America. But then he began to realize that each island was vastly different geographically from the next, that conditions were largely inhospitable, and that new species popped up on different islands. By studying the variations in finches he developed his theory of natural selection: that species change to adapt to their circumstances—and that the adaptations which make life easier are the ones that stick.

"Everyone thinks Darwin based his work on the finches," Gabriel says, "but everyone's wrong."

I turn. "Don't tell my AP Bio teacher that."

"Your what?"

I wave my hand. "It's an American thing. Anyway, I was taught that finches look different on different islands. You know, like one has a long beak because on one island the grubs are deep inside a tree; and on another island, their wings are stronger because they have to fly to find food . . ."

"You're right about all that," he says. "But Darwin was a pretty shitty naturalist. He collected finches, but he didn't tag them all properly. However—likely by accident—he *did* tag all the mockingbirds correctly." He tosses a pebble, and a mockingbird takes to the air. "There are four different types of *los sinsontes* on Galápagos. Darwin collected them and measured their beaks and their sizes. When he got back to England, an ornithologist noticed that the mockingbirds were significantly diverse from island to island. The modifications that helped them adjust to the climate or terrain on a given island had been replicated, because the mockingbirds that had them were the ones who lived long enough to reproduce."

"Survival of the fittest," I confirm. We are sitting now on the edge of the sand oasis, watching flamingos tightrope-walk along the water. Beatriz is at the far end of the lagoon, diving and surfacing, over and over. Gabriel's lips move in silence, and I realize that he is counting the seconds she stays beneath the water.

"Do you ever wonder what animals we'll never know about?" I ask. "The ones that *didn't* make it?"

Gabriel's eyes stay on the surface of the water, until Beatriz appears again. "History is written by the winners," he says.

FIVE

The day after I learn that the island is not reopening, I walk into town to the bank, hoping to figure out a way to transfer money from my account in New York here. The bank is closed, but near the docks a bright collection of tables have been set up underneath a tent. Masked for safety, locals move up and down the aisles, picking up wares and chatting with each other. It looks like a flea market.

I hear my name, and I turn to see Abuela waving at me.

Although Abuela and I do not speak a common language, I've learned a few Spanish phrases, and the rest of our communication is still gestures and nods and smiles. She worked, I now know, at the hotel where I was going to stay, cleaning the rooms of guests. With the business closed, she is happy to cook and watch her telenovelas and take an unscheduled vacation.

She is standing behind a card table that has been draped with an embroidered cloth. On it are a few folded aprons, a box of some men's clothing, two pairs of shoes. There is also a cake pan and a small crate of vegetables and fruits like the ones Gabriel brought me. A word-search magazine is open in front of her, with a little sheaf of G2 post-cards (does everyone have these?) stuck inside as a placeholder.

Abuela smiles widely and points to the folding lawn chair she has set up behind the table. "Oh, no," I say. "You sit!" But before she can respond, another woman approaches us. She picks up a pair of the shoes, looking at the tongue for the size, and through her mask asks Abuela a question.

They exchange a few more sentences, and then the woman sets on the table a large tote. Inside are jars of preserves, pickled garlic, red peppers. Abuela takes out one jar of jam and another of peppers. The woman slips the shoes into her tote and moves off to the next table.

I glance around and realize that although transactions are going on all around me under this tent, no one is exchanging money. The locals have figured out a barter system to combat their limited supply chain from the mainland. Abuela pats my arm, points to the chair, and then wanders down the aisle to survey the wares other locals have carted from home.

I can see double-jointed racks of used clothing, mud boots lined up in size order, kitchen utensils, paper goods. Some tables groan heavy with homemade bread or sweets, jars of beets and banana peppers. There are fresh cuts of lamb and plucked chickens. Sonny, from Sonny's Sunnies, has brought a full array of bathing suits and batteries and magazines and books. A fisherman with a cooler full of the catch of the day wraps up a fish in newspaper for a woman who hands him, in return, a bouquet of fresh herbs.

I could trade, too. But I don't have a surfeit of clothing or food I've grown or the ability to cook anything worth bartering for.

I run my hand back over my hair, smoothing my ponytail. I wonder what I could get for a scrunchie.

Just then, a zephyr of boys blows between the rows of tables. One small one straggles at the back, like the tail of a kite. He's red-faced and clearly trying to catch up to the bigger boys, the leader of whom is waving a battered comic book. As I watch, another boy sticks out his foot and trips the little one, who goes flying and lands headfirst under one of the tables. His crash stops the chase. Rolling onto his back, he sits up and shouts at the boy still holding the book. Even in Spanish, it's clear he has a lisp—which the bigger boy mocks. The bully rips the comic book in half and tosses it onto the smaller boy's chest before sauntering away.

The boy on the ground looks around to see who witnessed his humiliation. When his eye catches mine, I wave him closer.

Slowly, he walks toward me. He has dark brown skin and raven-wing hair that catches the sun. The mask he's wearing has the Green Lantern symbol on it. He clutches his torn comic book.

Impulsively I pull one of the G2 postcards from Abuela's maga-zine and root around for the pencil she was using to do the word searches. I flip the postcard to its empty side, and with quick, eco-nomical strokes, I begin to sketch the boy.

The summer between high school and college, I spent a month in Halifax, doing portraits of tourists in the Old City. I made enough money to stay at a hostel with my friends, and to spend the nights in bars. It was, I realize, the last time I traded in art of my own creation. After that, I spent every holiday building up my résumé for the in-ternship slot at Sotheby's.

Every artist has a starting point, and mine was always the eyes. If I could capture those, the rest would fall into place. So I look for the dots of light on his pupils; I draw in the flutter of lashes and straight slants of brow. After a moment, I pull at the strap of my mask, so that it swings free of my face, and then motion to him to do the same.

He's missing his front four teeth, so of course I draw that smile. And because confidence is a superpower, I give him a cape, like the hero in his torn comic book.

What feels rusty at first begins to flow. When I'm done, I pass the postcard to him, a mirror made of art.

Delighted, he runs the length of the tent, thrusting it toward a woman who must be his mother. I see some of the boys who'd been bullying him drift over, looking at what's in his hands.

I sit down, satisfied, and lean back in the lawn chair.

A moment later the boy returns. He is holding a fruit I've never seen before, the size of my fist, and armored with tiny spikes. Shyly, he sets it on the table in front of me and nods a thank-you, before darting back to his mother's table.

I scan the tent, searching for Abuela, and suddenly hear a small voice. *"Hola."*

The girl in front of me is thin as a bean, with dusty bare feet and braids in her hair. She holds out a dimpled green Galápagos orange.

"Oh," I say. "I don't have anything to trade."

She frowns, then pulls another postcard from Abuela's magazine. She holds it out to me, and tosses her braids over her shoulders, striking a pose.

Maybe I *do*.

When Abuela and I leave the *feria* two hours later, I am no richer in cash, but I have a straw sunhat, a pair of athletic shorts, and flip-flops. Abuela cooks me lunch: lamb chops, blue potatoes, and mint jelly that I received in return for my portraits. Dessert is the spiny fruit the boy gave me: guanabana.

Afterward, belly full, I leave Abuela's so I can take a nap at home. It is the first time, in my own mind, I've called it that.

To: DOToole@gmail.com
From: FColson@nyp.org

It's crazy—*everything's* been shut down. There are no flights out, and none in, and no one knows when that's gonna change. It's probably safer that way. Even if you could fly into the U.S., it's a shit-show. You'd probably have to quarantine somewhere for a couple of weeks, because we don't even have enough Covid tests right now for the people who are coming into the hospital with symptoms.

The truth is that even if you were home, I wouldn't be. Most of the residents who have families are staying at hotels, so they don't infect anyone accidentally. Even though I'm alone in the apartment, after I peel off my scrubs in the entry and stuff them in a laundry bag, the first thing I do is shower until my skin hurts.

You know Mrs. Riccio, in 3C? When I came home last night, I saw people I didn't recognize going in and out of her apartment. She died of Covid. The last interaction I had with her was five days ago, in the mailroom. She was a home health aide and she was terrified of catching it. The last thing I said to her was, Be careful out there.

One of my patients—she was extubated successfully but was in multiorgan failure and I knew she wasn't going to last the day—had a brief moment of consciousness when I went in to see her. I was in full PPE and she couldn't see my face well so she thought I was her son. She grabbed my hand and told me how proud she was of me. She asked if I'd hug her goodbye. And I did.

She was alone in her room and she was going to die that way. I was crying under my face shield and I thought: Well, if I catch it I catch it.

I know I took an oath. Do no harm and all that. But I don't remember saying I'd kill myself to do it.

Once we saw a movie, I don't remember the name, where there was a WWI soldier who was all of twenty, in a trench with a new recruit who was eighteen. The bullets were all around and the twenty-year-old was calmly smoking while the younger kid shook like a leaf. He asked, *How can you not be scared?* The older soldier said: *You don't have to be afraid of dying, when you're already dead.*

Whatever is going to happen is going to happen, I figure.

I read that the Empire State Building will be lit up red and white this week for healthcare workers. We don't give a fuck about the Empire State Building, or about people banging pots and pans at 7 P.M. Most of us won't ever see or hear it, because we're in the hospital trying to save people who can't be saved. What we want is for everyone to just wear a mask. But then there are people who say that requiring a mask is a gross infringement of their bodily rights. I don't know how to make it any more clear: you don't have any bodily rights when you're dead.

I'm sorry. You don't need to listen to me vent. But then again, this probably isn't even getting through to you.

Just in case it is: your mom's place keeps calling.

A few days later, while Beatriz is occupied making tortillas with her grandmother, I ask to borrow Abuela's phone to leave another mes-

sage for Finn. Gabriel has taught me how to dial direct internationally, but calls are expensive, and I don't want Abuela to incur the
costs, so I keep the conversation brief—just letting Finn know I'm all
right, and I'm thinking of him. I save everything else for the postcards Beatriz mails.

Then I call my mother's memory care facility. Although I haven't
received any emails or voicemail from them, that may be a function
of the internet here, since Finn said they've left messages on our
landline at the apartment. The last time The Greens reached out so
doggedly, there was a glitch in the direct deposit that paid my mother's monthly room and board. The administration was all over it like
white on rice, until I smoothed out the mistake and their money
came through the wire. It will not be easy to sort out another bank
error from a quarantined island.

I dial the number and a receptionist answers. "This is Diana
O'Toole," I say. "Hannah O'Toole's daughter. You've been trying to
reach me?"

"Hold please," I hear.

"Ms. O'Toole?" A new voice speaks a moment later. "This is Janice
Fleisch, the director here—I'm glad you finally called back."

It feels pejorative, and I try not to get my hackles raised.

I look over at the counter, where Abuela is showing a recalcitrant
Beatriz how to knead lard into flour to make dough. Curling the phone
line around me, I turn, hunching my shoulders for privacy. "Is there a
problem with my account? Because I'm not in New York at the—"

"No, no. Everything's fine there. It's just that . . . we've had an outbreak of Covid at our facility, and your mother is ill."

Everything inside me stills. My mother has been sick before, but
it's never merited a call.

"Is she . . . does she need to go to the hospital?" Were they calling
to get my permission?

"Your mother has a DNR," she reminds me, a delicate way of saying that no matter how bad it gets, she won't be given CPR or taken
to the hospital for life-sustaining measures. "We have multiple residents who've contracted the virus, but I assure you we're doing every-

thing we can to keep them comfortable. In the spirit of transparency we felt that you—"

"Can I see her?" I don't know what I could possibly do from here; but something tells me that if my mother is really, really sick, I will know by looking at her.

I think of Mrs. Riccio, in apartment 3C.

"We're not allowing visitors right now."

At that, a crazy laugh breaks out of me. As if I could even come. "I'm stuck, outside the country," I explain. "I barely have any phone service. There has to be something you can do. *Please.*"

There's a muffled sound, an exchange of words I can't hear. "If you call back this number, we'll get one of our aides to FaceTime with you," I hear, and I fumble around for a pen. Abuela has a marker attached to a whiteboard on her fridge; I grab it and write the digits down on the back of my hand.

When I hang up, my hand is shaking. I know that people who catch this virus do not always die. I also know that many do.

If my mother sees me on video, she might not even recognize me. She could get agitated, just by being forced to talk to someone she can't place.

But I also know I need to see her with my own eyes.

I am so focused on this, I forget I am in a place that lacks the technology to make this possible.

I hang up Abuela's phone and punch the new number into my cell, but there isn't a signal. "Dammit," I snap, and Abuela and Beatriz both look up. "I'm sorry," I mutter, and I dart out to the porch, holding my phone up in various directions as if I could attract connectivity like a magnet.

Nothing.

I smack my phone down beside me and press the heels of my hands to my eyes.

She has been an absent mother, and now I am an absent daughter. Is that quid pro quo? Do you owe someone only the care they provided for you? Or does believing that make you as culpable as they were?

If she dies, and I'm not there . . .

Well.

Then you won't be responsible for her anymore.

The thought, shameful and insidious, vibrates in my mind.

"Diana."

I look up to find Gabriel standing in front of me, holding a hammer. Has he been here the whole time? "My mother's sick," I blurt out.

"I'm sorry . . ."

"She has Covid."

He takes a step back involuntarily, and rubs his free hand across the nape of his neck.

"She's in an assisted living facility and I'm supposed to video-chat but my stupid phone still won't work here and—" I swipe at my eyes, frustrated and embarrassed. "This *sucks*. This just *sucks*."

"Try mine," he suggests. He pulls out his own phone, but it's not the device that's the problem. It's this whole damn island. While the local cellular network seems to function, anything that requires any real bandwidth is a complete loss.

Gabriel types something into his phone and then says, "Come with me." I fall into place beside him, but he is walking so fast I have to jog to keep up. He stops at the hotel I was supposed to stay at. Although I've tried to steal its Wi-Fi, as Beatriz suggested, the network hasn't shown up—likely because the business is shuttered. This time, however, Elena is standing outside the door, waiting with a ring of keys. "Elena," Gabriel says. *"Gracias por venir aquí."*

She dimples, combing her hands over the long tail of her braid. *"Cualquier cosa por ti, papi,"* she says.

I lean closer and murmur, "Do I want to know—"

"Nope," Gabriel cuts me off just as Elena loops her arm through his and presses herself up against him. She glances over her shoulder at me and whips her head back to Gabriel so fast her braid smacks against my arm.

Is a hotel with no guests even a hotel? The lobby feels small and stale, until Elena turns on the lights and an overhead fan. She boots up a modem behind the front desk, chattering to Gabriel in Spanish as we wait. She seems to be talking about her tan or a bra or something because she pulls aside the fabric and peers down at her bare shoulder, then sends a blistering smile toward him.

"Um," I say. "Is it ready?"

She glances at me like she's forgotten I'm here. When she nods, I find the network on my phone. I dial the memory care facility number I was given and wander off into a small room filled with tables, each wearing a bright cotton tablecloth.

When a face swims into view on my screen, I blink. The person on the other end is nothing more than a set of eyes above a mask, and that's behind a plastic face shield. She has a paper cap covering her hair, too. "It's Verna," the woman says, and she gives a little wave. I recognize her name; she is one of the aides who takes care of the residents there. "We were starting to wonder if you were ever going to call back."

"Technical difficulties," I say.

"Well, your mom's tired and she has a fever, but she's holding her own."

She holds up whatever device she's on and the view changes; from a distance I see my mother sitting on her couch with the television on, just like normal. My heart, which was racing, slows a little.

I let myself wonder, for the first time, what I was so afraid to see. Maybe vulnerability. My mother has been a gale force wind that blows in and out of my life before I can reorient myself. If she were still and silent in a bed, then I would know something is terribly wrong.

"Hi, Hannah," the aide says. "Can you look over here! Can you give me a little wave?"

My mother turns. She doesn't wave. "Did you take my camera?" she accuses.

"We'll find it later," Verna soothes, although I know my mother does not have a camera in her residence. "I have your daughter here. Can you say hello?"

"No time. We need to jump on the press convoy to the Kurdish village," my mother says. "If it leaves without us ..." She coughs. "Without ..." She dissolves into a fit of coughing, and the phone tumbles dizzily before coming to rest on a flat surface. The image goes black; I can still hear my mother hacking away. Then Verna's masked face reappears. "I have to settle her," she says, "but we're taking good care of her. Don't you worry."

The line goes dead.

I stare at the blank screen. There really isn't any way to tell if my mother's delirious, or if it is just her dementia.

Okay. Well. If she gets worse, they will call our apartment again. And if that happens, Finn will—somehow—update me.

Finn.

Immediately I try to video-chat him, too, making the most of the internet service. But it rings and rings and he doesn't pick up. I imagine him bent over a patient, feeling the buzzing in his pocket, unable to answer.

My mother has Covid, I type into a text. *So far she's stable.*

I tried to call you while I still had Wi-Fi but you were probably working.

I wish you were here with me.

I tuck my phone into my pocket and make my way back to the front desk. Everything about Elena's body language suggests she is trying to pin Gabriel against any wall she can. Everything about Gabriel's body language resists it. When he sees me, relief washes over his features. "*Gracias,* Elena," he says. He leans in to give her a quick kiss on the cheek, but she turns at the last minute and presses her mouth against his.

"*Hasta luego,* Gabriel," she says.

As soon as we are out the door, he turns to me. "Your mother?"

"She's sick," I tell him. "She has a cough."

His brows pinch together, then smooth. "So, that's not too bad, right? I bet she was happy to see you."

She had no idea who I was. The words are on the tip of my tongue, but instead I ask, "Is Elena your ex?"

"Elena was one night of extremely poor decision making," Gabriel says. "I don't have very good luck with relationships."

"Well, I'm ninety-nine percent sure my boyfriend was going to propose to me here on our vacation, so there's that."

He winces. "You win."

"More like both of us lose," I correct.

Gabriel misses the turn to Abuela's, heading further into town toward the docks.

I say, "Far be it from me to tell you you're going the wrong way, but . . ."

"I know. I just thought . . . maybe you didn't want to spend today worrying about your mother." We stop on the pier, near a string of small pangas, the little metal boats fishermen use.

"What about Beatriz?"

"I already texted her. My grandmother is watching her." He shields his eyes, looking up at me. "I *did* promise I'd show you my island." He steps into a boat and holds out his hand so I can follow.

"Where are we going?"

"The lava *túneles*," Gabriel says. "They're on the western side of the island, about forty-five minutes out."

"We'll break curfew."

He scrabbles for a key under the plank seat and turns over the engine. Then he glances up, one side of his mouth quirked. "That's not all. Where we're going is closed even to locals," he says. "What is it you *americanos* say? Go big or go home."

I laugh. But I think: *I wish.*

Fishing, Gabriel tells me, is dangerous here.

He expertly moves the panga he has borrowed from a friend beneath delicate lava arches formed by volcanoes. We weave through the formations like thread through needles, the tide edging us precipitously close to the narrow walls of rock. Columns rise from the water, capped by land bridges with cacti and scrub growing over them. For some, the connector has already crumbled into the sea.

"Fishermen can catch bluefin tuna, *blanquillo*, cod, swordfish. But I had friends who headed out, and never came back," he says. "Riptides . . . they're unpredictable. If your engine fails for some reason, you can get caught in one that moves three meters per second."

"So you mean . . . they died?" I ask.

He nods. "Like I told you," he says. "Dangerous." He navigates through the steampunk maze of risen rock. "Look, over there, on the *aa* lava."

"The what?"

He points. "The spiky rock," he explains. "*Pahoehoe* lava is the other kind—the stuff that looks like it's melting." I follow his finger to see two blue-footed boobies. They face each other, bowing formally to the left and then to the right and back again, twin metronomes. Then they attack each other with their beaks in a frenzy of nips and clacks. "They're going to kill each other," I say.

"Actually, they're going to mate," Gabriel says.

"Not if he keeps *that* up," I murmur.

He laughs. "That guy's a pro. The older the bird, the bluer the feet. This isn't his first shoot-out."

It takes me a moment. "Rodeo," I correct, grinning. I watch him hop out of the boat and drag it onto the beach. "I know Beatriz learned in school, but how come you speak English so well?"

"I had to for my job," he says. He reaches under the seat again and tosses me a snorkel and mask. "You know how to use these, yes?"

I nod. "But I'm not wearing a bathing suit."

Gabriel shrugs, kicks off his flip-flops, and wades into the water fully dressed. It laps at his hips, his waist, and then he dives forward, surfacing with a shake of his shaggy hair. He fits his own snorkel and mask to his forehead. "Coward," he says, and he splashes me.

The water is a dizzy mirror of the sky, the sand like sugar under my feet. It feels strange having my shorts float around my legs and my shirt plastered to my body, but I get used to the sensation as I tread water. Gabriel dives a few feet away and a moment later I feel him tug at my ankle. *"Vamos,"* he says, and when he ducks beneath the surface this time, I follow.

The undersea world explodes with color and texture—bright anemone jewels, runnels of coral, wispy fronds of seagrass. For a little while we follow a sea lion that keeps playfully slapping Gabriel with its tail. Gabriel squeezes my hand, pointing out a sea turtle rhythmically sawing through the water. A moment later, in front of my mask floats a bright pink sea horse, a question mark with a trumpet nose and translucent skin.

Gabriel surfaces, pulling me with him. "Hold your breath," he says, and still grasping me, he kicks us powerfully to the seafloor, where a rocky promontory juts, polka-dotted with sea stars and a ripple of octopus. Gabriel twists until we are hovering in front of a small crevice in the boulder. Inside I see two small silver triangles. Eyes? I swim closer for a better look. But when I do, one moves, and I realize I am staring at the white-tipped fins of sleeping reef sharks.

I kick backward so fast that I create a wall of bubbles. Without looking to see if Gabriel is following, I swim as hard and as fast as I can back to shore. When I crawl onto the sand and rip off my snorkel, he's right behind me. "That was," I gasp, "a fucking *shark*."

"Not the kind that would kill you." He laughs. "I mean, maybe just a good bite."

"Jesus Christ," I say, and I flop onto my back on the sand.

A moment later, Gabriel sits down next to me. He is breathing hard, too. He pulls off his soaked shirt and throws it to the side in a soggy ball. When he lies back, the sun glints off the medallion he wears.

"What is that?" I ask. "Your necklace."

"Pirate treasure," he tells me.

When I look at him dubiously, he shrugs. "In the sixteen and seventeen hundreds, pirates used the canal between Isabela and Fernandina Island to hide from the Spaniards after raiding their galleons. Back then, this was a place where you could disappear."

Still, I think.

"The pirates knew the galleons went from Peru to Panama, and after they stole the gold, they hid it on Isabela." He raises a brow. "They also nearly hunted the land tortoise population to extinction, and they left behind donkeys, goats, and rats. But that wasn't nearly as interesting to a seven-year-old boy who was digging for buried treasure."

I come up on an elbow, invested.

"It was back in 1995 on Estero Beach—that's near El Muro de las Lágrimas. Two sailboats showed up, full of Frenchmen who were exploring Isabela, digging for treasure. I helped them for a few days—or at least I thought I did, I was probably more of a nuisance—and they found a chest. I helped them dig it out."

My eyes fall on his medallion. "And that was inside it?"

"I have no idea what was inside it." He laughs. "They took it away, still sealed. But they gave this to me as thanks. For all I know, it came from inside a cereal box."

I smack him on the shoulder. He grabs my hand to stop me from swatting him again, but he doesn't let go. Instead, he squeezes it, and looks me in the eye. "Speaking of thank-yous," Gabriel says, "Beatriz—"

"Is a great kid," I interrupt.

He releases me, and seems to be carefully choosing his words. "When she would come home from school, there was always a wall between us. Every time I thought about knocking it down, every time I got close enough, I could feel so much heat on the other side—like a fire, you know. If you think there's a fire on the other side of a door, you don't rush in, because with even more oxygen, the flames are going to consume everything." He draws a line in the sand between us. "This past week, I don't feel as much heat."

"She's angry," I admit softly. "She was ripped out of her comfort zone. It's not fair, and it's not her fault. When you can't see light at the end of the tunnel, it's hard to remember to keep going."

"I know," Gabriel says. "I've tried to do things like this with her—distract her, you know, by taking her around the island? But she only goes through the motions, like it's a chore." He rubs his forehead. "For years, she lived with her mother, and God knows what Luz said about me. And then she was at school. And then when the virus hit, she called me, begging to come home."

Clearly, I misunderstood. "I thought she *had* to come home," I say.

"She's spent school vacations with her host family before—almost all of them," Gabriel says. "I don't know, maybe she was worried about the virus? Whatever it was, it was a gift. I was just happy she wanted to come back. I thought if we spent time together, she'd figure out that I wasn't actually a monster." He smiles a little. "I wish I could do what you do so easily."

"Talk to her?"

"Make her like me." He pulls a face. "That sounds pathetic."

I shake my head. "When you lose something that matters, you grieve," I say carefully. "Right now, Beatriz thinks she's lost her mom, her friends, her future." I hesitate. "So maybe there's a reason she keeps you at a distance. You can't grieve something if you don't let yourself get close enough to care."

His gaze snaps to mine—this seed of doubt is the absolution I can offer: the chance to think that Beatriz's aloofness might not be because she hates him, but the opposite.

Suddenly a marine iguana runs right between us, making me shriek and scurry backward. Gabriel laughs at me as the big lizard crawls with surprising speed into the water, bobbing a few times before it dives under the surface. "Why aren't those things as afraid of me as I am of them?" I mutter.

"They've had the run of the island longer than humans have," he says.

"Not surprising, since they look like baby dinosaurs."

"You should see the land iguanas in San Cristóbal. They turn turquoise and red during the mating season—we call them Christmas iguanas. That's how they get the ladies." He nods toward the water. "But the marine iguanas are my favorite."

I lie back down on the sand, looking up at the sky. "I can't imagine why."

"Well, they used to all be land iguanas. The ones that arrived came by accident ten million years ago, rafting in from South America on debris. But when they got here, there wasn't any vegetation. The only food was in the ocean. So their bodies changed, slowly, to make diving easier. They got salt glands around their nostrils to expel the salt when they went underwater. Their lungs got bigger so they could take bigger breaths and sink deeper."

Gabriel turns, rising on his elbow. Very slowly, he takes one finger, and traces the slope of my throat. "Evolution is compromise," he says softly. "When humans evolved to speak, our throats got longer to make room for that precise tongue, and with that came risks. Food had to travel further to get to the esophagus . . . but manage to miss the larynx."

His thumb rests in the spot where my pulse flutters at the base of my neck, and I swallow.

"So unlike animals, we can now sing and speak and scream . . . but unlike animals, we also can choke to death if our food goes down the wrong pipe." He looks at me, almost as if he is as dazed to find himself touching me as I am. "You can't move forward without losing something," Gabriel says.

I clear my throat and swiftly sit up.

Immediately, so does he, and the moment breaks like a soap bubble.

Before I can process what just happened, Gabriel scrambles to his feet. A boat putters closer to shore, idling where the waves are breaking. I shade my eyes with my hand and see a man in a khaki uniform and a brimmed hat. As he approaches I squint to read the patch on his shoulder, which looks official.

"Gabriel," the man says. *"Qué estás haciendo aquí?"*

"This is Javier." Gabriel's voice is perfectly even, but I can feel him stiffen. "He's a park ranger."

I remember what Beatriz said at the swimming hole with the mockingbirds—if the park rangers find you trespassing on a site that's closed due to Covid, you can be fined. And if you're a tour guide, you can lose your license.

Gabriel spills forth a river of Spanish. I don't know if he's trying to be placating or act clueless or justify our journey here.

I wing a wide smile at Javier and interrupt. *"Hola,"* I say. "This is all my fault. I'm the one who begged Gabriel to take me here—"

I do not know if the park ranger speaks English, but I hope I am rambling enough to draw attention away from Gabriel. And it seems to work, because Javier's gaze jerks toward me. "You," he says. "You were at the feria."

I feel sweat break out between my shoulder blades. Was it illegal to trade at that market, too? Will park rangers go after the locals, or just the tourist? And if I can't pay a fine, then what happens?

I know there is no hospital on the island, and no ATM. But with my luck, there's a functional jail cell.

"You drew pictures," the ranger continues.

"Um," I say. "Yes."

I can feel Gabriel's eyes on me, like the stroke of a brush.

"My son gave you a guanabana."

The boy, I realize, who was being bullied.

"You are talented," Javier continues, smiling a little. "But more important . . . you are kind."

I feel my cheeks heat with both compliments.

The ranger turns back to Gabriel. "You know, Gabriel, if I saw you here, I'd have to report you. But if I turned away and you were gone, it might just have been a trick of the light, *sí*?"

"Por supuesto," Gabriel murmurs. He reaches down for his shirt, stiff with dried salt, and pulls it on. I pick up the discarded snorkeling equipment and follow him to our panga. The surf whispers around my ankles while he holds the boat steady, letting me climb in before he pushes off from the shore and hops aboard, revving the engine in reverse.

I don't speak until we are out of the cove and through the túneles, bouncing over the chop of the ocean. "That was close," I say.

Gabriel shrugs. "I knew it could happen when I brought you here."

"Then why did you? He could have taken your tour guide license."

"Because this is Isabela," he says. "And you should see it."

On the way back to Puerto Villamil, we do not talk about what happened the moment before Javier interrupted us. Instead, I find myself thinking of the hollow bones of birds, of the long necks of giraffes. The changeable skin of leaf frogs, the insects that disguise themselves as twigs. I think of girls who are dragged from safe havens into the unknown, and men with secrets as deep as the ocean, and grounded planes.

It's not just animals that must adapt in order to survive.

Dear Finn,

Beatriz—the girl I wrote you about—told me that before there was a real mail service in the Galápagos, sailors would put their letters in a barrel in Post Office Bay, on Floreana Island. As other whalers showed up in their ships, they'd sort through the post, find ones addressed to their home port, and then hand-deliver them. Sometimes the mail wasn't delivered for years, but it was the only way the sailors had to communicate with the people they left behind.

Beatriz says now, tour boats go to Floreana. Tourists leave postcards in the barrel, and claim postcards others have left to deliver when they're back home.

The barrel's small; I wouldn't fit in it. Otherwise, I'd probably crawl in and hope someone would carry me back to you.

Love, Diana

The day I met Kitomi Ito, and found myself standing alone with her in front of her painting, I realized exactly what was wrong with the Sotheby's pitch, and why we would likely lose the opportunity to Christie's or Phillips. Everyone seemed to be concentrating on Sam Pride, who'd bought the painting. But no one had stopped long enough to think about who he gave it to, and why.

I began to talk fast. I didn't know if Eva would interrupt us, and if my boss heard me actively subverting her plan for the Toulouse-Lautrec painting, I'd be out of a job before the elevator hit the lobby.

"What if the auction wasn't about fame," I said, "but about privacy? It seems to me that everything was a big show for your husband—even, forgive me, his death. But this painting—it wasn't any part of that circus. It was just for you, and him." When Kitomi didn't respond, I took a deep breath and plunged ahead. "If it were up to me, I wouldn't use this to headline the Imp Mod sale. I wouldn't reunite the Nightjars. I wouldn't make this public at all. I'd build a private sale in a room with simple staging, good lighting, and a single love seat. And then I'd extend a confidential invitation to George and Amal, Beyoncé and Jay-Z, Meghan and Harry, other couples you might think of. It should be a privilege to be offered a showing. A nod to the idea that they have a love affair that's timeless, too." I turn back to the painting, seeing the vulnerability in the eyes of the pair, and the rock-solid belief that they were safe in sharing it with each other. "Instead of the buyer having the upper hand, Ms. Ito, you'd be choosing the couple that gets to continue the love story. You're the one giving it up for adoption; you should be the one to pick the new caretakers—not the auction company."

For a long moment, Kitomi just stared at me. "Well," she said, and a slow smile tugged at the corner of her mouth. "She speaks."

Just then Eva's voice cleaved between us like an ax. "What's going on here?"

"Your colleague was just presenting an alternate approach," Kitomi said.

"My *associate specialist* does not have the authority to present anything," Eva replied. She shot me a look that could cut glass. "I'll meet you at the car," she said.

The driver hadn't even closed the door behind Eva when she started lacing into me. "What part of 'do not speak' did you not understand, Diana? Of all the moronic, irresponsible things you could say, you managed to find something so . . . so . . ." She broke off, her face red, her chest heaving. "You do realize that the reason you have a salary is because the company survives on massive public auctions that attract an obscene amount of money, yes? And that silly little romantic love letter you proposed will make us look like kindergartners, compared to whatever spectacle Christie's is offering—for God's sake, they probably said they'd find a way to throw in a posthumous Kennedy Center Honor for Sam Pride—"

She was interrupted by the ring of her phone. Eva narrowed her eyes, warning me to be quiet under penalty of death, as she answered. "Kitomi," she said warmly. "We were just discussing how much—" Her voice broke off, and her eyebrows shot to her hairline. "Well, yes! Sotheby's is honored to know you trust us to showcase your painting at auction—" Her voice broke off as she listened to Kitomi speak. "Absolutely," she said, after a moment. "Not a problem."

Eva hung up and frowned down at her phone for a moment. "We got the account," she said.

I hesitated. "Isn't that . . . a good thing?"

"Kitomi had two conditions. She wants a private auction for couples only," Eva said. "And she insists that you're the specialist in charge."

I was stunned. This was my break; this was the moment I would talk about years later, when I was interviewed by magazines about how I'd advanced in my career. I had a vision of Beyoncé hugging me after she placed the winning bid. Of a corner office, where Rodney and I would close the door at lunchtime and share bowls from the Halal Guys and gossip.

I felt heat creeping up my collar and turned to find Eva staring, as if she was seeing me for the first time.

To: DOToole@gmail.com
From: FColson@nyp.org

Before I forget: The Greens called again and left a message at home.

It's 72 hours old, though, because that's how long I've been at the hospital.

Of course, a shift that long is technically against the rules, but there aren't rules anymore. It's Groundhog Day, over and over. We have it down to a routine. There's me, a junior resident, and four nurses. My job is to put in central lines and arterial lines, to manage a patient's other comorbidities. I put in chest tubes when they get air around their lungs, caused by the vents. I call the families, who ask for readings they don't understand on oxygenation, blood pressure, ventilation levels. *I hope she's getting better,* they say, but I can't answer because I know she's a mile from better. She's dying. All I hope is that she gets off the vent or ECMO, and that there's not a cytokine storm that sends her back to square one. The families can't visit, so they can't see the patients hooked up to wires and machines. They can't see with their own eyes how sick they are. To them the patient is someone who was perfectly healthy a week ago, with no chronic illness. They keep hearing on the news that there's a 99% survival rate; that it's no worse than the flu.

There's one patient who's been haunting me lately. She and her husband came in together; he died and she didn't. When she was extubated, her adult kids didn't tell her that her husband was dead. They were too afraid she'd panic and cry and her lungs couldn't take it. So she made it all the way to rehab thinking that her husband was still in isolation at the hospital. I think about her all the time. How she thought this was temporary, the separation between them. I wonder if she knows, yet, that it's forever.

Jesus, Diana, come back.

Sometimes I lie in bed at night and think: *What was I trying to prove? Why didn't I turn around and get on that ferry and go back to the airport?*

Sometimes I lie in bed and think: *What kind of partner was I then, if Finn wasn't in the forefront of my mind, when I stood on the brink between staying and leaving?*

For that matter, what kind of partner am I *now*, when there are times he is not in the forefront of my mind? When he's slogging through hell and I'm in a different hemisphere?

My father's father fought in World War II, and when he came back from it, he was never quite right. He drank a lot and wandered the house in the middle of the night, and when the car backfired once, he dropped to the ground and burst into tears. As a little girl, I was often told that the war did this to him, created an invisible scar he'd never lose. Once, I asked my grandmother what she remembered about the war. She thought for a long moment, and then finally said, *It was hard to get nylons.*

There's a part of me that thinks this is exactly what my grandfather would have wanted: to risk death every day so that my grandmother's life could stay mostly unruffled. But there's another part of me that recognizes how shallow, how privileged it is, to be the one who's an ocean away.

These days when I am swimming in pools as clear as gin or hiking green velvet mountains or frying a tortilla on a cast-iron pan in Abuela's kitchen, there are whole swaths of time when I forget the rest of the world is suffering.

I am not sure if that is a blessing, or if I should be cursed.

The *trillizos* are three collapsed lava tunnels in the center of the island. Beatriz and I start our hike there before dawn, which means we get to watch the breathtaking artwork of the sunrise as we climb into the highlands. I've been on island for just over three weeks now, and it keeps surprising me with its beauty. "How old are you?" Beatriz asks me, just as the last streak of pink becomes a bruise of blue sky.

"I'm going to be thirty on April 19," I tell her. "How old are *you*?"

"Fourteen," Beatriz says. "But emotionally, I'm older."

That makes me laugh. "You're a veritable crone."

We walk a little further and then, lightly, I ask if she's heard from her friends at school.

Her shoulders tense up. "Can't check social media when the internet sucks."

"Right," I muse. "It must be hard."

Beatriz doesn't look at me. "The silver lining is that I don't have to see what people are saying about me."

I stop walking. "Is that something you usually have to worry about?"

What if her cutting is tied to bullying somehow? I still don't know much more about Beatriz than I did when I first saw her on the ferry. She guards her secrets like her life depends on them. For a teenager, I suppose it does.

I have been wondering if I should intercede in Beatriz and Ga-briel's relationship. From my vantage point, all I see is misunder-standing. But then I think I have no right to involve myself in someone else's relationships when my own are a mess.

Finn's emails are now shorter and more desperate.

For the past two nights, I've awakened in the middle of the night, convinced I hear my mother's voice.

"When was the last time you talked to your mother?" Beatriz asks, as if she's reached right into my mind.

"Before I came here. I visited her," I say. "Although I can't really say it was a conversation. It's more like she talks *at* me and I try to keep up."

"My mother used to send me cards for my birthday, with money in them. But that stopped last year." Her mouth tightens. "She didn't want to have me."

"But she did."

"When you're pregnant and seventeen and the guy says he'll marry you, I guess you do it," Beatriz muses.

I tuck away this information about Gabriel.

"I think unconditional love is bullshit," Beatriz says. "There's al-ways a condition."

"Not true," I offer. "My father would have loved me no matter what." *But is that true?* I wonder. I adored the same things he did—visual art and painting. If I'd been obsessed with geology or emo rock, would we have clicked the same way? If my mother hadn't been absent, would he have been as attentive?

"And Finn," Beatriz says. "Don't forget about him. How did you know he was *the one*?"

"I don't know that," I bluster. "I'm not married to him."

"But if he proposed here, weren't you going to say yes?"

I nod. "I think that I used to believe that love was supposed to feel like a lightning storm—superdramatic, with crashes and thunder and all the hair standing up on the back of your neck. I had boy-friends like that, in college. But Finn . . . he's the opposite. He's steady. Like . . . white noise."

"He puts you to sleep?"

"No. He makes everything . . . easier." Saying this, I feel a surge of love so fierce for Finn that my knees go weak.

"So he's the first person you felt that way about?" Beatriz asks, probing.

She isn't looking at me, but there's a stripe of heat across her cheekbones, and I realize she isn't really asking about me. If not for this pandemic, Beatriz would be at school and would likely be confiding in a friend her own age about her own crush.

Then I think of what she said about being flamed on social media. I remember that Gabriel told me Beatriz begged to come back to Isabela.

Suddenly she breaks into a jog, and stops at the edge of a yawning hole that seems to reach to the belly of the earth. It's about sixty feet wide, with a ladder mounted at the lip, twined with several thick ropes. Ferns and moss grow on the walls, which narrow and narrow to a black hole further down. I peer into the abyss but it looks only dark and endless.

"People rappel to the bottom," Beatriz says.

I feel the walls of the tunnel pressing on me, and I'm not even inside it. "I am *not* rappelling to the bottom."

"Well, you can climb partway," she says. "Come on."

She scrambles down the slippery wooden rungs, wrapping the ropes around her arm as a safety measure. I follow her more cautiously. The tunnel narrows around us. The vegetation smells ripe and lush as I concentrate on stepping firmly with my foot down, down, down.

When Beatriz descends into the neck of the tunnel, I lose sight of her. "Beatriz!" I call, and her voice floats up to me.

"Come on, Diana, it's magic."

The further down we go, the hotter it gets, as if the tunnel is tapering toward hell itself. There is no more vegetation, just lava rock that is light and porous, and that shimmers in the faint light from above. I keep moving methodically and nearly scream when I feel Beatriz's hand close over my ankle. "Three more rungs," she says, "and then the ladder runs out."

She shifts so that we are clinging to the same bottom rungs, side by side. "Look up," Beatriz says.

I do, and the sky is a tiny pinprick of hope. When I glance back down and breathe in, it feels like the air from someone else's mouth. I can't see at first in the dim muscle of the tunnel, and then all of a sudden I can—just the shine of Beatriz's pupils. It feels like we're sharing a heartbeat.

"Remind me why we're here," I whisper.

"We're in the belly of a volcano," she says. "We could hide here forever."

For a few moments, I listen to the moan of wind from what must be a hundred feet above. Something wet drips onto my forehead. It is terrifying being here, yes, but it is also almost holy. It's like crawling back in time. Like preparing to be reborn.

It feels like the place to confide a secret.

"Truth or dare," I whisper, and I hold my breath, waiting.

"Truth," Beatriz says.

"Your father told me you wanted to come back here, but you don't want to be here."

"What's your question?"

I don't answer.

She sighs. "Neither of those," Beatriz says, "is untrue."

I wait for her to elaborate in this cocoon of darkness, but instead, she turns the game on me. "Truth or dare," she says.

"Truth."

"If you could change your mind three weeks ago and take the ferry home, would you?"

"I don't know," I hear myself answer, and it physically hurts to say it out loud, in the way that truth can sometimes be a knife.

The whole time I've been here, I've told myself that being stuck on Isabela was a mistake. But there is also a small, new part of me that wonders if it was meant to be. If I'm delayed because the universe decided Beatriz needed someone to depend on; if I had to distance myself from Finn to see our relationship more clearly—its strengths, and its flaws.

Unconditional love is bullshit. "Truth or dare. Is there someone at school you wish you could be with?"

I have wondered if, when I eventually leave, Beatriz will go back to Santa Cruz, back to her host family and, maybe, this crush. If that would stop the cutting. Would make her happy.

"Yes." The syllable is no more than a breath. "But she doesn't want to be with me."

She.

I hear the quiet hitch of Beatriz's breath. She's crying, and I'm pretending not to notice, which I suspect is what she wants.

"Tell me about her," I say softly.

"Ana Maria's my host sister," Beatriz whispers. "She's two years older than me. I think I've always known how I feel but I never said anything, not until there were rumors that school might close because of the virus. When I thought about not seeing her, like even just at breakfast, or walking back from classes, I couldn't breathe. So I kissed her." She curls herself closer to the ladder rungs.

"It didn't go well," I state.

"It did at first. She kissed me back. For three days—it was . . . perfect." Beatriz shakes her head. "And then she told me she couldn't. She said her parents would kill her, if they found out. That she loved me, but not like that." She swallows. "She said I was . . . I was a mistake."

"Oh, Beatriz."

"Her parents wanted me to stay during lockdown. I told them my father wouldn't let me. How could I live in the same house as her, and pretend it was all fine?"

"What will you do when school opens?"

"I don't know," Beatriz says. "I ruined it. I can't go back there. And there's nothing for me here."

There's something for you here, I think. *You just can't see it.*

"Will you tell my father?" she whispers into the dark.

"No," I promise. "But I hope you will, one day."

We cling to the ladder in the hot throat of the world. Her breathing evens again, in counterpoint to mine. "Truth or dare," she says, so softly I can barely hear it. "Do you ever wish you could do part of your life over?"

The truth is yes.

But . . . it's not these past three weeks. Instead, it's everything leading up to them. The more time I spend on this island, the more clarity I have about the time leading up to it. In a strange way, being stripped of everything—my job, my significant other, even my clothing and my language—has left only the essential part of me, and it feels more real than everything I have tried to be for years. It's almost as if I had to stop running in order to see myself clearly, and what I see is a person who's been driving toward a goal for so long she can't remember why she set it in the first place.

And that scares the fuck out of me.

"Dare," I reply.

A beat. "Let go of the ladder," Beatriz says.

"Absolutely not," I answer.

"Then I'll do it."

I hear her release her fingers from the rung, feel the shift in the air as she falls backward.

"No," I cry, and I somehow manage to snatch a handful of her shirt. With the ropes wrapped tight around my free arm, I feel her deadweight dangling.

Don't let go don't let go don't let go

"Bea," I say evenly, "you have to grab on to me. Can you do that? Can you do that for me?"

A thousand years later, I feel her fingers clutching my forearm. I grab back, forming a tighter link, until she is close enough to the ladder to grasp it again. A moment later, with a sob, she falls against me and I wrap my free arm around her. "It's okay," I soothe. "It's going to be okay."

"I wanted to know what it would be like," she cries, "to just let go."

I stroke her hair and think: *You cannot trust perception. Falling, at first, feels like flying.*

Six

Four weeks after I arrive on Isabela, I get an early birthday present: a strange and unlikely dump of old emails into my inbox. I have no idea why some were coming through, yet not others—but there are several from Finn, and two from my mother's facility, updating me on her health (no significant change, which I figure is good news). There is also a note from Sotheby's, saying that I have been furloughed, along with two hundred other employees, because of a massive downturn in the art sales industry. I stare at this for a while, wondering if Kitomi wasn't the only one to delay her auction, and trying to rationalize that being furloughed is better than being fired. There's also an email from Rodney, telling me that Sotheby's can suck a dick, and that the only people who weren't furloughed were tech support, because they're pivoting to online sales. He never thought he'd have to return to his sister's house in New Orleans, but who can afford rent in the city on unemployment?

The last line of his email is *Girl, if I were you, I'd stay in paradise as long as I could.*

On my actual birthday a week later, I am invited to Gabriel's farm. It's twenty minutes by car into the highlands, and he comes to pick me and Abuela up in a rusty Jeep with no side doors. "You don't look a day over forty," he deadpans when he sees me, and when I shove at him he starts laughing. "Women are so sensitive about their age," he jokes.

As we drive, we see more galapagueños out and about than I have in weeks. At first, when the island closed down, I could walk the beach or hike into the highlands and not see another soul. But now, by the fifth week of lockdown, with no actual cases of Covid on Isabela and no one new arriving to spread it, people have begun to sneak out of their houses and break curfew.

As we wind into the center of the island, the scrub and desert landscape at the shoreline gives way to lush, thick vegetation. The shipments of food and supplies to the island have been extremely limited, and I know that Gabriel isn't the only person here to rely on family farmland to supplement them during the pandemic. We pass dirty sheep in pens, goats, a lowing cow with an udder as full as the moon. There are banana trees, with green fruit defying gravity to grow upward, and girls squatting in fields pulling weeds. Finally Gabriel turns onto a dusty path that winds toward a small house. Beatriz had led me to believe that it was nothing more than a glorified tent, but only half of it is under construction. Gabriel isn't building a house as much as he is expanding it.

For Beatriz, I bet.

I've been thinking nonstop about her confession to me in the trillizos. I'd said that if Beatriz talked to me about suicide, I'd tell Gabriel—and her recklessness in the tunnel truly worried me. But I couldn't confess to Gabriel what had happened unless I explained why, and that would mean talking about Ana Maria not returning Beatriz's affections. That, I know, is not my secret to share. Gabriel doesn't strike me as the kind of parent who'd be upset if his daughter came out, but then, I do not truly know him. Whatever strides the LGBTQ+ community has made in the United States, they are not universal; moreover, this is a predominantly Catholic country and gay rights aren't exactly the mainstay of that dogma. I think about Abuela's house, where painted crosses decorate every bit of wall space. In the absence of church services, suspended because of Covid, she has created a small altar where she prays and lights candles.

Instead, I've found ways to see Beatriz every day, to take her emotional temperature, and hope I don't have to betray her in order to protect her.

Beatriz comes bounding out of the front of the house as Gabriel pulls the emergency brake on the Jeep. *"Felicidades!"* she says, smiling at me.

"Thanks."

I realize something is tugging at me and I turn to find a little white goat with brown ears chewing on the hem of my T-shirt. "Ooh," I say, kneeling down to rub its knobby horns. "Who's this?"

"I don't name my food," Gabriel says, and I gasp.

"You are not eating this sweetheart," I tell him, "and he has to have a name."

"Fine." He grins. "Stew."

"No." I fold my arms. "Promise me. Consider it my birthday gift."

Gabriel laughs. "Only because Stew's a terrible name for a lady goat. As long as we can milk her, she's safe. We trade her milk to the neighbor for eggs."

He helps Abuela up the steps into his house. The livable area is two rooms: one with a small kitchen, a tiny table, two mismatched wooden chairs, and a beanbag chair; the other a bedroom. I don't see a bathroom, just a little outhouse in the distance. While Gabriel and Abuela stand at the table, unpacking the food she's brought to cook and talking in Spanish, Beatriz pulls me into the bedroom.

There is a mattress on the floor and a scarred chest of drawers, but there is also a mirror with mosaic glass around it, and a quilt with flowers embroidered on it, and fairy lights strung on a series of nails that have been tacked to the wall. This must have been Gabriel's room, I realize. I wonder if he transformed it into this little oasis for her, hoping for the best before she came here from school. I wonder where he sleeps now.

"Oh," I say, pulling several postcards from my tote. "I brought some more."

"Cool." Beatriz takes them, setting them in front of the mirror.

Since our day at the trillizos, we haven't talked about the girl she left behind on Santa Cruz, or if she still feels like cutting. Only once in the past two weeks has she even alluded to what transpired. We were sitting in Puerto Villamil, watching boobies torpedo into the water to catch fish, our legs dangling off the pier, just letting the afternoon settle around us like cotton batting. "Diana?" Beatriz had said, apropos of nothing. "Thanks. For catching me."

What I wanted to do was wrap my arms around her tight. What I did instead was bump her shoulder with mine. *"De nada,"* I said, when I meant the very opposite. It wasn't nothing. It was *everything*.

I figure Beatriz will tell me what she wants to tell me and needs to tell me when she's ready. And God knows, right now, I have nothing but time.

There's a knock on the door and Gabriel pokes his head inside. "You ready to earn your supper? I need help picking fruit."

"It's my birthday," I protest.

"No problema." He shrugs. "We'll have the goat for dinner instead."

"Funny," I tell him, and turn to Beatriz. "Come help. I'm way too old for physical labor."

She shakes her head. "I've got other things to do. *Secret* things."

Gabriel leans toward her and in an exaggerated whisper asks, "Was that good?"

"Perfect," Beatriz says, and she skirts us on her way to the small table, where Abuela is already measuring out flour. "Go on," she shoos. "Leave."

I follow Gabriel outside. "She's making a cake for me, isn't she?"

"You didn't hear it from me," he says.

"That's sweet." I sit down on a stump near the front door as Gabriel untangles something from a pile of tools. He hands it to me—a wire basket on a stick—and then picks up a five-gallon plastic bucket.

"Vamos," he says.

"You mean we're really picking fruit? I thought that was just a ruse to get me out of the house."

"It was. But also, this is a farm." I follow him into the fields that stretch behind the house, where he points to yams and corn, lettuce and carrots. There is a patch of pineapple not ripe enough to harvest, and then we come to a small group of trees. "Papaya," Gabriel says. He takes the pole and squints up at the leaves, jostling the tool for a minute before he lowers it again and with a little flip of the wrist, drops the heavy fruit into my hand.

"I didn't know papaya grew on trees," I marvel.

We work in companionable quiet while he strips the tree of its ripe fruit, and then I kneel beside him to dig up a few yams. By the time we get back to the house, I'm filthy. Gabriel leads me to a water pump, jacking its handle so that I have a stream to wash my hands and my face. When I return the favor, he strips off his shirt and ducks his head and torso under the water, shaking off like a hound and making me shriek.

The noise draws Beatriz, who stands in the doorway. "Perfect timing," she says. Then she claps, and Abuela appears behind her holding a small one-tier chocolate cake on a plate. "*Cumpleaños feliz,*" they sing, "*te deseamos a ti . . .*" Beatriz runs ahead and whispers something to Gabriel, who takes out a lighter and flicks the flame to life with his thumb.

"No candle," he explains.

Abuela sets the cake down on a picnic table outside the house, which has been decorated with strewn flowers. "Make a wish," Beatriz orders.

Dutifully, I close my eyes.

I wish . . .

That I was back in New York with Finn.

That my mother will get better.

That this will be over soon.

These things are what I should be wishing for. But instead, all that runs through my mind is that it is hard to make wishes, when in the moment, it feels like you have everything you need.

I open my eyes again and lean toward the lighter in Gabriel's hand. Gently, I blow.

He winks at me, and snaps the lid so the flame disappears. "That means it will come true," he says.

After we finish the cake, Gabriel builds a fire in a ring of lava stones in the yard. He turns on a small transistor radio and we all sit on folding lawn chairs. To my shock, there are presents for me: Beatriz gives me a small box she has decorated with shells; Abuela gives me a necklace with a medal of the Virgin Mary on it and insists on securing it around my neck. Even Gabriel tells me he has a gift—but it's an experience, not a thing, and he'll take me in a few days. Afterward, Beatriz brings me a blank journal and demands I do a portrait of her, like the ones I did at the feria. When the last of the light leaves the sky it's decided that Beatriz will share her bed with Abuela, and that Gabriel and I will camp out under the stars.

When we are alone, I look at the medal nestled between my breasts. "Did I just get baptized or something?" I ask.

Gabriel grins. "It's called a miraculous medal. It's supposed to bring blessings to people who wear it with faith."

I glance at him. "So basically if I'm not Catholic, lightning could strike at any moment?"

"If it does, it will likely hit me first, so you're safe," he says. He pokes at the embers with a stick, stirring them, and then picks up the journal with the sketch I made of Beatriz. "You're very talented," he tells me, carefully closing the book and setting it on the picnic table.

I shrug. "Party trick," I say.

He disappears into the house for a moment. When he reappears with two rolled sleeping bags, the radio is playing a Nightjars song. "The first vinyl album I ever bought was Sam Pride's."

I look up at him. "Was it the one with Kitomi Ito naked on the cover?"

Gabriel blinks. "Well," he says, "actually, yeah."

"I know her," I tell him.

"*Everyone* knows her." He lays one of the sleeping bags at my feet, and shakes out the other on the opposite side of the fire.

"But I *know* know her," I tell him. "I was in the process of selling her painting. The one from that album cover, actually."

Gabriel pulls his own sleeping bag closer to the fire pit. The reflections of the flames dance over his forearms as he pours what looks like water from a bottle into two shot glasses. "That sounds like a story," he says, and he passes me a glass. "*Salud,*" he says, and clinks his own against mine.

Following his lead, I drain it in one swallow, and nearly choke, because it is most definitely not water. "Holy *fuck*," I gasp. "What is this?"

"Caña." He laughs. "Cane sugar alcohol. One hundred proof." Then he leans back on his elbows. "Now tell me why you know Sam Pride's wife."

I do, skirting over the fact that my last conversation with her may have cost me a promotion, if not my job. When I finish talking I look up to find Gabriel staring at me, puzzled. "So your job is to sell other people's art?" he asks, and I nod. "But what about your own?"

Surprised, I shake my head. "Oh, I'm not an artist. I just have an art history degree."

"What's that?"

"Useless arcane knowledge," I reply.

"I doubt that . . ."

"Well, at Williams I wrote a thesis on the paintings of saints and how they died."

He laughs. "Maybe that miraculous medal isn't such a stretch after all . . ."

I hold out my glass for another shot of liquor. "Hey, I'll have you know that Saint Margaret of Antioch was eaten by a dragon, but is usually painted with said dragon hanging out at her side. Saint Peter the Martyr's portraits *include* the cleaver in his skull. Saint Lucy—patron saint of eye problems—was always shown holding a dish with two eyeballs on it. Oh, and Saint Nicholas—"

"Papá Noel?" Gabriel pours me more caña.

"The very same. He's often painted holding three gold balls that look like candy, but they're actually dowries he'd give to poor virgins."

Gabriel's eyebrows rise. He lifts his own glass. "Merry Christmas," he says.

We toast, and I swallow; the second time, I'm expecting the burn. "So as you can see," I tell him, "my esteemed education has made me very good for trivia at cocktail parties." I shrug. "And it helped land me my dream job."

He leans back on the mattress he's made of his sleeping bag, his feet crossed. "People dream of making art," he says. "Nobody dreams of selling it."

This makes me think of my mother, gallivanting all over the world to take pictures that won awards, that graced magazine covers, that chronicled struggle and war and famine. How her images were in museums and even gifted to the White House but had never been sold in a public forum until I auctioned some off to pay for her assisted living facility.

I shake my head. "You don't understand. These pieces of art . . . they're worth millions. Sotheby's is synonymous with prestige."

"And that," Gabriel says, "is important to you?"

I stare into the fire. Flames are the one thing you can't ever really replicate in art. The moment you make them static in paint, you take away their magic. "Yes," I reply. "My best friend, Rodney, and I have been plotting our meteoric rise through the company since we met there nine years ago."

"Rodney," Gabriel repeats. "Your boyfriend doesn't mind that your best friend is a man?"

"No, Gabriel," I say sharply, "because my boyfriend and I do not live in the Dark Ages. Plus, Rodney is . . . well, Rodney. He's Black, Southern, and gay, or as he puts it, a golden trifecta." I look carefully at Gabriel as I say the word *gay*, gauging his reaction. Beatriz's confidences are still not mine to tell, but I can't help wondering what his reaction would be if she were brave enough to confide in him. Gabriel, however, doesn't bat an eye. "Are there a lot of LGBTQ people here?" I ask breezily.

"I don't know. What people do in private is what they do in private." He shrugs, a smile tugging at his mouth. "But when I was a tour guide, the gay couples always tipped best."

I hug my knees to my chest. "How did you become a tour guide?"

I don't expect him to answer, since he keeps that part of his life—and his subsequent departure from it—close to his chest, but Gabriel shrugs. "When my parents honeymooned on Isabela in the eighties, there were maybe like two hundred residents on island, and they wanted to stay. So they brought Abuela in from the mainland. My father loved it here. People used to call him *El Alcalde*—the mayor—because he would go on and on about how amazing Isabela is to anyone and everyone who landed in Puerto Villamil. He didn't have the scientific background to be a park ranger, so he became a tour guide."

Gabriel looks at me across the fire. "When I was growing up, it was expected that I'd join the family business. I'd been doing it unofficially with him for years. You have to train for seven months to be certified as a guide by the government of Ecuador—studying biology, history, natural history, genetics, languages. Professors come here from all over the world—the University of Vienna, and the University of North Carolina, and the University of Miami—they ask for the help of the guides to continue research for them when they're off-island. So you know, we might wind up taking pictures of green sea turtles, and sending them back to a scientist so he can track them around the island for his research. We might be asked to document penguin behaviors that seem unique."

"I was bit by one," I say, rubbing my arm. "When I first got here."

"Well, that's unique." Gabriel laughs. "They usually are pretty shy around people, but with the quarantine, they seem to crave human interaction a little more. Even if it hurts the humans." He pokes at the fire with a stick. "There was a time, believe it or not, that I thought I'd be the scientist doing marine biology. Not the tour guide doing the grunt work."

"What happened?"

"Beatriz," he says, smiling faintly. "My ex, Luz, got pregnant, when we were seventeen. We got married."

"So you didn't become a marine biologist."

He shakes his head. "Plans change. Shit happens."

"Beatriz told me her mother . . . left."

"That's a polite way of putting it," Gabriel says. "The truth is, we didn't stay together because we didn't belong together. Not even for a baby. I learned the hard way that you shouldn't stay with someone because of your past together—what matters more is if you want the same things in the future. Luz felt like she was too young to be trapped as a mother, and she was always looking for the escape hatch. I just didn't think it was going to take the shape of a *National Geographic* photographer." He glances at me. "Very different from you and your boyfriend, I'm sure."

I am glad for the darkness, because he cannot see the flush on my cheeks. Finn and I are the couple that our friends tag *#relationshipgoals*. Every time Rodney has cried over another breakup, I've curled up in Finn's arms in bed and silently given thanks that of all the people in the world, we found each other. I trust him and he trusts me. It's steady and stable and I know exactly what to expect: I'll get my promotion; he'll get a fellowship. We'll get married in a vineyard upstate (tasteful, no more than a hundred guests, band not DJ, justice of the peace officiating); honeymoon on the Amalfi coast; buy a house outside the city during the first year of his fellowship; have our first child during the second year and a sibling two years after that. Honestly, the only point of contention was whether we'd get a Bernese or an English springer spaniel. I had believed that Finn and I were so attuned that even a forced separation like this one wouldn't shake our rock-solidness. But it's taken only three weeks for me to feel disconnected; for doubt to grow like weeds, so insidious that it's hard to see what used to blossom in that bed instead.

There is still the niggling thought that Finn suggested I leave New York without expecting me to actually *do* it—as if this were some sort of relationship test I was supposed to pass, but failed. And maybe I am equally to blame for not insisting that I stay. But I also know that focusing on that one moment of miscommunication keeps me from examining a more painful, scarier truth: here on Isabela, there are times I forget to miss him.

I can explain it away: At first, I was distracted trying to figure out how to stay fed and housed. I've been thinking of Beatriz, and trying to keep her from cutting. I've been literally disconnected because of a lack of technology.

But if you have to *remember* to miss the love of your life . . . does that mean he's not the love of your life?

I pin a smile on my face and nod. "I'm lucky," I tell Gabriel. "When Finn and I are together, it's perfect."

And when we're not?

"Finn," he repeats slowly. "You know what finning is?"

"Is this a sex thing?"

His teeth flash white. "It's when massive Chinese fleets fish for tons of sharks. They cut off their fins for soup and traditional medicines—and then leave the sharks to die in the ocean."

"That is *awful*," I say, thinking that now I'll always associate this with Finn's name.

Maybe that's what Gabriel intended.

"That's the part of paradise you don't get to see," he says.

"Am I a terrible person?" I ask quietly. "For being here?"

"What do you mean?"

"It's been weeks. Maybe I should have been trying harder to get back to New York."

He glances at me. "Short of growing a pair of wings, I'm not sure how that would happen."

I lift my gaze. "Natural selection favors wings . . ."

His mouth curves. "I guess anything is possible. It just may take a few thousand years for you to evolve."

I scrub my hands over my face. "If you read his emails, Gabriel . . . it's so bad. It's killing him slowly to watch all those patients die, and I can't do anything to help him."

"Even if you were there," he says, "you might not be able to do anything. There's some shit that people have to work through on their own."

"I know. I just feel so . . . powerless."

He nods. "I imagine it feels like you're caged in and can't get to him," Gabriel says, "but maybe you're the only one who sees it as a cage."

"What do you mean?"

"If it were me," he says, looking down at the fire, "and if you were the person I love . . . I'd want you as far away as possible so that I could battle the monsters and not have to worry about you getting hurt."

"That's not a relationship," I argue. "That's . . . that's like a beautiful piece of artwork you don't display because you're afraid it will get damaged. So, instead, you crate it up and stick it in storage and it doesn't bring you any joy or any beauty."

"I don't know about that," Gabriel says softly. "What if it's something you'd fight like hell to protect so you can someday see it one more time?"

His words make a shiver run down my spine, so I unzip my sleeping bag and slide into it. It smells like soap and salt, like Gabriel. I lie down, my head still spinning a little from the caña, and blink at the night sky. Gabriel does the same, lying on top of his own sleeping bag, his arms folded over his stomach. The crowns of our heads are nearly touching.

"When I was a boy, my father taught me to navigate by stars, just in case," he murmurs. I hear a catch in his voice, and I think that of all he has told me tonight, the one thing he hasn't revealed is why he is a farmer, not a tour guide. *Plans change,* he'd said. *Shit happens.*

"How bad was your sense of direction?" I say, trying—and failing—for lightness.

The fire hisses in the quiet between us. "Everything you're seeing up in the night sky happened thousands of years ago, because the light takes so long to reach us," Gabriel says. "I always thought it was so strange . . . that sailors chart where they're going in the future by looking at a map of the past."

"That's why I love art," I say. "When you study the provenance of a piece, you're seeing history. You learn what people wanted future generations to remember."

The sky looks like an overturned bowl of glitter; I cannot remember ever seeing so many stars. I think of the ceiling at Grand Central Terminal, and how I restored it with my father. It is hard to piece out the constellations here, and I realize that's because on the equator, you can see clusters from both the Northern and Southern Hemispheres. There—I find the Big Dipper. But also the Southern Cross, which is normally hidden beneath the horizon for me.

It feels like a peek at a secret.

"I can't usually see the Southern Cross," I say softly. It makes me a little disoriented, like the whole planet has shimmied off course.

I wonder if I had to come to this half of the world just to see it a whole different way.

After a moment, Gabriel asks, "Did you have a good birthday?"

I glance at him. He has rolled to his side. While I've been looking at the sky, he's been looking at me.

"The best," I say.

To: DOToole@gmail.com
From: FColson@nyp.org

Sometimes I wonder if I'm ever going to do an appendectomy again. I'm a surgeon. I fix things. Your gallbladder's infected? I got it. Hernia repair? I'm your guy. If I have any ICU patients, it's temporary, a complication from surgery that I know how to fix. But with Covid, I can't fix anything. I'm just maintaining the status quo, if I'm lucky.

Also, I'm a resident, which means I'm supposed to be learning—but I'm learning nothing.

I'm good at my job. I just don't know if my job is still good for me.

Three days ago, when I left the hospital, 98% of the beds in the ICU were occupied, and all my patients were on oxygen and dying. On the way home, I called my dad to check in. You know he voted for Trump—so maybe I shouldn't have been surprised when he told me that the Covid numbers are inflated, and that the shutdown is a cure that's worse than the disease.

I get that not everyone is seeing this virus firsthand. It's another thing entirely to disavow it.

I hung up on him.

Fuck. I just remembered your birthday.

My mother was often asked how she "did it all"—juggled the roles of wife, mother, and one of the most renowned crisis photographers of the century. In real life, the answer was simple—she *didn't* do it all. My father did most of it, and if there was a balance between mother-hood and her career, it canted hard to the latter. In interviews, she would always tell the same story about the first time she took me to the pediatrician. She bundled me into my snowsuit, loaded her pock-etbook and the collapsible stroller and the diaper bag into the car, and drove off—leaving me buckled in my infant carrier on the floor of the kitchen. She was in the doctor's parking lot before she realized that she'd left her baby behind.

My mother never told me that story directly, but I had seen so many interview clips on the internet that I knew where she paused for dramatic effect, the part where she smiled wryly, the bit where she rolled her eyes in self-deprecation. It was an act, and my mother never broke character. She and the interviewer would both laugh, in a charming, what-can-you-do way.

What about the baby, I used to think, as if it were not me, as if I were a mere observer. *What about this is remotely funny?*

Finn—

Last night I had a supervivid dream of you. Someone had kid-napped me and drugged me and I was in a basement and there weren't any doors or windows where I could escape. I was tied to something—a pole, a chair? Then all of a sudden, you were there, wearing a costume. I couldn't see the bottom half of your face, but I knew it was you because of your eyes and because I could smell your shampoo. You kept telling me to stay awake so you could get me out of there, but I couldn't keep my eyes open. Then I realized we weren't alone. There was another woman with you, and she was in costume, too.

I was the only one who hadn't been invited to the party.

It's somewhere around the fourth hour of a seven-hour hike to the Sierra Negra volcano that I wonder why, exactly, Gabriel thought this was a birthday gift anyone would actually enjoy. I am hot and sweaty and sunburned when we reach a small tree with a black rock in a crotch of its limbs. "This is the spot where tourists leave their overnight packs," Gabriel says, and he shrugs off the gear he's been shouldering. "Some of them stay overnight before hiking down into the caldera. No one's allowed up here without a ranger or guide."

We are breaking curfew, Gabriel isn't really a guide anymore, and the volcano happens to be active. What could possibly go wrong?

Till this point, the climb has taken us along dirt paths, through lush, thick greenery. The trail begins 800 meters above sea level, Gabriel tells me, and by the time you reach the volcano, you're 1,000 meters up. From the pack he's carried, he takes out a lunch Abuela has made and spreads it between us. There are plastic bowls of rice and chicken, and a chocolate bar that is already soft with heat, which we share. I stretch my legs out in front of me, looking at the dust on my sneakers. "How much further?" I ask him.

He grins at me, his eyes shaded by a baseball cap. "You sound like Beatriz, when she was little."

I try to imagine Beatriz, smart and demanding, as a little girl. "I bet she was a handful."

Gabriel thinks for a moment. "She was just the right amount."

I open my mouth to explain the idiom to him, but then realize his answer is already perfect. "Don't think I didn't notice that you avoided my question . . ."

"You'll know," he says. "Trust me."

And, I realize, I do.

We gather up our trash and put it into Gabriel's pack, falling into an easy rhythm as we hike to the top of the caldera. "What are the odds," I ask, "that this is going to go all Mount St. Helens on us?"

"Slim to none," Gabriel assures me. "There are twelve geological systems tracking its tremors, and it gives out plenty of hints before it erupts, which happens every fifteen years or so. I was here the last time. My father and I hiked in and we slept on ground that was warm, like it had heated pipes underneath. He taught me how to gauge the wind and the slope, so that we wouldn't wind up in the path of the eruption. We took pictures, when it happened. I remember you could see the orange lava in the cracks of the earth, just a foot or so below. My shoes stuck to the rocks, because the soles had melted."

"When was this?"

"Two thousand five. I was a teenager."

I do the math. "So . . . this volcano is *overdue* to blow?"

"If it makes you feel better, the Galápagos are moving eastward on their tectonic plate, so even though the hot spot is in the same place, the lava flows mostly to the west now . . . which means the eruptions aren't as dangerous to the people living here anymore."

It does not make me feel better, but before I can tell him that, the caldera comes into view.

The crater stands out in stark relief to the lush green that cradles it. It's black, six miles of it, sprawled beneath a cloud of mist. It looks desolate and barren, otherworldly. From where we hike along the precipice, I can see the ocean and the rich emerald of the highlands to the right, but also the ropy, frozen black swirls of the caldera to the left. It feels like standing on the line between life and death.

We have to climb down into the caldera, trek across it, and then hike up to the fumaroles—the active part of the volcano. As we walk across the scorched belly of the crater, with its melted eddies of charred lava, it feels like we are navigating a distant planet. I follow behind Gabriel, stepping where he steps, as if one wrong move might plummet me to the middle of the earth.

"You know," he says over his shoulder. "You're different from when you first came."

I glance down at myself. I know, from looking in the mirror in the apartment bathroom, that my hair is streaked blonder from the sun. My shorts hang on my hips, likely because I'm not eating every day at Sant Ambroeus, the café in the Sotheby's building, and because I've been running and hiking instead of just briskly walking to work.

Gabriel has slowed, so that we are shoulder to shoulder, and he sees me doing a self-inventory. "Not like that," he says. "In *here*." He puts his hand over his heart.

He starts walking again, and I fall into pace with him. "You came here like every other tourist. Wound up supertight, with your check-list, to take a picture of a tortoise and a sea lion and a booby and put them on Instagram."

"I didn't have a *list*," I argue.

He raises a brow. "Didn't you?"

Maybe not literally, but sure, there were things I had wanted to do on Isabela. Touristy things, because what's the point of crossing off something on your bucket list if—

Shit. I did have a list.

"Visitors come here saying they want to see Galápagos, but they don't, not really. They want to see what they can already see in guide-books or on the internet. The real Isabela is made up of stuff most people don't care about. Like the feria, and how trading a pair of rubber wading boots can get you a meal of fresh lobster. Or how people who live here mark a path—not with a wooden sign, but with a lava rock set in the notch of a tree. Or what dinner tastes like, when you've grown it yourself." He glances at me. "Tourists come with an itinerary. Locals just . . . live."

"Gabriel Fernandez," I say. "Was that a compliment?"

He laughs. "This *is* your birthday present," he admits.

"You must have seen a lot of ugly Americans," I say. "Not physi-cally ugly. I mean the spoiled, entitled kind."

"Not too many. There were way more *turistas* who came here and saw what nature looks like when it's wild, when you haven't con-tained it and confined it into twelve square city blocks or an exhibit at a zoo, and they were just . . . humbled. You could see the gears turning: *How do we make sure these beautiful things are here for other people to see? How can I keep my corner of the planet alive, to help?* The best part of being a tour guide was planting a little seed in someone's mind, and knowing you wouldn't be there to see it, but that it would grow and grow."

Given how prickly he'd been about me being a tourist when we first met and the fact that he isn't a tour guide any longer, I wonder what changed.

My nose prickles—the first clue that we have reached the fumaroles. The ground bleaches from black to white and yellow. All I can smell is sulfur. Instead of the melted ice cream whirls of cooled lava, there are endless small light rocks that shift under my sneakers with a light, tinkling noise, and steam belching from thermal vents.

"There," Gabriel says, pointing to a spot where lime-green smoke oozes out of a pore in the earth.

I am six feet away from an active volcano.

"Why did you stop?" I ask.

He turns to me. "Because swimming in magma is overrated."

"No," I say. "Why did you stop being a tour guide?"

He doesn't answer, and I assume that he is going to ignore me, like he has before. But maybe there is something about the primeval landscape and our proximity to the beating heart of the planet, because Gabriel sinks down to the jaundiced ground, and starts from the beginning.

"We were taking out a scuba tour to Gordon Rocks," Gabriel says, as I settle across from him, our knees nearly touching. "It was a live-aboard boat, with twelve divers. It was a gig we'd done hundreds of times. My father and I went out early to check the conditions, because that's what you do. I was the one who went into the water, while he stayed in the boat. There was a slight current near the surface, no big deal."

He looks at me. "Gordon Rocks, it's a cliff under the water, where just a little triangle of rock peeks out above the surface. We went back to the clients' boat and we did the safety briefing. Because there were so many divers, we took two pangas. Everyone was given the same instructions for deboarding: get down twenty feet as quickly as possible, and bear to the right. But as soon as we were under the water it was clear that conditions weren't what I'd thought they were. The current was swift, and it was deep."

Gabriel stares out at the flat horizon, but I know he's not seeing what's in front of us. "Ten divers got spread out to the right of the cliff wall. But one, who wasn't quite as experienced at scuba, got sucked into the current to the left, and dragged down deep. My father, he pointed to the ten other divers and then he did this"— Gabriel touches his index fingers together—"he wanted me to stay close to them. I knew he was going to go after the other diver. I saw him swim into the current, and then when I couldn't see him anymore, I went after the others."

He shakes his head. "There was a clump of divers clinging to the rock face, together. After I got to them, I led them to the surface and set off a float so that the panga driver could get them. The boat was already a half mile north, picking up others who had surfaced a distance away. It went like that for a while—me treading water and trying to see the heads of the other divers and make sure the panga rounded them up. By the time that was done, I counted eleven divers and me, but my father and the last diver hadn't come up.

"We zoomed out to the left of the rock. I had binoculars, from the panga driver, and I was staring so hard at the surface of the water looking for a bobbing head or anything that moved, but the ocean . . ." Gabriel's voice caught. "It's just so goddamn big."

He fell silent, and I reached into his lap and squeezed his hand. I rested our fists on my knee.

"After an hour, I knew he couldn't have survived. At the depths he was at, he could have been dragged by the current a hundred feet or more. The percentage of oxygen in the tanks was meant for a shallow dive, and he knew going deeper would mess with his brain and his ability to function. He would only have had enough air for ten or fifteen minutes, that far down. Between swimming hard to catch up to the lost diver and inflating the diver's BC and unhooking his weight belt, my dad likely had even less time than that."

I think about my own father's death. I was not with him, and it happened too fast, but at the hospital, I was able to see his body. I remember holding his cold hand and not wanting to let it go, because I knew it would be the last time I ever got to touch him. "Did your father . . ." I start. "Did he ever . . ." But I can't seem to finish.

Gabriel shakes his head. "Bodies that drown in the ocean don't surface," he says quietly.

"I'm so sorry. What a terrible accident."

His gaze snaps up. "Accident? It was all my fault."

Dumbfounded, I stare at him. "How?"

"I was the one who tested the conditions. Clearly I got them wrong—"

"Or they changed—"

"Then I should have been the one to go after the diver," Gabriel insists. "So my father would still be alive."

And you wouldn't, I think.

He turns his head away from me. "I can't lead tours anymore, not without thinking about how bad I fucked up. I can't scuba-dive without thinking his body is going to drift in front of me. The reason I'm building the house and farming is because I have to be goddamn exhausted at the end of the day, or I have nightmares about what he must have been thinking in those last few minutes."

I'm quiet for a moment. "What he was thinking," I say finally, "is that his son would be safe."

Gabriel dashes a palm across his eyes, and I pretend not to notice. He stands up, using his weight to pull me to my feet. "We'd better get back," he says. "The return trip's not any shorter."

All around us, fumes rise from little pockets in the ground, as if we stand in a crucible. It is prehistoric and dystopian, but if you look closely, here and there are tiny green shoots and stalks. Something, growing out of nothing.

As we walk back across the fumaroles and the dark yawn of the caldera, Gabriel doesn't let go of my hand.

An hour later, the sun is skulking lower in the sky and we reach the crotched tree with the black lava rock where Gabriel left behind his heavier pack. We can see the huddled shape of it, propped against a tree, but there's another shadow as well, and as we get closer, it is clear that it's a person. I scramble in my pocket for the mask I haven't

worn when it was just me and Gabriel, only to realize that it is Beatriz. She breaks into a run as soon as she sees us.

"You need to come *now*," she says, and she pushes a piece of paper
into my hand.

It is an email, printed out on stationery from the hotel. *For im-
mediate delivery to guest Diana O'Toole*, it reads. *From: The Greens. We
have been trying to reach you. Please contact ASAP. Your mother is dying.*

On the way back to Gabriel's house, we sprint—and yet somehow,
the distance seems even further than it did this morning. Distantly I
hear Beatriz explain to Gabriel how the message arrived—something
about Elena and an electrical short that caused a small fire in the
hotel's utility room; how when she went to the hotel with her cousin
so he could rewire and fix the circuits, and to make sure everything
was in working order, she had powered up the front office computers
and seen a series of emails, each more urgent, trying to get in touch
with me. I hear Gabriel tell Beatriz to call Elena, to have the Wi-Fi
up and running by the time we get there.

Still, it's two hours before we drop Beatriz at the farm and continue in Gabriel's rusty Jeep into Puerto Villamil, to the hotel. This
time, there is no flirting from Elena. She meets us at the door, her
eyes dark and concerned.

My phone buzzes, automatically connecting to the network. I ignore the flood of emails and texts bursting through this tiny crack in
the dam of Isabela's radio silence. I pull up FaceTime, the last call I
made to the memory care facility, and dial.

A different nurse answers this time, one I don't recognize. She is
wearing a mask and a face shield. "I'm Hannah O'Toole's daughter,"
I say. All the breath seizes in my throat. "Is my mother . . . ?"

Those eyes soften. "I'll bring you in to her," the nurse says.

There's a lurching spin of scenery as whatever device she is holding is moved in transit. I close my eyes against a dizzy wave, expecting to see the familiar confines of my mother's apartment, but instead,
the nurse's face appears again. "You should be prepared—she's de-

compensated very fast. She has pneumonia, brought on by Covid," the nurse says. "But at this point it's not just her lungs that are failing. Her kidneys, her heart . . ."

I swallow. It has been a couple of weeks since I saw her on video chat. I had used Abuela's phone to call The Greens twice. Just days ago, they told me she was stable. How could so much have gone wrong since then?

"Is she . . . awake?"

"No," the nurse says. "She's sedated heavily. But you can still talk to her. Hearing is the last sense to go." She pauses. "Now is the time to say your goodbyes."

A moment later, I am looking at a wraith in a hospital bed, the covers pulled up to her chin. She is hollow-cheeked, faded, taking tiny sips of air. I try to reconcile this image of my mother with the woman who hid in bunkers in active war zones, so that she could chronicle the terrible things humans do to each other.

Anger washes over me—why isn't anyone *doing* anything to help her? If she can't breathe, there are machines for that. If her heart stops—

If her heart stops, they will do nothing, because I signed a do not resuscitate order when she became a resident at The Greens. With dementia, there was no point in prolonging her life with any extenuating measures.

I am uncomfortably aware that the nurse is holding up the iPad or phone and waiting for me to speak. But what am I supposed to say to a woman who doesn't remember me now, and actively forgot about me in the past?

When she reappeared in my life, already in the throes of dementia, I convinced myself that putting my mother in a care facility was more compassionate than any consideration she'd ever given *me*. She couldn't move into my tiny apartment, nor would she have wanted to, when we were little more than strangers. Instead, I had figured out a way to use her own work to fund her living expenses; I had done the research and found the best memory care facility; I had gotten her settled and had patted myself on the back for my good deeds. I was so busy being self-congratulatory for being more of a daughter to her than she was a mother to me that I failed to see I had really just underscored the distance between us. I hadn't used the time to get to know her better, or to become someone she trusted. I had protected myself from being disappointed again by not cultivating our relationship.

Just like Beatriz, I think.

I clear my throat. "Mom," I say. "It's me, Diana." I hesitate and then add, "Your daughter."

I wait, but there is absolutely no indication she can hear me.

"I'm sorry I'm not there . . ."

Am I?

"I just want you to know . . ."

I swallow down the hurt that roars inside me, the wash of memories. I see my father hanging a giant map on the wall of my bedroom, helping me press thumbtacks into each of the countries where my mother was when she wasn't with us. I think of how, when her returns were inevitably delayed, he would distract me by letting me pick a color and then he'd cook entire meals in that monochrome. The heat of my blush at age thirteen when I had to explain to my father that I'd gotten my period. Scratchy phone connections where I pretended my mother was saying something other than *You know I'd be there for your birthday/recital/Christmas if I could.* Nights I'd lie in bed, ashamed for wanting her to just be my mother, when what she was doing was so much more important.

Feeling forgotten.

And in that second, staring through a screen at someone I never knew, I cannot trust myself to speak, because I'm afraid of what I might actually say.

You weren't there for me when it counted, either.

Quid pro quo.

Just then, the connection dies.

Elena tries rebooting the modem three times. One of those times, the video call is picked up, but the image freezes immediately and goes black. It is when Gabriel and I climb back into his Jeep and we are driving down the main street of Puerto Villamil with its tiny sliver of cell service that the text comes in.

Your mother passed tonight at 6:35. Our deepest condolences for your loss.

Gabriel glances toward me. "Is that—"

I nod.

"Can I do anything?" he asks.

I shake my head. "I just want to go home," I tell him.

He walks me to the door of the apartment, and I can see he is trying to find the words to ask if he should stay. Before he can, though, I thank him and tell him I just want to lie down. I wait until I hear his footsteps on the ceiling above, and I imagine him telling Abuela and Beatriz that my mother has died.

I hold my breath, waiting for the words to beat through my blood.

I pick up my phone and stare at the text from The Greens, and then swipe my thumb to delete it.

That's how easy it is to remove someone from your life.

I realize, even as I think it, that this is not necessarily true.

This is nothing like when I lost my father. Back then, it felt like a rip in the fabric of my world, and no matter how hard I tried, I couldn't hold the edges together. Even now, four years later, when I am going about my day, sometimes I brush up against that seam and it hurts like hell.

I find a bottle of caña in the cupboard—Gabriel gave me my own supply after our campout, along with a box full of fresh vegetables for meals this week. Since I don't have a shot glass, I pour a little into a juice cup, and then—shrugging—fill it to the top. I take a healthy swig, letting the fire run through me.

Right now, I just want to get fucking drunk.

I peel off my clothes, the ones in which I had hiked to the volcano (was that *today*?) and run the shower. Standing in the stream of water, needles pelting at my skin, I say the word out loud: *orphan.* I am nobody's child now. I'm an isolated island, just like the one I'm stuck on.

There are logistics that will have to be sorted out: burial, funeral, liquidating her apartment at the facility. Right now even thinking about it is exhausting.

I pull on clean underwear and one of Gabriel's old T-shirts, which hangs down to my thighs. I braid my hair to get it out of my face. Then I sit down at the table with the bottle of caña and pour my second full glass.

"Well, Mom," I say, tasting the bitterness of that title. "Here's to you." I take another gulp of the liquor.

By tomorrow, the media worldwide will be reporting on her death. The obituaries will be retrospectives of her career—from her first embedding in a war zone to the Pulitzer she won in 2008 for photos of a street demonstration in Myanmar that turned violent.

The award ceremony for that was held at a swanky luncheon in New York City in late May. My mother attended. My father did not.

He was in the bleachers at my high school graduation, cheering as I crossed the stage to get my diploma.

I put my head down on my crossed forearms and sift through my mind for one pure pearl of a memory of my mother. Surely there's one.

I discard one after another as they start off positive—a work trip I tagged along for; an image of her opening a Mother's Day gift I'd made in preschool; a moment where she stood in front of my canvas at a student exhibition and canted her head, absorbing it. But each of those recollections devolves quickly, pricked by a thorn of self-interest: a sightseeing promise broken when something came up; a phone call from her agent that interrupted the gift giving; a blunt and brutal criticism of proportion in my painting, instead of a crumb of praise.

Did you really hate me that much? I wonder.

But I already know the answer: *No.* To hate someone, you'd have to consider them worthy of notice.

Then something drips into my consciousness.

I am little, and my mother is putting film into her camera. It is a magical black box and I know I am not supposed to touch it, just like

I'm not supposed to go into her darkroom, with its nightmare glow and chemical scent. She balances the little machine on her knees and gently winds the slippery film until the teeth catch. It makes soft clicking noises.

Do you want to help? she asks.

My hands are tiny and clumsy, so she covers my fingers with her own, to circle the little lever until the film is taut. She closes the body of the camera, then lifts it and focuses on my face. She snaps a picture.

Here, she says. *You try.*

She helps me lift it and positions my finger on the shutter. I've seen her do it a thousand times. Except I don't know to frame the shot through the viewfinder. I don't really know what to look at, at all.

My mother is laughing as I push down on the shutter so hard it takes a flurry of photos, the sound like a pounding heart.

It occurs to me that I never saw those images. For all I know she developed them and got a crazy collage of blurry wall and ceiling and rug. Maybe I didn't capture her at all.

But maybe that doesn't really matter. For one second, it *had* been my turn.

New memories are sharp, and I wait for this one to draw blood. But . . . nothing happens. If anything it's even more depressing to be sitting here half a world away, clinging to five seconds of motherhood, and wishing there had been more.

"Diana?"

I lift my head up from the table to find Gabriel standing in front of me. I blink at him as he turns on the light. I hadn't even noticed that it had gotten dark.

"I was headed back to the house," he says, "but wanted to see how you were."

"Still sober, that's how I am." I push the bottle across the table. "Join me." When he doesn't at first, I refill my glass. "I suppose you're going to tell me I shouldn't get wasted."

Gabriel takes a juice glass out of the cabinet and pours his own shot. He sits down across from me. "If ever there was a time to get wasted, it's when you're toasting someone you've loved and lost. I'm so sorry, Diana."

"I'm not," I whisper.

His gaze flies to mine.

"There," I say. "Now you know my terrible secret. I'm an awful, broken person. My mother died and I feel . . . nothing." I clink my glass to his. "*That* is why I'm drinking."

I gulp the alcohol, but it goes down wrong. Coughing and sputtering, I fold forward in the chair, trying—and failing—to catch my breath. It is like aspirating fire.

When I start to see stars at the edges of my vision, I feel a hand on the flat of my back, moving in circles. "Breathe," Gabriel soothes. "Easy."

My throat is burning and my eyes are streaming and I don't know if it's because I was choking or because I'm crying, and I'm not sure it matters.

Gabriel is crouched down next to me. He hands me a bandanna from his pocket so that I can wipe my face, but the tears don't stop. A moment later, with a soft curse, he wraps his arms around me. I sob into the curve of his neck.

I don't know when the air starts moving in and out of my lungs again, or when I stop crying. But I start noticing the rhythmic sweep of Gabriel's hand from the crown of my head to the tail of my braid. His lips against my temple. His breath falling in time to mine.

"You're not broken," Gabriel says. "You can feel."

When he kisses me, it feels like the most natural thing in the world. My fingers push through his hair as I fight to get closer. I'm struggling for breath again, but now I want to be.

Gabriel is still kneeling beside me. In one motion he picks me up and sets me on top of the table, standing between my legs. "I'm so glad I fixed this damn thing," he murmurs against my lips, and we both start to laugh. My hands slide up his forearms to his shoulders and my ankles hook behind his knees. He kisses like he is pouring himself into me. Like this is his last moment on earth, and he needs to leave his mark.

His palms move from my knees to my thighs, bunching the soft T-shirt. The whole time, we kiss. We kiss. When his fingers reach the elastic of my underwear, he stops and pulls back. He looks at me, his eyes so dark that I cannot see how far I've fallen. I nod, and he drags the T-shirt over my head. I feel his teeth scrape against my throat, against the chain of the miraculous medal, and then he paints words onto me with his tongue, moving between my breasts, down my belly, lower. *"Pienso en ti todo el tiempo,"* he says, hiking me to the edge of the table before kneeling again on the floor. His mouth is wet and hot through cotton. He feasts.

I am a lightning storm, gathering energy. I pull on Gabriel's hair, dragging him up, affixing myself to him like a second skin. The room spins as he picks me up and carries me into the bedroom, following me down onto the mattress in a tangle of limbs. He immediately rolls to his side so I don't bear his weight, and without him covering me I shiver beneath the ceiling fan. My hair has unraveled; he pushes it back from my face and waits. "Yes?" he asks.

"Yes," I say, and this time I crawl on top, pushing at Gabriel's clothes until they are gone; until I can sink onto him and into him and lose myself.

It isn't until afterward, when he has fallen asleep holding me tight, that I think maybe I've been found.

When I wake up, Gabriel is staring at me. I feel his hand flex on my shoulder, as if I am sand that might slip out of his grasp.

My head hurts and my mouth is dry but I know I cannot blame last night on the caña. I went into this with my mind clear, even if my heart was hurting.

Now, it's an anchor sinking in me.

Just one more second, I think.

I flatten my palm against Gabriel's warm chest, and I open my mouth to speak.

"Don't," he begs. "Not yet."

Because we both know what's coming. The slow untangling, the extraction. The excuses and the apologies and the veneer of friend-ship we will slap over this and never peek beneath.

He kisses me so sweetly, like it is a song in a different language. Even after he pulls back, I am still humming it. "Before you say any-thing," he begins.

But he doesn't finish. Because neither of us has heard the knock or the door opening, but we cannot miss the sound of breaking glass and china as Beatriz finds us knotted together, drops the breakfast she's kindly made me, and runs away.

By the time we have sorted out our clothes and hurried up to Abuela's, Beatriz is gone.

By unspoken agreement, I climb into Gabriel's Jeep with him. He is silent as he drives through town, scanning the empty streets for her. At the dock, he reverses direction, and heads for the highlands. "She could be back at the farm," he says, and I nod, because thinking of the alternative is too terrifying.

But I know that, like me, he saw the look on Beatriz's face. It wasn't just embarrassment at finding us. It was . . . betrayal. It was the expression of someone who realized she was well and truly alone.

It was a look I hadn't seen on her face since the very first time I saw her on the dock at Concha de Perla, watching her own blood drip from her fingertips.

In the time I'd been on Isabela, Beatriz had moved from despera-tion to resignation. If she hadn't been exactly joyous about this home-coming, at least now she seemed to be less tormented. She hadn't been cutting herself. Her old wounds were silver scars.

And now we'd ripped them open again.

I know that cutting does not always precede suicide. But I also know that sometimes, it does. Beatriz let her guard down with me; she trusted me to be her person. And then I gave myself to someone else.

A small sinkhole forms in me, filled with guilt. *Finn. My mother.*

There is so much wrong with what I did last night. But I push all that out of my head because right now nothing matters but finding Beatriz and talking her down from her ledge.

A whisper in my bones: *Coward.*

"This is a small island," Gabriel says tightly. "Until it isn't."

I know what he means. There are endless trails and furrows through Isabela that aren't accessible by car; there are poisonous plants and spined cacti in some places and thick greenery you can't see through in others. There are countless ways you can hurt yourself—unintentionally, or on purpose.

"We'll find her," I tell him. I lift my hand, planning to cover his on the stick shift, but on second thought, put it back in my lap.

I stare out the passenger-side window, scanning every flutter of movement to see if it might be a girl on the run. There's no way she could have outpaced us on foot. But maybe she took a bicycle from Abuela's. Maybe she got a head start on us when we made a false start by turning toward town.

When we finally reach the farm, I open the Jeep's door before we even come to a complete stop. I run into Gabriel's house, yelling for Beatriz. He is on my heels, wildly looking around the living room and throwing open the door to her bedroom to find it empty.

I stand in the doorway as he sinks down onto the mattress. "Shit," he mutters.

"Maybe she just needs time alone," I say quietly, hopefully. "Maybe she's on her way back right now."

His haunted gaze meets mine, and I realize this is not the first time he's searched far and wide for someone he loved who'd gone missing.

Suddenly he grabs Beatriz's backpack from beside the bed and dumps the contents on the mattress.

"What are you looking for?" I ask.

"Something she took? Something she didn't?" He unzips an inner pocket and stuffs his hand inside. "I don't know."

A clue. A hint to where, on this island, she would have gone to disappear.

I open the top drawer of the bureau, letting my hand sift through panties and bras, when my fingers brush against something that feels like a diary.

I dig deeper into the recesses of the drawer. It's not a diary or a journal or a book at all. It's a stack of postcards, banded together with a hair elastic.

It's all of the postcards I wrote Finn. The ones that Beatriz told me she mailed.

I feel like I've been run through with a sword. I pull off the elastic and shuffle through the cards, all G2 TOURS on one side, and my cramped handwriting on the other. This was the one connection I had to Finn. Even if I couldn't reliably speak to him or get his emails, I was hopeful that he was hearing every now and then from me.

Except . . . he wasn't.

Finn is thousands of miles away, without any word from me. Given our last abortive phone call, he must assume I'm pissed at him. At the very least he'll think I've put him out of my mind.

I look at Gabriel and realize that, last night, this was true.

The contents of Beatriz's backpack—textbooks and a phone charger and earbuds and some granola bars—are littered around him. But Gabriel is holding a Polaroid and frowning slightly. A line of tape runs down the middle, carefully piecing together something that was previously sliced apart.

On one side of the photograph is a pretty girl, with corkscrews of blond hair. She has her arm around Beatriz, her other hand extended to take the photo. Their eyes are closed, as they kiss.

Ana Maria.

The expression on Beatriz's face is one I've never seen: pure joy.

"Who is this girl?" Gabriel murmurs.

I wonder what he is thinking. "Her host sister, a friend from Santa Cruz."

"A *friend,*" he mutters, and at first I think he is reacting to Beatriz kissing a girl. But when he touches a fingertip to the Scotch tape down the center of the photograph, I realize he's angry at whoever broke Beatriz's heart so cleanly that she would tear apart this picture, and then regretfully patch it back together. "When her school closed, Beatriz begged to come back here. Is this why?"

I love that Gabriel has shoved aside the unimportant details—his daughter falling for a girl is inconsequential; what matters is that she was hurt. That she *still* is. That we are just the latest in a line of people she cared for who let her down.

I think of what Beatriz said to me when we were in the trillizos.

Truth or dare. Unconditional love is bullshit. She loved me, but not like that.

I wanted to know what it would be like to just let go.

"Gabriel," I breathe. "I think I know where she is."

The three volcanic tunnels are not that far from Gabriel's farm. We get as close as we can by truck and then Gabriel slings ropes and a rappelling harness over his shoulder. As we tramp through the thick ground cover, I call out Beatriz's name, but there is no answer.

I think about how far the ladder went into the shaft, how black it was below that. I wonder how much further she would have had to fall.

Curling my hand around Abuela's miraculous medal, I pray.

"Beatriz," I scream again.

The wind whispers through the brush and whips my hair around my face. Gabriel finds a sturdy tree and wraps one end of the rope around it, tying a series of impossible knots. It is an unfairly beautiful day, with puffy white clouds dancing across the sky and birdsong like a symphony. I stand in front of the three volcanic tunnels. If she's even here, she could be in any of them.

At the bottom of any of them.

"I'm going down," I tell Gabriel.

"What?" His head snaps up in the middle of securing the rope. "Diana, wait—"

But I can't. I start descending the ladder of the tunnel beside the one Beatriz and I climbed into, waiting for my eyes to adjust to the darkness. The distant sun bounces off minerals in the rock walls, glowing gold. I climb deeper, swallowed by this stone throat.

The only sound is the rhythmic drip of water on rock. *Plink. Plink.* And then a choked sob.

"Beatriz?" I cry, moving faster. "Gabriel!" I yell. "In here!" I lose my footing on the slick ladder in my hurry. "Hang on. I'm coming."

A beat, and then her voice threads toward me. "Just go away," Beatriz sobs.

Her words are disembodied, floating like ghosts. I can't see her anywhere below me. "I know you're upset about what you saw," I say, climbing down and down and down, until I reach the end of the ladder, and still she's not there. Wildly, I look between my feet on the bottom rung, wondering if I will see her broken body below me.

"I should never have talked to you," Beatriz says. I cannot see her; I go still and listen for the bounce of sound. I follow the soft hitch of her crying and—there—a shadow moving in a shadow. She clings to another ladder on the far side of the lava tube. There are a few straggling ropes left behind by others.

"I thought . . . you cared. I thought you meant what you said. But you're just like everyone else who says that and then leaves."

"You *do* matter to me, Beatriz," I say gently. "But I was always going to leave."

"Did you tell my dad that before or after you fucked him?"

I wince. "I didn't mean for that to happen."

"Yeah, sure. Keep digging that hole . . ."

"This isn't about him. This is about *you*," I say. "And I do care about you, Bea. I do."

Her sobs get louder. "Stop lying. Just fucking stop saying that."

The ladder shudders as booted feet strike the wall beside me. "She's not lying, Beatriz," Gabriel says, falling into view in the space between me and his daughter. He has the rappelling rope wrapped around him, a link to the world above. It is taut and seems too thin to support his weight. If it snaps, he is too far to grab either of the ladders Beatriz and I stand on. "When you care about someone, it just . . . happens," he says quietly. "None of us get to choose who we love."

I hold my breath. Is he talking about the two of us? About Beatriz and Ana Maria? About his ex?

As he is speaking, he has shifted his weight, canting his feet for balance on the slick wall. Incrementally, he's trying to make his way to Beatriz without startling her into doing something rash.

"You'd be better off without me," Beatriz sobs, the sentence torn from her throat. "Everyone else is."

Gabriel shakes his head. "You're not alone, even if you feel like you are. And I don't *want* to be alone." His breath catches. "I can't lose you, too."

He stretches out his hand toward her.

Beatriz doesn't move. "You don't even know who I really am," she says, her voice hushed in shame.

Their breathing circles, echoes.

"Yes I do," Gabriel says. "You're my baby. I don't care what else you are . . . or aren't. That's the only thing that matters."

His fingertips reach further through the void.

Beatriz meets him halfway. In the next moment, Gabriel has gathered her into his arms and lashed her tight against him with the ropes. He whispers to her in Spanish; she clings to his shoulders, drawing shuddering breaths.

Slowly, the three of us inch toward the light.

The next few hours pass in a blur. We take Beatriz down to Abuela's, because Gabriel doesn't want to leave her alone in the farmhouse while he ferries me back to the apartment. Abuela bursts into tears when she sees Beatriz and starts fussing over her. Beatriz is still weepy and silent and embarrassed, and Gabriel focuses all his attention and energy on her, as he should.

At some point, I slip out of Abuela's home and walk down to my basement apartment, sitting on the short retaining wall that separates it from the beach. With all the healing that has to happen in that family, I don't belong there.

But.

I'm starting to wonder where I *do* belong.

I think about the postcards in Beatriz's drawer that weren't sent. The things I wanted Finn to know. The things I will never tell him.

I don't know how long I sit on the little wall, but the sun staggers lower in the sky and the tide goes out, leaving a long line of treasure on the sand: sea stars and pearled shells and seaweed tangled like the hair of mermaids.

I can sense Gabriel walking up behind me even before he speaks. Space is different when he is in it. Charged, electrical. He stops just short of the spot where I sit, staring at the orange line of the horizon. I turn my chin, acknowledging him. "How is she?"

"Asleep," he says, and he steps forward. His hair is mussed by the breeze, as if it, too, sighs to see him.

He sits down next to me, one leg drawn up, his arm resting on his knee. "I thought you'd want to know she's all right," he says.

"I did," I tell him. "I do."

"We've been talking," Gabriel says hesitantly.

"About . . . school?" *About Ana Maria.*

"About all of it." He looks at me. "I'm going to stay with her to-night." A faint blush stripes his cheekbones. "I didn't want you to think that—"

"I wasn't expecting you to—"

"It's not that I don't—"

We both stop talking. "You're a good father, Gabriel," I say quietly. "You *do* protect the people you love. Don't second-guess that."

He takes the compliment awkwardly, his eyes sliding away from mine. "You know, I named her. Luz wanted something from a tele-novela she was obsessed with at the time—but I insisted on Beatriz. Maybe I knew what was coming."

"What do you mean?"

"Beatriz is the one who kept Dante going when he walked through hell. And every time I've found myself suffering, my Beatriz is the one who pulls me back."

This pushes on something so tender and bruised inside me, and instead of examining that reaction, I try to make light of it. "I'm shocked."

"That I named her Beatriz?"

"That you've read *The Divine Comedy*."

He smiles faintly. "There's so much about me you have yet to learn," he says, but there is a thread of sadness in the words, because we both know I never will.

He stands, blocking my view of the ocean. He holds my face in his palms and kisses my forehead. "Good night, Diana," Gabriel says, and he leaves me alone with the stars and the surf.

I pull the night around me like a coat. I think of New York City and Finn and my mother. Of commuter sneakers and Sunday brunch at our favorite café when Finn wasn't working and the blue Tiffany box hidden in the back of his underwear drawer. I think of the rush of relief when I manage to catch the subway car before it pulls out of the station and the taste of cheesecake I craved and bought at three A.M. and the hours I spent on Zillow dreaming of houses in Westchester we could not afford. I think of the smell of chestnuts from street vendors in the winter and asphalt sinking under my heels in the summer. I think of Manhattan—an island full of diverse, determined people hustling toward something better; a populace that doesn't sleepwalk through their days. But it all feels a lifetime away.

Then I think about *this* island, where there is nothing but time. Where change comes slowly, and inevitably.

Here, I can't lose myself in errands and work assignments; I can't disappear in a crowd. I am forced to walk instead of run, and as a result, I've seen things I would have sped past before—the fuss of a crab trading up for a new shell, the miracle of a sunrise, the garish burst of a cactus flower.

Busy is just a euphemism for being so focused on what you *don't* have that you never notice what you *do*.

It's a defense mechanism. Because if you stop hustling—if you pause—you start wondering why you ever thought you wanted all those things.

I can no longer tell the sky from the sea, but I can hear the waves. A loss of sight; a gain of insight.

When Finn and I booked a trip to the Galápagos, the travel agent told us it would be life-changing.

Little did she know.

To: DOToole@gmail.com
From: FColson@nyp.org

Whenever someone gets extubated in the Covid ICU, "Here Comes the Sun" plays on the loudspeakers. It's like in the Hunger Games movie, when someone dies, but the reverse. We all look up and stop what we're doing. But then again, days go by when we don't hear it at all.

Today, when I left the hospital for the first time in 36 hours, there was a refrigerated truck parked outside for the bodies we can't stuff into the morgue.

I bet every single one of those people came into the ER, thinking: it will only be a day or two.

I do not see Beatriz or Gabriel for five days. Even Abuela seems to be missing, and I assume that they are all up at the farmhouse together. I convince myself very easily that the reason I feel relieved has everything to do with Beatriz getting help and nothing to do with me being able to avoid Gabriel. The truth is, I don't know what to say to him. *This was a mistake* is what sits bitter on my tongue, but I'm not sure what it refers to: the night with Gabriel, or all the years that led up to it.

So every time I leave my apartment and do not see him, it is a reprieve. If I don't see him I can pretend it didn't happen, and postpone grappling with the consequences.

One day, I hiked to the Wall of Tears, hoping to find another miracle of cell service. When those bars appeared on my phone, I called The Greens first, arranging for my mother's cremation and explaining that

I was still stuck outside the country. Then I called Finn, only to be put through directly to his voicemail. *It's me*, I said. *I wrote you postcards, but they . . . didn't make it there. I just wanted to let you know I'm thinking of you*. And then I didn't trust myself to say anything else.

On another sunny, perfect day on Isabela, I pull on my bathing suit, take the snorkel and mask from Gabriel's apartment, and walk through the streets of Puerto Villamil, headed to Concha de Perla one more time. A couple of storekeepers—who, like everyone else, have become less strict with the rule about curfew—recognize me and wave, or call out hellos through their masks. A few have come up to me at the feria, trading me sunblock and cereal and fresh tortillas for portraits that they then hang in their establishments.

When I get to the dock at Concha de Perla, there is a massive sea lion lolling on one of the benches. It raises its head at my approach, twitches its whiskers, and then flings itself back into its nap. I strip to my bathing suit and walk down the stairway into the ocean, fitting the mask to my face and swimming with strong strokes into the heart of the lagoon.

A huge, dark shape rises in my peripheral vision. I turn to see a giant marble stingray moving in tandem with me. Its wings ruffle past, a hem sweeping the dance floor. It brushes my fingers gently, deliberately, as if to convince me there's no threat. It feels like stroking the soft, wet velvet underskirt of a mushroom.

Six weeks ago this would have sent me into a conniption. Now, it's just another living creature sharing space with me. I smile, watching it veer away from me underwater, until it becomes a dot in the deep blue field and then vanishes.

I float on my back for a while, feeling the sun warm my face, and then lazily breaststroke back toward the dock.

Once again, Beatriz is sitting on it.

She isn't wearing her ubiquitous sweatshirt. Her arms are bare, crossed with silver lines. She hugs her knees to her chest as I climb the stairs, drop my mask and snorkel, and wring my ponytail dry. I sink down beside her. "Are you okay?" I ask quietly, the same words I first spoke to her on Isabela, a bookend.

"Yeah," she says, and she looks into her lap.

We fall into a strained silence. Of all the time I've spent with Beatriz, we've never had nothing to say.

"What you saw . . . with me and your father . . ." I shake my head. "You know I have someone waiting at home for me. It shouldn't have happened. I'm sorry."

Beatriz rubs her thumbnail along a groove in the wood. "I'm sorry, too. About not sending your postcards."

I've thought a lot about what might have made her lie to me about mailing them. I don't think it was malicious . . . more like she wanted to keep me to herself, once she'd made me a confidante. All the more reason, of course, that she would have been shocked to find me in bed with her father.

She trusted me. Just like Finn had trusted me.

Suddenly I feel like I'm going to be sick. Because as much as I don't want to face Gabriel to discuss what happened between us, I want even less to confess to Finn.

Beatriz looks at me. "I talked to my dad about Ana Maria."

"How'd that go?"

"Not as bad as I made it out in my head to be," she says ruefully.

"The mind is an amazing thing," I reply.

She considers this. "Well, it's not like I didn't have a good reason to worry," she adds. "There are a lot of people in the world who'd hate me because I . . . like girls. But my father isn't one of them." Beatriz ducks her chin. "I kind of feel bad for Ana Maria. She doesn't have parents like him, so she has to pretend all the time. Even to herself."

I don't know what to say to her. She's right. The world can be a fucked-up place, and I suppose you're never too young to learn that.

"I'm not going to go back to school," Beatriz tells me. "My father said he'll let me do online courses here. But I had to promise to talk to a therapist, in return. We Zoomed for the first time, yesterday." She grimaces. "Something else that wasn't as bad as I thought it would be."

"*Online* school?" I repeat. "And *Zoom*?"

"My dad paid Elena to open the stupid hotel and turn on the Wi-Fi so I could get a decent signal," Beatriz explains.

I raise an eyebrow. "What's he paying her with?"

Beatriz cracks a smile, and then I do, too, and we both laugh. I put my arm around her, and she lays her head on my shoulder. We watch a sea lion playing in the distance.

"You know," Beatriz says, "you could stay. With us."

I feel myself soften against her. "I have to go back to real life sometime."

She pulls away, a wistful expression on her face. "For a while," she says, "didn't this feel real?"

Dear Finn,

It's possible you won't get this postcard until I come home and hand it to you myself. But there are things I need to say, and it can't wait.

I've been thinking a lot about the things we do that are simply unforgivable. Like me not being with my mother when she died, or my mother not being around when I was growing up. Leaving you alone during a pandemic. You encouraging me to go.

I've thought a lot about that last one. When you told me you were trying to keep me safe . . . you might just have been convincing yourself it was the smartest course of action. Did you really not think I could manage to stay healthy? Did you actually believe that when the world is falling to pieces, it's better to be apart from the person you love, instead of together?

I am overthinking this, of course, but these days I have a lot of time to think. And I can't even blame you. I've said and done things, too, that I shouldn't have.

I know everyone makes mistakes—but until recently I have held everyone to a standard where making mistakes is a weakness. Me in-cluded—I haven't given myself the grace to screw up, to do better next time. It is exhausting, trying to never step off the path, worrying that if I do, I'll never get back on track.

So here is what I've learned: if, in hindsight, you realize you've messed up—if you have done the unforgivable—that does not mean that the terrible thing wasn't meant to happen. Sure, we may wish otherwise, but when things don't happen according to plan, it may be be-

cause the plan was faulty. I'm not explaining this well. For example,
take my missing suitcase: I wonder if the person who found it needed
clothes more than I did. I wonder how Beatriz would have fared if I
had never come to Isabela. I imagine Kitomi having her painting for
company all these weeks, instead of it being crated up in a warehouse. I
picture all the people you've saved at the hospital and the ones you
couldn't, who you still walked with all the way to the edge of death. And
that's when I realize: Maybe things didn't get fucked up. Maybe I have
been wrong all along, and this is where I was always meant to be.

Diana

To: DOToole@gmail.com
From: FColson@nyp.org

I'm really too tired to rehash everything that happened at the hos-
pital today.
　I hope you're okay.
　One of us needs to be.

Two and a half weeks after Gabriel and I sleep together, I come
home from a run to find a note slipped under the door of my apartment, inviting me to join him on a hike to a place called Playa Barahona. He says he'll be waiting at the apartment at nine A.M. tomorrow,
in case I decide to come.

Although it would be easier to hide forever, I know I can't. It is
May 9. I've been here for almost two months. One day, that ferry will
start running again. I can't avoid Gabriel on an island this small. And
I owe him the grace of a conversation.

The next morning, I slip out the sliding glass doors and find him
waiting with two rusty bicycles and a thermos of coffee. "Hi," I say.

His eyes drink me in. "Hi."

I wonder how it is that you can be so shy with someone you've felt
moving inside you.

At that, a blush rushes over me, and I cover it with conversation. "Bikes? How far are we going?"

He rubs the back of his neck. "Further than El Muro de las Lágrimas, closer than Sierra Negra," Gabriel says. "It's a secret spot. It's closed to tourists *and* locals—I haven't been since I was a kid."

"Breaking more laws," I say lightly. "You're a bad influence."

At that, his eyes fly to mine.

I turn away, grabbing one of the bikes, and clear my throat. "I saw Beatriz," I say. "She says things are . . . good."

Gabriel looks at me for a long moment before he grabs the handlebars of the second bike. "Okay," he says softly, nodding to himself, as if he recognizes that I am signaling what we will talk about and what we won't. He starts walking the bike toward the main road, telling me how Beatriz schooled him on the 123 baby tortoises that were stolen from the breeding center in 2018, and how he's fighting a losing battle trying to explain to Abuela that she can't go play *lotería* at church, even if she wears a mask. As we pedal down dusty dirt paths, he tells me that he's almost finished building the second bedroom at his house—which is good, because Beatriz will be staying with him even after her school on Santa Cruz reopens.

For a half hour or so, we bike in silence.

"The first girl I fell for was Luz," Gabriel says suddenly. "She sat in front of me in class, alphabetically, and I stared at three freckles on her neck for months before I got the courage to speak to her." He glances at me. "Do you remember your first crush?"

"Of course. His name was Jared and he was a vegetarian, and I didn't eat meat for a month so that he'd notice me."

Gabriel laughs. "Do you remember *before* that, when you made the decision to like boys?"

I look at him quizzically. "No . . ."

"Exactly," he says, and his jaw sets. "No one gets to break her heart again."

Oh, this man. "Who would dare, with you in her corner?"

His gaze catches mine and I can't look away and I nearly crash into a tree, but Gabriel hops off his bike and interrupts the moment.

"We have to hide these," he tells me. "If the rangers see them, they'll come after us."

He drags his bike into a tangle of brush and rearranges the leaves to cover the rusty metal, then takes my bike and does the same. "Now what?"

"Now we walk the rest of the way," he says. "It's another forty-five minutes."

As we hike, he retreats into safe space—telling me about his childhood. His father used to read *Moby-Dick* to him before he went to bed, because Melville learned about whaling while on a ship in the Galápagos. He says Melville called the Galápagos "The Enchanted Islands." He tells me that the last time he was at Barahona, he was with a group called Amigos de las Tortugas—Friends of the Tortoises—a bunch of kids who went with the Charles Darwin Research Station to count sea turtle nests there. There were volunteers from all over the world who came to help, and one—a tourist from the United States—taught Gabriel how to surf.

When we finally crest a dune and see the beach spread below us, I catch my breath. It is beautiful in the way wild things are beautiful—with roaring sea and ungroomed sand, bordered by cacti and brush. Gabriel offers his hand, and after only a moment of hesitation I take it so that he can help me scuffle my way through the hillock to land on the beach. "Careful," he says, tugging me to the left so that I do not step on a tiny hole in the sand, like a bubble caught underground. "There," Gabriel says. "That's a sea turtle nest."

I look around, and with careful eyes spy another twenty little divots in the sand. "Really?"

"Yeah. And no matter how far they swim in the ocean, turtles come back to the same beach to lay their eggs."

"How do they find it?"

"Magnetic field. Each part of the coast has its own special fingerprint, basically, and the babies learn it and use memory as a compass."

"That's really cool," I say.

"That's not why I wanted you to see it," Gabriel says. He points to a wriggling line in the sand that tracks down to the water. "After the female turtles lay their eggs—around a hundred at a time—they leave." He looks at me. "They never come back to take care of those eggs."

I think of how the strongest memory I have of my mother is watching her pull a small carry-on out of our house.

"Here's the incredible thing," Gabriel says. "Two months later, those sea turtle babies hatch at night. They've got to get to the ocean before hawks and crabs and frigate birds can get to them. The only guide they have is the reflection of the moon on the water." I feel him standing behind me, a wall of heat. "Not all of them make it. But, Diana . . . the strongest ones do."

When my eyes sting with tears, I turn away, stumbling forward only to have Gabriel yank me back by my arm. *"Cuidado,"* he says, and I follow his gaze to the tree I nearly crashed into, a manchineel laden with poisoned apples.

I laugh, but it may just be a sob.

Gabriel's hand gentles on my arm. "Are we ever going to talk about it?"

"I can't," I say, and I leave it to him to dissect all the possible meanings.

He nods, letting go of me. He scuffs at the sand, careful to avoid the sea turtle nests. "Then *I'll* talk about it," he says quietly. "There have been a few times in my life when I thought all the stars had aligned, and I was exactly where I was meant to be. Once, when Beatriz was born. Once when I was diving near Kicker Rock on San Cristóbal and saw fifty hammerhead sharks. Once when the volcano came alive under my feet." He meets my gaze. "And once, with you."

If only these were normal times. If only I were an ordinary tourist. If only I didn't have a life and a love waiting for me at home. I draw in a breath. "Gabriel," I begin, but he shakes his head.

"You don't have to say anything."

I reach out my hand and catch his. I let myself look down at my fingers, curled in his. "Swim with me?" I ask.

He nods, and we pick our way back down the beach. I shuck off my shirt and shorts and wade into the surf in my bathing suit. Gabriel runs past me, splashing on purpose, and making me laugh. He dives shallowly, comes up shaking droplets off his hair, and shears a spray of water my way to soak me.

"You're gonna be sorry you did that," I tell him, and I dive under the water.

It is a baptism, and we both know it. A way to clean the slate and start fresh as friends, because that's the only path that's open to us.

The water is just cool enough to be refreshing. My eyes burn from the salt and my hair tangles in ropes down my back. Every so often Gabriel free-dives to the bottom and brings up a sea star or a piece of coral for me to admire, before letting it settle again.

I'm not sure when I realize I've lost sight of Gabriel. One moment his head is bobbing, like a seal's, and then he's gone. I turn in a circle, and try to swim closer to shore, but realize I'm getting nowhere. No matter how hard I paddle my arms, I am being pulled further out to sea.

"Gabriel?" I call, and swallow water. *"Gabriel!"*

"Diana?" I hear him before I see him—a tiny pinprick, so distant I cannot imagine how he got that far away. Or maybe I'm the one who has.

"I can't get back," I yell out.

He cups his hands so his voice carries. "Swim with the current, on the diagonal," he cries. "Don't try to fight it."

Somewhere in my consciousness I realize this must be a riptide— carrying me rapidly away from shore. I think of Gabriel's friends, the fishermen who never came back. I think of his father, swept away in a racing current under the surface of the ocean. My heart starts pounding harder.

I take a deep breath and start windmilling my arms in a strong crawl stroke, but when I lift my head I'm no closer to the beach. The only difference is that Gabriel is speeding toward me, swimming with the riptide, in the middle of its current, seemingly approaching at superhuman speed.

He's trying to save me.

It feels like forever, but in minutes, he reaches me. He grabs for me and snags his finger on the chain of the miraculous medal, but it snaps off and I drift further away from him. "Gabriel!" I scream, thrashing out as he floats closer. As soon as he is within reach I grab him and climb him like a vine, panicking. He shoves me under the water, and then jerks me back up.

I am sputtering, blinking. Now that he has my attention, Gabriel grabs my shoulders. "Hold on. Look at me. You are going to make it," he commands.

He slings one arm around me, swimming for both of us, but I can feel his strokes slowing and his body getting heavier.

My God. This can't happen to him again.

His fingers flex on my waist, trying to hike me closer to him. But I can tell he's losing steam. Alone, he might be able to get himself out of this hellish current, but my additional weight is sapping him of energy. If he keeps trying to save me, we will both drown. So I do the only thing I can.

I slip out of his hold.

The current immediately yanks me away from him, so fast it makes me dizzy. He treads water, desperately calling my name.

The waves are so big this far out that they crash over my head. Every time I try to answer him, I swallow water.

I think of what he told me as he touched my throat. Of the airway humans have evolved, of the promises we can speak to each other, of the compromises we suffer for that.

I have heard that the hardest part of drowning is the moment just before—when your lungs seize, about to burst; when you gasp for oxygen and find only water.

Our bodies try to fight the inevitable.

I've heard that all you have to do to be at peace, is give in.

SEVEN

Help

EIGHT

Hold on. Look at me. You're going to make it, Diana.

NINE

Do you know where you are?
Where is my voice.

TEN

Can you squeeze my hand? Wiggle your toes?
Do you know where you are?
Where is Gabriel

ELEVEN

"Blink once for yes," I hear. "Twice for no. Don't try to talk."

It is so bright, I have to close my eyes.

"Do you know where you are right now?"

There is something in my throat, some kind of tube. I can hear a whir and click of machines. This is a hospital. I blink once.

"Okay, Diana, cough for me."

The moment I try, that tube slips up and out, ridge by ridge, and my throat is raw and so so so dry—

I cough and cough and remember not being able to breathe. My eyes focus on writing on the plate-glass window of my room. The letters are in reverse, for whoever's on the outside coming in, and I have to puzzle them out in the right direction.

COVID +

Someone is holding my hand, squeezing tight. It takes all my strength to turn my face.

He is dressed like he's an astronaut, gowned and gloved, with a thick white mask covering his nose and mouth. Behind the plastic shield he wears, tears stream down his face. "You're going to be okay," Finn says, crying.

He is not supposed to be here.

He tells me that he begged a nurse to let him in, because even though I am in his hospital I am not his patient, and right now no visitors are allowed in the ICU. He says I gave everyone a hell of a scare. I've been on the ventilator for five days. He tells me that yesterday, when they dialed down the ventilator for a spontaneous breathing trial, my numbers on the gas looked good enough to extubate me.

None of this information fits into my brain.

Another nurse sticks her head into the room and taps her wrist—time's up. Finn strokes my forehead. "I have to go now before someone gets in trouble," he says.

"Wait." My voice is a croak. I have so many questions but the most important one blooms. "Gabriel."

Finn's brows draw together. "Who?"

"In the water, with me," I force out. "Did he . . . make it?" I pull air into my battered lungs; it feels like breathing broken glass.

"A lot of Covid patients experience delirium when they're taken off the vent," Finn says gently.

A lot of *what*?

"It's normal to be confused when you've been sedated for so long," he explains.

I'm not confused. I remember all of it—the current that swept me out to sea, the salt burning my throat, the moment I let go of Gabriel.

I clutch at the white sleeve of Finn's doctor's coat, and even that small motion is exhausting. "How did I get here?"

His eyes cloud. "Ambulance," he murmurs. "When you passed out brushing your teeth I thought I—"

"No," I interrupt. "How did I get back from the Galápagos?"

Finn blinks. "Diana," he says, "you never went."

TWO

TWELVE

Later, I would learn that when you want to take someone off a ventilator, you use the acronym MOVE to gauge readiness: mental status, oxygenation, ventilation, and expectoration. You want the blood vessels in the brain to be receiving and perfusing oxygen, so that the patient can process information and respond. You want the oxygen level to top 90 percent, and you want the patient to be able to overbreathe the ventilator. You have to make sure she can cough, so that she will not choke on her own spit when the tube is removed.

To determine this, a spontaneous breathing trial is done. First the patient is switched to pressure support mode, to see how much of a breath she is capable of taking. Then comes a spontaneous awakening trial, to see if the patient can wake up when the amount of sedatives being pumped into her veins is lessened. Finally, the pressure support is turned off to do a spontaneous breathing trial. If the patient can maintain low carbon dioxide levels, then she is ready for extubation.

This process is called a sedation vacation.

It is, according to my nurse, Syreta, the only vacation I've been on.

I am alone most of the time, but it seems there is always someone hovering outside my door, peering in. The next time Syreta comes in, I ask why, and she tells me that I'm a success story—and the staff has had precious few of them.

Syreta tells me that it's normal to feel wrung out. I can't sit up on my own. I am not allowed to eat or drink—I have a feeding tube down my nose, and will until I pass something called a swallow test. I am wearing a diaper. Yet none of this is as upsetting as the fact that everyone keeps telling me *this is real:* the moon-suited medical team, the wonkiness of my body, the television reports that schools and businesses are all closed and that thousands of people are dead.

Yesterday, I was on Isabela Island and I almost drowned.

But I'm the only person who believes that.

Syreta doesn't even blink when I tell her about the Galápagos. "I had another patient who was convinced there were two stuffed animals on her windowsill, and every time I left the room, they waved at her." She raises a brow. "There weren't any stuffed animals on her windowsill. She didn't even have a *window*."

"You don't understand . . . I *lived* there. I met people and made friends and I . . . I climbed into a volcano . . . I went swimming—Oh!" I try to reach my phone, on the table in front of me, but it is so heavy that it slips out of my hand and Syreta has to fish in the blankets to hand it to me. "I have pictures. Sea lions and blue-footed boobies I wanted to show Finn—"

I use my thumb to scrub across the screen, but the last picture on my phone is of Kitomi Ito's painting, from weeks ago.

That's when I notice the date on the screen.

"Today can't be March twenty-fourth," I say, the thought rolling like fog through my mind. "I've been away for two months. I celebrated my birthday there."

"Guess you get to celebrate again."

"It wasn't a hallucination," I protest. "It felt more real than any of this does."

"Honestly," Syreta mulls. "That's a blessing."

The Covid ICU is like a plague ward. The only people allowed to enter my room are my doctor, Syreta, and the night nurse, Betty;

even the residents who do rounds talk to me from outside the plate-glass wall. There are too many patients and not enough medical staff. Ninety-nine percent of the time, I am alone, trapped in a body that will not do what I need it to do.

I keep watching through the window, but I am the bug trapped in a jar—peered at occasionally by people who are mostly just grateful I am no longer sharing their space.

I am so fucking thirsty and no one will give me water. It feels like I have been in a wind tunnel for days, unable to close my mouth. My lips are chapped and my throat is a desert.

I still have oxygen being piped into my nose.

I have no recollection of getting sick.

What I do remember, vividly and viscerally, is the sparkle of the rock walls of the trillizos, and how the dock in Puerto Villamil smells of fish and salt, the taste of papaya warm from the sun, and the soft curves of Abuela's voice rounding out Spanish words.

I remember Beatriz, sitting on the beach with wet sand dripping from her fist.

I remember Gabriel treading water in the ocean, grinning as he splashed me.

Whenever I think of them, I start to cry. I am grieving people who, according to everyone here, never existed.

The only explanation is that in addition to catching this virus, I have gone insane.

I realize, when I try to breathe in and can't, when I feel the heaviness of my broken body, that I should believe everyone who tells me how sick I've been. But it doesn't feel like I was sick. It feels like my reality just . . . changed.

I've read about people who are medically sedated, and wake up fluent in Mandarin when there is no Chinese family history and they've never traveled to China; about a man who came out of a coma, demanded to have a violin, and went on to become a virtuoso who played sold-out concerts. I always took accounts like these with a grain of salt, because honestly, they sound too crazy to be true. I may not have a new linguistic or musical skill, but I would stake my life on the fact that the memories I have of the past two months are not delirium. I *know* I was there.

Wherever *there* was.

When I start to get so agitated that my pulse rate spikes, Betty comes into the room. It is telling that I am so grateful to see another human being in the same room with me that I begin to wonder if acting sicker means I will not be alone as much.

"What happens when you don't get enough oxygen?" I ask.

She looks immediately at my pulse ox numbers, which are steady. "You're fine," Betty insists.

"Now," I clarify. "But clearly, I was bad enough that I needed a vent, right? What if it messed my brain up . . . permanently?"

Betty's eyes soften. "Covid fog is a real thing," she tells me. "If you're having trouble stringing thoughts together or remembering the end of a sentence before you finish speaking it, that's not brain damage. It's just . . . an aftereffect."

"The problem isn't *not* remembering," I say. "It's that I *do* remember. Everyone is telling me I've been in the hospital and that I have Covid but I don't have any recollection of that. All my memories are of me in a different country, with people you're all telling me are make-believe." My voice is thick with tears; I don't want to see the pity on Betty's face; I don't want to be thought of as a patient who doesn't have a grasp on reality. What I want is for someone to fucking believe me.

"Look," Betty says, "why don't I page the doctor on call? That's what intensivists are for. Someone who's come through the kind of experience you have is likely to experience some PTSD; and we can get you some medication to take the edge off—"

"No," I interrupt. "No more drugs." I don't want to lose these memories because of a pharmaceutical that makes me a zombie. I don't want my mind erased.

Since I sort of feel like it already *has* been.

When I refuse to let Betty call in the doctor, she suggests that we try to reach Finn. She uses my phone to FaceTime him, but he doesn't pick up. Ten minutes later, though, he knocks on the glass outside my room. Seeing him there—seeing someone who cares about me—I am flooded with relief. I wave, trying to get him to come in, but he shakes his head. He mimes holding a phone to my ear, and then flags down Betty in the hallways. She comes inside to hold my own cellphone for me, because my arms are too weak.

"Hey," Finn says softly. "I hear the patient is rowdy."

"Not rowdy," I correct. "Just . . . frustrated. And really, really lonely."

"If it's any consolation, isolation must be doing wonders, because you look better already."

"You liar," I murmur, and through the glass, he winks.

This is real, I tell myself. *Finn is real.*

But I feel the concavity of that statement, too: Gabriel is not.

"Finn?" I say. "What if I can't tell the difference anymore between what was a dream and what wasn't?"

He's silent for a moment. "Have you had . . . any more . . . episodes?"

He doesn't want to say the word *hallucination,* I can tell. "No," I reply. What I don't say is that every time I've closed my eyes today I have expected to return to where I was yesterday.

I want a do-over, even as my conscience reminds me this *is* one.

"Your nurse said you were getting a little worked up," Finn says.

Tears spring to my eyes. "No one will tell me anything."

"I will," he vows. "I'll tell you anything you want to know, Diana."

"I don't remember getting sick," I begin.

"You woke up in the middle of the night with a headache," Finn says. "By the next morning, you had a fever of a hundred and three. Your breaths were so shallow, you were panting. I called an ambulance to bring you here."

"What about the Galápagos?" I ask.

"What about it?" he says. "We decided not to go."

Those five words wipe clean all the noise in my mind. Did we?

"Your pulse ox was seventy-six, and you tested positive," Finn continues. "They took you to a Covid ward. I couldn't believe it. You were young and healthy and you weren't supposed to be the kind of person who could get this virus. But the biggest thing we know about Covid is that we don't know anything about it. I was reading everything I could, trying to get you into trials for drugs, trying to figure out how even six liters of air pushed through a cannula to you couldn't raise your pulse ox. And meanwhile, all around me, I had patients on vents who weren't ever coming off them." He swallows, and I realize that he's crying. "We couldn't keep you lucid," Finn says. "They called me to tell me they needed to intubate you *now*. So I gave them the go-ahead."

My heart hurts, thinking of how hard that must have been.

"I'd sneak in whenever I could, sit by the bed, and talk to you— about my patients, and about how fucking scary this virus is, and how I feel like we're all just shooting in the dark and hoping to hit a target."

Those sporadic emails from him, then, weren't really emails.

"I bullied your medical team into proning you—putting you on your belly, even on the vent. I read where a doctor on the West Coast had success with Covid patients by doing that. They thought I was crazy but now some of the pulmonologists are doing it, because what the hell, it worked for you."

I think about all the time I spent at Concha de Perla, floating facedown with a mask and snorkel, peeking into a world undersea.

"I'd be working—rounding on my own patients, whatever—and I'd hear the call for codes, and every time, every *goddamn* time, I would freeze and think, *Please God, not her room*."

"I . . . I've been here ten days?" I ask.

"It felt like a year to me. We tried to bring you out of sedation a few times, but you weren't having it."

Suddenly I remember the vivid dream I had when I was in the Ga-lápagos: Finn, not costumed as I had assumed, but wearing an N95 mask like everyone else here. Telling me to stay awake, so he could save me. The woman I pictured beside him, I realize now, was Syreta.

There is one overlapping part of both realities, I realize. "I almost died," I whisper.

Finn stares at me for a long moment, his throat working. "It was your second day on the vent. Your pulmonologist told me that he didn't think you'd last the night. The vent was maxing out and your O-two levels were shit. Your blood pressure bottomed out, and they couldn't stabilize you." He draws a shuddering breath. "He told me I should say goodbye."

I watch him rub a hand over his face, reliving something I do not even recall.

"So I sat with you . . . held your hand," Finn says softly. "Told you I love you."

One tear streaks down my cheek, catching in the shell of my ear.

"But you fought," he says. "You stabilized. And you turned the corner. Honestly, it's a miracle, Diana."

I feel my throat get thick. "My mother . . ."

"I'm taking care of everything. Your only job is to rest. To get better." He swallows. "To come home."

Suddenly there is a code blue over the loudspeaker and Finn frowns. "I have to go," he says. "I love you." He runs down the hall, presumably to the room where one of his patients is tanking. Someone who is not as lucky as me.

Betty takes the phone away from where she's been holding it to my ear with her gloved hand. She puts it on the nightstand and a moment later presses a tissue gently to the corner of each of my eyes, wiping away the tears that won't stop coming. "Honey, you're through the worst of it," she says. "You have a second chance."

She thinks I'm crying because I nearly lost my life.

You don't understand, I want to tell her. I *did.*

Everyone keeps telling me I have to focus on getting my body back in shape, when all I want to do is untangle the thicket of my mind. I want to talk about Gabriel and Beatriz and the Galápagos but (first) there is no one to listen to me—the nurses spend quick, efficient moments in my room changing me and giving meds before they step out and have to sanitize and strip off their gear—and (second) no one believes me.

I remember how isolated I felt when I thought I was stuck on Isabela, and wonder if that was some strange distillation of my drugged brain filtering what it is like to be a quarantined Covid patient. I was alone a lot in the Galápagos, but I wasn't lonely, like I am here.

I haven't seen Finn for a whole day.

I can't read, because words start to dance on the page and even a magazine is too heavy for me to hold. Same with a phone. I can't call friends because my voice is still raspy and raw. I watch television, but every channel seems to carry the president saying that this virus is no worse than the flu, that social distancing should be lifted by Easter.

For endless hours I stare at the door and wish for someone to come in. Sometimes, it's so long between visits from nurses that when Syreta or Betty arrive, I find myself talking about anything I can seize upon, in the hope that it will keep them with me a few minutes longer.

When I tell Syreta that I want to try to use the bathroom, she raises a brow. "Easy, cowgirl," she says. "One step at a time."

So instead I beg for water, and I'm given a damp, spongy swab that's moved around my mouth. I suck at it greedily, but Syreta takes it away and leaves me thirsty.

If I'm good, she promises, I can have a swallow test tomorrow and my feeding tube might come out.

If I'm good, physical therapy will come in today to assess me.

I resolve to be good.

In the meantime, I just lie on my side and listen to the beep and whir of machines that prove I'm alive.

Even though I'm alone, when I soil my adult diaper, my cheeks burn in humiliation. I scrabble for the call button. The last time I needed to be changed (my *God*, even thinking that embarrasses me) it took forty minutes for Syreta to come. I didn't ask why she was delayed; it was written all over her face: disappointment, exhaustion, resignation. Sitting in my own mess just doesn't compare to another patient who's crashing.

To my relief, this time the door opens almost immediately. But instead of my day nurse, the most beautiful man I've ever seen walks into my room. He is young—early twenties—with raven-black hair and eyes so blue they are like looking into the sky. Beneath his mask, his jaw is square; his shoulders are wide, and his biceps strain the sleeves of his scrubs. "Need something?" he says.

I feel like I'm going to swallow my tongue. "I . . . um. You're not Syreta."

"I definitely am not," he agrees. I can tell he is smiling from the way his eyes crinkle, but I bet beneath that mask and shield he has perfect teeth. "I'm Chris; I'm a certified nursing assistant."

"Why?" The word springs from my mouth before I can stop it. This man could be a movie star, a model. Why would he choose to be in a Covid ward taking care of contagious people who can't wipe their own bottoms?

He laughs. "I actually like the work. Or I did, before it became a potential death sentence." His cheeks darken above his mask with a fierce blush. "I'm sorry," he says quickly. "I didn't mean to say that out loud."

I imagine how, in another time or place, patients might have requested him when they wanted to be moved from the bed, or lifted into a wheelchair.

Those arms.

Suddenly I am blushing as much as he is, because I remember why I pushed the call button.

"So, what can I do for you?" Chris asks.

My voice dries up. I weigh the thought of sitting in this disgusting diaper against the mortification of telling him why I needed help.

Apparently, he is also psychic, or accustomed to women making idiots of themselves around him. Because he just nods briskly, as if we've had an entire conversation, and efficiently moves to the supply cabinet to extract a fresh diaper. He gently pulls down the bedding, rips the elasticized side panels of the diaper, and swiftly cleans me before getting me sterile and swaddled again. The whole time, I keep my eyes closed, as if I could will away this entire experience.

I hear the swish of debris in a trash can and water being run and the snap of new elastic gloves. "All set," Chris says lightly. "Anything else?"

Before I can answer, another person comes into the room. I haven't seen two human beings in the same space with me since I was extubated, and Finn was there. This is a tiny woman who is swathed in PPE, like everyone else. "Stop hogging the patient," she says. "It's my turn."

Chris winks at me. "See you later," he says.

The woman watches him leave. "Hot CNA," she muses, "is sex on legs."

"His name is Chris," I reply.

She raises a brow. "Oh, I know." She walks toward the bed. "I'm Prisha. I'm a physical therapist."

"Nice to meet you," I say.

"We've met, kind of. When you were sedated, I moved your limbs around so your joints and muscles would stay healthy." She shrugs. "You're welcome."

"I want to go to the bathroom," I tell her. "I mean, not now. But when I have to."

She nods. "That's a great goal. But you've been on a vent for five days, so we have to see how you're moving, and how you'll respond to being upright, first." Prisha draws one of my arms over my head, encouraging me to take a breath. Then she does this with the other arm. I can feel my rib cage expanding. She gives me a few breathing exercises to try, and I do, until I cough. "We can try to get out of bed, but to do that, we're going to need a second set of hands and a blood pressure cuff," Prisha says.

"Please," I beg. "The bathroom?"

She narrows her eyes, as if assessing me. Then she calls in Chris, the CNA, again. Prisha helps me roll and lowers my legs off the bed. With Chris's help, she gets me to a sitting position. Prisha slides an arm around me, and at the embrace, I almost gasp. Everyone else— even Finn, that first night—is tentative about coming close to me, as if my skin itself is contaminated. To have someone touch me, so willingly and without fear, nearly brings me to tears.

Everything hurts as I move it, but I am driven. I do not want Chris wiping my ass again.

"Why," I grind out, "is this so hard?"

"You're lucky," Chris says, from my other side. "The other post-vent Covid patients—and there aren't many—have a lot of complications. Renal failure, heart failure, encephalopathy, pressure ulcers . . ."

Prisha interrupts him just as I'm starting to get panicked hearing about complications I haven't even anticipated. "Okay," she says. "Let's try sitting up on your own for a few seconds."

Sitting? I'm not an invalid; it's only been a few days. "I just need help standing. I haven't been in the hospital that long—"

"Humor me," Prisha says, and she removes her arm so that I have to support myself upright.

For about fifteen seconds, I do.

Then everything swims. Around me, inside me. Being vertical feels like hurtling through space. I see stars, start to tip forward, and Chris's strong arms catch me and gently lower me back onto the bed.

Prisha looks down at me. "You've been effectively paralyzed for nearly a week. When you sit up, all the blood rushes down from your head because the muscles around the blood vessels have been on hiatus and need to remember how gravity works. Baby steps, Diana. You almost died. Cut your body a break."

I feel exhausted, like I have run a mile. I think about how, on Isabela, I would swim or run or snorkel for hours without getting tired.

But then again, that was fake.

Prisha tugs the blanket up around me. "I've got patients who can't even manage five seconds," she says, patting my shoulder. "Fifteen seconds today. Tomorrow's going to be better."

When Prisha and Chris leave, I watch them through the plate-glass window, stripping off their PPE and stuffing it into special bins for Covid-exposed gear.

The sound of my own failure pounds like a headache. I reach for the smooth plastic tail of the TV remote, fishing it closer. It slips out of my hand twice before I manage to drag it onto my belly and turn the TV on.

The channel is CNN. "At least 215 million Americans are under shelter-in-place orders," the anchor says. "At this point, the United States has surpassed China and Italy for most known cases worldwide, with over 85,000 cases and 1,300 deaths."

My mother being one of them.

"One of the hardest hit locations is the New York City area. A hospital official in Queens said that they have only three remaining ventilators, and that if this continues into April, patient care may have to be rationed. Bodies are being stored in freezer trucks—"

I smack at the remote until I hit the button that turns the TV, blessedly, off.

Twice, I see a ghost.

She comes into my room so quietly that at first I am not sure what wakes me. She moves in the shadows and is gone soundlessly before I can even blink her into focus.

So the third time I am waiting. She is a dark blur of activity at the edges of the room, and I turn toward the disturbance and narrow my eyes. An older woman with dark hair and darker skin, who is holding her own shadow in one fist.

"Hello," I whisper, and she turns. She looks startled.

"Are you real?" I ask.

Like everyone else, she is masked and gloved and gowned. She points to the trash can. I realize, then, that what she holds is just a black plastic bag. That she is an essential worker who's come to clean the room.

"What's your name?" I ask.

She says, haltingly, "No English."

I tap my chest. "Diana," I say, then point to her.

"Cosima," she replies, and she bobs her head.

It strikes me that nobody willingly connects with either of us. Cosima, because she is beneath the notice of the medical staff; me, because I'm a walking potential death sentence.

"I don't know what's real anymore, and what's not," I confess to Cosima, as she wipes down the faucets and the sink basin.

"I've lost time," I tell her. "And people. And maybe my mind."

She pulls the bag out of my garbage can and knots its neck. She nods and takes away my trash.

There aren't clocks in hospital rooms, and your sleep keeps getting disturbed, and the lights never really go out fully, so it's hard to get a sense of time passing. Sometimes I am not sure if hours have gone by, or days.

Instead, I begin to count the spaces between the fits of coughing that leave me spent and exhausted. My lungs may have rallied enough to take me off a ventilator but they aren't anywhere near being healthy. When I start coughing, I can't stop; when I can't stop, I gasp for air; when I'm gasping, the edges of my vision turn dark and starry.

It's exactly what it felt like when I thought I was drowning.

When it happens again, I press the call button, and Chris the Hot Nursing Assistant comes in. He sees me struggling to breathe and adjusts the bed so I am sitting up. He takes a suction tube, like the kind from the dentist, and slips it into my mouth. What comes out makes me think of hoarfrost, little crystal shards, that I've coughed out of my chest. No wonder I can't breathe, if this is what's inside me.

"Okay," Chris soothes. "Now, try to even out those breaths."

I cough again, my ribs seizing and my eyes watering.

"In . . . and out. In . . . out," he says. He grasps my hand firmly and looks into my eyes. I don't blink. I hold on to his gaze like a lifeline.

My gasps level out. Chris squeezes my fingers, an acknowledgment. But I still can't keep that tickle from my throat, that urge to cough, from taking over. "Just match me," he instructs, exaggerating his breathing so that I can follow along.

It takes a few moments, but eventually, I am doing my best to breathe along with him.

A few more moments, and I find my voice again. Now that I am breathing, he will leave. And I don't want to be alone again. "Are you single?"

"Are you asking?" He laughs.

I shake my head. "I have a boyfriend. But one day, you're going to make someone an incredible partner."

He smiles, clasping his other hand over our joined ones. Just then, the door opens, and as if I've conjured him, Finn enters in his PPE.

"Since you just lit up like a Christmas tree," Chris says, "I'm guessing this is the boyfriend."

"Dr. Colson," Finn corrects, narrowing his eyes.

Chagrined, Chris drops my hand. "Of course," he says, and he glances at me. "Just breathe," he reminds me, winks, and slips out of my room.

Finn sits down in the chair Chris has vacated. "Should I be jealous?" he asks me.

I roll my eyes. "Yes, because the first thing I'm thinking about after almost dying is cheating on you."

The sentence hasn't even left my mouth before I feel a furious blush on my cheeks.

With the exception of how Finn and I met, I haven't really had a chance to see him in his professional mode. It's impressive to see him cut a swath through the hospital, but the way he just used his title to bully Chris makes me cringe a little . . . even though I should probably be flattered by the fact that he was possessive.

What he said or did, though, pales by comparison to the fact that he's *here*. He's in my room; he's not on the other side of the glass; I'm not alone. It makes me giddy. "Where have you been?"

"Earning our rent," he says. "But I missed you."

I reach out my hand to touch him. Just because I can. "I missed you, too."

I want him to take off his mask; I want to see his whole face as if everything between us is normal. But I also know that he's already taking a risk being in this room with me, even trussed up in all that gear.

It strikes me that Covid isn't the only thing that can take your breath away.

I remember the first time I saw Finn in a suit instead of scrubs—on an official date, waiting for me at a table at an Italian place in the Village. When I came in, late because of subway delays, he stood up and the room narrowed to the size of just us. I had to actively remember to draw in air.

A week later, in the middle of a heated kiss, his fingers found the strip of skin between my sweater and my jeans. It was like being branded, and all the breath rushed out of me in a sigh.

Months into our relationship as I reached for him in the dark, I remember thinking how lovely it was to have a body you knew as well as your own. How he gasped when I touched him the way he liked; how *I* gasped at the miracle of knowing exactly what that was.

Suddenly I realize how lucky I've been to have had Finn with me when I got sick. If he hadn't realized that I passed out from a lack of oxygen; if he hadn't gotten me to the hospital—well, I might not be sitting here now. "Thank you," I say, my voice thick. "For saving me."

He shakes his head. "You did that yourself."

"I don't remember any of it," I tell him. "I don't even remember being in the hospital before going on the vent."

"That's normal," Finn says. "And that's what I'm here for." The corners of his eyes crinkle, and I think that of all the horrible things about the masks everyone has to wear, this must be the worst: it is so hard to tell when someone is smiling at us. "I'll be your memory," he promises.

A part of me wonders how his recollection could be any less faulty than mine. For one thing, he wasn't here the whole time. And, in my mind, neither was I.

There are experiences our brains probably forget on purpose, so we don't have to suffer through them again. But there are experiences our brains remember that serve as some kind of red flag or warning: *Don't touch that stove. Don't eat that rotten food.*

Don't leave your boyfriend in the middle of a pandemic.

"The last thing I remember is you telling me I should go on vacation without you," I say quietly.

He closes his eyes for a moment. "Great. That's the part I was hoping you *wouldn't*," Finn admits. "You were pretty pissed at me for saying that."

"I . . . was?"

"Uh, yeah. You asked how I could even suggest that, if I really believed things were going to get so bad here."

In other words, everything I had felt in the Galápagos.

"You said clearly we had very different interpretations of a relationship. You kept talking about *Romeo and Juliet* and how if Romeo had just stayed in Verona, all the rest of the bullshit wouldn't have happened." He looks at me, confused. "I had no idea what you were talking about. I've never read it."

"You've *never* read *Romeo and Juliet*?"

Finn winces. "You said that, too." He looks at me. "You accused me of caring more about the money we were going to lose on the vacation and less about you. You said if I really loved you, I wouldn't let you out of my sight when all hell was breaking loose. The truth is, I made a mistake. I spoke without really thinking it through. I was tired, Di. And scared about working here, and taking care of patients who had the virus, and—" His voice breaks, and he bows his head. To my shock, I see that he's crying.

"Finn?" I whisper.

Those beautiful blue eyes, the color of his scrubs, the color of the sea in a country I never flew to, meet mine. "And I'm probably the one who brought it home to you," he forces out. "I'm the reason you got sick."

"No," I say. "That's not true—"

"It is. We don't know a lot, but it's pretty clear some people are carriers and they never show symptoms. I work in a *hospital*." He spits out that last word, and I realize he is nearly bowed over with the guilt he's been carrying. "I almost killed you," Finn whispers.

"You don't know that," I say, squeezing his hand. "I could have caught this at work or on the subway—"

He shakes his head, still steeped in remorse. "I was so tired that night that I didn't want to fight anymore. I didn't try to stop you when you went to bed early, and you were already asleep when I turned in for the night. When you woke up in the middle of the night to get some Tylenol I heard you and I pretended to be asleep, because I was afraid to pick up where we left off. And then the next morning, when I wanted to apologize, I could barely wake you up." He turns away, wiping his eyes with the shoulder of his scrubs.

Other things that leave you breathless: love so big that it tumbles you like a wave.

"I almost lost you. If I ever needed a lesson that saying goodbye isn't something you do casually, I sure as hell got one." Finn brings my hand to his cheek, laying my palm along it, leaning into my touch. "I will never ask you to go anywhere without me again," he says softly. "If you swear to me you'll never leave."

I close my eyes and see two blue-footed boobies, bobbing and weaving in an ancient dance, then snapping at each other's beaks.

They're going to kill each other.

Actually, they're going to mate.

My eyes fly open, my gaze fixes on Finn. "I promise," I say.

The intensivist comes to see me. His name is Dr. Sturgis, and Finn doesn't know him very well; he only started in the ICU at New York–Presbyterian at Christmas. He runs down my list of medications; he says my oxygen levels are improving. He asks me if I have any questions.

I am careful not to talk to Betty or Syreta about my memories of the Galápagos, because the response always involves Xanax or Ativan, and I don't want any more pharmacological interference in my mind. But contrary to what they've said in passing about how the hallucinations patients have on ventilators fade away, mine have not. If anything, they've been honed sharper and more brilliant, because I revisit them when I am alone in my room for hours on end.

"The . . . dreams," I say to the intensivist. "The ones I had while I was on the ventilator. They aren't like any other dreams I've ever had." I force myself to continue; this is a physician, he can't dismiss my concerns as foolish. "I'm having a hard time believing they're not real."

He nods, as if he's heard this before. "You're worried about your mental state."

"Yes," I admit.

"Well. I can tell you there's a physical explanation for anything that doesn't make sense. When you're not oxygenating right, your mental status changes. You have trouble interpreting what's actually happening to you. Add to that pain meds and very deep sedation— it's a recipe for all kinds of delirium. There are even some scientists who think that the pineal gland, under stress, produces DMT—"

"I don't know what that is."

"It's the main ingredient in ayahuasca," Dr. Sturgis says, "which is a psychedelic drug. But that's still just a theory. The truth is, we don't really know what happens when we medically sedate someone, and how your mind syncs your reality with your unconscious. For example, at some point, you were likely restrained—most of the Covid patients on vents try to rip out their IVs otherwise. Your brain, in its drugged state, tried to make sense of the insensible, and maybe you hallucinated a scenario in which you were tied down."

What I hallucinated wasn't confinement, but freedom. Now that I'm constrained again it chafes. I want to wander to Sierra Negra. I can still smell the sulfur. I can feel Gabriel's hand on my bare skin.

"Neurons fire and rewire during a near-death experience," the doctor says. "But I can promise you, it was just a dream. A particularly three-dimensional one, but still a dream." He looks down at my chart. "Now, your nurse says you're having trouble sleeping?"

I wonder why everyone's answer involves more medication. This will be Tylenol PM or zolpidem or something that will knock me out. But that's not what I want. It's not that I can't sleep; it's that I don't *want* to.

"Is it because you're worried about having more hallucinations?" Dr. Sturgis asks.

After a moment, I nod. I can't admit the truth: I'm not afraid of revisiting that other world.

I'm afraid that if I return there, I won't want to come back.

I am moved to a step-down unit that isn't the ICU, which means I no longer have Syreta or Betty or the Hot CNA taking care of me. Instead, I am now in the ward I was in when I was first brought to the hospital, the one I don't remember. The nurses here are flat out, with more patients to attend to. It is impossible for Finn to sneak in to visit me here, because he's stationed in the Covid ICU and he's not allowed elsewhere due to safety protocols.

If anything, I feel even more isolated.

There are a *lot* of codes on this floor.

I realize that the vast majority of patients who move from this space to the ICU do not return. That I am the anomaly.

When a speech therapist comes in to see me, I am so grateful to interact with someone that I don't want to tell her I can already talk—even if it's raspy. Sara reads my mind, though, and says, "Speech therapy isn't just about talking. You're getting a swallow test. We'll try different consistencies of food to make sure you don't aspirate. If you pass, you get to have your NG tube removed."

"You had me at *food*," I answer.

By now, I can sit up for nearly a half hour without getting dizzy, which is what makes me eligible for this swallow test. I dutifully sit with my legs swung over the side of the bed. Sara scoops some ice chips onto a spoon and places them on my tongue. "All you have to do," she says, "is swallow."

It's hard to do on command, but it almost doesn't matter, because the ice melts in the heat of my mouth and drips blissfully down, quenching my raw throat. As I do it, Sara holds a stethoscope up to my throat and listens. "Can I have more?" I ask.

"Patience, young grasshopper," Sara says, and I give her a blank look. "You millennials," she sighs, and she holds a cup with a straw to my lips. I suck up a mouthful of water, which is just as satisfying.

By the time we move on to applesauce, I am in heaven. When Sara moves to take the little dish from me I curl around it, hoarding, and hurriedly scoop another spoonful into my mouth.

I graduate to a graham cracker, which requires chewing—muscles that my jaw has to actively remember how to use. Sara watches my throat work. "Good job," she says.

I wait until I am sure no crumbs remain. "It's so weird," I muse. "To have forgotten how to eat."

She resettles the oxygen cannula into my nostrils as I lean back in bed again. "You'll have plenty more practice. I'm going to give the green light for the feeding tube to be removed. Tomorrow, you get to eat a whole meal while I watch."

A half hour later, a nurse I haven't seen before comes in to remove the nasogastric tube. "I cannot tell you," he says as he works quickly and efficiently, "how glad I am to see you again."

I try to read the name on the badge clipped onto his lanyard. "Zach?" I ask. "Did you take care of me before?"

He holds a hand to his heart. "You don't remember me. I'm crushed." My eyes fly to his, but they're dancing. "I'm *kidding*. But clearly, I'm going to have to up my game."

I rub the bridge of my nose, itchy without the tape adhering the feeding tube. "I don't . . . I don't remember being in this ward."

"Totally normal," Zach assures me. "Your O-two levels were so low you kept passing out. I'd be surprised if you *did* remember."

I watch him briskly wash his hands in the sink and towel-dry before snapping on a new pair of gloves. He seems competent and kind, and he holds a part of my history I may never recover. "Zach?" I ask quietly. "Would it be a surprise if I remembered things . . . that didn't happen?"

His eyes soften. "Hallucinations aren't uncommon for people who are sick enough to be in an ICU," he says. "From what I've heard, Covid patients are even more likely to have them, between the lack of oxygen and the deep sedation and the isolation."

"What you've heard," I repeat. "What else have you heard?"

He hesitates. "I'll be honest, you're only the second patient I've had who has gone to the ICU and survived to talk about it. But the other one was a man who was absolutely convinced that the roof of the hospital opened up like the Superdome, and twice a day light would shoot out of it, and one lucky person would be chosen to be lowered from a crane into that beam of light and get instantly healthy."

I probe the corners of my mind for hallucinations that are hospital-based, like this, but cannot find any.

"I was in the Galápagos," I say softly. "I lived on the beach and made friends with local residents and swam with sea lions and picked fruit right off the trees."

"That sounds like an awesome dream."

"It was," I say. "But it wasn't like a dream. Not like anything I've ever dreamed when I'm asleep anyway. This was so detailed and so real that if you put me on the island, I bet I could find my way around." I hesitate. "I can see the people I met like they're standing in front of me."

I watch something change in his eyes, as he puts on his professional regard. "Are you still seeing them now?" Zach asks evenly.

"You don't believe it was real," I say, disappointed.

"I believe *you* believe it was real," he says, which isn't an answer at all.

Although I am still testing Covid-positive—which Finn assures me is normal—he lobbies to get me out of the step-down Covid ward as fast as possible, because if you're in the hospital long enough you wind up getting sick with something else—a UTI, hospital-acquired pneumonia, *C. diff.* I feel ridiculous being in a rehabilitation unit when I'm not even thirty, but I also realize that there's no way I'm ready to go home yet. I still haven't managed to do more than sit upright in a chair, and even that took Prisha and a Hoyer lift for the transfer. I can't get myself to the bathroom.

To qualify for rehab, you have to be able to tolerate three hours of therapy a day. Some of it is physical therapy, some occupational, and for those who need it, speech therapy. The silver lining is that I will see people again. The therapists are completely covered in PPE to keep them safe, but at least three times a day I will have company.

And the more time I spend with people, the less time I spend replaying my memories of Isabela.

I am moved into a small room with a private bathroom, and I haven't been there for more than a half hour when the door opens and a tiny hurricane with red hair and snapping blue eyes blusters in. "I'm Maggie," she announces. "I'm your physical therapist."

"What happened to Prisha?" I ask.

"She doesn't leave the hospital; I don't leave the rehab unit. It's theoretically a single building, but it is like there's a special force field between us." She grins; there is a sweet gap between her front teeth. "Big Star Wars fan here. You watch *The Mandalorian*?"

"Um, no?"

"The guy's hotter with his helmet on," she says. She has approached the bed and already has stripped back the covers; her hands are firm and strong on my feet as she rotates my ankles. "My kids got me into that show. I have three. One came back home from college because of Covid. I can't believe it. He's a freshman; I thought I'd just gotten rid of him." She says this with another smile as she moves to my arms, pulling them over my head. "You got kids?"

"Me? No."

"Significant other?"

I nod. "My boyfriend is a surgeon at the hospital."

She raises her eyebrows. "Ooh, better be on my best behavior," she says, and then she laughs. "I'm just kidding. I'm gonna put you through the paces like I do everyone else."

As she moves my limbs as if I'm a rag doll (which, to be fair, I might as well be), I learn that she lives on Staten Island with her husband, who is a policeman in Manhattan, plus her displaced college student, as well as a seventh grader who wanted to be a nun last week but has, as of Tuesday, decided to convert to Buddhism, and a ten-year-old boy who will grow up to be either the next Elon Musk or the Unabomber. Maggie says she's already had Covid, which she's pretty sure she contracted while volunteering to sew costumes for her son's elementary school play, which is about a *T. rex* afraid to tell its parents it is vegan, which is what you get when you take your retirement fund and apply it instead to a private school for the gifted and talented. She talks about her apartment building, and the constantly rotating stream of morons who live just below them. One started feeding a skunk on the fire escape. After he was evicted, a woman moved in who slipped a note under their door, asking if they'd have objections to her putting in a skylight in her ceiling—which, of course, was Maggie's floor. She keeps me so busy laughing that I do not realize I've maxed out my physical capacity until every muscle in my body is screaming.

Finally, she stops stretching my arms and my legs. I collapse against the bed, wondering how I can be so exhausted from someone else doing the motions for me. "Okay, sunshine," she says. "Time for you to sit up."

I push myself upright, swinging my legs over the side of the bed. It takes a lot of effort and concentration, so at first I don't notice Maggie sliding a recliner wheelchair closer. She takes off one arm, locks the wheels, and then puts a board as a bridge from the bed to the chair. I look at it, then down at my unfamiliar body. "Oh hell no," I say.

"If you do it, I'll get you a Popsicle. I know where the stash is."

"Not even for a *Fudgsicle*," I mutter.

Maggie folds her arms. "If you can't transfer to a chair, you can't get to the bathroom. If you can't get to the bathroom, you can't leave rehab."

"I can't get in that chair," I tell her.

"You can't do it *alone*," Maggie corrects.

She leans in front of me and uses all of her compact body for me to lean into as she slides my butt onto the edge of the board. Then she shifts my legs a bit, then leans forward again to help me amass the strength to creep sideways on the board. We do this a few more times until I am seated in the chair, and then she pops its arm back on.

I am sweating and red-faced, shaking. "Orange," I grind out.

"Orange what?"

"Popsicle."

She laughs. "Double or nothing. Can you kick your leg out for me? Yeah, like that. Ten times."

But ten times with the left leg leads to ten times with the right. And then come toe tapping and arm lifting. When Maggie asks me to grip the armrests and try to lift my body weight an inch, I can't even budge a finger.

"Come on, Diana," Maggie urges. "You got this."

I can't even raise my head from the back of the chair. I could sleep for a week. "Rehab," I say, "is staffed by sadists."

"True," Maggie agrees. "But when you're a dominatrix, the pay is shit."

At that, I start to sob.

Immediately, her demeanor changes. "I'm sorry. I crossed a line. My mouth just doesn't know when to stop—"

"I was on a vent for five days," I wail. "Five *fucking* days. How could I get this bad this fast?"

Maggie crouches down in front of me. "First, it's not as bad. Not compared to some others I've seen—people who've been on a vent or ECMO for months; people who have suffered through amputations. It may feel ridiculous to you to sit in a chair and tap your toes, but that's how you're eventually going to walk out of here. I promise you, these are small things, with exponential benefits." She meets my gaze fiercely. "You can be pissed at your body, or you can celebrate it. Yes, it sucks that you got Covid. Yes, it sucks that you were on a vent. But a lot of people who did the same aren't going home, and you are. You can look at this situation and feel bitter, or you can choose not to be negative. Most adults don't have many firsts left to them—but you get to experience yours all over again." She takes a deep breath. "Give me two weeks, and your body will belong to you again."

I narrow my eyes. I look down at my lap and grit my teeth. Then I grab the sides of the chair, squeeze, and start to push myself up.

"Atta girl," Maggie says.

It is after a session of occupational therapy—which involves me taking off and putting on clothes, and during which I decide that socks are the work of the devil—that I see the news story: a funeral director in Queens, talking about how backed up they are for cremations; how you can pick up the ashes of your loved one with contactless delivery.

It makes me think, again, that being sore from all this therapy is not the worst that could happen, but rather the best. The majority of people in the Covid ICU ward will only come out of it in a body bag.

Instead of ringing for help, I cantilever my body upright so that I can reach for my phone, which sits on the table hovering across my bed. After I've hauled my body weight around, the phone feels light as a feather—an improvement since yesterday.

I do not want to make this call, but I know I have to.

I dial the main switchboard of The Greens. "Hello," I say, when I am connected to the business office. "I'm Diana O'Toole. My mother, Hannah, was one of your residents. I've been sick in the hospital, but I wanted you to know that once I'm discharged I can pick up her things. If you need to put someone else in the room, you can store—"

"Ms. O'Toole," the director of the facility says. "Are you saying you want to move your mother from our facility?"

"I . . . what?"

"I can assure you she's being well taken care of. I know that there have been a lot of care facilities in the news recently because of Covid, but we have had zero cases here and we're maintaining a level of vigilance—"

My heart starts galloping in my chest. "Zero cases," I repeat.

"Yes."

"My mother is alive."

The director hesitates. "Ms. O'Toole," she says gently, "why would you think otherwise?"

The phone drops out of my hand, and I bury my face in my hands and burst into tears.

What else didn't actually happen?

If my mother is alive, if I was never in the Galápagos, are there other things I believed as fact that aren't necessarily true?

Like . . . do I still have a job?

I find myself logging in to my email, something I've avoided, because my eyes still have trouble focusing on a tiny screen and the number of unread messages is so high it makes me feel like I'm about to break out in hives.

But before I can even begin to do a specific search for work emails, a text pings from Finn, with a Zoom link and an emoji heart. It's been two long, endless days that I haven't seen him or talked to him, because he's been at work, so I immediately log on. It is the first time I've seen him without a mask, and there are bruises along the bridge of his nose. His hair is wet; he is freshly showered. His face lights up when I join the call.

"Why didn't you tell me my mother was alive?" I blurt out.

He blinks, confused. "Why *wouldn't* she be?"

"Because when I was . . . sedated I thought she died."

His breath gusts out. "Oh my God, Diana."

"I saw her on a FaceTime call, fighting to breathe," I tell him. "And then she . . ." I can't say it. I feel like I'll jinx this unexpected resurrection. "I asked you about her, when I first woke up. You said you'd take care of everything. So I assumed that meant you *knew* what had happened. That you'd been talking to the memory care place and the funeral home and everything."

"Well," he says tentatively, "silver lining, right?"

"When I thought she'd died, I didn't feel anything. I thought I was a monster."

"Maybe you didn't feel anything because on some unconscious level you knew it wasn't real—"

"*It felt real,*" I snap, and I swipe at my eyes. "I want to visit her."

"Okay. We will."

"I think I need to go by myself," I say.

"Then that gives you even more incentive to get better," Finn replies, gentling his voice. "How's rehab?"

"Torture," I say, still sniffling. "Every inch of me aches and my bed has plastic under the sheets so I'm sweating bullets."

"You won't be there that long," he says confidently. "It usually takes three times as long to get back to where you were after you're intubated. So that would be fifteen days for you."

"My physical therapist said two weeks."

"You've always been an A student," Finn says.

I peer through the screen at his face. "Did someone punch you?" I brush my finger along the orbital bones of my own face, mirroring where his is bruised.

"They're from the N95 mask," Finn says. "That's how tight they have to be fitted to keep us safe. I don't even notice it anymore. Of course, that's probably because I'm always wearing the damn mask."

All of a sudden, I am ashamed. I jumped all over Finn the minute the call connected, all but accusing him of not being more clear that my mother was healthy. Of course he couldn't have known that I'd be doubting this. Plus, given the limited exposure I've allowed my mother in my life, she would not be anywhere near Finn's first, fifth, or even fiftieth topic of conversation after I awakened from a medically induced coma. "I haven't asked about your day," I say. "How was it?"

Something in Finn changes, like a shade being drawn down, not to keep me out but to protect him from having to see what he doesn't want to revisit. "It's over," Finn says. "That's about the best thing I can say about it." He smiles at me, and his eyes light again. "I thought maybe both of us could use a little treat right now."

I snuggle down further in bed, curling on my side so that the phone is propped on the pillow beside me. "Does it involve a bath? Please tell me it involves a bath."

He laughs. "I was thinking more like . . . porn."

My jaw drops. "What? No! Someone could walk in here any minute . . ."

Finn starts typing, sharing his screen, and a moment later the Zillow website loads. "I didn't specify what *kind* of porn," he says.

I cannot help but grin. Finn and I have spent so many lazy Sunday mornings in bed with coffee and bagels and a laptop balanced between us, surfing through the real estate of our dreams. Most homes were out of our price range, but it was fun to fantasize. Some were just ridiculous—sprawling mansions in the Hamptons, a functional ranch in Wyoming, an actual treehouse in North Carolina. We would scroll through the pictures, scripting our future: *This screened porch is where we'll eat the saved piece of wedding cake on our first anniversary. This is the alcove room we'll paint yellow when we find out we're having a baby. This is the yard where we build her swing set when she's old enough. The carpet in this room has to go, because our Bernese puppy will pee on it.*

Finn loads a modest Victorian with an actual turret. "That's cute," I say. "Where is it?"

"White Plains," he says. "Not a bad commute."

The house is pink, with violet trim. "It's a little Hansel and Gretel."

"Exactly. Perfect for a fairy-tale ending."

He is trying so hard, and I am dragging my feet. So I throw myself into the game of it. When Finn clicks to the interior, I say, "That Aga stove will take us months to figure out. We may starve."

"That's okay, because look, there's a pantry the size of Rhode Island. We can stock it with ramen." He clicks again. "Three bedrooms . . . one for us, one for our daughter . . . but what are we going to do with the twins?"

"If you want twins, *you're* going to have to have them," I say.

"Look, a claw-foot tub. You always wanted one."

I nod, but all I can think about is that I cannot even stand in a shower; how on earth am I going to ever master climbing into a tub like that?

Finn is happily leading me on a virtual tour of the house, through the living room with the woodstove and the study that he can convert into a home office and the cute little hidden dumbwaiter that can be retrofitted as a liquor cabinet. Then he clicks on the basement, which has a dirt floor and feels uncomfortably ominous. The last room has an iron door and metal bars across it, like a jail cell. "This just took a turn," I murmur.

Finn scrolls again, and we are inside the room, which is papered in red velvet, with a padded floor and walls sporting whips and iron manacles. "Look, our own sex dungeon!" he proclaims, and at the sight of my face, he bursts out laughing. "Wait, you know what's the best part? This room is listed as the den." He pauses. "Den of *iniquity,* maybe."

I realize that, a few weeks ago, this real estate listing would have had me giggling for a full quarter of an hour. That I would have texted screenshots of it to Finn in the middle of the workday just to make him laugh. But right now, it doesn't feel funny. All I can think of is that whoever is selling that house had a whole hidden, secret life.

"You know," I say, forcing a smile. "I think physical therapy just caught up with me. I can't keep my eyes open."

Immediately, Finn pulls out of the screen share and looks at me with the assessing eyes of a physician. "Okay," he says after a moment, apparently finding whatever answer he needed to in my face. Then his mouth curls on one side. "Although this one might be snapped up off the market if we don't act soon."

I look at his beautiful, familiar face. The shock of blond hair that never stays out of his eyes, the dimple that flirts in only one cheek. "Thank you," I say quietly. "For trying to make it all feel normal."

"It will," he promises. "I know how hard it must be to have to re-learn everything. I know it seems like you've lost a whole chunk of time. But one day, you'll barely remember any of this."

I nod. And think: *That's what I'm afraid of.*

The next morning, after Maggie bullies me into standing with a walker in spite of my Jell-O legs, I call my best friend. Rodney picks up on the first ring. "My therapist says I shouldn't talk to people who ghost me," he says.

"I'm in the hospital," I tell him. "Well, rehab. I *was* in the hospital. With Covid. On a ventilator."

Rodney is silent for a beat. "The *fuck*," he breathes. "You are officially forgiven for not answering any of my texts and just ignore the part where I called you a faithless bitch. Jesus, Diana. How did you get it?"

"I don't know. I don't even remember getting sick."

I walk him through every detail Finn has given me, but it feels like trying on clothes that don't quite fit. Then I hesitantly ask, "Rodney? Did we really get furloughed?"

He snorts. "Yup. You should have seen that bloodbath—Eva and all the other senior staff bargaining to save their salaries. There was never any question that the rest of us were expendable. And let me tell you, an apartment in Dumbo isn't cheap. Not all of us have sexy surgeons pitching in to pay the rent."

"What am I supposed to do without a job?" I ask.

"The same thing everyone else in the United States is doing. You sign up for unemployment and bake banana bread and hope Congress gets its shit together to pass a stimulus plan."

"But . . . what did Sotheby's say? I mean, do we get our jobs back . . . eventually? Or do we start looking for new ones?"

"They didn't say shit," Rodney answers. "Just a lot of *circumstances beyond our control* and *we remain committed to the field of art sales* blah blah blah. Didn't you see the email?"

It is somewhere, I'm sure, buried under the 2,685 others I haven't read yet. I wonder why *this* detail of my sedation dream would be the one that turns out to be true. "Isabela didn't have internet service," I reply automatically.

"Who's Isabela?"

"Rodney," I say quietly, "I want to tell you something. But it's going to be hard for you to believe."

"Like, how hard? On a scale from bike shorts and blazers during Fashion Week to Lady Gaga's Meat Dress?"

"Just listen," I say, and I sketch my other life: my arrival on Isabela and the closed hotel and Beatriz self-harming and her broody father. My mother's death. The fierce and foolish night Gabriel and I spent together. The waves closing over my head.

When I finish, Rodney is silent. "Well?"

"I don't know what to say, Di."

I roll my eyes. "Rodney, I've seen you pass judgment on a five-year-old's unicorn backpack. You have thoughts. You always have thoughts."

"Mmm. It reminds me of something . . . oh, I know. Remember the guy who sleeps outside the Sephora on East Eighty-sixth? The one in the rainbow onesie who preaches End of Days?"

My face flames. "You're an asshole. I didn't make this up, Rodney."

"I know that," he says. "Because as it turns out, Isabela Island in the Galápagos did indeed close for two weeks, starting on March fifteenth."

"What?" I gasp. "How do you know that?"

"Gooooogle," Rodney says slowly.

"That's the day I got there, on the ferry. Or dreamed I got there. Whatever."

"Well, if you were running a high fever in the hospital that day, you probably weren't doing Web searches."

"Maybe it was in the background, on the television . . ."

"Or maybe," Rodney says, "it wasn't."

When I hear those words, my eyes fill with tears. I don't think I realized how much I needed someone to believe me.

"Look, baby doll, I got too many relatives who dabble in the occult to not give you the benefit of the doubt. Who's to say you didn't tumble into some fourth-dimension shit?"

"Okay, that sounds even more insane," I mutter.

"More insane than having an affair with a figment of your imagination?"

"Shut *up!*" I hiss, although no one but me has heard him.

"So the million-dollar question is: have you told Finn about your, um, extracurricular excursions?"

"He thinks it's a symptom from Covid, from the sedation on the ventilator."

Rodney pauses. "If it was real . . . even just to *you*," he says, "you're going to have to tell him."

I rub the heel of my hand between my eyebrows, where a dull ache has started up. "I can't even see him. He's working around the clock, and I'm not allowed to have visitors here. I feel like a leper. I can barely stand on my own feet, I haven't had a shower in so long I can't remember the date, and based on my experience trying to dress myself, bras may be a thing of my past. When I'm too tired to do therapy, my mind starts going in circles and I can't remember what's real and what's not and then I start panicking even more." I let out a shuddering breath. "I need a distraction."

"Girl, I have two words for you," Rodney says. *"Tiger King."*

Other things that happen on my second day in rehab:

1. I put on my own shoes and socks.
2. CNN reports that eighty percent of people on ventilators have died.

I am actively fighting against my own body. My mind is laser-focused, screaming things like *lift, hoist, balance.* My muscles do not speak the language. Like any other kind of dissonance, it's exhausting. The only good thing about working so hard during the day is that at night, I am so exhausted, I don't resist sleep. It fells me with blunt force, and I am too tired to dream.

I wonder, too, if the reason that I can fall asleep here the way I did not in the step-down ward is that I know every morning, Maggie will appear with a new torture device. I may not trust her with my physical progress yet, but I do trust her to bring me back to the real world.

On my third day, my occupational therapist, Vee, comes into the room and watches me struggle to squeeze toothpaste onto a toothbrush. It's something that I used to do without thought but now requires Zen focus. I finish brushing my teeth just as Maggie enters. She is pushing a weird, squat box, which she sets at the side of the room. "Time to stand," she says.

She glances around, her gaze landing on the walker she brought in for yesterday's dose of therapy. She sets it on the side of the bed. "Let's get up close and personal with Paul," she says.

"Alice." (We've been arguing about the best name for a walker, which is already a misnomer because I'm using it to stand, not move.) But I swing my legs over the side of the bed, and this time, I barely have to think to make it happen. Maggie wraps a belt around me, waits till she is sure I'm not dizzy, and helps me scoot to the edge of the bed. When I stand for thirty seconds, my legs don't quiver beneath me.

I look up at her, a smile spreading over my face. "Bring it on," I challenge.

"What did you tell me you wanted to do when you got here?"

"Leave," I say.

"And what did I tell you you needed to be able to do first?"

Vee, I realize, has not left the room but has instead shoved the weird little box that Maggie dragged in so that it is kitty-corner to Alice the Walker.

She flips the top up, and I realize it's a commode. "Ta-da," Maggie says.

Day four of rehab:

1. I transfer to a wheelchair by myself.
2. I wheel it into the bathroom and brush my teeth.
3. I get so tired, halfway through, that I put my head on the counter and fall asleep.
4. That is how a nurse finds me to tell me that, finally, I've tested negative for Covid.

Now that I'm no longer Covid-positive, Maggie tells me that for physical therapy I will go to the gym. She wheels me into the large space, where multiple patients are working with multiple physical therapists. It is almost shocking to see so many people in one place, after so much time in isolation. I wonder how many of these people had Covid.

She gets me settled on a mat and begins moving my arms and legs, assessing joint tightness and strength in my deltoids and biceps. The whole time, she is grilling me about my apartment. *Do you live with someone who's there full-time? Is there an elevator? How many steps from the elevator to your apartment? Are there carpets or throw rugs? Stairs?*

By the time she leads me to the parallel bars, I am grateful to concentrate on something other than rapid-fire questions. My mind still is foggy; I will start a sentence only to forget where it was going.

Maggie stands in front of me, belly to belly, with a wheelchair behind me. "Lift your left leg," she says.

I feel sweat bead on my forehead. "If I go down," I tell her, "you're going with me."

"Try me," Maggie challenges.

I am dizzy and terrified of losing my balance, but I lift my leg an inch off the floor.

"Now your right one," Maggie says.

I grit my teeth and try and my knee buckles. I collapse into the wheelchair, scooting back a few inches.

"That's okay," Maggie tells me. "Rome wasn't built in a day."

I look up at her. "Again," I demand.

She narrows her eyes and then nods. "Okay," she says, and she hauls me back up to my feet. "Let's start with a knee bend."

I do it, the world's ugliest plié.

"Now shift your weight to your left foot," she says, and I do. "Now. Lift your right leg."

My knee wobbles, and I have to clutch the bars in a death grip, but I do it.

"Good," Maggie says. "Now . . . march."

Left leg. Right. Left. Right.

I force myself to move in place. I am bathed in sweat now, and grimacing, and depending on the support of the parallel bars like they are an extension of my own skeleton. I'm so busy concentrating, in fact, that I do not realize I have advanced a foot.

Maggie whistles. "Look who's walking."

Vee tells me that if I can wash my own hair, she has a surprise for me. I cannot imagine anything better than the shower itself. Sitting on the little plastic stool, with water pounding against my skin, I begin to feel human again.

I feel like an Olympian when I bend down to get the shampoo bottle, squeeze some into my palm, and scrub my scalp. I don't fall off the chair. I hold my face up to the weak stream of water and think that this is better than any spa in a four-star hotel could ever be.

As I watch the suds spool down the drain, I think of all the things that I am washing away. This weakness. This fucking virus. The ten lost days I can't remember.

I felt like a failure in the hospital, dependent on tubes and medications and IVs and nurses to do every little thing I've done independently since I was a child. But here, I'm getting stronger. Here, I'm a survivor. Survivors adapt.

I am seized by a mental image of Gabriel gesturing toward a marine iguana. I find myself folding forward into the spray, closing my eyes against it.

I rap my knuckles on the side of the shower. "I'm done," I say thickly, wondering how long before I'm no longer ambushed by these memories. I hear the click of the door, and Vee comes in with a towel. She yanks open the plastic curtain and turns the faucet off. Not even being stark naked in front of her can rob me of the joy of finally being clean.

Vee watches me drag on my sweatpants and sweatshirt and then hands me a brush for my hair. I try, but the snarls and mats after all this time are impossible for me to deal with. She sits behind me on the bed and starts to pick through the knots, combing the hair back from my face.

"I think I'm in heaven," I tell her.

She laughs. "No, we're happy you *didn't* wind up there." Her fingers fly over my scalp in an intricate pattern. "I do French braids for my girls all the time."

"I never learned how."

"No?" Vee asks. "Your mama never taught you?"

I feel her weave and pull and twist. "She wasn't around much," I reply.

And now that she isn't far-flung and hightailing it all over the world, I haven't been around her much, either.

That could change.

I have always believed we are the architects of our own fates—it's why I so carefully planned my career steps and why Finn and I dreamed in tandem about our future. It is also why I could blame my mother for choosing her career over me—because it was just that: a decision she *made*. I have never really subscribed to the mantra that things happen for a reason. Until, maybe, now.

If I was so sick that it nearly cost me my life . . . if I was one of only a handful to survive ventilation . . . if I returned to this world, instead of the one embedded in my mind . . . I would like to believe that there is an explanation. That it isn't random or the luck of the draw. That this was a lesson for me, or a wake-up call.

Maybe it is about my mother.

Vee ties the braid off with a rubber band. "There," she says. "You're like a whole new person."

Not yet.

But I *could* be.

She pulls over a wheelchair and sets the brakes and then positions Alice nearby so that I can do the stand-pivot-transfer move to seat myself. "I believe I promised you a surprise," Vee says.

It's probably a trip down to the multipurpose gym to do more physical therapy. "Do we have to?" I ask.

"Trust me," Vee says, and she opens the door to my room.

She gives me a surgical mask and pushes me down the hallway, past patients who are carefully moving behind their own walkers or with four-footed canes. A couple of the nurses smile at me and comment on my appearance, which makes me wonder how terrible I looked before. Instead of heading into the elevator, though, Vee turns right at the end of the hallway and hits an automatic door button with her elbow, so that a glass panel slides open. She rolls me into a tiny courtyard that is walled in by four sides of the hospital building. It's unseasonably warm, and the sun falls in an amber slant. "Fresh air?" I gasp, tilting my face, and that's when I see him.

Finn stands at the far end of the narrow courtyard, holding a little bouquet of tulips.

"I think you can take it from here, Doc," Vee says, and she winks at me and slips back inside.

Finn stares at me, and then unloops his mask so that it dangles from one wrist. The bridge of his nose is still dark and bruised, but my God. To see that smile.

I cry out, frustrated by my inability to get to him, and as if I've willed it, Finn is at my side a second later. He kneels, his arms coming around me. "Look who tested negative," he says.

I unhook my mask and set it in my lap. "You read my labs?"

He grins. "Professional perks."

Finn rests his forehead against mine. He closes his eyes. I know that this moment is too big for him, too. To hold him, to be held. It is as if I've been trapped underneath ice, and suddenly, I'm back in a place where there is sound and warmth and sun.

"Hi," Finn whispers against my lips.

"Hi."

He closes the distance between us, feathering his mouth against mine, before pulling away with a stripe of pink on his cheeks, as if he knows I'm still recovering but couldn't help himself.

I wait for it, that last click of the lock, that satisfying final puzzle piece, that familiar sigh of reaching home.

This is where you belong, I tell myself.

"You were so lucky," Finn says thickly, as if he's struggling to push away the shadows of what could have happened.

"I *am* so lucky," I correct. I grab both sides of his face and press my lips to his. I show him that this is what I want, what I've always wanted. I consume him, to convince myself.

I steal his breath for safekeeping.

Since we aren't supposed to have visitors and Finn has bribed his way in with donuts for the staff, I get to spend only an hour with him in the courtyard. By then, it's getting colder, and I'm getting tired. He helps me hook my mask over my ears again, wheels me back to my room, and tucks me into bed. "I wish I could stay with you," he murmurs.

"I wish I could *go* with you," I tell him.

He kisses my forehead. "Soon," he promises.

He leaves me with a reusable grocery bag full of books—books that I asked him to bring to the front desk for me, before I knew he would be able to deliver them in person. They are the guidebooks on Ecuador and the Galápagos that I had used to plan our trip.

Obviously, they are not in a missing suitcase somewhere. They've been on the kitchen counter all along, with our passports and our e-ticket confirmations, ready to pack.

I take a deep breath and open one.

Isabela is the largest island in the Galápagos and much of it is unreachable, due to lava flows and thorny brush and rocky, inhospitable shores.

Puerto Villamil remains relatively untouched by visitors; it's a tiny hamlet of sandy roads and homes bordered by cacti on one side and a gorgeous beach on the other.

I've highlighted some of the sights that I wanted to make sure Finn and I saw:

The path to Concha de Perla leads to a protected bay with good snorkeling.

After passing several small lagoons with flamingos, the turnoff to the Tortoise Breeding Center is marked.

A two-hour walk from Playa de Amor will take you to El Muro de las Lágrimas—the Wall of Tears.

Around the half-submerged lava tunnels at Los Túneles, the water is sparkling and clear and home to a variety of marine species.

One after another, I read about the places I visited while I was unconscious and watch them blossom into fully dimensional memories full of sound and color and scent.

I put the book on the nightstand and pull Finn front and center in my mind. I think about how his hair felt, sifting through my fingers. How he smelled of pine and carbolic soap, like he always does. How his kiss wasn't a discovery, but the reassurance that I had been on this journey before and knew where to go, what to do, what felt right.

That night, I don't let myself fall asleep.

Rodney is angry at me because we are supposed to be watching reruns of *Survivor* together on our phones and live-texting our predictions about who will be voted off the island, but I keep drifting off, trying to catch up on the rest I'm not getting.

Hello? he texts. *Are you dead?*

. . .

Too soon?

The last ding wakes me up, and I read his messages. *Very funny,* I type.

Imma find a new bff in NOLA.

Rodney is moving to his sister's house in Louisiana, because he can't afford his rent in the city. That sobers me. We are in lockdown, I know, and I'm likely the last person anyone wants to be in close contact with, but the thought of not seeing Rodney again before he moves makes something shift in my chest.

Sorry. I won't fall asleep again. I swear.

On my tiny phone screen I watch a contestant who is a preschool teacher climb into a barrel to be maneuvered through an obstacle course to win some peanut butter.

#claustrophobia, Rodney types. *Remember when you got locked in that vault at work and lost it?*

I take this to mean I've been forgiven for napping.

I didn't lose it, I just freaked out a little, I lie. *Plus I've crawled down a tunnel that was as wide as my hips.*

Like hell you did. Proof?

I hesitate. *On Isabela,* I write.

For a moment I watch those three dots appear and disappear while Rodney figures out what to say.

Suddenly the *Survivor* screen freezes and a FaceTime call pops up. I answer it and Rodney's face swims into view. "I don't know if it counts as conquering your fears when you do it unconscious," he says.

"Definitely a blurry line."

He regards me for a long moment. "You wanna talk about it?"

"It's a place called the trillizos. They're like these gopher holes into the middle of the earth. I guess tourists rappel down them."

He shudders. "Give me a beach and a frozen marg."

"Beatriz brought me there the first time, and the second time, she ran away and I crawled down to try to save her."

"How come she needed saving?"

"She kind of found me in bed with her father and it didn't go well."

Rodney hoots with laughter. "Diana, only you could hallucinate yourself into an ethical mess."

At that word—*hallucinate*—something in me shutters. Rodney notices, and his eyes soften. "Look, I shouldn't have said that. Trauma is trauma. Just because someone else hasn't experienced it themselves doesn't make it any less real to you."

Maggie has talked to me about other patients who have come off ECMO or the vent who suffer from PTSD. I have some of the same symptoms—that fear of falling asleep, the panic attacks when I start to cough, the obsessive checking of my pulse ox numbers. But I can still feel what it was like to have water fill my lungs as I drowned, too. In the middle of the night, my heart pounds in my throat and I'm right back in the tunnel I shimmied down looking for Beatriz. I am having flashbacks of experiences everyone here tells me I never had, and now—more than a week after being weaned off any sedation drugs—they still haven't gone away.

"Maybe I shouldn't talk about it," I mull out loud. "Maybe that's only going to make it harder in the long run. It's just . . ." I shake my head. "Remember that guy who came into Sotheby's convinced that he had a Picasso and it wasn't even a fake or a forgery—it was a flyer for a shitty band, and he was completely delusional?"

Rodney nods.

"I get it now. To him, that was a goddamn Picasso." I pinch the bridge of my nose. "I don't know why it hasn't just . . . gone away. Or why I can't wrap my head around it being a detailed, incredibly weird dream."

"Maybe because you don't want it to be?"

"If the reality is that I nearly died, then sure. But it's more than that. These people were *so real.*"

Rodney shrugs. "For a smart girl, you're a dumbass, Di. You're holding a phone in your hand, aren't you? Tell me you've Googled them."

I blink at him. "Oh my God."

"Yes, my child?"

"Why didn't I think of that?"

"Because you still can't do the word scramble puzzles that OT gives you, and your brain isn't firing right."

I pull up the search engine, Rodney shrinking to a little green dot in the background. I type *Beatriz Fernandez.*

There are results, but none of them are her.

The same happens when I type in Gabriel's name.

"Well?" Rodney asks.

"Nothing." But that's not surprising, given the fact that the internet there was so bad that social media profiles would be useless.

Unless the internet *isn't* bad there, and I just created that obstacle in my dream.

My head starts to hurt.

"Let me try something," I murmur.

I type in *Casa del Cielo Isabela Galápagos.*

Immediately, a picture loads of the hotel I had booked—it looks nothing like the one I visited in my imagination. But . . . it *exists.*

My thumbs fly over my phone again. *G2 TOURS.*

Tours/Outfitter, I read. And in red: *CLOSED.*

I suck in my breath. "He's real, Rodney. Or at least his company is."

"And you don't remember ever coming in contact with them before you went, like when you were planning the trip?"

I don't. But maybe my brain did.

"Hang on, Rod." I put my phone down, hoist myself up on Alice, and use the walker to make my way to the nightstand. There, I sit on the edge of the bed and pick up the guidebook I was reading the night before. Thumbing through the pages, I find the ones about Isabela Island.

I skim the categories: *Arrival and Getting Around.*

Accommodation.

Eating and drinking.

Tour operators.

The third one down: *G2 TOURS. Open M–Sun 10–4. Private land/water excursions, SCUBA certified.*

I did not highlight it. But I must have skimmed over it. My imagination clearly was working overtime to create a whole backstory and family around one tiny line item in a guidebook.

I shuffle back to the chair and pick up my phone again. "Gabriel's tour company is listed in the guidebook I read."

"He's mentioned by name?"

"Well . . . no," I say. "But why else would I have invented a place called G2 unless I'd seen something about it?"

"True," Rodney points out. "That's pretty basic. You'd probably have called it something like Happy Holidays or Galápagoing."

"Do you think that's all it was?" I ask him. "Do you think I unconsciously memorized all this while I was planning our vacation and somehow imagined it when I was on the vent?"

"I think there's a lot of stuff we don't know about the way the brain works," Rodney says carefully. "But I also think there's a lot of stuff we don't know about how the world works." He raises his brows. "Oh," he adds. "And get yourself a shrink."

Since the days in rehab bleed into each other, I mark time by progress. I stop using a death grip on the bars and instead graze my palm over them while I take steps. I graduate to using Alice the Walker, keeping my own balance and pushing it forward. Maggie helps by giving me verbal progress reports: "Yesterday I had to help you and you lost your balance three times, but today you're doing it all by yourself. Yesterday I was right next to you, today I'm within shouting distance." Vee brings me puzzles, word searches, and a deck of cards. I start by sorting cards by suit and color and number, and then move on to playing solitaire. She has me tie my own sneakers and braid my own hair. She makes me pull beads out of putty to finesse my fine motor skills, and by the next afternoon, when I text on my phone my fingers are flying the way they used to. She brings me to a fake kitchen, where I use my walker to move from dishwasher to cabinet, putting away plastic glasses and dishes.

On the twelfth day of rehab, I maneuver Alice into the bathroom, assess my balance, tug down my sweatpants, and pee on an actual toilet. I get to my feet, straighten my clothing, wash my hands.

When I step out into my room, Maggie and Vee are cheering.

There is a checklist of things I must be able to accomplish before I can leave rehab. Can I brush my hair? Can I walk with a device? Can I dial my phone? Can I go to the bathroom? Can I shower? Can I balance? Can I do light meal prep? Can I walk up and down steps?

On the day I'm discharged, Finn comes to take me home. "How did you get the day off?" I ask.

He shrugs. "What were they gonna do? Fire me?"

It's true, they need him too much right now to risk him leaving for good. Which reminds me I will be alone in the apartment when he goes back. Which makes me terrified.

Even though I've been able to walk for a few days—even trading up from Alice for a quad cane—the protocol for rehab is that I be wheeled out. I've packed my limited stash of clothing and toiletries and the travel guides in a small duffel. "Your chariot," Finn says, with a flourish, and I gently lower myself into the sling seat. I put on the blue surgical mask I've been given, and Finn sets the duffel on my lap.

Maggie comes rushing into the room. "I'd hug you if I could do it from six feet away," she says.

"You've been up in my face for weeks," I point out.

"But that was when you were a *patient*," she says. "I brought you a gift." She pulls out what she's hidden behind her back—a shiny new quad cane for me to take home. "Candis," she says, and I burst out laughing. *Candis Cayne.*

"Perfect."

"So much cooler than *Citizen*."

"For sure," I tell Maggie. "I'm going to miss you."

"Ah, fuck it," she says, and she gives me a quick, fierce hug. "I'm gonna miss you more."

She opens the door to my room and Finn pushes me into the hall.

It is lined with people.

They are all masked and gowned, with their hair restrained in surgical caps. And they are all staring at me.

Someone starts clapping.

Someone else joins in.

There is a rolling wave of applause as Finn wheels me past. I see tears in some of the eyes of the staff and I think: *They're not doing this for me. They are doing it for themselves, because they need hope.*

I feel my cheeks heat underneath my mask, with embarrassment, with unease. I am reentering a society that has moved one month ahead without me, a place where every emotion is now hidden— a casualty of safety.

I keep my eyes straight ahead. I am the world's loneliest soldier, limping back from war.

Getting home is an adventure. After I settle into the Uber, Finn squirts hand sanitizer into my palms and his, too. We lower the windows for ventilation even though it's only fifty degrees out, because he's read studies about aerosol transmission and viral droplets. Driving is eerie; the city is a ghost town. Stores are shuttered and the streets are so empty that we make record time. New York City is usually teeming with people—businessmen, tourists, dreamers. I wonder if they're locked in the high-rises or if, like Rodney, they've just given up and left town. I think about the Empire State Building and Central Park and Radio City, the iconic locations that stand resolute and lonely. I used to get so frustrated when the subways were packed solid or when Times Square was swarming with sightseers. I didn't realize how much I actually loved the congestion of Manhattan until I saw the alternative.

When we reach our apartment building, Finn hovers at my side until I shout at him because he's making me nervous. We have to wait for two elevator cycles before we get a car to ourselves, which Finn insists on, because not everyone is taking precautions as seriously as he is.

There was a time when I thought having an apartment at the end of the hall, away from the ding of the elevator, was a bonus, but now it feels Herculean to make it all the way there. Finn unlocks the door and helps me take off my coat and then immediately goes to wash his hands. He washes them like a surgeon, long minutes elapsing, scrubbing under his nails and up past his wrists. I follow his lead.

I see the pile of household bills that Finn's been too busy to pay and take a deep breath. All of this I can deal with tomorrow. The only thing I have to do now is remember how to live a normal life.

Finn carries my duffel into the bedroom and unpacks my things. "Are you hungry?" he asks.

"Can we get Thai?" I ask, and then I frown. "Is there still delivery?"

"If there wasn't I'd be dead by now," Finn says. "The usual?"

Spring rolls, satay, and massaman curry. I love that I don't have to tell him. I nod and glance toward the bathroom. "I'm going to take a shower," I announce, more to myself than to him, because there's a tub I have to lift my leg over. But I'm going to have to do it sooner or later, and it might as well be while Finn is home to help me if I wind up sprawled on the floor.

As it turns out, I do fine. I am so proud—and so grateful to smell like my own soap and shampoo, instead of hospital versions. I brush and braid my hair, thinking of Vee, and put on clean leggings and my softest sweatshirt.

When I come into the living room, Finn grins. "You clean up nicely."

"I really have nowhere to go but up."

I sit down on the couch and turn on the television, skipping quickly away from MSNBC to a rerun of *Friends*. "Have you watched *Tiger King*?" I call out.

"*Tiger* what?" Finn asks.

"Never mind." I remind myself that the whole time I've been fighting for my life, Finn has been fighting for other people's.

Suddenly he's standing in front of me, holding out a steaming mug. "What's this?"

"Hot milk."

"I don't like hot milk," I say.

Finn frowns. "You drank it the last time you were sick."

Because he'd made it for me without asking if I wanted it. Because his mom used to make it for him, when he was feeling under the weather. Because I didn't want him to think I wasn't grateful.

"I'm not sick," I tell him.

He looks at me skeptically.

"You're a doctor. You should know," I say. With a sigh I pat the couch next to me and set the mug on the side table. Finn sits down. "I know something really bad almost happened," I say quietly. "But it didn't. And I'm here. And I'm better."

I slide closer to him and feel him go still. Immediately, I pull back to look at Finn's face. "Are you worried you'll catch it from me?"

A shadow of pain crosses his face. "More like the other way around."

"If I just beat this motherfucker," I say, "my veins must be full of antibodies." I flex my arm. "I'm basically a superhero."

That, finally, makes him smile. "Okay, Wonder Woman."

I lean a little closer. "I wonder if antibodies are contagious."

"I can categorically tell you they're not," Finn says.

"I mean, just in case," I murmur against his neck. "Maybe we should try to get some into you." I loop my arms around his neck and press my mouth against his. Finn hesitates, then kisses me back. I slide my hands under his sweater, feeling his heart beat against my palm.

"Diana," he breathes, a little desperate. "You just got out of rehab."

"Exactly," I say.

I don't know how to explain to him that when you find out you nearly died, there is a crucial need—a compulsion, really—to make sure you're alive. I need to feel healthy and vital and desired. I need to burn with something that is not fever.

"Let me show you what I've learned," I say to Finn, and I pull my sweatshirt over my head. I shimmy my leggings down to my ankles and kick them off. "And watch this." I get to my feet, turn to face him, and sit down on his lap with my knees on either side of him. "Stand, pivot, transfer," I whisper.

Finn's arms come around me as I grind against him. It is a matter of moments before his clothes are off, before the feel of his skin against mine sets me on fire. Teeth and lips and fingertips, my nails on his scalp, his palms bracketing my hips. I sink onto Finn and he flips us so that I am lying on the couch, dissolving around him. I succumb to the here and the now, focusing on the symphony of our breath, the percussion of our bodies, the crescendo.

When the buzzer rings, we are both so surprised we roll onto the floor.

"Shit," Finn says. "Dinner."

He scrambles to his feet and I am jealous of his easy, unthinking movement. In his hurry, he pulls on my sweatshirt instead of his own, and it stretches too tight across his chest. As Finn hops into his boxers, I watch. "Don't forget the . . . tip," I say.

A laugh bursts out of him. "I *cannot* believe you said that."

He is back a few minutes later, holding a brown paper bag full of Thai food. He looks at me, almost shyly. "Hungry?"

"Starving," I say.

I watch him put the food on the counter, take out some disinfectant spray and paper towels, and start wiping everything down. "What . . . what are you doing that for?"

He blinks at me. "Oh, right. You don't know. It's for safety. You should use gloves, too, when you go to the mailbox, and let the mail sit for two days, just to make sure—"

"To make sure of what?"

"That there's no virus on it."

He washes his hands again vigorously as I stand up and walk toward him. "You know what has no virus on it?" I ask, and I pull his head back down to mine.

The food cools on the counter as we tangle ourselves on the couch. When I finally unspool in Finn's arms, I open my eyes to find him watching me. He brushes my hair off my face. "Something's different about you," he murmurs.

"I like being back here," I whisper.

What he likely thinks I mean: *not in the hospital.*

What I actually mean: *not wandering in my clouded, confused thoughts. In his embrace and wholly, blissfully present.*

Finn is, and always has been, my anchor.

We eat in our underwear, and make love again, knocking over the sanitized cartons of food. At some point, we stumble to the bedroom and crawl under the covers. Finn's arm comes around me, holding my back tight against his front. It's not the way we usually sleep—we have a king bed and we tend to retreat to our corners; I get cold too easily and Finn throws the covers off. But, oddly, I don't mind. If he is holding me tight, I can't disappear.

I wait until he falls asleep, until I feel his breath falling in even puffs on the back of my shoulder. "I have to tell you something," I whisper. "Everything I dreamed in the hospital? I think it was . . . real."

There is no response.

"I was in the Galápagos," I say, testing the words out loud. "There was a man there."

Almost imperceptibly, Finn's arm tightens around me. I hold my breath.

"As long as you know who you're really having sex with," he murmurs.

He does not let go of me. And I do not sleep.

THIRTEEN

The next morning when Finn leaves for work, we do not talk about what I said in the middle of the night. He asks me a hundred times if I'm all right here on my own, and I spackle a smile on my face and tell him yes, and then the minute he walks out the door I have a panic attack.

What if I trip and fall?

What if I cough so hard I can't stop?

What if there's a fire and I can't move fast enough?

All I want to do is call Finn and tell him to come back, but it's both selfish and impossible.

So instead, I take Candis into the kitchen with me, leaning on the quad cane when I have to balance to get a mug from the cabinet. I fill up the kettle with water and put it on the stove, moving slowly and deliberately. I grind enough coffee for the Aeropress and congratulate myself on doing all this without stumbling. I slosh hot coffee all over my hand on the way to the table, and the first day of the rest of my life begins.

In the past, when Finn wasn't working tirelessly through a pandemic, we'd spend our days off lingering over coffee, reading *The New York Times* and *The Boston Globe* online. Finn would read aloud highlights about politics and sports. I gravitated toward the arts pages, and the obituaries. It sounds morbid, but it was actually for work: I kept a running list on my computer desktop of those who might have collections to be sold posthumously at Sotheby's.

Of course, I don't have a job at Sotheby's now. I don't know when or if I will again. Finn says I shouldn't worry about that; he thinks we can make do on his salary for a while if we are careful. But I have a feeling there are financial hurdles we're going to face that we can't even imagine yet. We are only a month into this pandemic.

The first *New York Times* banner I read: NYC DEATH TOLL SOARS PAST 10,000 IN REVISED VIRUS COUNT.

The *Boston Globe* headlines are only marginally less anxiety-producing: CHELSEA'S SPIKE IN CORONAVIRUS CASES CHALLENGES HOSPITALS AND STATE; BOSTON SCIENTIFIC GETS OK TO MAKE A LOW-COST VENTILATOR.

I click on the link to the obituaries.

Couple married more than 75 years dies within hours of each other: After Ernest and Moira Goldblatt got married in the summer of 1942, they spent the rest of their lives together, right up until the very end. On April 10, the couple passed away at the Hillside Nursing Home in Waltham, less than two hours apart. Moira, 96, had recently tested positive for Covid-19. Ernest, 100, had been sick but his test for the disease was still outstanding. In an effort to reduce the spread of the virus, nursing home residents who were infected were transferred to a separate space. But there was no doubt that the Goldblatts would be staying together.

I click to turn the page and scan the names. I click again.
And again.
Again.
There are twenty-six pages of obituaries today in *The Boston Globe*.
With shaking hands, I close my computer.
There are already so many people who have lost someone, who'll

never receive another lopsided grin or smooth a cowlick or cry on a shoulder that smells like home. They'll always see the empty seat at a wedding, a birthday, breakfast.

Why did I survive, when those they loved didn't?

It's not like I did anything right—I don't even remember going to the hospital.

But it's also not like they did anything wrong.

I feel a crushing sense that if I am here, there has to be an explanation. Because the alternative—that this virus is random, that anyone and everyone could die—is so overwhelming that it is hard to breathe.

Again.

I'm not conceited enough to think that I am special; I'm not religious enough to think I was spared by a higher power. I may not ever know why I'm still here and why the people in the rooms on either side of me at the hospital are not. But I can pivot on this point of the axis, and make sure whatever happens from here on in is worthy of this second chance I've been given.

I just don't know what that looks like, exactly.

I reopen my computer, and type into Google: *Jobs in art business*.

A string of them pop onto my screen: Senior Business Development Manager, Artsy. Adjunct faculty, Institute of Art. Creative Director, Omni Health Corp. Art Director—Business Banking Division, JPMorgan Chase.

All look equally uninspiring.

I truly enjoyed my work at Sotheby's. I loved the people I met and the art I helped sell.

Or at least that's what I'd told myself.

I let my mind drift back to the last time I saw Kitomi and her painting.

If I got sick that night, and if asymptomatic people can spread the virus—could I have infected her?

Panicked, I look her up online. As far as I can tell, she is still alive and well in New York with her painting.

I remember how it felt to stand in the presence of that kind of artistic greatness. In front of that Toulouse-Lautrec, my fingers had itched for a brush, even though I was no Toulouse-Lautrec, no Van Gogh. I was a competent artist, but not a great one, and I knew it. Like my father, I could make a decent copy—but that's different from creating an original masterpiece.

I had grown up in the shadow of my mother's prize-winning photography. So instead of trying to create my own legacy—and failing—I reshaped my skill set to fit a field adjacent to art.

I erase one word in the search bar.

Jobs in art.

Fashion designer. Animator. Art teacher. Illustrator. Tattoo artist. Interior designer. Motion graphics designer. Art therapist.

Art therapy is the practice of incorporating visual art media to improve cognitive and sensory-motor function, self-esteem, and emotional coping skills for mental health treatment.

Immediately I am back on a beach in Isabela, making tiny dolls out of flotsam and jetsam and setting them in a sandcastle with Beatriz. I am writing our names on lava rocks and making them part of a standing wall. I am explaining to her why monks make beautiful mandalas and then brush the sand away.

I've already been thinking of another career, without even realizing it. I've practiced it, with Beatriz.

I rub my hand over my face. I imagine filling out an application for admission to a graduate program in art therapy, listing my imaginary experience in the field.

But maybe that's the point. Maybe the Galápagos wasn't something that happened, but something that is *supposed* to happen.

When it starts to feel like a chicken-and-egg logic bomb, I decide that I have done enough job searching for the day. Instead, I open up Instagram and see college friends giving thumbs-up on planes, cashing in on cheap vacation deals. Another friend has posted a picture of her aunt, who died yesterday of Covid, with a long tribute. A celebrity I follow is doing a fundraiser for Broadway Cares/Equity Fights AIDS. My former neighbor posts a teary video about postponing her wedding when they were totally going to do it in a *safe way*. It's like there are two different realities unfolding at the same time.

I do not post often on Facebook, but I have an account. When I open it, there are dozens of notifications from acquaintances: *Sending healing thoughts! I'm praying for you, Diana. You got this.*

Frowning, I click onto the post that inspired these comments. Finn must have logged in to my account, because he's written a short paragraph explaining that I have been hospitalized with Covid and put on a ventilator.

I tamp down the annoyance at the thought of him logging in as me.

The comments are supportive, effusive, heartfelt. Some are political, claiming that the virus is a hoax and I have the flu. Other friends attack that poster on my behalf. All this while I was unconscious.

On a whim, I type *Covid-19 survivors* into the search tab, and a string of articles comes up, as well as a list of support groups. Most are private, but I dive into one that is not and start reading through the timeline.

Has anyone else found their taste has changed? I used to love spicy, and now not so much. Plus, everything smells like bacon.

Sleep is impossible—getting migraines every night.

Am I the only one losing hair? I had long, thick curls and now my hair's super thin; how long will this last?

Hang in there, someone else has responded. *Mine's stopped falling out!*

Try zinc.

Try vitamin D.

Tested positive 3/11, tested positive again on day 10, still testing positive a month later—is it safe for me to be around people?

Question for the ones who have had Covid-19: have y'all been getting nosebleeds on just one side?

Can I get this virus again if I've already had it?

My doctor won't believe me when I say that I didn't have heart palpitations before . . .

I am getting more and more freaked out. What if leaving the hospital is only just the start? What if I have long-term effects that haven't even shown up yet?

And if I *don't* get them, is that something else to feel guilty about?

I am about to close my laptop, crawl back into bed, and give up when I see another post: *Anyone else who was on a vent have weird dreams/nightmares?*

I fall into this rabbit hole and start reading.

I was bike riding around town with my husband. Now, we don't bike ride, we're large people. We went to a crowded diner and he went inside to put our names down for a table. He was gone for a while. Finally I went in and started looking around. I asked the greeter if she'd seen him. She said no and I went back outside and one of the bikes was gone. When they took me off the vent I found out he had passed while I was under. I didn't even know until two weeks later.

I was in a hospital that was Broadway-themed, but in a bad way, like being trapped in It's a Small World at Disney, you know? Every hour everything stopped and there was a big musical revue. It was so crowded that I couldn't even be in the room to watch it. The only way to get anyone's attention was by hitting a buzzer, and if you did, the song changed to one of shame, because you weren't supposed to stop the performance.

I was in space trying to contact people to get help before I ran out of oxygen.

I was at an electronic dance festival and I was some kind of creature in a tank of water, and the people who came to the festival kept feeding me through tubes while I floated.

I was in a videogame and I knew that I had to beat the other players if I wanted to survive.

I was sitting at my childhood kitchen table and my mother was making pancakes. I could smell them so distinctly and when she brought them over with maple syrup I could taste that, too. When my plate was empty she put her hand on my shoulder and she told me I had to stay at the table because I wasn't finished. My mom's been dead for 32 years.

I can't remember anything clearly but it was SO REAL. Not like a dream with jump cuts, or how you're supposed to wake up the minute before you die. I could feel and smell and see ALL of it. And I died. A whole bunch of times over and over.

I was being kidnapped by the hospital staff. I knew they were Nazis and I didn't know why no one else could see that. When I woke up for real, they had tied my hands down because I kept trying to hit the nurses.

I was being held captive.

I was in a room that was crawling with bugs and someone told me that this was how you got Covid, and I shouldn't go near the bugs. But they were already covering me.

My brother and I were in a freight car and we had monitors on us that showed our heart rates going lower and lower because we didn't have enough air. There was all this garbage in there with us and I found a Christmas card and wrote HELP on it and told my brother to hold it through the slats in the car's wooden side.

I was tied to a pole and I knew I was going to be sold as a sex slave.

I was in the basement of NYU (I've never even been to New York City, so don't ask me why) and someone was trying to give me medicine and I knew it was poison.

I was locked in a basement and tied down and I couldn't get out.

I pause, thinking of my dream about Finn when I was in the Galápagos, or my not-dream, or whatever it was. It, too, had been in a basement. And I was tied down.

I dreamed that my four-year-old grandson, Callum, drowned. I went to the funeral with my daughter and helped her grieve and lived through her having two more kids, twin girls, Annabelle and Stacy. When I woke up for real, I asked her if I could see the twins and she thought I was crazy. She said the only grandkid I had was Callum, and sure enough he was alive and well.

I think about my mother's face, still and white on the iPad, her chest barely rising.

I read for hours, stopping only to eat leftover Thai food for lunch. There are hundreds of posts from people who have been delirious from lack of oxygen or who have, like me, survived ventilation. I read lush, sprawling dreamscapes. Some are terrifying, some are tragic. Some have common threads—the videogame scenario, the basement entrapment, and seeing someone who's died. Some stories are detailed, some are a scant few words. All are described as painfully, unequivocally real.

As one person in the Facebook group puts it: *If I'd never woken up, I wouldn't have been surprised. Everything I was seeing, feeling, EXPERIENCING was genuine.*

For the first time since I've awakened, I realize that I'm not crazy. That I'm not alone.

That if all my good memories of the Galápagos didn't actually happen . . . then neither did my bad ones.

Which is why, come hell or high water, I am going to visit my mother.

That day, Finn calls me three times from work. Once he asks if he left his phone charger in the bedroom (no). The second time he asks if I want him to pick up dinner on the way home (sure). The third time I tell him he should just ask me how I'm doing, since that's why he's really calling.

"Okay," he says, "how are you doing?"

"Not bad. I've only fallen once and I'm pretty sure that the burn on my hand is second degree, not third."

"What?"

"Kidding," I tell him. "I'm fine."

I do not tell him that I have been reading obsessively about other Covid survivors. Or that I am trying to figure out how to get to The Greens safely, given that I can barely walk the length of a city block without resting.

He tells me that he will check in again later, but he doesn't. I don't hear from him again till his keys jingle in the lock a full hour after he told me he'd be home. Immediately I get up and start toward him—I'm not even using Candis, just cruising on the furniture when I need a little extra support, and I want to show him—but before I can reach him he holds out his hand like a stop sign. He proceeds to strip off his clothes and stuff them into a laundry bag that he's wedged underneath the table by the door where we keep our phones and keys and wallets. When he's wearing only his boxers and a surgical mask, he edges past me in the hallway. "Just let me rinse off," he says.

Five minutes later he reappears, dressed and smelling of soap, his hair still wet. I am in the kitchen, awkwardly dragging a Clorox wipe along the wax paper of the two deli sandwiches he's brought home. I wonder if we will all die from ingesting cleaning solutions.

I scrub my hands thoroughly and bring the plates to the table. Finn immediately takes a giant bite and groans. "First thing I've eaten since this morning."

"So I shouldn't ask how your day was."

He glances at me. "This is the best part of it," he says. "What did *you* do?"

"Skydiving," I tell him. "Then a little light lion taming."

"Underachiever." His face lights up. "Wait. I have something for you."

He goes to the entryway and digs inside the backpack he carries to work, coming out with a sealed Ziploc bag. He pulls out a fabric mask, printed with sunflowers. "Thank you?" I say.

"An ICU nurse made it. God knows the last thing I'd want to do after a shift is sit down with a sewing machine, but it was really nice of her. I haven't had a chance to buy any reusable masks yet, and you can't wash the blue surgical ones."

"How does she even know about me?"

"She's the one who snuck me in to see you."

"I don't want to take your mask—"

"Oh, it's okay. Athena made me one, too. Without sunflowers."

His cheeks have gone pink.

"Athena," I repeat. "That's a real name?"

"Greek mom. Dad's from Detroit."

I wait for him to say, *She's sixty-five.* Or, *She's been married longer than we've been alive.* Or even to be amused by my jealousy. But Finn doesn't say anything else, and I put the mask down carefully beside my plate. "You seem to know a lot about her," I say.

"I guess that's how it is, when you're fighting against death together every day," Finn answers.

I am resentful of a woman who may have helped save my life. I am suspicious of Finn, even though I cheated on him in my dreams.

I force myself to swallow. "Please thank Athena for me," I say.

While Finn finishes his sandwich, I tell him about a tutorial I saw online today on how to make a homemade mask from the cup of a bra.

Finn smiles, and I achieve my goal: to see his shoulders relax and the tension release. I was the one who made this happen, and that's who Finn needs me to be.

If there's one thing we are both good at in this relationship, it's being predictable.

"I've been trying to remember getting sick," I say. "I know you said you'd tell me anything I want to know. Did I have a headache, before things started getting bad, or—"

"Diana?" Finn cuts me off, rubbing his temples. "Can we . . . just . . . not?" He looks up at me, his eyes pleading. "It's been a *day.*"

I abandon everything I was about to ask.

"How about a movie?" he says, realizing that he's shut me down. He stands and yanks me into his arms and buries his face in the curve of my neck. "I'm sorry," he whispers.

I comb my fingers through his hair. "I know," I say.

We settle onto the couch and turn on the TV, looking for something completely escapist. *Avengers: Endgame* is on and we are quickly absorbed. Well, Finn is. I mostly pepper him with questions like why Captain Marvel can't just use the gauntlet by herself. I do not realize at first that Finn is crying.

It's the end of the movie, and Pepper Potts is bent over Tony Stark, who's sacrificed himself to save the universe. She tells him they're going to be okay, and Tony just *looks* at her, because he knows that's not true, and she kisses him. *You can rest now,* she says.

Finn's shoulders tremble and I pull away to look at him. He sinks forward, burying his face in his hands, trying to stifle his sobs. I do not think, in all the years I've known Finn, I have ever seen him fall apart like this. It is scary.

"Hey," I say, touching his arm. "Finn, it's okay."

His hand shakes as he wipes it over his eyes. "They asked me to sign a DNR for you," Finn says. "I didn't know what to do. I came in and I sat with you and I told you that if you needed to go, it was okay."

You can rest now.

Maybe, in my sedated haze, I heard him. Maybe I rested, then fought my way back to the land of the living. But Finn, he hasn't had any time to rest.

He takes a shuddering breath and looks up at me sheepishly. "Sorry," he murmurs.

I lay my palm on his cheek. "You don't have to apologize."

He grasps my hand and turns his face to kiss it. "I didn't think this was going to happen quite like this," he says under his breath, and then he looks me directly in the eye. "I knew I wanted to spend my life with you. The thing is, I didn't really understand what that meant until yours nearly ended." He ducks his head. "I had a whole plan for how to do this—but I don't think I can wait—"

I rocket off the couch, yanking my hand from his. My fingers feel like ice. "I have to . . . use the bathroom," I blurt out, and I stumble away from him, closing the door behind me. Inside, I run the faucet and I splash water on my face.

I know what Finn was about to do. It is a moment I've dreamed about. So why can't I let it happen?

I am sweating and I am cold and shaking. I've known what I wanted for years. And now that it's here—

Now that it's here—

I'm not sure I'm ready.

I turn off the water and open the door. Finn is still on the couch, watching the television. His eyes are dry, and they track me as I sit down next to him. "What did I miss?" I ask, looking at the screen.

I can feel his stare on me. I think I hear him say, *Okay.*

There are topics, I guess, that neither of us is ready to talk about.

I settle myself under Finn's arm and lean into him again. After a long moment, I feel his words whispered against the crown of my head. "Maybe you should talk to someone. Like . . . a shrink."

I don't look at him. "Maybe I should," I say.

I focus on the television, as Tony Stark's ashes are set adrift on a lake.

I know that you can't run a marathon without training. And I can't get to The Greens if I can barely make it to the end of the hallway. So the next day I gather all my courage and go for a walk. The streets are empty. I move deliberately and slowly to the end of the block, where there is a wine and liquor store around the corner.

To my surprise, it's open. But then again, what business could be more essential?

When Finn comes home that night, I am nearly bouncing with excitement. "Guess what I did," I say, as soon as he finishes stripping and showering. From behind me on the couch, I hold up a bottle of red wine. "I walked all the way to the liquor store. And now we get to celebrate."

To my surprise, Finn doesn't seem happy. "You *what?*"

My smile falters. "I didn't break lockdown," I tell him. "We're allowed to go out for food." I look down at the bottle in my hands. "This counts, right?"

"Diana, you shouldn't have gone out by yourself," Finn says. He sits next to me, looking me over like he's expecting to find a bleeding head wound or a broken bone. "You just got out of the goddamn hospital."

"I got out of *rehab*," I say gently, "and I'm supposed to be challenging myself. Besides, I had to do it sometime. The toilet paper isn't going to buy itself."

This is not going the way it is supposed to. Finn should be pleased that I'm getting stronger, that I was brave enough to venture out alone. But at the same time, I realize that when Finn kisses me now, he always presses his lips to my forehead, too, like he's checking for a temperature. He watches me when I get up to go to the bathroom or into the kitchen, in case I fall.

I nestle closer until he's holding me. "I'm fine," I whisper. I wonder when he is going to stop treating me like a patient, rather than a partner.

"Promise me you'll wait for me if you need to leave the apartment?" he murmurs.

I hold my breath for a moment, because I can't take that oath. I'm heading to The Greens tomorrow, no matter what. "One day," I say gently, "you're going to have to let me go."

There is a theory of dementia called retrogenesis, meaning that we lose life skills in the reverse of the order in which we gained them. A doctor told me this when my mother was first diagnosed at age fifty-seven with early-onset Alzheimer's. A person with dementia, he said, starts out like a ten-year-old. She can be trusted to follow directions on a note that you leave behind. Eventually, the patient will suffer mental decline until she's at the stage of a toddler—she can't be expected to remember to get dressed or to feed herself. The next skills that are lost are continence, speech. The very first things we master as an infant are the last things we lose: the ability to lift one's head from a pillow. The ability to smile.

What I remember from that initial visit was asking the doctor how long my mother's life expectancy would be. *Most people with Alzheimer's survive from three to eleven years,* he told me. *But some have been known to live for twenty.*

And I had thought, at the time: *My God. What am I going to do with her for all that time?*

All of this was before I lost her/didn't lose her in a dream.

Although there is a lockdown in the city, I can easily argue why seeing my mother face-to-face is necessary. I know the trains are running, but decide to splurge on an Uber.

I haven't told Finn I'm going. I haven't told anyone.

When my ride arrives, the driver looks at me in my sunflower mask and I look at him in his KN95 mask, as if we are assessing each other for risk. He glances at my quad cane and I think about telling him that I actually just got over Covid, but that would be counter-productive.

At The Greens, to my surprise, the front door is locked.

I ring the bell, and knock a few times. After a moment, the door opens, revealing a nurse in a surgical mask. "I'm sorry," she says, "we're not open."

"But these are visiting hours," I reply. "I'm here for Hannah O'Toole."

The woman blinks at me. "We're closed by order of the *governor.*" She says this with judgment, like I should know better.

Which, I mean, I do.

"I've been away for a while," I tell her, which isn't a lie. "Look, I don't have to stay long. It's kind of a crazy thing—I was under the impression that my mother had passed away but—"

"I'm really sorry," the nurse interrupts. "But this policy is meant to keep your mother safe. Maybe you could . . . just call her?"

She closes the door in my face. I stand in the chilly breeze, leaning on my quad cane, thinking about her words. Normally, every few weeks, that's exactly what I do.

I am about to dial my mother's number when a car pulls into the parking lot. An elderly man gets out with a bag of birdseed. Instead of going to the front door, however, he walks around the side of the building. Near one of the patient's screened porches there is a bird feeder. He pours a little of the seed into it and then notices me watching. "I've been with her for fifty-two years," he says. "I'm not going to let a virus ruin a perfect record."

"You're visiting your wife?"

He nods.

"How?"

He jerks his chin in the direction of the porch. Like my mother's, it's a sealed box without an entrance—no one can enter the apartment from out here, but the resident can be outside in a safe way. A door slides open from inside the apartment, and an aide wheels out a woman. She has white cotton-candy hair piled on her head, and a blanket over her narrow shoulders. She is staring vacantly past the man.

"That's my Michelle," he says proudly. "Thank you!" he calls to the nurse, who waves and disappears back inside. He walks closer to the screen, pressing his hand against it. "How's my doll?" he asks, and the woman doesn't respond. "You have a good week? I saw a cardinal yesterday, at home. First one this year."

He doesn't even seem to notice or care that I'm eavesdropping as he talks to her. His wife is motionless, expressionless. It makes my heart hurt.

As I am about to leave, he starts singing in a clear tenor the Beatles song with her name as the title. *"Très bien ensemble,"* he says, *"très bien ensemble."*

Suddenly his wife sparks alive. "I love you, I love you, I love you," she says.

"That's right." A grin splits his face. "That's right, honey."

I hurry away around the corner, toward my mother's screened porch. I dial her phone number. A moment later, she answers. "Hi, it's Diana!" I say brightly. "It's so good to talk to you!"

Those sunny, bright inflections at the ends of my sentences, I know, are how she will figure out how to respond. It will have nothing to do with my name, or our relationship, which she doesn't remember.

"Hi," she says, tentative but upbeat. "How are you?"

"It's such a beautiful day," I say. "You should come out on the porch. I'm right here, enjoying the sunshine."

She doesn't respond, and to be honest, I don't even know if she can manage the sliding door onto the porch. But a moment later, she steps out into the little space, looking around like she can't remember why she went there.

I wave the hand that's not holding the phone. I rip my mask off my face. "Hi!" I say, almost desperately. "Over here!"

She sees me and walks to the edge of the porch. I do the same, and the phone falls away from my ear. She looks healthy and steady and all the things she was not in my dream. Unexpectedly, my throat is so tight I can't speak.

She flattens her hand to the screen and tilts her head. "Is it warm for this time of year?"

I know she has no idea what time of year it is, but this is her way of trying to pry open a conversation.

"It *is* warm," I manage.

"Maybe they'll let the fire hydrants run," she says. "My daughter loves that."

I am afraid to move, to speak, because I am afraid to ruin this moment. "She does," I say.

I move closer and press my palm against hers. There's a screen between us. *Where are you?* I wonder. The world that my mother inhabits, it's not this one. But that's not to say it isn't real to her.

It might be the first thing we've had in common.

If you had asked me a few weeks ago, I would have said my mother was a burden, an albatross, a grudging responsibility. She was someone I owed a debt to. But now?

Now I know everyone has their own perception of reality. Now I'm thinking that when we're in crisis, we go to a place that comforts us. For my mother, it's her identity as a photographer.

And for me—right now—it's *here*.

"You look good, Mom," I whisper.

Her vision clouds; I can see the exact moment that she slips away from me. I pull my hand back from the screen and tuck it into the pocket of my jacket. "I think I might come visit you more often," I say softly. "Would you like that?"

She doesn't respond.

"Me, too," I say.

When I get back to the parking lot, the old man is sitting in his car with the windows open, eating a sandwich. I order my Uber and awkwardly smile at him.

"Good visit?" he asks.

"Yes. You?"

He nods. "I'm Henry," he says.

"Diana."

"My wife, she's got white matter disease," he says. He taps his head, as if to underscore this is a brain thing. But then, everyone in the building has a brain thing. Alzheimer's affects the gray matter, not the white, but the outcome is the same.

"She only has three words left," he says. He takes a bite of his sandwich, swallows. Then he smiles. "But they're the three words I need to hear."

The sound of ambulance sirens is constant. It gets to the point where they become white noise.

In the middle of the night, I wake up and roll over to realize Finn is missing. I have to shake myself out of sleep to remember whether he's pulling a night shift. It's hard to tell time when every day is the same.

But no, we brushed our teeth together and climbed into bed. Frowning, I sit up and pad in the darkness to the living room, calling softly for him.

Finn sits on the couch, limned by moonlight. He is bent like Atlas, bearing the weight of the world. His eyes are closed and his hands are pressed tight against his ears.

He looks at me, his face bruised from his mask, shadows ringing his eyes. "Make it stop," he whispers, and it's only then I hear the whine of another ambulance, racing against time.

My therapy session with Dr. DeSantos—like everything else—is going to take place over Zoom. She has been recommended to Finn, and apparently is doing him a favor to schedule a session with me so quickly. When I ask Finn how he knows her, the tips of his ears go red. "She was made available to residents and interns," he says, "when a bunch of people started losing it during their shifts."

Finn is at the hospital during our session, for which I am grateful. I have not told him about my excursion to see my mother—I know he'll be angry that I went out. I have convinced myself it is kinder *not* to tell Finn.

I can convince myself of virtually anything these days, it seems.

"What you're talking about," Dr. DeSantos says, "is ICU psychosis."

I've told her about the Galápagos—haltingly at first, and then with more abandon when it became clear she wasn't going to interrupt. "Psychosis?" I repeat. "I wasn't psychotic."

"An elevated dream state, then," she points out. "Why don't we call them . . . ruminations?"

I feel a prickle of frustration. Rumination. Like what cows do.

"It wasn't a dream," I reiterate. "In dreams you do things like fly through walls or come back to life or breathe water like a mermaid. This was a hundred percent realistic."

"You were on an island . . . one you've never been to . . . and you were living with local residents," the doctor says. "That sounds pleasant. The mind is remarkable when it comes to protecting us from pain we might otherwise feel—"

"It was more than just a vacation. I was sedated for five days, but in my head, I was gone for months. I went to sleep dozens of times there, and I woke up in the same place, in the same bed, on the same island. It wasn't a . . . a hallucination. It was my reality."

She purses her lips. "Let's stick to *this* reality," she says.

"This *reality*," I stress. "What about this feels real? I lost ten days of my life that I can't remember, and when I woke up suddenly everyone is standing six feet away and we wash our hands twenty times a day and I lost my job and there's no more sports or movies and all the borders are closed and every time my boyfriend goes to work he runs the risk of catching this virus and winding up—"

I break off.

"Winding up . . . ?"

"Like me," I finish.

Dr. DeSantos nods. "You're not the only one with PTSD," she says. "Dr. Colson tells me that you work for Sotheby's?"

"Worked," I correct. "I've been furloughed."

"You know what surrealism is, then."

"Of course." It was a twentieth-century art movement that elevated the subconscious and the stuff of dreams: Dalí's dripping clocks and Magritte's *The False Mirror*. The whole point is for the art to make you uneasy, until you realize the world is just a construct. An image that doesn't make sense to you forces your mind to free-associate—and those associations are key to analyzing reality on a deeper level.

"The reason this all feels surreal is that we're in uncharted territory," the doctor says. "We've never been through something like this—well, at least most of us haven't. There aren't too many people who survived the 1918 Spanish flu who are currently alive. Humans love to find patterns and to make sense of what we see. When you can't find those patterns, it's unsettling. The CDC tells us that we have to social distance, and then the president is on TV without a mask, shaking people's hands. Doctors say if you feel sick you should get a test, but the tests are nowhere to be found. Your kids can't go into a classroom, even though it's the middle of the school year. You can't find flour on the grocery shelves. We don't know what's going to happen tomorrow, or six months from now. We don't know how many people will die before this is over. The future is completely up in the air."

I stare at her. This, this is exactly how I feel. Like I'm in a little panga, adrift in the middle of a great, wide ocean.

With no motor and no oars.

"Of course, that's not really accurate," Dr. DeSantos says. "The future is going to come, in some form, whether we like it or not. What we really mean is that we can't *plan* for the future. And when we can't plan—when we can't find those patterns that make sense—we lose the skeleton of life. And no one can remain upright without that."

"But if everyone's experiencing this right now," I ask, "then how come I'm the only one who got dropped into an alternate life?"

"Your *rumination*," she says gently, "was your brain doing its damnedest to make sense of a very stressful situation for which you had no reference. Plus, you were on medications that mess with consciousness. You created a world that you could understand, from building blocks that were lying around your mind."

I think about the guidebooks I had highlighted. The places I'd seen on Isabela. G2 Tours.

"What you keep referring to as another life," Dr. DeSantos says, "was a defense mechanism." She pauses. "Are you still having dreams of the Galápagos?"

"No," I say. "But I don't sleep much."

"That's very common for people who have been in the ICU. But it's also possible that you're not dreaming because you don't *need* to anymore. Because you survived. Because the outcome isn't as vague anymore."

My mouth is suddenly dry. "Then how come I still feel lost?"

"Build your scaffolding again, but while you're conscious. Use the bricks that you've still got, in spite of the pandemic. Make coffee in the morning. Meditate. Watch *Schitt's Creek*. Have a glass of wine at dinner. FaceTime the friends you can't see in person. Whatever habits you used to have, stack them up and give yourself structure. I promise. You won't feel as unsettled."

I think about surrealist paintings, how you can be startled out of your understanding of what the world should be. To my surprise, tears spring to my eyes. "What if that's not the problem?"

"What do you mean?"

"I *wish* I could dream about the Galápagos," I whispered. "I liked it better there."

The psychologist tilts her head, pity written on her face. "Who wouldn't," she says.

In my past life, I'd groan when my alarm went off and choke down a piece of toast with my coffee and join the millions of people in New York City getting from point A to point B. I'd spend my days buried in work, a mountain that only seemed to get higher the more I climbed it, and when I came home I was too tired to deal with groceries or cook so I ordered in. Sometimes Finn was here, sometimes he was doing an overnight at the hospital. There were weekends I worked but also weekends when I took walks to Chelsea Piers, down the High Line, through Central Park. I'd force myself not to think about office politics or what I could be hammering away at on my laptop to get a head start on the coming week. I'd go to the gym and watch rom-coms on my phone while running on the treadmill.

Now, I have nothing to do and nothing but time. I can cook, but only if I can find a time slot for grocery deliveries, and only if they have the actual ingredients I ask for. And there's only so much home-made bread a single human can consume.

I finish *Tiger King*. (I think she's totally guilty.) I binge *Nailed It!* I become obsessed with Room Rater, and after seeing a pundit on television I immediately go to see how their home space fared. I hold virtual happy hours with Rodney from his sister's home in New Orleans. I stop wearing pants with buttons. Sometimes, I just cry until I can't anymore.

One day, I type *Coma dreams* into the search bar of Facebook.

There are two videos and a link to a story in the Cedar Rapids *Gazette*. The first video is a woman who was in a coma for twenty-two days after giving birth. When she woke up, she did not recognize her baby, or remember that she had been pregnant. While unconscious, she'd found herself in a palace and her job there was to interview cats—all of which were dressed like courtiers, and all of which could talk. In the video, she shows sketches she has created of each of them, with tiny ruffs or dangling diamond eardrops or velvet doublets.

"My God," I whisper out loud. Do I sound as unhinged as that?

The second video is another woman. "When I was in a coma," she says, "my brain decided that the hospital was a conspiracy theory. My ex-boss—I was a barista, before the accident—owned the hospital and millions of other corporations. In real life, she's kind of flaky and has a misspelled Chinese tattoo. Anyway, she wanted me to sign a contract with her and I didn't want to. She got so mad she kidnapped my mother and my brother and said that if I didn't sign the contract, they'd die. Now, I was in a coma just for two days, but this went on for weeks. I went all over the country trying to find friends who had money I could borrow. I flew on jets and stayed at hotels and saw things at places I've never been to in my life—but when I came out of the coma and looked them up on the internet, there they were." There's a muffled question, and she shrugs. "Like that shiny mirrored bean in Chicago," she says. "And this place in Kansas that has a twenty-thousand-pound ball of twine inside. I mean, *why* would I have known that?"

The video ends before she can give me what I really want: an explanation. More than the cat lady's, this woman's experience resonates with mine. She, too, lived through more time while she was unconscious than she did while she was hooked up to machines. And her journey was filled with real-world details that weren't part of her life pre-accident. But then, who knows what cognitive thorns caught in the folds of her brain? Like Dr. DeSantos said—maybe she had read the Guinness World Records when she was younger; maybe the facts she unconsciously retained bubbled up to the surface of her subconscious like a hot spring.

The third story is a newspaper article about a fifty-two-year-old man named Eric Genovese, who has lived in Cedar Rapids since birth. He was a Poland Spring truck driver and he got hit by a car as he was crossing the street with a corporate water delivery. In the time it took

EMTs to resuscitate him—a matter of minutes—he said he lived an entirely different life. "When I looked in the mirror I knew it was me, but I was completely different. Younger, and with a new face, and that felt right. I had a different job—I was a computer engineer," he was quoted as saying. "The woman who worked next to me in a cubicle, she had an abusive boyfriend, and I spent months trying to get her to ditch the guy and to realize I was in love with her. I proposed and we got married, and a year later we had a little girl. We named her Maya, after my wife's mother. When I woke up, after I was revived . . . none of it made sense. I kept asking where my wife was, and my baby girl. For me, years had passed, but for everyone else it was like twenty minutes. I had this burning urge to pray a bunch of times during the day and I knew whole passages of religious text that no one could identify, not even me. Turned out to be the Quran. I was raised Catholic; I went to parochial school. But after I woke up, I was Muslim."

Even though this is an article and I cannot *hear* his voice, there is something in his words that speaks to me. A desperation. A discombobulation. A . . . wonder.

I type his name into Facebook. There are a plethora of Eric Genoveses, but only one in Cedar Rapids.

I click the message button. My hands hover over the keyboard.

The psychologist has encouraged me to find a footing in this world, even if it feels strange. There is more than enough scientific evidence that the medication used to sedate me could have messed with my mind sufficiently to create what I thought was an alternate reality, but what everyone else recognizes as a drug dream. There are dozens of witnesses to the fact that I was lying in a hospital for ten days; I am the only person who thinks differently. Or to put it another way: the facts add up to one explanation that anyone rational would accept.

But none of those people experienced what I did.

And there are all kinds of things that used to be considered inconceivable but that turned out to be the opposite—from the earth circling the sun to black holes to diseases that jump from bats to humans. Sometimes the impossible is possible.

I don't know why I keep feeling the tug back to that other place. I don't know why I'm not thanking my lucky stars to be alive and *here*. But I do believe that there's a reason I cannot let go of this—science and doctors and logic be damned.

And I think Eric Genovese might know what I'm talking about.

Hello, I type. *You don't know me, but I read your story in the newspaper.*

I was on a ventilator for five days.

I think I lived a different life, too.

On April 19, we celebrate my birthday.

Finn orders a fat slice of cake from one of our favorite delis. "Carrot cake?" I ask, when he sets it on the table.

"It's your favorite," Finn says. "We always split it when it's on the menu."

Because it is *his* favorite, but I don't say that. He's gone out of his way to make sure he's not working tonight, and he's trying to make the day special for me, even if it looks and feels exactly like yesterday and I haven't left the apartment in days.

When he sings to me, I have an uncanny sense that I've done this before, because I *have*. I think about how Beatriz made me a cake; how Gabriel and I slept outside by a campfire. How he gave me a volcano as a present.

Since we don't have birthday candles, Finn scrounges up a fancy Jo Malone scented candle that Eva gave me for Christmas and lights it. When he hands me a jewelry-size box, my blood thunders in my ears.

Thisisitthisisitthisisit. The thought becomes a second pulse. It feels like more than just the biggest question I will ever be asked; it is the understanding that the answer will be for life.

For life.

Which one?

Finn bumps his shoulder against mine. "Open it," he urges.

I manage to stretch a smile over my face and I tug at the improvised wrapping paper—yesterday's *Times*. Inside is a little bracelet that says WARRIOR.

"That's how I think of you," Finn admits. "I am so fucking glad you're a fighter, Di."

He leans in, threading his hand through my hair and kissing me. When I pull away, I lift the bracelet from the box and he helps me put it on. "Do you like it?"

It is rose gold, and catches the light, and it's not an engagement ring.

I love it.

I look up to find Finn already digging into the slice of cake. "Get in here," he says, his mouth full, "before I finish it all."

I feed my sourdough starter. I watch YouTube tutorials so I can cut Finn's hair. I have another session with Dr. DeSantos. I FaceTime Rodney and we dissect the new email we received from Sotheby's, saying that we will continue to be furloughed through the summer.

The United States crosses a million cases of Covid-19.

I stop using my quad cane. Although I get tired if I am on my feet too long and even one flight of stairs leaves me winded, balance is no longer an issue. I go to put Candis away in my closet and when I do, I remember the shoebox with my old art supplies inside.

Carefully, I tug it loose and set it on the bed.

I peel back the cover and find acrylic paints and a crusty palette and brushes. My fingers sift through the cool metal tubes and my nails catch on dried bits of paint. Something unfurls in me, like the thinnest green shoot from a seed that's been buried.

It has been so long since I painted that I don't have an easel, I don't have gesso, I don't have a canvas. The wall is the perfect surface to work on, but this is a rental and I can't. Finally I manage to tug the dresser away from the wall. It's something we picked up at a second-hand shop and primed with the intent of repainting one day—but we never got around to it. The wood on the back is smooth and white and waiting.

I sit down on the floor with a pencil and begin, in rough, sweeping strokes, to draw. It feels otherworldly, like I'm a medium channeling from somewhere else, watching the unlikely manifest before my eyes. I tumble into the zone, blocking out the sounds of the city and the occasional ping of my phone. I squeeze a rainbow of color on the palette, touch the tip of a brush to a carmine line, and draw it over the wood like a scalpel. There's a sense of relief at having made contact, and anxiety at not knowing what comes next.

I don't notice the sun going down and I don't hear Finn's keys in the door when he comes home. By then, I have covered the back of the dresser with color and shape, sea and sky. There is paint in my hair and under my fingernails, my joints are stiff from sitting, and I am thousands of miles away when I realize Finn is standing in front of me, calling my name.

I blink up at him. He's showered and a towel is wrapped around his waist. "You're home," I say.

"And you're painting." A smile ghosts over his lips. "On our bureau."

"I didn't have a canvas," I tell him.

"I see." Finn moves to stand behind me, so that he can view what I've done. I try to stare at it, too, through a stranger's eyes.

The sky is an unholy cobalt, with breaths of clouds like afterthoughts. They're mirrored in the still surface of a lagoon. Flamingos goose-step across a sandbar, or sleep with their legs bent into acute angles. A manchineel tree squats like the old crone in a fairy tale, poison at her fingertips.

Finn crouches down beside me. He stretches out a hand toward the art, but acrylics dry so quickly I know he cannot smudge anything. "Diana," he says after a moment. "This is . . . I didn't know you could paint like this." He points to two small figures, far in the distance, so tiny they would easily be overlooked if you weren't paying attention.

"Where's this supposed to be?" Finn asks.

I don't answer. I don't have to.

"Oh," he says, standing again. He takes a step away, and then another, until he has found a smile to wear. "You're a very good artist," Finn says, keeping his voice light. "What else are you hiding from me?"

By the time we go to bed that night, Finn has maneuvered the dresser back into position so that the lagoon I've drawn is flush against the wall, hidden away. I don't mind. I like knowing there is a side to it that nobody would ever guess is there.

Finn, coming off a forty-hour shift at the hospital, is asleep nearly as soon as his head hits the pillow. He clutches me against him the way a child holds tight to a stuffed animal, a talisman to keep the monsters away from them both.

The first night Finn and I slept together, as he trailed his hands over my skin, he told me that you can never really touch anything, because everything is made of atoms, and atoms have electrons inside them, which have a negative charge. Particles repel other particles that have a similar charge. This means when you lie down in bed, the electrons that make up your body push away the electrons that make up the mattress. You're actually floating an infinitesimal distance above it.

I had stroked my hand down the center of his chest. *So you're hallucinating this feeling?* I said.

No, he replied, catching my hand and kissing it. Or so I felt. *It's our brains working overtime. The nerve cells get a message that some foreign electrons got close enough in space and time to repel our personal electromagnetic field. Our brains tell us that's the sensation of touch.*

You're saying this is all make-believe? I asked, rolling on top of him. *This is why I shouldn't date a scientist.*

He held my hips in his hands. *We're all in our own little worlds.*

Come visit mine, I had said, and I let him slide inside.

Now, I feel Finn's heat surrounding me and the rough of his skin pressed to mine and I close my eyes. Even wedged against him, I imagine that invisible seam between us.

My throat is on fire and there is an anvil on my chest. I feel hands on me, tugging and rolling and smacking me hard between the shoulder blades. My eyes are crusted and stinging and the pressure under my ribs is unbearable. *Breathe,* I command myself, but the mandate dies in a vacuum.

Then suddenly the heel of a hand presses on my forehead and my nose is pinched shut and my mouth is covered. A gust of heat inflates me like a balloon. I use all my strength to push away, to roll to the side, and the dam bursts. I cough and vomit fluid that burns, that cramps my belly and my sides. I cough and cough and finally gasp in the sweetest, cleanest stream of air.

I fall back, spent, becoming aware of other sensations: the rasp of sand on my skin and the bite of stones, blood coursing from a cut on my lip, the weight of the sun on my brow. A strand of hair is caught across my face and I don't have the energy to brush it away.

Suddenly it's gone, and the bright light shining in my eyes is, too. A shadow spreads over me like a protective wing.

Diana.

I force my eyes open and there is Gabriel, dripping wet, leaning over me. His hands frame my face, and when he smiles, it pulls at me, like we have been sewn together with invisible thread.

Everything hurts and he is the sun I shouldn't stare into but cannot turn away from. *"Dios mío,"* he says. "I thought I lost you."

Coffee. I can smell it. I burrow deeper into the covers and then I feel a warm hand on my shoulder. A kiss on the back of my neck.

I turn, a smile lighting me up from tip to toe.

I push myself up against the pillows. Finn hands me the mug and I cup my hands around the ceramic, feeling its heat and its solidity.

Then, to my shock and his, I burst into tears.

FOURTEEN

"What did you tell Finn?" Rodney asks me, when we video-chat two days later.

"The truth," I say. "Kind of."

He raises an eyebrow. "Girl."

"I said that I had a dream and I thought I wasn't going to wake up."

"Hm," Rodney says. "That's like when you bought a vibrator and said it was for neck massages."

"First, *you* bought me the vibrator for my birthday because you're an asshole. Second, what was I supposed to say when Finn found it? 'Thought you might like a little help'?"

I watch as Rodney's adorable little niece, Chiara, toddles up to him with a baby-size plastic cup. "You sit!" she orders, pointing to the floor.

"Okay, baby," Rodney says, plopping cross-legged onto the carpet. "I swear to Jesus, if I have to have one more tea party I'm gonna lose my shit."

Chiara starts lining up stuffed animals and dolls around Rodney. "The thing is, I was trying," I tell him. "I did what Dr. DeSantos said. I started making routines and sticking to them. And since I'm stuck here all day in an apartment, I now clean and cook, too. I have dinner on the table for Finn every time he comes home."

"Wow, so you single-handedly set back womyn's rights by like fifty years? You must be so proud."

"The only thing I did different that day was paint from memory. A little swimming hole that Gabriel and Beatriz took me to. I've been out of rehab for a couple of weeks, Rodney, and I haven't dreamed my way back there until now." I hesitate. "I tried. I'd lie in bed and hold on to an image in my head and hope I could still hang on to it after I was asleep, but it never worked."

"Alternative thought," Rodney suggests. "Gabriel's been trying this whole time to break through to you. Kind of like the way Finn was, when he sat next to you at the hospital and talked to you while you were unconscious."

"Then which one's the real me?" I ask, in a small voice.

From a purely scientific standpoint, it would seem to be this world—the one where I love Finn and am talking to Rodney. Certainly I have been here the longest, and have more memories of it. But I also know that time doesn't correspond equally, and that what is moments here might be months there.

"Wouldn't it be weird if I were talking to you in this world and you were trying to convince me I don't belong here?" I ask.

"I don't know," Rodney says. "That kind of shit makes my head hurt. It's like the Upside Down in *Stranger Things*."

"Yeah, like with fewer demogorgons and more coconuts."

"You already talked to a shrink ... ," Rodney mulls.

"Yeah. So?"

"Well, I want you to talk to someone else. Rayanne."

"Your sister?" I ask.

"Yeah," Rodney says. "She has the sight."

Before I can respond, the camera tumbles sideways and then rights itself and there is a woman standing next to Rodney who looks like a bigger, more tired version of Chiara. "This her?" Rayanne asks.

"Hi," I say, feeling ambushed.

"Rodney told me all about what happened to you," she replies. "This virus sucks. I work in a group home for developmentally disabled folk, and we lost two of our residents to Covid."

"I'm sorry," I say, that familiar wash of survivor's guilt flushing my face.

"When I'm not working there," Rayanne says matter-of-factly, "I'm a psychic."

She says this the way you'd say, *I'm a redhead* or *I'm lactose intolerant*. A simple and indisputable fact.

"He says you're salty because you feel caught between two lives."

I make a mental note to kill Rodney.

"I mean, I don't know if I'd put it quite like that," I qualify. "But then again, I *did* almost die."

"No *almost* about it," Rayanne says. "That's your problem."

A laugh bubbles out of me. "I promise you, I'm very much alive."

"Okay, but what if death wasn't the ending you've been told it is? What if time is like fabric, a bolt that's so long you can't see where it starts or it ends?" She pauses. "Maybe at the moment a person dies, that life gets compressed so small and dense it's like a pinprick in the cloth. It may be that at that point, you enter a new reality. A new stitch in time, basically."

I feel my heart start to pound harder.

"That new reality, it takes place for you at a normal pace, but within that giant fabric of time. What felt like months to you was actually days here, because again, time was compressed the minute you left that other life."

"I don't really understand," I say.

"You're not supposed to," Rayanne tells me. "Most lives end and get compressed into that tiny, tiny hole and we pick up a new thread—a brand-new existence that goes on and on until it's over and gets condensed down into a single stitch in the fabric again. But for you, the needle jumped. For you, death wasn't a stitch. It was a veil. You got to peek through, and see what was on the other side."

I imagine a universe draped with the gauzy textile of millions of lives, tangled and intersecting. I think of needles that might have basted together me and Finn, me and Gabriel, for just a moment in time. I think of yards and yards of cloth as black as night, every fiber twisted into it a different life. In one I am an art specialist. In another, a stranded tourist. There could be infinite versions, some where I cure cancer, or fall in battle; some where I have a dozen children, break a heart, die young.

"We don't know what reality is," Rayanne says. "We just pretend we do, because it makes us feel like we're in control." She looks at my face on the screen and laughs. "You think I'm loony tunes."

"No," I say quickly.

"You don't have to believe me," Rayanne replies. "But just remember . . . you don't have to believe *them*, either." She shrugs. "Oh, and you're not done with all this yet."

"What does that mean?"

"Damned if I know. I just get the message, I don't write it." She glances to her left. "Real talk, though, right now the universe is telling me to change Chiara's diaper before the stench wipes us all out like an asteroid."

She hands Rodney the phone again. He raises his eyebrows, as if to say, *I told you so.*

Then he lifts the plastic toy cup in his free hand. "And that's the tea," he says.

On the days I visit my mother at The Greens, I pack a picnic lunch and always bring extra. I can't give any to her, because I am still not allowed inside, but I always have a cinnamon roll or a slice of pumpkin bread for Henry, who is there every time I go, no matter what day of the week it is. I always leave a wrapped offering at the front door, too, for the staff, with a note thanking them for keeping the residents safe.

I start bringing a blanket with me, which I set up on the lawn outside my mother's screened porch. When I call her, she answers, and I tell her the same thing each time: It's a beautiful day, would she like to join me?

We talk like strangers who have only recently been introduced, which isn't really that far off the mark. We watch recorded episodes of *American Idol,* and she points out her favorite singers, who are now being filmed from their garages and living rooms without a studio audience. We look over the weekly menus at The Greens. I tell her about the little dog in a yellow raincoat that I saw in the park, and the plots of the books I read. Sometimes she takes out photo albums and walks me through her journeys, while I sketch her in an unlined journal. She can remember the most minute details about the flooding rains in Rio de Janeiro in the eighties, a dynamite explosion in the Philippines, landslides in Uganda. She was in New York City when the Twin Towers collapsed and the air was white with ash and grief. She captured the aftermath of the Pulse nightclub shooting. She did an entire series on the coyotes who brought children over the Mexican border. "I got into a lot of trouble for that one," she tells me, running her finger over a grainy photograph of a man and a little girl walking across a barren wasteland.

"How come?"

"Because I didn't show a clear villain," my mother says. "It's hard to blame someone for breaking the law when all your choices have been taken away from you. Nobody's all good or all bad. They just get painted that way."

I think about what my life would have been like if she had come home and sat down at the kitchen table with me and told me these stories. Surely I would have understood better what captured her attention and drew her away from my father and me, instead of only feeling jealous of it.

These days I am thinking a lot about loss. Because of this pandemic, everyone feels like they've been robbed of something, or—in the most extreme and permanent of cases—some*one*. A job, an engagement, a painting for auction. A graduation, a vacation, a freshman year. A grandmother, a sister, a lover. Nobody is guaranteed tomorrow—I realize that viscerally now—but that doesn't keep us from feeling cheated when it's yanked away.

During the past two months, the things we are missing have come to feel concentrated and acute, personal. Whatever we forfeit echoes the pain from all the other times we have been disappointed in our lives. When I was sedated and I thought I had lost my mother, it was amplified by all the times she left me when I was little.

She looks up and finds me watching her. I do that, now, trying to see myself in the curve of her jaw or the texture of her hair. "Have you ever been to Mexico?" she asks.

I shake my head. "I'd like to go, one day. It's on my bucket list."

Her face lights up. "What else is on there?"

"The Galápagos," I say softly.

"I've been," she replies. "That poor tortoise—Lonesome George. He died."

I was the one to tell her that, a day before my life changed. "So I hear." I lean back on my elbows, glancing at her through the screen. She is pixelated and whole at the same time. "Did you always want to travel?" I ask.

"When I was a girl," my mother says, "we went nowhere. My father was a cattle farmer and he used to say you can't take a vacation from the cows. One day an encyclopedia salesman came to the house and I begged my parents to subscribe. Every month there was a new volume showing me a world a lot bigger than McGregor, Iowa."

I am entranced. I try to connect the dots between her childhood and her move to New York City.

"The best part was that we got a bonus book—an atlas," she adds. "There weren't computers back then, you know. To see what it looked like thousands of feet up a mountain in Tibet or down in the rice paddies of Vietnam or even just the Golden Gate Bridge in San Francisco—I wanted to be there. All the places. I wanted to put myself in the frame." She shrugs. "So I did."

My mother, I realize, mapped out her life literally. I did mine figuratively. But it was for the same reason—to make sure I didn't get trapped someplace I didn't want to be.

I don't know what makes me ask the next question. Maybe it is because I have never struck a tuning fork in myself and heard it resonate in my mother; maybe it's because I have spent so many years blaming her for not sharing her life with me, even though I never actually asked her to do so. But I sit up, legs crossed, and say, "Do you have children?"

A small frown forms between her brows, and she closes the photo album. Her hands smooth over its cover, nails catching at the embossed gold words. A LIFE, it says. Banal, and also spot-on.

"I do," my mother says, just when I think she will not answer. "I *did*."

Let this go, I tell myself. Alzheimer's 101 says do not remind a person with dementia of a memory or event that might be upsetting.

She meets my gaze through the screen. "I . . . don't know," she says.

But the cloudiness that is the hallmark of her illness isn't what I see in her eyes. It's the opposite—the memory of a relationship that wasn't what it might have been, even if you do not know why.

It's blinking at your surroundings, and not knowing how you got to this point.

And I am just as guilty of it as she is.

I've spent so much time dissecting how different my mother and I are that I never bothered to consider what we have in common.

"I'm tired," my mother says.

"You should lie down," I tell her. I gather up my blanket.

"Thank you for visiting," she says politely.

"Thank you for letting me," I reply, just as gracious. "Don't forget to lock the slider."

I wait until she is inside her apartment, but even in the space of those few seconds, she's forgotten to secure the latch. I could tell her a million times; she will likely never remember.

While I'm waiting for my Uber, I laugh softly at my foolishness. At first, I thought maybe I'd come back to this world so that I could give my mother a second chance.

Now I'm starting to think I'm here so she can give *me* one.

Every night at seven P.M., New Yorkers lean out their windows and bang pots and pans for the frontline workers to hear, in a show of support. Sometimes Finn hears them when he is headed home from work.

On those days, he comes into the apartment and strips and showers and goes right to the cabinet over the refrigerator to take out a bottle of Macallan whiskey. He pours himself a glass and sometimes doesn't even speak to me until he's drunk it.

I didn't know Finn even liked whiskey.

Each night, the amount he pours gets a little bigger. He is careful to leave enough in the bottle for the next night. Sometimes he passes out on the couch and I have to help him to bed.

During the day, when he's at work, I climb on a step stool and take out the Macallan. I pour some of the whiskey down the sink. Not an amount that would raise suspicion; just enough for me to protect him a little from himself.

By the end of May we aren't washing the groceries anymore or waiting to open our mail, but we're freaked out about slipstreams, and whether you can catch the virus from a jogger who runs past you. I start receiving the unemployment benefits I became eligible for when I was furloughed, but they certainly don't cover my half of the rent.

When I start to feel like I'm going stir-crazy, I remind myself of how lucky I am. I scour forums of long-haul Covid survivors, who are still suffering weeks later with symptoms no one understands and no doctors have the bandwidth or knowledge to address. I read articles about women who are balancing work and online education for their kids; and profiles of frontline workers who get paid scandalously little to risk their exposure to the virus. I see Finn stagger in after his long shifts, haunted by what he's seen. Sometimes it feels like the whole world is holding its breath. If we don't gasp, soon, we will all pass out.

One Saturday when Finn has the day off, we spend the afternoon getting back to ground zero: cleaning the apartment, doing laundry, sorting through the mail that has piled up. We play Rock Paper Scissors to choose chores, which leaves me scrubbing toilets while Finn fishes through piles of envelopes and junk mail for the cable bill and the bank statements. Every time I pass by him at the kitchen table, I feel ashamed. Usually we split the cost of utilities and rent, but with my contributions reduced to a trickle, he's paying the lion's share.

He picks up a stack of glossy catalogs he has separated out from the bills and tosses them into the milk crate we use as a recycling bin. "I don't know why we keep getting these," he says. "College brochures."

"No, wait." I put down my dustrag and sift through them, pulling a bunch back out and cradling them in one arm. "They're for me." I meet his gaze. "I'm thinking of going back to school."

He blinks at me. "For *what*? You already have a master's in art business."

"I might change careers," I tell him. "I want to find out more about art therapy."

"How are you paying for tuition?" Finn asks.

It stings. "I have some savings."

He doesn't respond, but implicit in his look is: *You may not by the time this is over.*

It makes me feel equally guilty—for wanting to spend money on myself when I haven't been carrying my own weight on household expenses, and angry—because he's right. "I just feel like this could be . . . a wake-up call."

"You're not the only one who lost a job, Di."

I shake my head. "Not only getting furloughed. *Everything.* There has to be a reason that I got sick."

Finn suddenly looks very, very tired. "There doesn't have to be a reason. Viruses don't need reasons. They strike. Randomly."

"Well, I can't believe that." I lift my chin. "I can't believe I'm alive because of the luck of the draw."

He stares at me for another moment, and then shakes his head and mutters something I don't hear. He rips open another envelope and eviscerates its contents.

"Why are you mad?" I ask.

Finn pushes his chair away from the table. "I'm not mad," he says. "But, I mean—going back to school? Changing *careers*? I can't believe you didn't happen to mention this anytime over the last month."

I blurt out, "I've been visiting my mother."

"Wow," Finn says quietly. Betrayal is written all over the margins of his face.

"I didn't say anything because . . . I thought you'd tell me not to go."

His eyes narrow, as if he is searching to find me. "I would have gone with you," he says. "You have to be careful."

"You think I could get hurt taking the trash into the hallway to dump it."

"My point exactly. You shouldn't be doing that, either. You're only a month out of rehab—"

"You treat me like I'm on the verge of dying," I snap.

"Because you *were*," Finn counters, rising from his chair.

We are standing a foot apart, both of us crackling with frustration.

He wants to gently set me down exactly where I was before this happened, like he's been holding that place for me in a board game, and we are going to pick up where we left off. The problem is that I'm not the same player.

"When I thought you were going to die," Finn says, "I didn't believe there could be anything more awful than a world you weren't in. But this is worse, Diana. This is you, in the world, not letting me be a part of it." His eyes are dark, desperate. "I don't know what I did wrong."

Immediately, I reach out, my hands catching his. "You've done nothing wrong," I say, because it is true.

The relief in his eyes nearly breaks me. Finn's arms come around my waist. "You want to go back to school?" he says. "We'll figure out how. You want a PhD? I'll be in the front row at your dissertation defense. We've always wanted the same things, Di. If this is a detour on the way to everything we've dreamed about, that's okay."

A detour. Inside, where he cannot see, I flinch.

What if I don't want what I used to?

"What did you want to be when you grew up?" I murmur.

A laugh startles out of Finn. "A magician."

I'm charmed. "Really? Why?"

"Because they made things appear out of thin air," Finn says, with a shrug. "Something from nothing. How cool is that?"

I nestle close to him. "I would have come to all your shows. I would have been that annoying superfan."

"I would have promoted you to magician's assistant." He grins. "Would you have let me saw you in half?"

"Anytime," I tell him.

But I think: *That is the easy part. The trick is in putting me back together.*

The next morning, I video-call Rodney and tell him that Finn doesn't want me to go back to school. "Remind me why you need his permission?" he says.

"Because it changes things, when you're a couple. Like how much we can pay in rent, if I'm not making a salary. Or how much time we'll actually spend together."

"You hardly spend any time together now. He's a resident."

"Well, anyway, I didn't call to talk to you. Is Rayanne there?"

Rodney frowns. "No, she's working."

"Like . . . doing a reading for someone?"

"Nursing home," he says. "The only thing that pays worse than a career in art is being a psychic." His eyes widen. "*That's* why you want to talk to her."

"What if I'm being an idiot, thinking about starting over now? Finn could be right. This could be some weird reaction to having a second chance, or something."

Rodney slowly puts it all together. "So you want Rayanne to take a peek a few years out and tell you if you're gluing pom-poms together with kids who have anxiety from gluten allergies—"

"—That is *not* art therapy—"

"—or if you're wearing stilettos and in Eva's old office? Mmnope. It doesn't work that way."

"Easy for you to say," I tell him, pressing my hand to my forehead. "Nothing makes sense, Rodney. *Nothing*. I know Finn thinks that I shouldn't make any radical changes, because I've been through so much. Instead of trying new things, I should find the stuff that feels comfortable."

Rodney looks at me. "Oh my God. Nothing bad's ever happened to you before."

I scowl at him. "That's not true."

"Okay, sure, you had a mother who didn't know you existed, but your daddy still doted on you. Maybe you had to go to your second-choice college. You had a share of white lady problems, but nothing that's knocked the ground out from under your feet. Until you caught Covid, and now you understand that sometimes shit happens you can't control."

I feel anger bubbling inside me. "What is your point?"

"You know I'm from Louisiana," Rodney says. "And that I'm Black and gay."

My lips twitch. "I'd noticed."

"I have spent a great deal of time pretending to be someone that other people want me to be," he says. "You don't need a crystal ball, honey. You need a good hard look at *right now*."

My jaw drops open.

Rodney scoffs. "Rayanne's got nothing on me," he says.

In late May, the strict lockdown of the city is eased. As the weather improves, the streets become busier. It's still different—everyone is masked; restaurant service is solely outdoors—but it feels a little less like a demilitarized zone.

I get stronger, able to go up and down stairs without having to stop halfway. When Finn is at the hospital, I take walks from our place on the Upper East Side through Central Park, going further south and west every day. The more people venture outside, the more I tailor my outings to odd times of the day—just before dawn, or when everyone else is home eating dinner. There are still people out, but it's easier to social-distance from them.

Early one morning I put on my leggings and sneakers and strike off for the reservoir in Central Park. It's my favorite walk, and I know it is because it makes me remember another static body of water and a thicket of brush. If I close my eyes and listen to the woodcock and the sparrows, I can pretend they are finches and mockingbirds.

This is exactly what I'm doing when I hear someone call my name. "Diana? Is that you?"

On the running path, wearing a black tracksuit and a paisley mask and her trademark purple glasses, is Kitomi Ito.

"Yes!" I say, stepping forward before I remember that we are not allowed to touch, to hug. "You're still here."

She laughs. "Haven't shuffled off the mortal coil yet, no."

"I mean, you haven't moved."

"That, too," Kitomi says. She nods toward the path. "Walk a bit?"

I fall into step, six feet away.

"I admit I thought I would have heard from you by now," she says.

"Sotheby's furloughed me," I tell her. "They furloughed almost everyone."

"Ah, well, that explains why no one's been beating down the door asking for the painting." She tilts her head. "Isn't the big sale this month?"

It is, but it has never crossed my mind.

"I must say, I've never been more grateful for a decision than I was to not auction the Toulouse-Lautrec. For weeks now, it's just been the two of us in the apartment. I would have been quite lonely, without it."

I understand what she's talking about. I was just staring at a man-made reservoir, after all, and pretending it was a lagoon in the Galápagos. I could close my eyes and hear Beatriz splashing and Gabriel teasing me to dive in.

I remember, again, that the last normal thing I did before getting sick was go to Kitomi's penthouse. "Did you get the virus?" I ask, and then blush beneath my mask. "I don't mean to intrude. It's just—I had it. I went to the hospital the day after our meeting. I worried that I might have given it to you."

She stops walking. "I lost taste and smell for about a week," Kitomi says. "But it was so early that nobody knew that was a symptom. No fever, no aches, nothing else. I've been tested for antibodies, though, and I have them. So maybe I should be thanking you."

"I'm just glad it was mild."

She tilts her head. "But for you . . . it wasn't?"

I tell her about being on the ventilator, and how I almost died. I talk about rehab, and explain that's why I am trying to walk further and further each day. I tell her about my mother, who was dead to me, and then wasn't. She doesn't ask questions, she just lets me speak into the gap between us and fill it. I remember, then, that before she was married to Sam Pride, she was a psychologist.

"I'm sorry," I say after a moment. "You should probably bill me for this."

She laughs. "I haven't been a therapist for a very long time. Maybe it's a muscle memory."

I hesitate. "Do you think that's the only way memories work?"

"I'm not sure what you mean."

"What if your body or your brain remembers something you *haven't* done before?"

She looks at me. "You know, I used to study different states of consciousness. It's how I met Sam, as a matter of fact. That was during the hard drug years of the Nightjars, and after all, what's an acid trip but an altered state?"

"I think I was in two places at one time," I say slowly. "In the hospital, on a ventilator. And in my head, somewhere completely different." I do not look at her as I sketch the story of my arrival on Isabela, my adoption by Abuela, my conversations with Beatriz.

My time with Gabriel.

Including the moment I let myself drown.

"I used to do past life regressions for clients," Kitomi says. "But this isn't a past life, is it? It's a simultaneous one."

She says this mildly, like she's pointing out that there's a lot of humidity today. "Have you returned there?" she asks.

"Once," I admit.

"Do you want to go back?"

"I feel . . ." I begin, trying to choose the right words. "I feel like I'm on loan here."

"You could go to the Galápagos," Kitomi points out.

"Not now," I say wryly.

"One day."

I don't have a response. Kitomi and I walk a little further. We are passed by a jogger with a headlamp. "I could have moved to Montana during any of the past thirty-five years," Kitomi says. "But I wasn't ready yet." She tilts her head to the sky, and the rising sun glints off the lenses of her glasses. "When I lost Sam, I lost all my joy. I tried to find it—through music and art and therapy and writing and Prozac. Then I realized I'd been looking in the wrong place all along. I was trying to find meaning in his death—and I couldn't. It was violent and tragic and random and wrong. It always *will* be. The truth is, it doesn't matter how or why Sam died. It never will."

Just then, the sun breaks over the tree line, setting the trees aflame. It is the kind of art that no master could ever capture on canvas, but it's here for the viewing every single day.

I understand what Kitomi is telling me: Trying to figure out what happened to me isn't important. It's what I do with what I've learned that counts.

There are more people on the reservoir trail now.

All of us are grieving *something*.

But while we are, we're putting one foot in front of the other. We're waking up to see another day. We're pushing through uncertainty, even if we can't yet see the light at the end of the tunnel.

We are battered and broken, but we're all small miracles.

"I'm here most days before the sun comes up," Kitomi says. "If you want to join me."

I nod, and we walk a little further. Just after we part ways, my phone dings with a notification.

It is a Facebook message from Eric Genovese, with a cellphone number and an invitation to call.

Eric Genovese tells me that in his other life, he lives in Kentwood—a suburb of Grand Rapids he'd never heard of before and had never been to, before he was hit by a car. "My wife's name is Leilah," he says. "And my little girl is three."

I notice he uses the present tense. *Lives. Is.*

"I do computer programming there, which if you know me here is laughable," Eric says. "I can't even figure out my TV remote."

"When I was in the Galápagos, months passed," I tell him. "But here, it was days."

We have been on the phone for an hour, and it is the most liberating conversation I've had in over a month. I had forgotten that I messaged him, it's been so long—but Eric apologizes and says he doesn't use Facebook much anymore. He completely understands what I'm talking about when I say that I was somewhere else while I was lying in a hospital bed; that the people I met there are real. He doesn't just give me the benefit of the doubt—he dismisses the people who are too narrow-minded to know what we know.

"Same," he says. "My wife and I have been together for five years in Kentwood."

"How did you get back here?"

"One night we were watching *Jeopardy!* like we usually do, and I was eating a bowl of ice cream. And it was the damnedest thing—my spoon kept going through the bowl. Like it was a ghost spoon, or something. I couldn't stop staring at it. I couldn't go to bed, either, because I had the weirdest premonition that this was just the beginning." He sighs. "I don't blame my wife. Leilah thought I was going crazy. I called in sick to work and stared at the spoon and the bowl the whole day. I kept telling her that if the spoon wasn't real, maybe *nothing* was. She begged me to call the doctor, and when I wouldn't, she took Maya and went to her mom's place." He hesitates. "I haven't seen them since then."

"What happened to the spoon?"

"Eventually, it got bright red, like a coal. I went to touch it and burned my hand and it hurt like hell. I started screaming, and then the room fell away like it was made out of paper, and all I heard was yelling and all I felt was pain. When I opened my eyes, there was a paramedic pounding on my chest and telling me to stay alive."

I swallow. "What about after that? When you came back?"

"Well," he says. "*You* know. Nobody believed me."

"Not even your family?"

He pauses. "I had a fiancée," he admits. "I don't anymore."

I try to reply, but all the words are jammed in my throat.

"Do you know what an NDE is?" he asks.

"No."

"Near-death experience," Eric explains. "When I got out of the hospital, I became obsessed with finding out more about them. It's when someone who's unconscious remembers floating over his body, or meeting a person who died years ago, or something like that. Ten to twenty percent of people report having them after an accident, or if their heart stops."

"On Facebook, I read about this farmer," I say excitedly. "In the middle of bypass surgery, while he was under anesthesia and his eyes were taped shut, he swore he saw his surgeon do the Funky Chicken. When he said something after surgery, his doctor was shocked, because he does wave his elbows around in the OR—it's how he points, so he doesn't contaminate his gloves."

"Yeah, exactly. It even happens during cardiac arrest, when there's no brain activity. Have you ever seen the MRI scan of someone with end-stage Alzheimer's?"

I feel a shiver run down my spine. "No."

"Well, you can literally *see* the damage. But there's hundreds of reports of patients with dementia who can suddenly remember and think clearly and communicate just before they die. Even though their brains are destroyed. It's called terminal lucidity, and there's no medical explanation for it. That's why some neurologists think that there might be another reason for NDEs other than messed-up brain function. Most people think that the cerebral cortex *makes* us conscious, but what if it doesn't? What if it's just a filter, and during an NDE, the brain lets the reins go a little bit?"

"Expanded consciousness," I say. "Like a drug trip."

"Except not," Eric replies. "Because it's way more accurate and detailed."

Could it be true? Could the mind work, even when the brain doesn't? "So if consciousness doesn't come from the brain, where does it come from?"

He laughs. "Well, if I knew that, I wouldn't be working for Poland Spring."

"So, this is what you do now? Armchair neuroscience?"

"Yeah," Eric says, "when I'm not doing an interview. I can't tell you how awesome it is to talk to someone about this who doesn't think I'm a whack job."

"Then why do them?"

"So I can find her," he says flatly.

"You think your wife is real."

"I *know* she is," he corrects. "And so is my little girl. Sometimes I can hear her laughing, and I turn around, but she's never there."

"Have you been to Kentwood?"

"Twice," Eric says. "And I'll go back again, when we don't have to quarantine anymore. Don't you want to find them? The guy and his daughter?"

My throat tightens. "I don't know," I admit. "I'd have to be ready to accept the consequences of that."

He's lost a fiancée; he understands. "Before my accident, I was Catholic."

"I read that."

"I never even met anyone Muslim. I wasn't aware there was a

mosque in my town. But there are things I just *know* now, part of me, like my skin or my bones." He pauses. "Did you know that the Sunni believe in Adam and Eve?"

"No," I say politely.

"With a few differences. According to the Quran, God already knew before he created Adam that he'd put him and his offspring on earth. It wasn't a punishment, it was a plan. But when Adam and Eve were banished, they were put on opposite ends of the earth. They had to find each other again. And they did, on Mount Ararat."

I think I like that version better—it's less about shame, and more about destiny.

"Don't you feel guilty?" I ask. "Missing a person everyone else thinks you invented? When all around us, because of the virus, people are losing someone they love? Someone *real*, someone they'll never see again?"

Eric is quiet for a moment. "What if that's what people are saying to him, now, about you?"

Kitomi tells me that someone has made an offer on the penthouse. A Chinese businessman, although neither of us can imagine why someone from China would want to come to a country where the president refers to the virus as the Wuhan flu. "When would you move?" I ask.

She looks at me, her hands resting lightly on the railing that borders the reservoir trail. "Two weeks," she says.

"That's fast."

Kitomi smiles. "Is it? I've been waiting thirty-five years, really." We watch a flock of starlings take flight. "How disappointed would you be if I decided not to auction the Toulouse-Lautrec?" she asks.

I shrug. "I don't work for Sotheby's, remember."

"If I don't consign it," she asks, "will you *ever* work there again?"

"I don't know," I admit. "But you shouldn't make a decision based on me."

She nods. "Maybe I will have the only ranch in Montana with a Toulouse-Lautrec."

"You do you," I say, grinning.

For a moment I just hold on to this: the wonder that I am walking at dawn with a pop culture icon, as if we are friends. Maybe we are. Stranger things have happened.

Stranger things have happened *to me*.

Kitomi tilts up her head, so that she is looking at me from under the rims of her purple glasses. "Why do you love art?"

"Well," I say, "every picture tells a story, and it's a window into the mind of the—"

"Oh, Diana." Kitomi sighs. "Once more, minus the bullshit."

I burst out laughing.

"Why art?" Kitomi asks again. "Why not photography, like your mother?"

My jaw drops. "You know who my mother is?"

She raises an eyebrow. "Diana," she says, "Hannah O'Toole is the Sam Pride of feature photography."

"I didn't know you knew," I murmur.

"Well, *I* know why you love art, even if you don't," Kitomi continues, as if I haven't spoken. "Because art isn't absolute. A photograph, that's different. You're seeing exactly what the photographer wanted you to see. A painting, though, is a partnership. The artist begins a dialogue, and you finish it." She smiles. "And here's the incredible part—that dialogue is different every time you view the art. Not because anything changes on the canvas—but because of what changes in *you*."

I turn back to the water, so that she can't see the tears in my eyes.

Kitomi reaches across the distance between us and pats my arm. "Your mother may not know how to start the conversation," she says. "But you do."

On my way back home through the park, I discover that I have three messages from The Greens.

I stop walking in the middle of the path, forcing joggers to flow around me. "Ms. O'Toole," a woman says, moments later when I redial. "This is Janice Fleisch, the director here—I'm glad you finally called back."

"Is my mother all right?"

"We've had an outbreak of Covid at our facility, and your mother is ill."

I have heard these words before; I am caught in a cyclone of déjà vu. I even remember my lines.

"Is she . . . does she need to go to the hospital?"

"Your mother has a DNR," she says delicately. No matter how sick she gets, she will not get any life-saving measures, because that's what I deemed best when she moved there a year ago. "We have multiple residents who've contracted the virus, but I assure you we're doing everything we can to keep them comfortable."

"Can I see her?"

"I wish I could say yes," the director says. "But we aren't letting visitors in."

My heart is pounding so hard that I can barely hear my own voice thanking her, and asking her to keep me updated.

I start walking as fast as I can back home, trying to remember where Finn put the toolbox we use for emergencies in the apartment.

They may not be letting visitors in. But I don't plan to ask permission.

I ask the Uber to drop me off at the end of the driveway, so that I can detour across the lawn away from anyone who might see my approach. For once, Henry's car is not at The Greens, and the bird feeder outside his wife's porch is empty. I can think of only one reason.

I push that thought out of my mind. The only silver lining is that there will be no witnesses for what I'm about to do.

Although I have wire cutters, I don't really need them. One of the lower corners of my mother's screened porch is peeling at the base, and all I have to do is hook my fingers underneath and tug hard for the screen to rip away from its moorings. I create just enough space to wriggle through and step around the wicker chair and table where my mother usually sits when I come for my visits. I peer into her apartment, but she isn't on the couch.

I don't even know, really, if she's here. For all I know, they've moved all the Covid-positive residents to a completely different place.

I pull on the door of the slider that opens into the porch. Thank God my mother never remembers to lock it.

I tiptoe into the apartment. "Mom?" I say softly. "Hannah?"

The lights are all turned off, the television is a blind, blank eye. The bathroom door is open and the space is empty. I hear voices and follow them down the short hallway toward her bedroom.

My mother is lying in bed with a quilt thrown down to her waist. The radio is chattering beside her, some program on NPR about polar bears and the shrinking ice caps. When I stand in the doorway, her head turns toward me. Her eyes are feverish and glassy, her skin flushed.

"Who are you?" she says, panic in her words.

I realize that I am still wearing the mask I wore in the Uber, and that all the times I have visited her, I have stood in the fresh air not wearing one. She may not know me as her daughter, but she recognizes my face as a visitor she has had before. Right now, though, she is sick and scared and I am a stranger whose face is half-obscured by a piece of cloth.

She has Covid.

Finn has drummed into me, daily, how little we know about this virus, but I'm counting on the fact that I still have antibodies. I reach up and unhook one side of my mask. I let it dangle from my ear.

"Hi," I say softly. "It's just me."

She reaches toward her nightstand for her glasses, and has a coughing fit. Her hair is matted down in the back and through pale strands I can see the pink of her scalp. There's something so tender and childlike about that it makes my throat hurt.

She settles her glasses on her face and looks at me again and says, "Diana. I'm sorry, baby . . . I don't feel so good today."

I fall against the frame of the door. She hasn't called me by name in years. Before Covid, she referred to me as "the lady" to staff, when they talked about my visits. She has never given me any indication that she knows we are related.

"Mom?" I whisper.

She pats the bed beside her. "Come sit."

I sink down on the edge of the mattress. "Can I get you anything?"

She shakes her head. "It's really you?"

"Yeah." I remember what Eric Genovese said about terminal lucidity. Terminal. Whatever is causing this clarity from her dementia—whether it's fever, or Covid, or just sheer luck—is it worth it? If the trade-off is knowing that it means she's probably going to die? "I've been here before," I tell her.

"But sometimes I'm not," she says. "At least not mentally." She hesitates, frowning, like she's probing her own mind. "It's different, today. Sometimes I'm back in other places. And sometimes . . . I like it better there."

I understand that viscerally.

She looks at me. "Your father was so much better at everything than I was."

"He would have argued about that. He thought your work was brilliant. Everyone does."

"We tried to have a baby for seven years," my mother says.

This is news to me.

"I tried fertility treatments. Traditional Chinese medicine. I ate bee propolis and pomegranates and vitamin D. I wanted you so badly. I was going to be the kind of mother who took so many photos of my baby that we had a whole closet full of albums. I was going to chronicle every step of your life."

This is so far from the Hannah O'Toole I know—that *everyone* knows. An intrepid photographer of human tragedy, who didn't realize the shambles she'd made of her own deserted family. "What happened?"

"I forgot to take you to the pediatrician when you were a week old," she says.

"I know. I've heard the story."

"It was an appointment for *you*, and I left you sitting at home, in your little baby car seat," she murmurs. "That's how awful I was at being a mother."

"You were distracted," I say, wondering how it's come to this: me making excuses for her.

"I was determined," she corrects. "There couldn't be more mistakes if I wasn't around to make them. Your father . . . he was so much better at taking care of you."

I stare at her. I think of all the times I thought that I was a distant runner-up to her career, that photography held her captive in a way I never could. I never imagined she'd had so little confidence parenting me.

"I used to get asked why I photographed catastrophes," my mother says. "I had a whole list of stock answers—for the excitement, to commemorate tragedy, to humanize suffering. But I mostly shot disasters to remind myself I wasn't the only one."

There is a difference, I realize, between being driven and running away from something that scares you to death.

"I forgive you," I say, and everything inside me shifts. I may not have had much of my mother, between her career and her dementia, but something is better than nothing. I will take what I can get.

"Do you remember the time Dad and I went with you to chase a tornado?" I ask.

She frowns, her eyes clouding.

"I do," I say softly.

Maybe that's enough. It's not having the adventures or crossing off the line items of the bucket list. It's who you were with, who will help you recall it when your memory fails.

My mother coughs again, falling back against the pillows. When she glances at me, something has changed. Her eyes are a painted backdrop, instead of a dimensional landscape. There's nothing behind them but anxiety. "We have to get to higher ground," she says.

I wonder where she is, what other time or place. I hope it's more real to her than here and now. That in the end it's where she will choose to remain.

I imagine her existence shrinking down to the point of a pin, a hole in the fabric of the universe, before she jumps into another life.

She seems to be falling asleep. Gently, I reach for her glasses and slide them from her face. I let my hand linger along the soft swell of her cheek, her paper-thin skin. I set the folded glasses beside a paperback novel on the nightstand, and notice the deckled edge of an old photo that is sticking out from between the pages, like a bookmark.

I don't know what makes me open the book to better see the image.

It's a terrible picture of my mother, when she was young. The top half of her head is cut off, and her wide smile is blurry. Her hand is outstretched, like she's reaching for something.

Someone.

Me.

I remember being the one behind the shutter, when I was no more than a toddler.

Here. You try.

I must make some small noise, because my mother blinks at me. "Have we been introduced?"

Surreptitiously, I slip the photo into my pocket. "Yes," I tell her. "We're old friends."

"Good," she says firmly. "Because I don't think I can do this alone."

I think of the staff, who might come in to check on her at any moment. Of this virus, and how if I catch it again, I may not survive a second time. "You don't have to," I tell her.

I don't realize how late I am until I am in the Uber on my way back to the apartment, and see that Finn has left me a barrage of texts and six phone messages. "Where have you been?" he says, grabbing me when I walk through the door. "I thought something terrible happened to you."

Something already did, I think.

I set down the toolbox I took with me. "I lost track of time," I tell him. "My mother tested positive for Covid. There's an outbreak at The Greens. But they told me I couldn't visit."

Finn's fingers flex on my arms. "God, Diana, what can I do? It must be killing you to not be able to see her."

I don't say anything. My gaze slides away from his face.

"Diana?" he says softly.

"She's dying," I say flatly. "She has a DNR. The odds of her getting through this are virtually nonexistent." I hesitate. "No one even knows I was in her apartment."

Yet. Eventually someone will notice the torn screen.

He suddenly lets go of me. "You went into the room of a Covid-positive patient," he states.

"Not just some patient—"

"Without wearing an N95 mask..."

"I took off my mask," I admit. Now, in retrospect, it seems ridiculous. Risky. Suicidal, even. "She was scared and didn't recognize me."

"She has dementia and *never* recognizes you," Finn argues.

"And I wasn't about to let that be the last experience we had!"

A muscle leaps in his jaw. "Do you realize what you've done?" He spears a hand through his hair, pacing. "How long were you in contact?"

"Two hours ... maybe three?"

"Unmasked," he clarifies, and I nod. "For *fuck's sake,* Diana, what were you thinking?"

"That I could lose my mother?"

"How do you think I felt about *you*?" Finn explodes. "*Feel* about you?"

"I already had Covid—"

"And you could get it again," he says. "Or do you know more than Fauci? Because as far as we know right now, it's a crapshoot. You want to know what we *do* know? The more time you spend in a closed-in space with someone contagious the more likely you are to catch the virus, too."

My hands are shaking. "I wasn't thinking," I admit.

"Well, you weren't thinking about me, either," Finn shoots back.

"Because now I have to quarantine and get tested. How many patients am I not going to be able to take care of, because you *weren't
thinking?*"

He turns like a caged animal, searching for an exit. "God, I can't
even get away from you," Finn snaps, and he stalks into the bedroom
and slams the door.

I am shaky on the inside. Every time I hear Finn moving around in
the bedroom I jump. I know that he will have to come out sooner or
later for food or drink or to use the bathroom, even as the shadows
of the afternoon lengthen into the dark of night.

I don't bother to turn on the lights. Instead, I sit on the couch and
wait for the reckoning.

I've already learned today that caretaking is not a quid pro quo;
that if someone neglects you in your past, that doesn't mean you
should abandon them in their future. But does it hold the other way?
Finn's as good as any other reason for why I survived such a bad case
of Covid—he tethered me. So what do I owe him, in return?

Obligation isn't love.

It stands to reason that Finn and I might have disagreements
while we're locked together during a quarantine. He's exhausted and
I'm recovering and nothing in a pandemic is easy. But our relationship used to be. I don't know if I'm just noticing the hairline fractures
for the first time, or if they've only just appeared. Where we used to
be marching toward the future in lockstep, I'm now stumbling or
trying to catch up. Something has changed between us.

Something has changed in *me*.

At about nine o'clock, the door of the bedroom opens and Finn
emerges. He goes to the kitchen and opens the fridge, taking out the
orange juice and drinking from the carton. When he turns around,
he sees me in the blue glow of the refrigerator light. "You're sitting in
the dark," he says.

He puts the carton down on the counter and comes to sit on the other end of the couch. He flicks on a lamp, and I wince at the sudden brightness.

"I thought maybe you left."

At that, a laugh barks out of me. "Where would I go?"

Finn nods. "Yeah. Well."

I look down at my hands, curled in my lap like they do not belong to me. "Did you . . . do you want me to leave?"

"What makes you think I'd want that?" Finn seems honestly shocked.

"Well," I say. "You were pretty pissed off. You have every right to be." *And I'm not paying any rent right now,* I think.

"Diana? Are you happy?"

My gaze flies to his. "What?"

"I don't know. You just seem . . . restless."

"It's a pandemic," I say. "Everyone's restless."

He hesitates. "Maybe that's not the right word. Maybe it's more *trapped.*" He looks away from me, worrying the seam of the couch. "Do you still want this? Us?"

"Why would you ask that?" I choose those words carefully, so that I don't have to lie, so that he can interpret them however he wants.

Reassured, Finn sighs. "I shouldn't have yelled at you," he says. "I'm really sorry about your mother."

"I'm sorry I contaminated you."

The corner of his mouth tips up. "I needed a vacation anyway," he says.

Two days later, my mother is actively dying. You would think that FaceTiming her while she was unconscious would be old hat, after all the energy I expended on her while I was a child and receiving nothing in return. Instead, I only feel silly. A staff member holds up the iPad near her bed and pretends she isn't listening. I stare at my mother's sedated body, curled like a fiddlehead under the covers, and try to find things to talk about. Finn tells me it's important to talk to her, and that even if I think she can't hear me, on some level, she can.

He's right. The message might be garbled, but it will get through. My voice might be a breeze in the weather of whatever world she's in.

Finn sits with me, and when I run out of words, he jumps in and charms with the story of how we met and how he's teaching me the rules of baseball and that he thinks the apartment is haunted.

The last thing I say during our call is that it's okay for her to leave, if she has to.

I realize she's been waiting to hear those words from me her whole life, because less than an hour later, The Greens calls to tell me she has passed away.

I make the necessary arrangements in a strange, detached way—deciding to cremate her body, deciding not to have a funeral. I remember learning, as a child, how the Shinnecock made dugout canoes—by burning out the middle of a log and carving the insides away. That's how I feel. Hollow, scraped, raw.

For someone I was angry at for so long, someone I rarely saw—I miss her.

It's amazing how easily someone can leave your life. It's standing on a beach and stepping back to see the hole of your footprint subsumed by the sand and the sea as if it were never there. Grief, it turns out, is a lot like a one-sided video conversation on an iPad. It's the call with no response, the echo of affection, the shadow cast by love.

But just because you can't see it anymore doesn't make it any less real.

The day that we get a message saying my mother's ashes are ready to be picked up, *The New York Times* runs her obituary in their Covid section, Those We've Lost. They talk about her rise as a feature photographer and her Pulitzer Prize. There are quotes from colleagues from *The New York Times* and *The Boston Globe* and the Associated Press, from Steve McCurry and Sir Don McCullin. They call her the greatest female photographer of the twentieth century.

The very last line of the obituary, however, is not about her art at all.

I take the paper with me into the bedroom, crawling under the covers. I read that sentence, and read it again.

She leaves behind a daughter.

For the first time since I got the call about my mother's death, I cry.

FIFTEEN

Go away.

SIXTEEN

My eyes are swollen shut.
The sun rises.
I don't.

SEVENTEEN

Am I the only person in the world whose mother has died twice?

EIGHTEEN

"All right, Rip van Winkle," Finn says. "Let's go."

He yanks the covers away from me and I groan. When I scrabble for them again, he sits down and curls my hand around a mug of coffee.

I've been here before, I think.

How easy it would be to follow his lead. I roll over and blink up at him.

"You're going to take a shower," Finn orders, "and then we're going to go for a walk."

We are on day nine of quarantine. We have five more left, before we can leave the apartment. "How?" I ask.

Finn smiles shyly, and I realize he is telling me that he'll bend the rules for me. That he knows why I had to, when I visited my mother. "One step at a time," he says.

I've spent three days in bed, after she died. I was asleep more than I was awake.

Not once did I ever slip back to the Galápagos, or see Beatriz's sunburned face, or hear the lilt of Gabriel's accent.

I am not sure why I thought, while I was drowning again—this time in grief—this alternate reality would come for me.

I'm even less sure what it means that it didn't.

Finn and I walk along Ninety-sixth Street, under the FDR, toward the East River. We wear our masks and leave extra distance when we pass by people, because even if Finn is being a rebel, he's still too much of a do-gooder to risk infecting anyone. We pass a couple of guys shooting up, and a lady with a jogging stroller. The grass along the edge of the walkway is lush and green, and flowers crane their throats to the sun.

There is nothing like early summer in Manhattan. There are usually pop-up concerts—boys with drums made of five-gallon containers, hip-hop dancers defying gravity; businessmen eating shawarma during fast lunch breaks; little girls with shiny white patent-leather shoes clutching their American Girl dolls. There are taxi drivers who wave instead of shout and sprays of daylilies and everyone has a dog to walk. Now, people are out and about, but moving in furtive, cautious bursts. No one lingers. The few people who wear their masks beneath their noses are glared at. It is leaner and less crowded, as if half the population has been removed, and that makes me wonder if this is the way it will always be.

The new normal.

"Do you think we'll ever go back to the way it was?" I ask Finn.

He glances at me. "I don't know," he says thoughtfully. "When I used to talk to patients before surgery, they always asked if they'd be able to do everything they used to do before the operation. I mean, technically, the answer should be yes. But there's always a scar. Even if it's not right across your belly, it's in your head somewhere—the brand-new knowledge that you weren't invincible. I think that changes you for the long haul."

We have reached Carl Schurz Park—one of my favorites. There are trees and green velvet gardens and two sets of curved stone steps that always feel like a spot where a fairy tale should start. There's a playground for kids. A bronze of Peter Pan.

We sit down on a bench across from the statue. "You were right. I needed to get out." I knock my shoulder against Finn's. "Thanks for taking care of me."

"That's what I'm here for," he says.

I take a deep breath through my mask. "I've always liked this park."

"I know."

He leans back, tilting his face to the sun, his hands in his jacket. If not for the fact that we are still mired in a pandemic, it would be an absolutely perfect day.

By the time I realize that Finn isn't just relaxing, he's no longer rummaging through his pockets. A small ring box is balanced on his knee.

"I know this doesn't seem like the most opportune time," he says, "but the more I think about it, the more I realize it is. I almost lost you. And now, with your mom . . . well, every day counts. It doesn't matter to me if nothing ever goes back to normal, because I don't want to go backward. I want to go forward, with you. I want kids that we can bring here and push on the swings. I want the dog and the yard and all the things we've been dreaming about all these years."

Finn sinks down to one knee. "Marry me?" he says. "We've done the sickness part. How about we try the health?"

I open the box and see the solitaire, simple and lovely, light winking at me.

Three feet away, Peter Pan is frozen in time. I wonder how many years he spent in Wendy's company here before forgetting that he used to know how to fly.

"Di?" Finn says, laughing nervously. "Say something?"

I look at him. "Why aren't you a magician?"

"What? Because . . . I'm a surgeon? Why are we talking about this—"

"You wanted to be a magician, you said. What changed?"

Awkwardly, he slides back into the seat beside me, knowing the moment is gone. "No one grows up to be a magician," he mutters.

"That's not true."

"But it's different. The people who do it professionally aren't making magic happen. They're just distracting you from what they're really doing."

Finn has always been my anchor. The problem is that anchors don't just keep you from floating away. Sometimes, they drag you down.

I could paint Finn from memory—every freckle and shadow and scar. But suddenly it is like seeing someone you recognize in a crowd and getting closer to realize that the person is not who you thought he was.

He rubs his hand on the back of his neck. "Look, if you need time . . . if I misjudged . . ." He meets my gaze. "Isn't this what you want? What we planned?"

"You can't plan your life, Finn," I say quietly. "Because then you have a plan. Not a life."

There may not be a reason that I survived Covid. There may not be a better man than the one sitting beside me. But I'm not the same person I was when Finn and I imagined the future . . . and I don't think I want to be.

You may not be able to choose your reality. But you can change it.

I am still holding the ring. I put it into his palm, curl his fingers around it.

Finn stares at me, broken. "I don't understand," he says, hoarse. "Why are you doing this?"

I feel impossibly light, like I am made of air and thought, instead of flesh. "You're perfect, Finn," I tell him. "You're just not perfect for me."

EPILOGUE

May 2023

Ask anyone who's nearly died: you should live in the moment. Unfortunately, that's impossible. Every moment keeps slipping past.

You can only go on to the next moment and the one after that, seeking out *what* you love most with *whom* you love most. All those moments, tallied up? That's your life.

Bucket lists aren't important. Benchmarks aren't important. Neither are goals. You take the wins in small ways: Did I wake up this morning? Do I have a roof over my head? Are the people I care about doing okay? You don't need the things you don't have. You only need what you've got, and the rest? It's just gravy.

It's been three years since I recovered from Covid; two years since I was vaccinated; one year since I finished my degree in art therapy and started my own practice. I've been saving since then, and it's all led to this.

I turn my face into the wind. The spray keeps hitting my sunglasses, so I take them off and let my face get wet. I laugh, just because I can.

It took a while for the country to reopen, and even longer for the borders to do so. I had to gather the courage to take the smallest of steps: Eat *inside* a restaurant. Not freak out when I left my mask at home. Fly on a plane.

The ferry is crowded. There is a family with three rowdy kids and a knot of teenagers bent over a cellphone. A tour group from Japan is listening to their leader point out the different kinds of fish they might see during a dive, complete with a flip-book of underwater photographs. The driver of the boat calls out as we approach a dock, where several water taxis are waiting to take us the final stretch.

It's only a five-minute ride; I pay the boat driver and alight on the dock at Puerto Villamil. There is a sea lion stretched across the sand in front of me, wide and immobile as a continent. I take out my phone and snap a picture, then text it.

Immediately, Rodney pings me back. *LATINX DUDES ARE SO HOT.*

My thumbs fly over the phone. *You got this message, right?*

No, Rodney writes back.

Rodney and I have been living together in Queens since I moved out of Finn's place. Breaking up with your boyfriend is never easy, even less so during a pandemic. But two hours after I called Rodney and told him about my mother's death and Finn's proposal, he got on a plane. We scraped by on our unemployment checks until Sotheby's hired Rodney back. By then, I'd matriculated at NYU.

Rodney wanted to come with me to the Galápagos, but it was something I had to do on my own. It's the last chapter; it's time for the book to end.

I've seen Finn only once since we broke up. We crossed paths, of all places, on the running path along the East River. He was coming home from the hospital and I was jogging. I hear that he's engaged to Athena, the nurse who made me the sunflower mask.

I hope he's happy; I really do.

Puerto Villamil is packed. There are open-air bars with music and patrons spilling into the street, and a taco stand with a long line of customers, and barefoot kids kicking a soccer ball. It has the lazy, boozy atmosphere of a tourist town, and I'm not the only person dragging a little roller bag down the gritty dust of the street.

A Gordian knot of iguanas untangles and scatters when the wheels of my bag get too close. I check my phone for the address of Casa del Cielo, but the hotels are all arranged in a neat line, like sparkling white teeth along the edge of the ocean. Mine is small—a boutique. Its stucco reflects the sun, and a blue mosaic sign spells out its name.

It looks nothing like the hotel I dreamed.

When I walk up to the front, there is a couple leaving. They hold the door for me, and I pull my bag inside and approach the front desk.

The air-conditioning blows over me as I give my name. The clerk, a college-age kid, has dyed white-blond hair and a nose ring. He speaks perfect English. "Have you ever visited before?" he asks, when I hand him my credit card.

"Not really," I tell him, and he grins.

"That sounds like a story."

"It is," I say.

He gives me a room key, affixed to a little piece of polished coconut shell. "The Wi-Fi code is on the back," he says. "It's a little unreliable."

I can't help it; I laugh.

"If there's anything you need, just dial zero," he says.

I thank him and reach for the handle of my bag. Just before I get to the elevator, I turn around. "Does someone named Elena work here?" I ask.

He shakes his head. "Not that I know of . . ."

"That's okay," I tell him. "I must have been mistaken."

I wrote my master's thesis on the reliability of memory, and how it fails us. In Japan, there are monuments called tsunami stones—giant tablets on the coastline that warn descendants of earlier settlers not to build their homes past a certain point. They date back to 1896, when two tsunamis killed 22,000 people. The Japanese believe that it takes three generations to forget. Those who experience a trauma pass it along to their children and their grandchildren, and then the memory fades. To the survivors of a tragedy, that's unthinkable—what's the point of living through something terrible if you cannot convey the lessons you've learned? Since nothing will ever replace all you've lost, the only way to make meaning is to make sure no one else goes through what you did. Memories are the safeguards we use to keep from making the same mistakes.

In my art therapy practice, I started working with people whose lives had been affected in different ways by Covid—those who'd lost jobs or loved ones, or those who'd survived the virus and (like me) were left wondering why. Over the course of the past three years, my patients and I have created three pandemic stones—ten feet high by three feet wide, painted and carved by survivors with images and words that call forth the wisdom they have now, which they didn't have back then. There are pictures of stick figure families, some grayed out by death. There are mantras: *Find your joy. No job is worth killing yourself for.* There are images of Black fists raised in solidarity, of a globe in the shape of a heart, of a syringe filled with stars. The first one that we finished was installed in the lobby of the MoMA on the most recent anniversary of the pandemic.

The obelisk sits three floors below one of my mother's photos.

Exploring Isabela is a little bit like revisiting a city you toured when you were high as a kite. Some things look exactly the way I remember—like the flat black of the *pahoehoe* lava and the elbow of beach beyond the hotel. These must have been photographs I saw when I was planning my trip there that embedded themselves some-where in my subconscious, enough for me to call them up with le-gitimacy. But other pieces of the island are startlingly different, like the place the pangas come with their daily fishing catch, and the ar-chitecture of the small houses that freckle the road leading out of town. Abuela's little home, with the basement apartment, simply does not exist.

Tomorrow, I will arrange to take a tour of the island. I want to see the volcano and the trillizos. But right now, because it's been a long flight and I want to stretch my legs, I change into shorts and sneakers and a tank top, pull my hair into a ponytail, and walk down to the water's edge. I take off my shoes and wade up to my knees, watching Sally Lightfoot crabs polka-dot the rocks. I put my hands on my hips and look up at the clouds, then across the ocean at a small island that never existed in my dream. I breathe deeply, thinking that last time I was here, I couldn't breathe at all.

I sit on a rock with an iguana that is completely unbothered by the company and wait for my feet to dry before putting on my sneakers again. This time, I start jogging away from town. Another thing that looks nothing like it did in my imagination: the entrance to the tortoise breeding ground. It's touristy, with signs and maps and cartoon pictures of eggs and hatching tortoises.

There's a couple leaving; they smile at me as I pass them on my way in. "It's closed," the woman says, "but you can still see the babies in the pens outside."

"Thanks," I say, and I walk toward the horseshoe of enclosures. Beneath cacti, tortoises huddle together, stretching their old-man necks toward whatever danger lies six inches ahead. One unhinges his jaw and sticks out a triangular pink tongue.

The tortoises are arranged in size order. Some pens have only two or three, others are crammed. The babies are no bigger than my fist, and they are clambering over each other, creating their own obstacle course.

One of the little ones manages to get its feet on the shell of another, double-stacked for a breathtaking moment before it topples over onto its back.

Its feet are pedaling in the air, its head snicked back inside its shell.

I look around, wondering if there's an attendant who will flip this poor little guy back over.

Well. They're babies; they can't be dangerous.

The retaining wall is only thigh-high. I put my foot on it, intending to climb over, complete a rescue mission, and leave.

I have no idea why the sole of my sneaker slips.

"Cuidado!"

I feel a hand grab my wrist the moment before I fall.

And I turn.

AUTHOR'S NOTE

Humans mark tragedy. Everyone remembers where they were when Kennedy was shot, when the Twin Towers fell, and the last thing they did before the world shut down due to the Covid-19 pandemic.

I was at a wedding in Tulum. The bride was an actress who—in a month—was going to star in the off-Broadway musical adaptation of *Between the Lines,* a novel I co-wrote with my daughter. I attended her wedding with the librettist and his husband, and our director and his husband. We all sat together at a table, drank margaritas, and had a wonderful time. From there, I met up with my husband in Aspen, where my son was about to propose to his girlfriend. There was buzz about coronavirus, but it didn't seem real.

Then we got notice at our hotel that a guest had tested positive. By the time we flew home, New Hampshire was going into lockdown. My last trip to a grocery store was March 11, 2020 (and as of this moment, I still haven't gone to one since). One week later I learned that all of the other people at my table at the wedding in Mexico had contracted Covid. Two were hospitalized.

I never caught it.

I have asthma, and I took quarantine very seriously. I can count on one hand the number of times I've left my house in the past year—

when, in previous years, I would travel cumulatively six months out of the year. Two of my kids and their partners came down with Covid, with fortunately mild symptoms. When my husband would go food shopping, and a clerk would dismiss the need for masks or social distancing, he always made sure to let them know that our kids had been sick. As Finn experiences in this novel—they usually jumped back a few feet, as if merely speaking of illness makes you contagious.

And me? I was at home, paralyzed with fear. I couldn't breathe well on a *good* day; I couldn't even imagine what Covid would do to my lungs. I was so anxious that I couldn't concentrate on anything—which meant that I couldn't distract myself with my work. I couldn't write. I couldn't even read. After only a few pages, I was unable to focus.

My reading slump broke first, thanks to romance novels, the only genre I could get lost in at the time. I think I needed to know there was a happy ending, albeit fictional. But writing was still elusive. I started working on a novel that I was supposed to co-write for a 2022 release, attempting to jog my muscle memory by doing research (via Zoom, this time), and somehow my brain remembered how to craft a book. But the whole time I was working on that story, I was wondering: How are we going to chronicle this pandemic? Who will do it? How do we tell the tale of how the world shut down, and why, and what we learned?

Several months into the pandemic I stumbled across an article about a Japanese man who got stranded in Machu Picchu during Covid. He was trapped there due to travel restrictions and, out of necessity, stopped being a tourist and became a resident of the community. Eventually the locals petitioned the government to open the historic site just for him, and he finally got to experience it as a visitor. Suddenly, I knew how to write about Covid.

The most pervasive emotion that we have all felt this past year is isolation. What's odd is that it's a shared experience, but we still feel alone and adrift. That got me thinking of how isolation can be devastating . . . but can also be the agent of change. And *that* made me think of Darwin. Evolution tells us that adaptation is how we survive.

I had never been to Machu Picchu . . . and I obviously couldn't go there to do any research. But I *had* been to the Galápagos years ago, and I wondered whether there might have been a tourist stranded there during the pandemic. Sure enough, a young Scottish tourist named Ian Melvin found himself on Isabela Island in the Galápagos for months while travel was restricted. I tracked down Ian to interview him, as well as some of the residents he met there—Ernesto Velarde, who works with the Darwin Foundation, and Karen Jacome, a naturalist guide. I wanted to write about what it felt like to be stuck in paradise while the rest of the world was going to hell.

But I also wanted to talk about *survival*. About the resilience of humans. It is impossible to attribute meaning to the countless deaths and smaller losses we have all suffered—and yet, we're going to have to make sense of this lost year. For that, I began by interviewing the medical professionals who have been in the trenches fighting Covid from the beginning. I heard their frustration, their exhaustion, and their determination to not let this damn virus win. I poured their hearts into Finn's voice, and I hope I've done them justice. We will never be able to thank them for what they've done, or to erase the memories of what they've seen.

Then I turned to those who had such severe Covid that they were on ventilators—and who lived to tell me about it. It is worth noting that when I put out a social media call for survivors who had been on vents, I received over one hundred responses in an hour. Overwhelmingly, the people I spoke with (who were all ages, sizes, races—this virus doesn't discriminate) wanted others to know that Covid *isn't* "just the flu"; that there's a reason for masking up and social distancing, and politics has no role in it. Like Diana, nearly every person I interviewed experienced incredibly detailed, lucid dream states—some that were snippets of time and others that lasted for years.

I'm pretty sure I'm the only person so far cataloging these experiences, because there's much more important stuff we need to know about Covid, but I found it fascinating that these dreams could mostly be categorized into four types: something involving a base-ment, an experience of restraint or kidnapping, a dead loved one re-appearing, or a loved one dying (who, when the Covid patient returned to consciousness, turned out to be very much alive). The lucid dreams of my interview subjects became the Facebook posts that Diana reads. Caroline Leavitt, an author I love, has written mul-tiple times about her own experience in a medically induced coma, and shared details with me about this "other place" she still visits in her sleep sometimes—where she is not a writer but a teacher; where she is unmarried; where she looks different but knows it's her; where she has spent *years*. There are all sorts of explanations for these lucid, unconscious experiences—the bottom line is that we just don't know enough about the brain to understand why they happen and what they mean.

The last question I asked each of my interview subjects was *How has this experience changed the way you think about the rest of your life?*

Their responses brought me right back to the concept of isolation. When you find yourself utterly alone—on a rocky outcropping or on a ventilator—the only place to find strength is in yourself. As one woman told me, "I'm not looking for anything outside of me any-more. I'm like, this is it. I've got everything I need." Whether or not we have been hospitalized for Covid in the past year, we all have a much clearer sense of what matters. Go figure—it's not the promo-tion, or the raise, or the fancy car, or the private jet. It's not getting into an Ivy League school or completing an Ironman or being fa-mous. It's not adding an extra shift or staying late because your boss expects it of you. Instead, it is taking the time to see how beautiful frost looks on a window. It's being able to hug your mom or hold your grandchild. It's having no expectations but taking nothing for granted. It's understanding that an extra hour at your desk is an hour you don't spend throwing a ball with your kid. It's realizing that we could wake up tomorrow and the world could shut down. It's know-ing that at the very end of life, no matter what your net worth is and the length of your CV, the only thing you want is someone beside you, holding your hand.

When I try to make sense of the past year, it feels to me like the world pressed pause. When we stopped moving, we noticed that the ways we have chosen to validate ourselves are lists of items or experiences we need to have, goals that are monetary or mercenary. Now, I'm wondering why those were ever even goals. We don't need those things to feel whole. We need to wake up in the morning. We need our bodies to function. We need to enjoy a meal. We need a roof over our head. We need to surround ourselves with people we love. We need to take the wins in a much smaller way.

And we need to remember this, even when we're no longer in a pandemic.

—Jodi Picoult, March 2021

ACKNOWLEDGMENTS

I'm known for being a fast writer, but I think I broke a land-speed record with this book. It would not have been possible without the help of the following people:

For refreshing my memory about the Galápagos: Ian Melvin, Karen Jacome, Ernesto Velarde. (NOTE: Although Isabela Island did indeed close to visitors, it happened on March 17, 2020—not March 15, as in this book. That's my fictional prerogative, rather than the failure of my experts!)

For insight into what it was like to work as a medical professional during Covid: Dr. Barry Nathanson, Dr. Kim Coros, Dr. Vladislav Fomin, Carrie Munson, Kathleen Fike, Meghan Bohlender, Dr. Grecia Rico, Dr. Ema-Lou Ranger, Dr. Alli Hyatt, Dr. Samantha Ruff, Meghan Summerall, Kendal Peters, Megan Brown, Lewis Simpson, Stefanie Ryan, Jennifer Langford, Meagan Campuzano, Dr. Francisco Ramos.

For sharing her imaginary town with me (and for her openness, her honesty, and her wonderful talent as a writer): Caroline Leavitt.

For helping me kill someone via scuba: Christopher Crowley.

For frantic texts about New York City and the geography of Central Park: Dan Mertzlufft.

For teaching me about art therapy, and adolescents who self-harm: Dr. Sriya Bhattacharyya.

For teaching me about art, art business, and creating a remarkably convincing faux Toulouse-Lautrec (and also for loving my son Jake): Melanie Borinstein.

For being survivors, and for their candor about what it's like to have severe Covid: Vicki Judd, Kabria Newkirk, Caroline Coster, Karen Burke-Bible, Chris Hansen, Don Gillmer, Lisa and Howard Brown, Felix Torres, Matt Tepperman, Shirley Archambault, Alisha Hiebert, Jennifer Watters, Pat Conner, Jeri Hall, Allison Stannard, Sue McCann, LaDonna Cash, Sandra and Reggie McAllister, Teresa Cunningham, Katie White, Lisa Dillon, Nancee Seitz.

For introducing me to tsunami stones: Dr. Daniel Collison.

For plotting fictional deaths while on insufferable hills, and for being in my Covid walking bubble: Joan Collison, Barb Kline-Schoder, Kirsty DePree, Jan Peltzer.

For encouraging me to write this when I kept saying I probably shouldn't, and/or for reading early drafts: Brigid Kemmerer (who is the *best* critique partner), Jojo Moyes, Reba Gordon, Katie Desmond, Jane Picoult, Elyssa Samsel.

Now on to the MVPs of publishing. Creating a book takes a long time. It's not just the writing, it's the editing and copyediting and design and marketing and placement and all the other things that have to happen so you can read it. One day in March I showed up in my editor's inbox with an email that said, *Surprise, here's a book I never planned to write!* Jennifer Hershey, who is the world's most brilliant editor and fiercest cheerleader, reacted in the best possible way: she loved the book, and she wanted to publish it while we were all still trying to wrap our heads around this past year. My agent/friend/partner-in-crime, Laura Gross, was equally instrumental in achieving this Herculean feat. My publicist, Susan Corcoran, has the biggest heart and the sharpest mind and I would not do any of this without her by my side. And then there is the rest of the well-oiled Ballantine machine, which made this publication possible in record time: Gina Centrello, Kara Walsh, Kim Hovey, Deb Aroff, Rachel

Kind, Denise Cronin, Scott Shannon, Matthew Schwartz, Theresa Zoro, Kelly Chian, Paolo Pepe, Erin Kane, Kathleen Quinlan, Corina Diez, Emily Isayeff, Maya Franson, Angie Campusano. You are my army, and that makes me feel invincible.

Endless thanks to the family that kept me sane when I was crawling the walls this past year: Kyle and Kevin Ferreira van Leer, who did the *New York Times* crossword and Spelling Bee with me daily; and Four Square Team Extraordinaire Sammy and Frankie Ramos, Jake van Leer and Melanie Borinstein.

Finally, thanks to the only guy I'd want to be stuck in an enclosed space with for over 365 days: Tim van Leer. Even though you edited my grocery lists to make them healthier, I will love you forever, no matter what world we're in.

JODI PICOULT is the author of twenty-seven novels, with forty million copies sold worldwide. Her last twelve books have debuted at #1 on the *New York Times* best-seller list, including her most recent, *The Book of Two Ways*. Five novels have been made into movies and *Between the Lines* (co-written with daughter Samantha van Leer) has been adapted as a musical. She is the recipient of multiple awards, including the New England Bookseller Award for Fiction, the Alex Award from the YA Library Services Association, and the New Hampshire Literary Award for Outstanding Literary Merit. She is also the co-librettist for the musical *Breathe,* and the upcoming musical *The Book Thief.* She lives in New Hampshire with her husband.

jodipicoult.com
Facebook.com/jodipicoult
Twitter: @jodipicoult
Instagram: @jodipicoult

ABOUT THE TYPE

This book was set in Caslon, a typeface first designed in 1722 by William Caslon (1692–1766). Its widespread use by most English printers in the early eighteenth century soon supplanted the Dutch typefaces that had formerly prevailed. The roman is considered a "workhorse" typeface due to its pleasant, open appearance, while the italic is exceedingly decorative.